710分 新题型

大学英语 ⑥ 级考试

直击考点

综合测试

主　编：王长喜

副主编：白玉宽

编　者：王　莉

《长喜英语》图书编委会 编

U0116820

中国社会出版社

特色内容 先睹为快

（改 错）

熟悉常见错误 炼就火眼金睛

一、词法层面的考查

3 代词

代词错误是短文改错中出现频率较高的几类错误之一，几乎每套题中都有。代词常见的错误有：

(4) 不定代词及反身代词的误用

【示例】 (03-9)

…the entire family — mother, father, children, even grandparents — live in a small house and working together to support each other. Anyone understood the life and death importance of family cooperation and hard work.

【答案】Anyone → Everyone。

【解析】上一句中的 the entire family 指整个家庭，故应把 Anyone 换成 Everyone。anyone 指"任何人"，强调个体，而 everyone 指"每人，人人"，强调整体的一致性。

二、句法层面的考查

4 并列句

并列连词所连接的两个并列部分在语法上必须是对等的，也就是说名词对名词（短语），介词短语对介词短语，动词过去时态对动词过去时态。这点是并列连词的最基本用法，但却常被英语学习者所忽略，因此也成为六级改错中的一个重要考点。

【示例】 (03-9)

West, was to find a piece of place, build a house for one's family, and started a farm.

【答案】started → start。

【解析】根据分析可知，to find…，(to) build… 以及 (to) started… 为并列表语。started 的形式须与 find、build 一致，同为不定式作表语，故应把 started 改为动词原形 start。

三、篇章层面的考查

1 上下文一致（观点、事实、态度等）

篇章层面的改错视角更宽，需识别内容更多，照应范围也更大，需要考生联系上下文敏锐识别。

【示例】 (00-6)

…We asked a lady, who replied that she thought you could tell a well-mannered person in the way they occupied the space around them — for example, when such a person walks down a street he or she is constantly unaware of others…

【答案】unaware → aware。

【解析】这位女士的回答是，她认为从一个人占据周围空间的方式就能判断他是否有良好行为。比如：一个有良好行为的人在街上走路时总能意识到他人的存在。这样的人决不会撞到别人身上。显然，若用"unaware"则前后意思矛盾，应将其改为"aware"。

四、逻辑层面的考查

3 转折与启承

转折与启承是短文改错中考查最多的逻辑关系，几乎每次试题中都出现，需要考生仔细梳理。这里列举出其中主要的 9 种关系。

(8) 因果关系

【示例】 (03-9)

…they dreamed of buying houses and starting families. But there was a tremendous boom in home building.

【答案】But → So。

【解析】but 是表示转折关系的连词，所以确定其前后句子逻辑关系是解答本题的关键。But 前一句的 they dreamed of buying houses and starting families 与其所在句的 there was a tremendous boom in home building 在逻辑上是因果关系，故应将 But 换成 So。

特色内容 先睹为快

（完 形）

悟透四类题型 上场成竹在胸

一、逻辑推理题

1 对语境的把握

语境就是我们通常所指的上下文。段与段之间，句子与句子之间、句子之间以及词语之间都有一定的语义联系。而这一切的联系都尽在语境之中，因此对语境的理解对解题至关重要。

【示例】 (07-06)

But a __69__ of the past year in disaster history suggests that modern Americans are particularly bad at protect themselves from guaranteed threats.	[A] review [B] reminder [C] concept [D] prospect

【解析】选 [A]。逻辑推理题。四个选项都能和介词 of 连用，但能和空格后的 the past year in disaster history 形成语义场共现的只有 [A]"回顾"。[B]"暗示，提醒"；[C]"观念，概念"；[D]"前途，前景"均脱离了上下文语境。

三、短语搭配题

短语搭配题考察的是学生基本的知识储备，这就需要学生平时多加积累。尤其是一些短语动词（look in, let out, make off 等一些固定下来作为动词使用的结构）、动词短语（动词和一些常用的名词的短语搭配）、名词短语和介词短语。

【示例】 (05-06)

They are thereby shut __61__ from the world of books and newspapers, having to rely on friends to read aloud to them.	[A] up [B] down [C] in [D] off

【解析】选 [D]。[D] shut off 常与 from 连用，表示"与…隔离，隔绝"，填入原文构成的句意为"与书籍和报刊隔绝"，符合题意。[A] shut up"住口"；[B] shut down"（使）关闭，（使）停工"；[C] shut in"把…关在里面，禁闭"都不符合题意。

理解实用技巧 做题思路清晰

二、解题技巧

1 动词

(3) 看动词的属性——是及物动词还是不及物动词。空格后如有宾语则应该选及物动词，反之则应选不及物动词。

【示例】 (07-06)

So what has happened in the year that __75__ the disaster on the Gulf Coast?	[A] ensued [B] traced [C] followed [D] occurred

【解析】选 [C]。该句后面的内容表明本段主要阐述 the disaster on the Gulf Coast 之后所发生的事情，因此本空应填入表示"后续"意义的词，从而答案在 [A] 和 [C] 之间，但 [A] ensue 表示"跟着发生"时为不及物动词，后面不能跟宾语，故排除。[C] 项完全符合题意，故为答案。

二、解题技巧

3 形容词

(2) 当形容词直接修饰名词或名词性词组时，要看它们的合适性和褒贬意义的一致性。

【示例】 (07-12)

...he rush to give as lectures to Berlin's Prussian Academy of Sciences on four __77__ Thursdays.	[A] successive [B] progressive [C] extensive [D] repetitive

【解析】选 [A]。根据上下文可知，此处说的是"连续四个星期四"，故答案为 [A] successive"连续的"。[B] progressive"前进的，进步的"；[C] extensive"广大的，广泛的"；[D] repetitive"重复的，反复性的"均与文意要求不符。

特色内容 先睹为快

（翻 译）

驾驭各类句式　准确地道表达

二、语句层次

1 否定句

(3) 双重否定句

其形式一为："主语+cannot+help/refrain/keep+from+动名词"。其形式二："主语+cannot+but/choose but/help but+动词原形"。

【示例】

I ＿＿＿＿＿＿＿＿（忍不住表达我的崇拜之情）his insight and resolution.

【答案】cannot refrain from expressing my warm admiration for。

【解析】本题主要考查 cannot+help/refrain/keep 在双重否定句中的应用，from 后接动名词。

If you insist on having been here yesterday, I ＿＿＿＿＿＿（不得不认为你在说谎）。

【答案】cannot but think you are lying。

【解析】本题主要考查 cannot+but 在双重否定句中的应用，注意 but 后面接动词原形。

二、语句层次

6 倒装让步句型

其形式一："表语+as+主语（代词）+系动词，+主句"。

【示例】

＿＿＿＿＿＿（虽然他还是个孩子），he has to learn how to earn his living.

【答案】Child as he is。

【解析】本题主要考查"表语+as"构成的倒装让步句型。

其形式三："副词或动词原形+as+主语…，+主句"。

【示例】

＿＿＿＿＿＿（虽然他确实很努力），he never seems able to do the work satisfactorily.

【答案】Try hard as he does。

【解析】本题主要考查"表语+as"构成的倒装让步句型，does 在这是强调动词，后面接动词原形。

适当提升技巧　句子立即生辉

一、十大翻译技巧

1 词语层次

(4) 正反译法

由于语言习惯的不同，汉英两种语言在正说与反说方面也常常不同。英语中有些从正面说的，汉语则从反面来解释；而对那些从反面说的句子，汉语则可以从正面来解释。

【示例1】

The above facts＿＿＿＿＿＿（使人不能不得出以下结论）。

【答案】insist on the following conclusions。

【解析】"不能不得出"，双重否定，而 insist on"坚持，强调"，表示肯定。

【示例2】

She＿＿＿＿＿＿（要等你答应帮助以后才肯走）。

【答案】won't go away until you promise to help her。

【解析】"才走"，汉语是肯定形式，翻译成英语用 not…until 表示。

一、十大翻译技巧

2 语句层次

(3) 成分转译法

英汉两种语言，由于表达方式不尽相同，在具体英译汉时，有时往往需要转换一下句子成分，才能使翻译达到逻辑正确、通顺流畅、重点突出等目的。

【示例】

China's national ball is Table tennis, ＿＿＿＿＿＿（中国到处都打乒乓球）。

【答案】and it's played all over China。

【解析】题干包含两个分句，前分句的末尾提到了 Table tennis，因此后分句用 Table tennis 作主语能起到一个很好的衔接作用。又因为"Table tennis"是受动者，故应用被动语态。"中国到处"译为"all over China"，简洁而精确。

目　录

第一篇　改　错

第二篇　完形填空

第三篇　翻　译

第四篇　预测试题

第一篇　改　错

第一章 题型透视

一、题型特征

在历年的六级考试中，改错是一种常见题型。考生在复习备考时，一定要对这种题型加以重视。

根据《大学英语六级考试大纲》的规定，改错部分占总分 710 分的 10%。该部分共 10 题，考试时间为 15 分钟。在一篇题材熟悉，难度适中的短文（约 200~300 词）中有 10 行标有题号，每一行均只有一处错误.（不含拼写或标点错误），可能需要改正某个词，也可能需增添或删去某个词。

"综合运用语言能力"，"在全面理解内容的基础上指出并改正错误"，"短文的意思和结构正确、完整"这三点，概括了综合改错题的性质和内容。这是一种主观性测试题，考查学生的语言运用能力。它要求学生具备篇章层面的理解能力，能够依靠系统、扎实的语法知识，充分理解全文的语义、逻辑关系，识别并能够改正词汇搭配、语法结构、篇章结构和逻辑意义上的错误。

综合改错题是一种综合性强、要求高、难度大的题型。考场上正确快捷的答题依赖于考生敏锐的语感和扎实的训练。因此，考生一方面要在阅读过程中积累词汇、语法知识、表达式等，最好能背诵一些优秀的英语短文，强化自己的英语语感，另一方面，还要对改错题的命题思路、常见错误设置、改错要领等有清楚的了解。

二、错误形式

◆错词（words mistaken）：在标有题号的一行中有一词在词法、搭配或语义连贯等方面有错误，要求考生找出错误并换上正确的词，这类错误在所有错误中占绝大多数。

◆缺词（words missing）：在标有题号的一行的任何位置（包括行首词前和行末词后）缺了一词，要求考生按语法、搭配或上下文语义的需要找出缺词的位置并补上所缺的，而且还要注意该词的形式。

◆多词（words redundant）：在标有题号的一行中有一词从语法、搭配或上下文语义上看纯属多余，要求考生找到这个多余的词并删去。

三、答题要求

◆改正（correction）：将文中错词用斜线（／）划去，在后面横线上填入正确的词，表示替换该错词。

◆增添（add）：在文中两词间加"∧"号，表示有遗漏，然后在横线上填入遗漏的词的正确形式。

◆删除（delete）：在文中将需要删除的词用斜线（／）划去，在后面横线上也划一斜线（／），表示该错词是多余的。

【例】

Television is rapidly becoming the literature of our ~~periods~~. Many of the arguments ~~having~~ used for the study of literature as a school subject are valid for ∧ study of television.	time
	／
	the

四、专项练习

Exercise 1

In the years 1095-1450, many large armies were sent to Middle East by European countries. They carried banners with a cross on them. These armies were called "crusades", that means "marked with a cross".

At first, these crusading armies tried to recover Jerusalem from the Muslims. Later, they became mainly business adventures, sometimes financed by wealth merchants who hoped to make a profit from them.

In the early years of the thirteenth century, a French boy named Stephen led a strange crusade of its own. He went to Paris to see King Philip II. The boy claimed that Christ had sent him a letter, calling in him to organize a crusade of children. Philip II rightly refused to help, so Stephen started to walk to Marseilles. He claimed that when he reached the coast, the sea would disappear so that the children could walk to Jerusalem. That is said that as many as thirty thousand children joined in him on the long march to the port. At that time, the south of France suffered from drought and crop failures. Thousands of children died before they even reached the coast.

At Marseilles, the remained children were disappointed when the Mediterranean continued to wash the French coast as usually. Eventually two traders put them on broad seven small ships. The children believed that they were going eastwards to Palestine. In fact, the ships sailed to the south. Two ships sank in a storm but the other five reached the North African coast.

1. _____

2. _____

3. _____

4. _____

5. _____

6. _____

7. _____

8. _____

9. _____

10. _____

Exercise 2

More people than ever are drinking coffee these days — but in small quantities than they used to. Some manufacturers of coffee makers are trying to make advantage of this trend by developing diminutive machines that *brew* (煮) smaller amounts of coffee. Two U. S. appliance companies — Black & Decker, basing in Towson, Maryland, and Toastmaster Inc. of Columbia, Missouri — has recently introduced "drip" coffee makers that brew one or two cup servings of coffee. Neither of the products brew the coffee directly into a cup or mug, eliminating the need for a separate carafe. Since many people make a pot of coffee in the morning and drink only a single cup, the new coffee makers should reduce the wasted coffee. Black & Decker's Cup-at-a-Time spends $ 27, while Toastmaster's Coffee Break retails for $ 20.

Black & Decker also makes a coffee maker drips coffee directly into a carry-around thermal carafe. The carafe, a glass vacuum bottle, is supposed to keep the coffee fresh for hours. The product, called the Thermal Carafe Coffee-maker, comes with a built-in lid that opens during the brewing process, closes when it is completed. There are several models, including one that firs under the counter, ranging from $ 60 to $ 110 at price.

1. _____
2. _____
3. _____
4. _____
5. _____
6. _____
7. _____
8. _____
9. _____
10. _____

答案与解析

Exercise 1

1. 【答案】to ∧ Middle —— ∧ the。
   【解析】本题考查定冠词的用法。由普通名词构成的专有名词多数要加冠词，the Middle East "中东"符合此规则。类似的还有 the United Kingdom，the Department of Education，the New York Times 等。

2. 【答案】that → which。
   【解析】本题考查非限制性定语从句的关系代词。该从句用逗号与先行词分开，是非限制性定语从句，因此关系代词不可用 that，只能用 which。

3. 【答案】wealth → wealthy。
   【解析】本题考查形容词的用法。中心词 merchants 为名词，不能被名词 wealth "财富"修饰，将 wealth 改成形容词 wealthy "富有的"。

4. 【答案】its → his。
   【解析】本题考查代词的用法。own 前要用物主代词，该代词代替的是前面的 a French boy，为第三人称阳性单数，其相应的物主代词为 his。

5. 【答案】in — on。

【解析】本题考查动词短语。call in 的意思是"邀请"，call on 的意思是"要求，号召"。根据句意，应为"救世主送给他一封信，要他组织一支儿童十字军"，所以应把 call in 改为 call on。由 call 构成的短语还有 call back"召回"，call for"要求"，call off"取消"等。

6. 【答案】That — It。

【解析】本题考查形式主语。该句的真正主语是 that 引导的从句，形式主语必须用 it 而不能用 that 来充当。It is said that...已成习惯用法，译为"据说"。

7. 【答案】in — in。

【解析】本题考查动词的用法。动词 join 既可作及物动词也可作不及物动词。当 join 为及物动词时，意思是"成为…一员，与…一起"，如 Will you join me in a walk?（你愿和我一起散步吗?）；而 join 为不及物动词时，和介词 in 连用，意思是"参加（活动等）"，如 Everyone joined in the game.（每个人都参加了游戏。）。根据句意，应该是前一种情况，即 join 为及物动词，因此去掉 in。

8. 【答案】remained — remaining。

【解析】本题考查非谓语动词作定语。remain 为不及物动词，因此其过去分词不能作定语，故将 remained 改成 remaining，the remaining children 意思是"剩下的孩子"。

9. 【答案】usually — usual。

【解析】本题考查形容词和副词。as usual"照例，像往常一样"是习惯用法，而 usually"通常，大抵"是副词，不和 as 搭配构成短语。例如：As usual, I slept late that Saturday morning.（和平时一样，那个星期六早晨我睡得很晚才起。）

10. 【答案】broad — board。

【解析】本题考查形近词辨析。broad 是形容词或副词，意思是"宽阔的（地）"，不能同 on 搭配，显然是和拼写近似的 board 相混淆了。board 为名词，构成副词短语 on board"到船上，在船上"，符合句子的意思。

Exercise 2

1. 【答案】small — smaller。

【解析】本题考查形容词比较级。句中有 than，这说明句子应该用比较级，故将 small 改成比较级。

2. 【答案】make — take。

【解析】本题考查固定搭配。take advantage of 为固定搭配，意为"利用"。

3. 【答案】basing — based。

【解析】本题考查非谓语动词。base 和它的逻辑主语是被动关系，所以要用它的过去分词形式。

4. 【答案】has — have。

【解析】 本题考查主谓一致。句子的主语为 two U. S. appliance companies，故谓语动词要用复数形式。

5. 【答案】Neither — Both。

【解析】 本题考查逻辑一致。Neither of the products brew…mug 和 recently introduced "drip" coffee makers…coffee 矛盾。neither 表否定，意为 "两者都不"，将其改为表肯定的 both。

6. 【答案】and — but。

【解析】 本题考查连接词。make a pot of coffee in the morning 和 drink only a single cup 之间呈现的显然是一种转折关系，意为 "大部分人都是早上煮一壶咖啡但是却只喝一小杯"。因此应将 and 改成 but。

7. 【答案】spends — costs。

【解析】 本题考查近义词辨析。spend 的主语是人，而此处的主语是物，而且是单数第三人称，故用 costs。

8. 【答案】maker ∧ drips — ∧ that。

【解析】 本题考查定语从句中的关系代词。定语从句的关系代词在从句中作主语时不能省略，所以要在 drips 前加 that。

9. 【答案】process，∧ closes — and。

【解析】 本题考查句子结构。opens during the brewing process 和 closes when it is completed 是两个并列的谓语，因此它们之间必须要用连接词 and。

10. 【答案】at — in。

【解析】 本题考查介词。表示 "在…方面" 应该使用介词 in，而不是 at。

考 点 透 视

在综合改错这种题型中，无论词汇、语法、还是篇章层次的理解都能成为改错设题的对象。下面，我们结合对历年六级考试综合改错题的分析，分别从词法、句法和篇章三个层次给同学们以具体详实的讲解。

一、词法层面的考查
名词与代词

1 可数名词与不可数名词

常见的不可数名词有：advice，assistance，education，equipment，furniture，luggage，work（工作）等。这些不可数名词是没有复数形式的，应特别注意。

【示例】   (04-6-S3)

... abstract creations like values, beliefs, customs and institutional arrangements — and material culture — physical object like cooking pots, computers and bathtubs.	3. _____

【答案】object — objects。
【解析】object 为可数名词，在没有被表单个概念的词修饰限定时，通常要用复数形式。从后面列举的炊具、计算机和浴缸的复数形式也可以判定 object 须用复数形式，即 objects。

2 名词单复数形式

（1）规则名词复数

foot→feet；mouse→mice；goose→geese；crisis→crises；analysis→analyses；hypothesis→hypotheses；phenomenon→phenomena。

（2）集体名词

这类词多用复数，有时也可用单数形式，视情况而定。如果表示的是整体概念，谓语动词就用单数形式；如果指具体成员，谓语动词就用复数形式。常见的这类名词有 army，audience，class，club，committee，crowd，crew，couple，family，jury，staff，faculty，village 等。试比较下面两个句子：

【示例1】

The committee is divided into opinion.	＿＿＿＿＿＿

【答案】is — are。

【解析】根据 divided into opinion 可以判断出此处的 committee 指的应该是具体成员，所以谓语动词应该用复数。

一些有生命的集体名词作主语时，谓语动词只用复数形式。这类词有：cattle，people，police，youth，mankind，personnel（全体人员）等。无生命的集体名词作主语时，谓语动词用单数，例如：scenery，clothing，jewelry，poetry，underwear，sugar，rice 等。

【示例2】

The set of furnitures the newly married couple bought at the store are very well finished.	＿＿＿＿＿＿

【答案】furnitures — furniture。

【解析】furniture 是集合名词，只用单数形式。单位量词 the set of 放在前面，表示"这件家具"。

（3）特殊名词复数形式

有一些特殊名词复数形式需要记住。由-man 或-woman 构成的复合名词，前后两个都要用复数形式。例如：gentleman-farmer 的复数形式是 gentlemen-farmers。有些合成词的第一个词是名词或重要的词，它们的复数形式词尾应在这些词上。例如 comrade-in-chief 的复数形式是 comrades-in-chief；father-in-law 的复数形式是 fathers-in-law；还有 lookers-on；standers-by 等。

【示例】

The two man servants rushed in with frightened expression on their faces.	＿＿＿＿＿＿

【答案】man — men。

【解析】man servant 的复数形式应该是 men servants。

3 代词

代词错误是综合改错中出现频率较高的几类错误之一，几乎每套题中都有。代词常见的错误有：

（1）指代错误

题中出现代词时，要注意分析其指代的对象。

【示例】 (03-9-S9)

…The new houses, typically in the suburbs, were often small and more or less identical, but it satisfied a deep need. Many regarded the single-family house the basis of their way of life.	9. _____

【答案】 it —— they。
【解析】 根据前句内容可知，but 后面的代词 it 指代的应该是 the new houses，故应将 it 改为 they。

（2）关系代词的误用

此类错误主要指非限定性定语从句和主语从句中先行词的误用（主要为 that 与 which、who 与 which、where 与 which 的误用；what 与 that 等常见先行词的混用）请看下面的例子。

【示例1】 (06-6-S5)

…There's also convincing evidence which dyslexia is largely inherited…	5. _____

【答案】 which —— that。
【解析】 evidence 为抽象名词，后通常接由 that 引导的同位语从句，故将 which 换成 that。下一句中 that 为本行 that 的原词复现，stereotype 也为抽象名词。

【示例2】 (06-6-S2)

…illiterate（文盲的），unable to ever meet their potential. But in the last several years, there's been a revolution in that we've learned about reading and dyslexia…	2. _____

【答案】 that —— what。
【解析】 a revolution in 为 "在…方面的一次革命"，in 为介词，in 后为其宾语，并且 we've learned 中 learned 须有宾语，that 不能满足这里的语法要求，故将 that 改成 what（= the thing which）。

（3）代词 it 与 this，that 误用

【示例】 (98-1-S5)

While technology makes this possible for four or even six billion of us to exist, it also eliminates our job opportunities.	5. _____

【答案】this — it。

【解析】makes 后面的宾语是不定式。makes 后接形式宾语 it。真正宾语是带有逻辑主语的不定式短语 for four or even six billion of us to exist。形式宾语 it 不能由 this，that 代替。

（4）不定代词及反身代词的误用

【示例1】 (03-9-S5)

... the entire family — mother, father, children, even grandparents — live in a small house and working together to support each other. Anyone understood the life and death importance of family cooperation and hard work.	5. _____

【答案】Anyone — Everyone。

【解析】上一句中的 the entire family 指整个家庭，即包括 mother，father，children，even grandparents。本句句首的代词应指代上述的所有家庭成员，故应把 Anyone 换成 Everyone。anyone 指"任何人"，强调个体，而 everyone 指"每人，人人"，强调整体的一致性。

【示例2】 (98-1-S10)

But if 98 percent of us don't need to work, what are we going to do with oneself?	10. _____

【答案】oneself — ourselves。

【解析】oneself 所在的句子的主语是 we，因此要用 ourselves。ourselves 指代不清。

形容词与副词

英语中的形容词、副词有三种最基本的比较方式：原级比较、比较级比较和最高级比较。下面分别对这三种方式在运用中易出现的错误进行讲解。

1 原级比较 ≫

（1）as...as 原级比较形式

在该形式中，第一个 as 后应是形容词或副词。the same ...as 表示比较时；same 后应跟名词，二者不可混淆。

例如：The girl was as pretty as her mother.

My car is the same color as his.

（2） like，alike 的用法

like 作动词时表示"喜欢"，反义词是 dislike；作介词时表示"像"，反义词是 unlike。alike 是个表语形容词（即只能作表语，不能作定语）。

【示例】

Alike many other immigrants, Mr. Wang finds it is quite difficult to adopt the value system of Americans'.

【答案】 Alike — Like。

【解析】 句子大意为：像许多其他移民一样，王先生发现要接受美国人的价值体系相当难。所以 Alike 错，应改为 Like。

2 比较级比较

（1） 有"极限"含义的词语

从语义上看，英语中有些形容词和副词本身已有"极限"的含义，所有没有比较级和最高级。例如：perfect（ly），excellent（ly），unique（ly），（im）possible，empty，final（ly），absolute（ly），entire（ly），eternal（ly），square，dead，round。

（2） 有"比较"含义的词语

另外，英语中有些词本身有"比较"的意思，它们的用法如下：

$$A\ is\ \begin{cases} superior \\ inferior \\ senior \\ junior \\ prior \\ previous \end{cases} to\ B.$$

【示例】

People tend to think that the quality of goods for the domestic market is more inferior to that of goods to be exported.

【答案】 more — more 。

【解析】 根据以上解释，inferior 本身已经具备比较含义，所以其前面的 more 为多余。

（3） -er 和 more 不能并用

做改错时，要特别注意句子里有没有把-er 和 more 并用的情况。例如，more longer，more happier，more cleverer 都是不正确的。

【示例】

| When we met him for the second time, he appeared to be more friendlier. | |

【答案】friendlier — friendly。

【解析】"我们第二次遇见他的时候，他似乎友好一些了。" -er 和 more 不能并用。

3 最高级比较

（1）最高级比较的标志

最高级比较中，常出现 in，among，of 等表示比较范围的介词。of all，of the whole，of the entire...，of the three 等是最高级比较的标志。

（2）the 的省略

形容词最高级前一般都加 the。但当最高级作后置短语修饰名词、代词时，the 省略。例如：On the stage are those most popular in the entertainment world. 另外 most 不表示"最"，而表示"非常，很"的时候，前面也不加 the。例如：Jane is most distinguished in arts. 但一般序数词前一定要加 the。

【示例】   (05-12-S1)

| We've seen it all：CVs printed on pink paper, CVs that are 10 pages long and CVs with silly mistakes in ∧ first paragraph. | |

【答案】in ∧ first — ∧ the。

【解析】本行错误不容易发现，本行中出现序数词 first，其前要加定冠词 the。

4 常见错误

（1）形容词与副词混淆

【示例】   (04-6-S8)

| Culture is essentially to our humanness. It provides a kind of map for relating to others. | 8. _____ |

【答案】essentially — essential。

【解析】因为 essentially 是副词，而 essential 是形容词，原文中 be 动词后面只能跟形容词或名词，不能跟副词。

（2）形容词与副词的原级、比较级和最高级的误用

【示例】
(02-6-S10)

…and the myth of the country as a Garden of Eden, which, a few generations late, sends them flooding out again to the suburbs.	10. ＿＿＿＿＿

【答案】late — later。

【解析】Late 强调在安排的、规定的或预期的时间之后"迟地，晚地"，与 early 对应，均与持续较短的时间连用。显然本行中的 a few generations 不是安排或规定好的时间，故此处应改用 late 的同根异义副词 later。later 意为"后来，过一会儿"，强调"在所谈论的时间之后"，与 ago 对应，均与持续较长的时间连用。

（3）形容词与副词的比较句式的混淆和误用

同级比较句式，如 as…as；非同级比较句式，如 more…than…；升级比较句式，如 the more…the more…。

【示例】

The *gorilla*（大猩猩）, while not quite as curious than the *chimpanzee*（黑猩猩）, shows more persistence and memory *retention*（记忆力）in solving a problem.	

【答案】than — as。

【解析】这里是同级比较句式 as…as 与非同级比较句式 more…than…的混用。

（4）比较对象的疏忽

各种比较，都应该在同类事物之间进行。

【示例】

Young readers, more often than not, find the novels of Dickens far more exciting than Thackeray.	＿＿＿＿＿

【答案】Thackeray — Thackeray's。

【解析】相比较的两部分不是 Dickens 和 Thackeray 本人，而是两人的小说。

并列连词与从属连词

1 并列连词

并列连词，如 and，or，so 等。它们反映出前后两个语法地位对等的并列分句，即 A = B。因此 though，although 等引导的复合句不能与 but 引导的并列句并列；because/since/as 引导的复合句不能与 so 引导的并列句并列。

2 从属连词 ⌄

反映主从关系的从属连词中，

表示时间关系的有 before，after，when，while，as，as soon as，since 等；

表示目的关系的有 in order that，so that；

表示让步的有 even if/even though，though/although，no matter what（who，when，where，how）等；

表条件的有 if，unless，once，as long as 等；

表因果的有 as，since，because 等。

这些连词反映的是主句（A）在语法地位上高于从句（B），即 A > B。这种语法地位的不等就会导致分词、with 等复合宾语结构、独立主格结构等。

3 常见错误 ⌄

◆并列连词和从属连词的混淆；

◆并列连词连接的两部分不是对等成分，从属连词连接的两个分句逻辑意义不清；

◆并列连词、从属连词与其他词类的混淆；

◆带有并列连词或从属连词的单、复句结构混乱；

◆引导从句的固定词组的搭配错误等。

【示例1】 (05-1-S6)

This alliance guarantees that all leprosy patients, even they are poor, have a right to the most modern treatment.	6. ＿＿＿＿＿

【答案】 even ∧ they — ∧ if/ though。

【解析】 句子为复合句，This alliance guarantees 为主句，that 引导宾语从句，patients 为宾语从句主语，本行中的 have 为从句谓语，与 patients 在数上一致。have a right to sth. ≈ have access to sth.，故本句中 have a right to…中不存在错误。所以，把错误锁定在逗号前的内容中。even they are poor 中，even 不能引导从句；由 they are poor 与宾语从句构成转折关系断定，应在 even 后加入 if 或 though。even if/ though 意为"即使，虽然"，引导让步状语从句。

【示例2】 (03-9-S6)

Although most people in the United States no longer live on farms, but the ideal of home ownership is just as strong in the twentieth century as it was in the nineteenth.	6. ＿＿＿＿＿

【答案】 but — ~~but~~。

【解析】 表示转折关系的 although 不能和 but 连用，二者只能保留其一，故此处需将 but 去掉。

动词与非谓语动词

六级改错中非谓语动词部分是重要的出题点。非谓语动词通常分为不定式、分词、动名词三类。非谓语动词不能作句子的谓语动词，而是作除谓语动词以外的其他句子成分。

1 非谓语动词的句法功能　　》

	主语	宾语	表语	定语	状语	补语
不定式	+	+	+	+	+	+
分词	−	−	+	+	+	+
动名词	+	+	+	+	−	−

2 非谓语动词语态　　》

非谓语动词又称非限定动词，这意味着它不跟随主语发生人称和数的变化。但是，非谓语动词毕竟是由动词变化而来，因而，仍保留一定的动词特征。它也有几种时态形式，即一般式、完成式、动词不定式还有进行式和完成进行式，以及主动与被动的区别。非谓语动词的时态是以谓语动词的动作为参照的，也就是说，非谓语动词的时态只表示其动作发生的时间是在谓语动词的动作之前、之后或同时。

非谓语动词	时态	主动形式	被动形式
动词不定式	一般时	to do	to be done
	完成时	to have done	to have been done
	进行时	to be doing	/
	完成进行时	to have been doing	/
分词	一般时	doing	being done
	完成时	having done	having been done
	过去分词	/	done

非谓语动词	时态	主动形式	被动形式
动名词	一般时	doing	being done
	完成时	having done	having been done

3 常见错误 ⌄⌄

（1）谓语动词与非谓语动词的混淆

【示例】

In prison you get your own toilet, while at work you having to share with others.	＿＿＿＿＿

【答案】having — have。

【解析】while 表示转折、对比，前后两句是平行对等的句子结构，都要用完整的主谓结构，用谓语动词。

（2）非谓语动词语态、时态错误

【示例】

Having given such a good opportunity, how could she let it slip away?	＿＿＿＿＿

【答案】Having ∧ given — ∧ been。

【解析】作状语的-ing 分词语态错误。give 和 she 之间是被动关系。

（3）谓语动词的主语与非谓语动词的逻辑主语的关系不清

　　如果分词的逻辑主语与谓语动词逻辑主语不一致时，语法上要求分词必须带上自己的逻辑主语，这种带有自己的逻辑主语的分词结构叫独立主格结构。独立主格结构在句中作状语，表示时间、原因、条件等。这种题目是我们在学习和考试时的难点，请大家格外留心。

【示例】

Few years ago, while traveling through Italy, the idea of the history of Florentine architecture occurred to him.	＿＿＿＿＿

【答案】while ∧ traveling — ∧ he。

【解析】"while traveling through Italy" 是时间状语，traveling 的逻辑主语是 he，"the idea … occurred to him" 是主句，occurred 的主语是 idea。traveling 的逻辑主语与 occurred 的主语不一致，因此 traveling 必须带上自己的逻辑主语 he。

（4）非谓语动词——不定式、-ing 分词、-ed 分词的混淆

【示例】 (02-6-S2)

And any large or rich city is going to attract poor immigrants, who flood in, filling with hopes of prosperity which are then often disappointing.	2. _____

【答案】filling — filled。

【解析】由 filling with 的逻辑主语为 immigrants 可知，immigrants 与 fill 为被动关系，故应改为过去分词形式。

助动词与情态动词

1 助动词和情态动词的作用

助动词和情态动词都是特殊动词，非常有用。没有了它们，疑问句不能成立，否定句也难形成。没有了"have，has，had"，完成时无法存在；没有了"be，is，are，am，been，was，were，being"，就无法表示被动语态。

2 助动词的用法

助动词一般没有词义，主要作用是帮助构成谓语，表示时态、语态、语气或构成疑问或否定形式等。有的时候有一些词义。比如，be 和不定式构成谓语，表示按计划要发生的事，应该做或能够做的事。例如：They had a good discussion on the evening before actual work was to start.。这个句子的意思是，在实际工作头一天晚上他们好好讨论了一次。实际工作是将要开始的，要用 be to do 的结构。be 和不定式构成谓语时，表示按计划要发生的、应该做或能够做的事。

3 情态动词的具体用法

◆情态动词 may（might）加动词的完成式，相较于 must 加动词的完成式，语气上要弱，把握要小。例如，She might have seen the doctor last week, but I am not sure. 上星期她或许去看医生了…。

◆can（could）加动词的完成式，表示过去可能或不可能发生的事，或本来可以做却没做的事。例如，I couldn't have called you. I wasn't near any telephone.

◆should（ought to）加动词的完成式，表示责备、不满；表示本该发生却没发生或（否定句）表示本不该发生却发生了的事。例如，You should have apologized to her for not giving her an immediate reply.

◆needn't 加动词的完成式，表示过去不必做的事情却做了，意思是"其实不必"。例如，You needn't have carried all these parcels yourself. The shop would have delivered them if you had asked a shop assistant. 其实你没必要自己把那些东西搬回

来。只要你对任何一位店员说一下，店铺会把它们送过来的。

【示例】

| You had better not to follow his suit. Or sooner or later you would end in prison. | _____ |

【答案】 to — ⱡo̶。

【解析】 固定用法是 had better do sth. ，否定句式是 had better not do sth. 。

语义选择与词组搭配

　　英语的副词、介词数量很多。与这些副词、介词搭配组合的名词词组、动词词组及其他词组的数量更是不计其数。有些活跃的动词与其他词组合，能构成十几个、甚至几十个不同含义的词组。如 make，take，have，get，go 等。这些词组在日常交流中占有很重要的位置，在考试中是不可少的考点。请同学们平日有意识地积累、扩大自己的词组数量，对词组中的副词、介词保持敏感，注意区别。各个副词、介词、名词、动词都有自己的基本词义，因此容易辨别记忆。因篇幅有限，此处不再一一列举。可参照本书完形填空部分里列举的固定短语。

【示例】　　　　　　　　　　　　　　　　　　　　　　　　　　　(04-1-S7)

| … improvements in yield. In Africa, by instance, improved seed, more fertilizer and advanced growing practices… | 7. _____ |

【答案】 by — for。

【解析】 本题较简单，因为 for instance（或 for example）是固定搭配。

词形、词义、词性混淆、多词与漏词

　　词形、词性混淆、多词与漏词的错误多半是由于基础不扎实，正确的语感未形成造成的。还有一些是由固定的用法或特殊要求没掌握好造成的。这需要多看多背。只有平日大量、艰苦、细致地练习，才能培养出语言的敏感性、精确性，才能在考题设计者的圈套中保持清醒，做到答题准确、迅速。

【示例1】　　　　　　　　　　　　　　　　　　　　　　　　　　(96-6-S5)

| The framer aroused at dawn or before and had much work to do, with his own muscles like his chief source of power. | 5. _____ |

【答案】 aroused — arose。

【解析】 此处是词形、词义混淆。arouse 是及物动词，表示"唤醒…"。arose 是 arise 的过去式，是不及物动词，表示"起床"。

【示例2】　　　　　　　　　　　　　　　　　　　　　　　　　(01-6-S5)

… With occasional breaks for war, the rates of death and infection in the Europe and America dropped steadily through the 19th and 20th centuries…	5. _____

【答案】the — ~~the~~。
【解析】人名、地名等专有名词前不加冠词。

【示例3】　　　　　　　　　　　　　　　　　　　　　　　　　(00-1-S10)

…But perhaps we should look at both sides of the coin before arriving hasty conclusions.	10. _____

【答案】arriving ∧ hasty — ∧at。
【解析】hasty conclusions 意思是"草率的结论","得出草率结论"在英语中用 arrive at hasty conclusions，其中 arrive 是不及物动词，后面要接宾语，只能借助介词 at。

二、句法层面的考查
时态与语态

1 时态

（1）各种时态的具体表现形式

　　综合改错中，时态是常考的一项内容。时态中的过去完成时、将来完成时、过去进行时、完成进行时等，语态中的被动语态，特别是非谓语动词的时态和被动语态都是考点。此部分所占比例较低，但通常会有一题。

以 do 为例	一般时态	进行时态	完成时态	完成进行时态
现在	does do	am/are/is doing	has/have done	has/have been doing
过去	did	was/were doing	had done	had been doing
将来	will do	will be doing	will have done	will have been doing
过去将来	should/would do	should/would be doing	should/would have done	should/would have been doing

（2）常见时态及对应的时间状语

◆一般现在时：every，sometimes 等

◆一般过去时：yesterday，last week，an hour ago，the other day，just now 等

◆一般将来时：next week（month，year），tomorrow，in a week（month，year）等

◆现在完成时：for，since，so far，ever，never，just，yet，till/until，up to now，in past years，always 等

◆过去完成时：before，by，until，when，after，once，as soon as 等

◆过去进行时：the whole morning，all day，while 等

（3）常见的时态错误

最常见的时态错误一般是现在时和过去时的误用，或者是现在完成时和过去完成时的误用。就其表现形式而言，主要有两种：固定时间状语与配合错误；上下文时态矛盾。

【示例】　　　　　　　　　　　　　　　　　　　　　　　　　　　　（06-6-S6）

Studies indicate that many girls are affecting as well — and not getting help.	6. ————

【答案】affecting — affected。

【解析】affecting 为及物动词，用作主动语态时后须接宾语，故可断定 affecting 形式错误，应成 affected。affected 后省略了 by dyslexia。此外，下一段中 discouraged 为 affected 的下义词复现。

2　语态

（1）各种语态的具体表示形式

英语有两种语态，即主动语态和被动语态。被动语态表示主语是谓语动词动作的承受者，其构成为"be + 过去分词"。在综合改错题中最常见的语态错误是被动语态被误用为主动语态。被动语态的各种时态形式如下：

	一般时态	进行时态	完成时态
现在	am（is，are）done	am（is，are）being done	has（have）been done
过去	was（were）done	was（were）being doned	had been done
将来	（will）be done		（will）have been done
过去将来	should（would）be done		should/would have done

【示例】　　　　　　　　　　　　　　　　　　　　　　　　(06-6- S6)

Studies indicate that many girls are affecting as well — and not getting help.	6. _____

【答案】affecting — affected。

【解析】通读本行可知，本行中不存在主谓不一致或引导词使用错误等问题。affecting 为及物动词，用作主动语态时后须接宾语可断定，affecting 形式错误，故换成 affected。affected 后省略了前文中提到的 by dyslexia。

（2）不及物动词（短语）不能用于被动语态

　　常见的不及物动词有：appear，belong to，break out，occur，depart，happen 等。

【示例】

Great changes have been taken place in my hometown.	_____

【答案】been — ~~been~~。

【解析】take place 是不及物动词短语，所以不能用于被动语态。

（3）被动语态中常见介词用法的区分

　　注意区别被动语态中的几个常用介词用法：by 表示动作的执行者或施动力；with 表示用某种工具；of 表示由某种原料制成（原料能直接看出）；from 表示源于某种物质（但不能直接看出原料）。请看下面几个句子：

The article was written by Jack.

The pencil was sharpened with a knife.

The bridge is made of stones.

Wine is made from rice.

主谓一致

1　主谓关系与句子结构

　　初学英语时我们就知道，主语与谓语需要保持数的一致，如 She is…，Those are…，Were you…? Is there…? 等。然而随着语言程度的加深，我们认识到它们并不简单，在使用和辨别时出现一些难点。

　　在涉及主语与谓语保持数的一致之前，有必要提一下句子结构分隔。由于行文需要，常常出现这样的情况：主语与谓语的分隔，谓语与宾语的分隔，定语与被修饰词的分隔，或者并列成分的分隔等。有时句子省略、倒装等等都会给理解造成一定的困难，甚至造成误解。因此，我们平时要养成难句分析的习惯。句子结构清晰，各个部分关系明确，难点就一一化解了。

【示例】

An iron and steel works, with several satellite factories, are to be built here.	_____

【答案】are — is。

【解析】短语 with several satellite factories 不是并列主语, 是插入语, 是状语。An iron and steel works "一座钢铁厂" 是主语, 为了保持主谓一致, 必须用单数。

2 主谓一致的六种特殊情况

(1) 和单数连用的短语

在 together with, as well as, no less than, like, but, except, in addition to, accompanied by 等短语前, 如果主语是单数, 谓语仍然用单数。例如, Nobody but Mary and Tom was there. (只有 Mary 和 Tom 在那里。) No one except my parents knows anything about it. (除了我父母谁也不知道这件事。)

each, either, neither, none 和由 some, any, no, every 构成的复合词按单数看待。例如: Neither of these care is exactly what I need.

None of us is entitled to the privileges.

Has either of them told you?

Someone is using the phone.

(2) 抽象概念

请看下面的句子:

That we made amazing achievement is an undeniable fact.

Growing vegetables needs constant watering.

时间、距离、钱的数额等复数名词表示一个整体概念时, 按单数看待; 侧重具体的数量时, 按复数处理。请看下面的句子:

Five years is already long enough for children to imagine.

Ten thousand dollars was provided for the research project.

Three hours of his last twelve were gone.

(3) 以 -ics 结尾的表示学科的名词

此类名词有: politics, mathematics, statistics, acoustics, linguistics 等。

(4) 临近原则

由 there, here 引起的句子, 主语不止一个时, 谓语和最近的主语一致。请看下面两个句子:

There was carved on the board a dragon and a phoenix. 板子上雕着一条龙和一只凤。

Here is a pen, a few envelopes and some paper for you.

（5）概念原则

集体名词可用作单数，也可用作复数，这取决于表达者心中的概念。表示整体用单数，表示成员用复数。请看下面两个句子：

His family isn't very large. （指整体）

His family are all music lovers. （指各个家人）

（6）名词的可数与不可数的变化

有些不可数名词，在一些特殊的语境中，也可以作为可数名词使用。这时，这些名词前一般都有使这些名词具体化的形容词，此时，这些名词表示具有某种特点的一种事物。如：three colorful waters "三种彩色的水"。

【示例】

Computer, as we know, has many possible use in different fields.	_____

【答案】use — uses。

【解析】句中名词 use 前的修饰语 many 是用来修饰复数名词的，所以 use 应改为 uses。

否定

在否定句中，应该注意区别全部否定和部分否定。

All that glitter is not gold. （= Not all that glitter is gold.） 闪光的不都是金子。

All of my friends are not in Hong Kong. （= Not all of my friends are in Hong Kong.）

All of them are not honest. （= Not all of them are honest.）

Both are not mine. （= One of them is mine）

"Do both of them speak English well?" "No, both of them don't." （= "No, it isn't that both of them do." = "One speaks English well, while the other doesn't."）

Everything is not expensive here. （= It isn't that everything is expensive here.）

以上都是部分否定。由此可见，all，both，every 的否定式是"并不是…都"的意思。以上句子改为全部否定就是：

None that glitter here is gold. 在这里，闪光的都不是金子。

None of our friends are in Hong Kong. （They are all away）

None of them are honest.

Neither is mine.

"Neither of them speaks English well."

Nothing is expensive here.

全部否定的句子一般用 none，neither，nothing，not a single 等词汇手段作彻底否定，句式仍然是肯定形式。

　　每个句中的副词 not 都有一个否定范围。它可以否定主语，也可以否定谓语，也可以否定定语、状语或其他成分。

【示例】

Get someone to check for spelling and grammatical errors, because a spell-checker will pick up every mistake.	6. ＿＿＿＿＿＿

【答案】will ∧ pick —— ∧ not。

【解析】spell-checker will pick up every mistake 表明"拼写检查装置将检查出所有的错误"，这与上一行中 Get someone to check for spelling and grammatical errors（叫人检查拼写和语法错误）矛盾，即原因与结果矛盾。get someone to check for...errors 暗示拼写检查装置并不能检查出所有的错误，故 will 和 pick 之间加入否定词 not。

虚拟语气

　　虚拟语气中，与过去、现在、将来相反的表达形式，同学们都应该熟悉。一些要求用虚拟语气的词汇、句式要记牢。比如，suggest，order，recommend，propose，insist，wish，It's high time…，would rather，If only…等。在六级改错中，值得注意的是虚拟语气的错综条件句、虚拟语气在一些句型中的用法、虚拟语气的一些特殊用法、虚拟语气的省略和倒装情况。本书在完形填空部分对虚拟语气进行了详细的阐释，考生可参照。

【示例】

"Shall I go downstairs?" inquired Oliver. "No," replied a Mr. Brown. "I had rather you remain here."	＿＿＿＿＿＿

【答案】remain —— remained。

【解析】had rather 接从句时，从句谓语要求用虚拟语气。

并列句和复合句

1 并列句

　　并列连词所连接的两个并列部分在语法上必须是对等的，也就是说名词对名词，介词短语对介词短语，从句对从句。这点是并列连词的最基本用法，但却常被学习者所忽略，因此也成为六级改错中的一个重要考点。

【示例】　　　　　　　　　　　　　　　　　　　　　　　(03-9-S3)

West, was to find a piece of place, build a house for one's family, and started a farm.	3. ＿＿＿＿＿＿

【答案】　started — start。

【解析】　根据分析可知, to find…, (to) build…以及 (to) started…为并列表语。由 build 前的逗号以及 started 前的并列连词 and 可知, started 的形式须与 find, build 一致, 故应把 started 改为动词原形 start。

2　复合句

与并列句一样, 复合句的构成方式是把几个简单句连接在一起。但是复合句的各个组成部分并非同等重要, 其中总有一个独立小句 (即"主句") 和一个或一个以上从属小句 (即"从句")。主句常常可以单独成句。

从句可以分为以下三种:

① 名词从句: 像任何名词一样, 名词从句也可以作动词的主语, 但更多的是用作动词的宾语, 或用作动词 be 或其他系动词, 如 seem 和 appear 的表语。

② 关系 (或形容词) 从句: 这种从句起的作用和形容词一样, 用以修饰人、事、物。

③ 状语从句: 状语从句可表示时间、地点、方式、目的、条件、让步等等。

【示例1】　　　　　　　　　　　　　　　　　　　　　(02-6-S4)

…century London or early nineteenth-century Paris. This is new is the scale.	4. ＿＿＿＿＿＿

【答案】　This — What。

【解析】　本行中 century London or early nineteenth-century Paris 不存在错误。错误范围在 This is new 中。本句为"主＋系＋表"结构, This is new 为完整的句子, 如果正确, 那么后面不能再接系表结构 (is the scale), 如果 is the scale 正确, 前面的部分应是主语, 故把错误锁定在 This 上。this 不能引导从句, 故用能引导主语从句并在从句中作主语的 What 来换掉 This。

【示例2】　　　　　　　　　　　　　　　　　　　　　(04-6-S7)

But to sociologists, to be human is to be cultured, because of culture is the common world of experience we share with other members of our group.	7. ＿＿＿＿＿＿

【答案】　of — ~~of~~。

【解析】　由 because of 后为完整的句子可知, 这里是个原因状语从句。because of 和 because 均可以表原因, 但 because of 后接的是名词或名词性短语, 而 because 后接的是完整的句子, 即引导的是原因状语从句。

平行结构

　　平行结构是各类考试题型中使用频率相当高的一种语言现象，在综合改错、完形填空、阅读和写作中都要用到。平行结构是指用相同的语法结构表示几个意思上密切相关的内容。平行结构主要用于表达两个或两个以上的同等重要意义的事物，表示比较或对照等。

　　平行结构内可以是词、短语，也可以是句子。例如 hot and humid（形容词），too much complaint but not any suggestion（名词短语），when they leave and where they go（从句）。

　　连接平行或并列结构的有单个的连词，如 and，but，or 或是成对出现的并列连词，如 both…and…，not…but…，not only…but（also）…，either…or…，neither…nor…，as well as…等。

【示例1】　　　　　　　　　　　　　　　　　　　　　　　　　　（05-12- S7）

Restrict yourself to one or two pages, and listing any publications or referees on a separate sheet.	7. ＿＿＿＿＿＿

【答案】listing — list。
【解析】本句为并列祈使句，语气与第四、五、七段首句一致，均提出建议，这也正符合整篇文章构成为问题解决型特点。Restrict 为原形动词，后用了并列连词 and，故 listing 的形式应与 Restrict 一致，即用原形动词。

【示例2】　　　　　　　　　　　　　　　　　　　　　　　　　　（04-1- S6）

…if the population doubles by the mid-21st century, although feeding 10 billion people will not be easy for politics, economic and environmental reasons.	6. ＿＿＿＿＿＿

【答案】politics — political。
【解析】名词误用作定语。politics 是名词不可用作定语，应用形容词形式 political，与 economic and environment 保持一致。

三、篇章与逻辑意义的考查

　　我们在词法、句法改错部分应用的一些语法规定、基本原则和技巧，在本部分也大都是适用的。区别在于，不像词法、句法改错部分那样微观细致，篇章层次需要的视角更宽，识别内容更多，照应范围也更大。

上下文一致（观点、事实、态度等）

　　综合改错以阅读为基础，以语法为指针，以一篇短文的形式、改错的题型考该学生较高程度的英语综合应用能力。因此，同学们在阅读短文时，要力求扩大自己的迅速、短时记忆容量，把那些有用信息 keep at the back of your mind，以备答题时使用。在改错题中，词义不当、信号词或是过渡词误用以及连接词、助动词、情态动词的误用都会造成文章中观点、事实、态度等不符的情况。这时对比大脑中的记忆，就能敏感地觉察出错误。

【示例1】　　　　　　　　　　　　　　　　　　　　　　　　　(01-6-S9)

They are wrong. In the mid-1980s the frequency of infections and deaths started to pick up again around the world. Where tuberculosis had vanished, it came back; in many places where it had never been away, it grew better...	9. _____

【答案】 better — worse。

【解析】 根据上文，医学研究人员认为抗菌素的使用能对付结核病，于是便宣布治疗结核病取得了成功。然而，他们错了。二十世纪八十年代中期，结核病又开始在世界各地蔓延滋生。原先消灭了结核病的地区又发现了这种病症；而原先就没有根治的地区情况比以前更糟了，而不是更好了。因此，"better"应改为"worse"。

【示例2】　　　　　　　　　　　　　　　　　　　　　　　　　(00-6-S2)

...We asked a lady, who replied that she thought you could tell a well-mannered person in the way they occupied the space around them — for example, when such a person walks down a street he or she is constantly unaware of others...	2. _____

【答案】 unaware — aware。

【解析】 ...本文的主旨是 good manners，前文中提到许多人的看法，本句是问一位女士的看法。她的回答是，她认为你可以从一个人占据周围空间的方式来判断他是否有良好行为。比如：一个有良好行为的人在街上走路时总能意识到他人的存在。这样的人决不会撞到别人身上。显然，若用"unaware"则前后意思矛盾，应将其改为"aware"。

前后指代一致

代词 it，that，they，those，its，theirs，one，ones，such，so 等应该和它们指代的名词、词组、句子，或它们指代的文章中的人物、事物保持数、性、人称等方面的协调一致关系。我们把这种协调一致关系称作为指代一致关系。指代关系错误是六级改错中经常出现的考点。

【示例】 (04-1-S2)

...The fast-growing population's demand for food, they warned, would soon exceed their supply, leading to widespread food shortages and starvation.	2. _____

【答案】 their — its。

【解析】 应把 their 改成 its。本题犯了名词与代词指代不一致的错误。因为 supply 对应的是前文中的 demand。两个名词词组相对，这里 their 应改为 its，指代前面的 food。

转折与启承

　　文章的表达与人脑的逻辑思维是一样的。句子之间，段落之间都有一定的关系。这些逻辑关系主要有时间关系、空间关系、比较关系、因果关系，还有表示并列、条件、目的、方式、让步、主次、大小等关系。

　　表达这些关系可以使用句子手段，如并列句、主从复合句等；也可以使用词汇手段——信号词或过渡词。这些词可以确保内容连贯，条理清晰，可以使文章的承上启下、语气转折显得自然流畅。一篇文章如果缺少了过渡连接词语，就显得生硬，甚至使人不明白。常用的过渡连接词有如下几类：

（1）表示空间

　　beside, between, beyond, across, over, at, from, into, here, inside, outside, to the left, in the middle, next to, opposite to 等。

（2）表示时间

　　now, then, not long after, soon, after a while, meanwhile, immediately, before, next, after that, in time, later, following, finally, eventually, earlier, at first, at last, just then, while, from then on, ever since, first, firstly, to begin with, in the first place 等。

（3）表示举例

　　for example, for instance, to illustrate, such as, namely, for one thing 等。

（4）表示递进

　　also, moreover, then, first, second 等。

（5）表示转折

　　but, however, yet, though, although, in spite of 等。

（6）表示强调

　　surely, certainly, indeed, above all, most importantly 等。

（7）表示总结

finally, at last, to conclude, in conclusion, to sum up, in summary, in brief 等。

（8）表示因果

because, thus, since, so as, so that, for, as a result, consequently, therefore, for this reason, hence, accordingly, because of 等。

（9）表示比较、对比

similarly, like, however, but, yet, still, also, equally, nevertheless, unlike, although, whereas in the same way, on the contrary, on the other hand, in contrast 等。

【示例1】 (03-9-S8)

…they dreamed of buying houses and starting families. But there was a tremendous boom in home building.	8. _____

【答案】But — So。

【解析】but 是表示转折关系的连接词，所以确定其前后句子逻辑关系是解答本题的关键。But 前一句的 they dreamed of buying houses and starting families 与其所在句的 there was a tremendous boom in home building 在逻辑上是因果关系，故应将 But 换成 So。

【示例2】 (96-6-S2)

In 1860 because some of the farm population had moved to the city, yet eighteen percent of the American population was still in the country.	2. _____

【答案】because — although。

【解析】下文中出现了 yet，是明显的转折。这句是让步状语从句，应改为 although。

四、专项练习

Exercise 1

The term "virus" is derived from the Latin word for poison, or slime. It was originally applied to the noxious stench emanating from swamps that was thought to cause a variety of disease in the   1. _____
centuries before microbes were discovered and specifically linked to illness. But it was until almost the end of the nineteenth century   2. _____
that a true virus was proven to be the reason of a disease.   3. _____

The nature of viruses made them impossible to detect for

many years, even after bacteria had been discovered and studied.
Not only are viruses too small to be seen with a light microscope,
but also can be detected through their biological activity,   4. _____
except as it occurs in conjunction with other organisms. In fact,
viruses show no traces of biological activity by themselves. Unlike
bacteria, they are not living agents in the strictest way. Viruses are   5. _____
very simple pieces of organic material composing only of *nucleic*   6. _____
acid (核酸), either DNA or RNA, enclosed with a coat of protein   7. _____
made up of simple structural traits. (Some viruses also contain
carbohydrates and lipids.) They are *parasites* (寄生虫) require   8. _____
human, animal, or plant cells to live. The virus replicates by
attaching to a cell and inject its nucleic acid; once inside the cell,   9. _____
the DNA or RNA that contains the virus' genetic information
takes on the cell's biological machinery, and the cell begins to   10. _____
manufacture viral proteins rather than its own.

Exercise 2

From Boston to Los Angeles, from New York City to Chicago to   1. _____
Dallas, museums are both planning, building, or wrapping up wholesale
expansion programs. These programs already have radically altered facades
and floor plans or are expecting to do so in the not-too-distant future.   2. _____

In New York City alone, six major institutions have spread up and
out into the air space and neighborhoods around them or are preparing   3. _____
to do so. The reasons for this confluence of activity are complex,
but one factor is a consideration somewhere — space. With collections   4. _____
expand, with the needs and functions of museums changing, empty space   5. _____
has become very precious commodity.   6. _____

Probably nowhere in the country is this truer than at the Philadelphia
Museum of Art, which has needed additional space for decades and which
receive its last significant facelift ten years ago. Because of the space crunch,   7. _____
the Art Museum has become increasingly cautious on considering   8. _____
acquisitions and donations of art, in some cases passing up opportunities to
strengthen its collections.

Deaccession — or selling off — works of art has taken on new
important because of the museum's space problems. And increasingly,   9. _____
curators have forced to juggle gallery space, rotating one masterpiece into   10. _____
public view while another is sent to storage.

答案与解析

Exercise 1

1. 【答案】disease — diseases。

【解析】本题考查名词单复数。词组 a variety of 修饰的是复数名词，指"各种各样的…"，因此将 disease 改为 diseases。

2. 【答案】was ∧ until — ∧ not。

【解析】本题考查特殊句型。It was not until…that…为固定句式，意为"直到…才…"。

3. 【答案】reason — cause。

【解析】本题考查近义词辨析。reason 常与介词 for 搭配，指某事的原因、理由。cause 与 of 搭配，指某事的起因。由此可知，应该将 reason 改成 cause。

4. 【答案】can — cannot。

【解析】本题考查句型。not only…but …为固定句型"不但…而且…"表示递进关系，前面用了"too…to…"表示否定意义的关联词，所以这里应将 can 改为 cannot。

5. 【答案】way — sense。

【解析】本题考查固定搭配。虽然 in a way 与 in a sense 都可指"在某种程度上，在某种意义上"，但 in a sense 可加定语构成 in a broad/narrow/the strictest sense 等搭配，而 way 无此用法，因此要将其改成 sense。

6. 【答案】composing — composed。

【解析】本题考查非谓语动词。viruses 是由 nucleic acid 构成的，因此应该用 compose 的过去分词形式而不是现在分词形式。

7. 【答案】with — in。

【解析】本题考查介词搭配。enclose with sth. 意为"附带某物"，根据常识我们知道 nucleic acid，DNA，RNA 不是附带着一层蛋白质的，而是被蛋白质外层包围着的，因此将 with 改成 in。enclose in sth. 意为"包在某物中"。

8. 【答案】require — requiring。

【解析】本题考查非谓语动词。跟在 parasites 后面的 require… to live 是作它的定语，因此要用 require 的现在分词或过去分词形式。由于 parasites 即是动作的发出者，因此要用现在分词形式，即 requiring。

9. 【答案】inject — injecting。

【解析】本题考查平行结构。and 所连接的两个平行结构在语法上必须是对等的，也就是说其形式应该保持一致。又由于介词后面应该用动词-ing 形式，因此将 inject 改成 injecting。

10. 【答案】on — over。

【解析】 本题考查短语搭配。根据 and the cell begins to manufacture viral proteins rather than its own 可知 the virus' genetic information 对 the cell's biological machinery 具有控制力，take on "雇佣" 不能使语义通顺。take over 可以表示 "接管，接收" 之意，因此将 on 改为 over。

Exercise 2

1. 【答案】 both — either。
   【解析】 本题考查固定搭配。both 和 or 不能搭配，both 和 and 搭配，either 和 or 搭配。文中提到的博物馆的做法不止两种，故应使用 either...or...这一搭配。

2. 【答案】 expecting — expected。
   【解析】 本题考查语态。expect 的逻辑主语并不是句子的主语 These programs，故此处应用被动语态，be expected to do sth. 是固定用法。

3. 【答案】 them — it。
   【解析】 本题考查代词指代问题。此处的代词指代的是上文的 the air space，故应使用单数形式 it。

4. 【答案】 somewhere — everywhere。
   【解析】 本题考查逻辑一致。根据上下文逻辑，这个因素是无论何地均要考虑的，故用 everywhere。

5. 【答案】 expand — expanding。
   【解析】 本题考查非谓语动词。with 是介词，后面要用动名词，故将 expand 改为 expanding。

6. 【答案】 become ∧ very — ∧ a。
   【解析】 本题考查冠词的用法。commodity 是可数名词单数，故在前面加不定冠词 a。

7. 【答案】 receive — received。
   【解析】 本题考查时态。根据句中的时间状语 ten years ago 可知此处应该用过去时，故将 receive 改为 received。

8. 【答案】 on — in。
   【解析】 本题考查固定用法。"很谨慎地做某事" 用英语表达为 be cautious in doing sth. ，故将句中的 on 改成 in。

9. 【答案】 important — importance。
   【解析】 本题考查词性。take on 后面应使用名词，故将 important 改成 importance。

10. 【答案】 have ∧ forced — ∧ been。
    【解析】 本题考查语态。curators 不是 force 这一动作的逻辑主语，因此本句应用被动语态。但其中缺少构成被动语态的 been。

技 巧 熟 悉

从上一章的考点和错误类型分析可知，做改错题一定要具有一双"慧眼"。重要的不是自己会运用一个语法点或知识点，而是能够识别出错误的用法，以审查的眼光去看每一道改错题。这就需要掌握必要的解题步骤和技巧。

一、解题步骤

◆一般来说，做题时千万不要拿起来就改。先花一两分钟从头到尾通读全文，对文章大致内容和行文结构有所了解，做到心中有数。

◆然后把重点放在有错误项的标题号行，寻找较容易辨认的语法错误，如主谓不一致、时态、语态使用错误、非谓语动词错误等等。

◆如果错行中不存在上述明显错误，则应查看是否有词语搭配错误，易混词错误、词性错误等等细节错误。如果错行中既不存在语法错误，也不存在词汇错误，则从整体上查看上下文意思是否连贯，连接词是否使用正确，是否有逻辑混乱的现象，如否定句误用成肯定句造成句意不通等。注意：有时没有错项的行对改错很有帮助。

◆找到错误项之后，按要求形式进行改正、增添、删除，并设法找到一个正确项使句子在语法、语义和逻辑上都成立。

二、解题要点

◆文章要读懂读细；

◆要善于利用文中有关信息，更正原文中语意、逻辑上的错误；

◆不要受前一步改错的影响；

◆最后通读全文，再次核查。

三、时间安排建议

此题考试时间为 15 分钟。建议同学们用 3 分钟迅速浏览短文，明确文章主题、内容、结构和作者态度等；10 分钟仔细阅读短文，并寻找标号行中的错误点，找到以后按照词法、句法、上下文的逻辑关系更正错误；2 分钟检查答案。简单地说就是：3 - 10 - 2。当然，同学们也可以自测一下，做个记录，在我们给出的时间分配上做些调整，那就是适合你自己的时间安排了。

四、专项练习

Exercise 1

A new era is upon us. Call it which you will: the service economy, the information age, the knowledge society. It all translates to a fundamental change in the way we work. Already we're partly there. The percentage of people who earn their live by making things has fallen dramatically in the Western World. Today the majority of jobs in America, Europe and Japan (two thirds or more in of these countries) are in the service industry, and the number is in the rise. More women are in the work force than ever before. There are more part-time jobs. More people are self-employed. But the breadth of the economic transformation can't have measured by numbers alone, because it also is giving rise to a radical new way of thinking about the nature of work itself. Long-held notions about jobs and careers, the skills needed to succeed, even the relation between individuals and employers — all these are being at challenged.

We must only to look behind us to get some sense of what may lie ahead. No one looking ahead 20 years possibly could have foreseen the ways in which a single invention, the *chip* (集成块), would transform our world thanks in its applications in personal computers, digital communications and factory robots. Tomorrow's achievements in biotechnology, artificial intelligence or even some still unimagined technology could produce a similar wave of dramatic changes. But one thing is certain: information and knowledge will become even more vital, and the people who possess it, whether they work in manufacturing nor services, will have the advantage and produced the wealth. Computer knowledge will become as basic a requirement as the ability to read and write. The ability to solve problems by applying information instead of performing routine tasks will be valued all else. If you cast your mind ahead 10 years, information services will be predominant. It will be the way you do your job.

1. _____

2. _____

3. _____

4. _____

5. _____

6. _____

7. _____

8. _____

9. _____

10. _____

Exercise 2

Acting is so an over-crowded profession that the only advice which should be given to a young person thinking of going on the stage is "Don't!" But that is useless to try to discourage someone who feels he must act, although the chances of his becoming famous is small. The normal way to begin is a drama school. Usually only students who show promise and talent are accepted, and the course lasts two years. Then the young actor or actress takes in work with a *repertory company* (剧团). They have to do everything there in the theater: painting scenery, looking after the furniture, taking the care of the costumes, and even act in very small parts. It is very hard work indeed, the hours are long and the salary is tiny. But, young actors have the stage in their blood are happy, waiting for the chance.

Of course, some people have unusual chances which lead to famous and success without this long and dull training. Connie Pratt, for example, was just an ordinary girl working in a bicycle factory. A film producer happened to catch sight of her one morning being waiting at a bus stop. They gave her some necessary lessons and within a few weeks she was playing the leading part in the movie. Of course, she was given a more dramatic name, which is now world-famous. But chances like this happen once in a blue moon!

1. _____
2. _____
3. _____
4. _____

5. _____

6. _____
7. _____
8. _____

9. _____

10. _____

答案与解析

Exercise 1

1. 【答案】which — what。
   【解析】本题考查引导词，which 引导的名词性从句中，which 含义为"哪一个"，是指从既定的选择范围中选出某一个，冒号前面的部分中不存在这样一个选择范围，所以 which 不对。将 which 改为 what，冒号后面所列举的正是各种叫法。此句意为：你愿意怎么叫它就怎么叫。

2. 【答案】live — living。
   【解析】本题考查固定短语。earn one's living 为固定搭配，意为"赚钱、谋生"。

3. 【答案】第一个 in — on。
   【解析】本题考查固定短语。be on the rise 为固定搭配，意为"在上升"。像这样的词组还有：on the increase "增加"，on the decrease "减少"，on the de-

cline "下降"。

4. 【答案】have — be。

　　【解析】 本题考查语态。measure 这个动作的逻辑主语不是句子的主语，故此处应该用被动语态，而不是完成时态。句子大意为：经济改革的广度不能仅仅靠数字来衡量。

5. 【答案】at — at。

　　【解析】 本题考查句子结构。该部分为现在进行时的被动语态，介词 at 是多余的。此句意为：所有这些都受到了挑战。

6. 【答案】must — have。

　　【解析】 本题考查动词。must 后不跟 to do sth.，have to 为固定词组，意为"不得不，必须"，相当于 must。此处错误。

7. 【答案】第一个 in — to。

　　【解析】 本题考查固定搭配。thank 不和介词 in 连用，thanks to 为固定词组，意为"因为，由于"。

8. 【答案】nor — or。

　　【解析】 本题考查固定搭配。whether…or…为固定搭配，意为"不管…还是…"，此句意为：不管他们是在工厂工作还是在服务业工作。nor 通常和 neither 连用，含有否定的意义。但此处是表选择而非表否定，故应将 nor 改为 or。

9. 【答案】produced — produce。

　　【解析】 本题考查并列谓语的形式一致。由 and 连接的并列的谓语动词时态，在形式上要保持一致，and 前是（动词）have，故将 produced 改为 produce。

10. 【答案】valued ∧ all — ∧ above。

　　【解析】 本题考查惯用法。valued above all else 是习惯表达，意为"比其他一切更重要，更有价值"，其中介词 above 不能省略。

Exercise 2

1. 【答案】so — such。

　　【解析】 本题考查近义词的辨析。so 与 such 都可以表示"这样，如此"之意，但它们的用法不同。so 为副词，应修饰形容词、副词或动词，如 The dream he had had for so many years ended there.（他多年来所抱有的幻想就这样结束了。）而 such 是形容词，可用来修饰名词。句中的中心词是名词短语 an overcrowded profession "过度拥挤的职业"，显然应该用 such。

2. 【答案】which — that。

　　【解析】 本题考查定语从句中的关系代词。该定语从句的先行词是 advice，关系代词可用 which 或 that，但因为前面有 the only 修饰，所以只能用 that。

3. 【答案】that — it。

【解析】 本题考查形式主语。该句结构中真正的主语应该是 to try to…must act，that 不能代替它作形式主语，只能用 it。

4. 【答案】 is — are。

【解析】 本题考查主谓一致。句子的主语是 the chances，为可数名词复数，谓语动词应与其保持一致，故改成复数形式。

5. 【答案】 in — up。

【解析】 本题考查动词短语。take in 的意思是"吸收"，不能同句中的宾语 work 构成合理搭配。应改为 take up "从事（工作）"，使语意通顺。与 take 相关的动词短语还有：take after "像，学…的样子"，take down "拿下，记下"，take off "拿掉，脱下"，take over "接收，接管" 等。

6. 【答案】 第二个 the — the。

【解析】 本题考查固定短语。take care of "照顾" 是固定短语，名词前不加冠词。care 是抽象名词，通常不加冠词，但在特指时要加定冠词，如 I bought a product for the care of fine floors yesterday. （我昨天买了保养考究地板的产品。）

7. 【答案】 act — acting。

【解析】 本题考查平行结构中的一致性。句中的 act 是与前面的 painting，looking after 并列作 everything 的同位语，应保持形式上的一致，改成 acting。

8. 【答案】 have — with。

【解析】 本题考查句子结构。原句中有两个动词 have 和 are，显然 are 是谓语动词，应把 have 改掉。with 具有 have 的含义，既可保持结构正确，又能维持句子的原意。

9. 【答案】 famous — fame。

【解析】 本题考查句子成分。动词短语 lead to 后应接宾语，famous 是形容词不能做宾语，应改成其名词形式 fame。

10. 【答案】 being — being。

【解析】 本题考查非谓语动词中的现在分词。现在分词本身就有主动和进行的意思，不需要用 being。在强调主动的动作在谓语所表示的动作前完成时可用 having done 的形式。

The National Endowment for the Arts recently released the results of its "Reading at Risk" survey, which described the movement of the American public away from books and literature and toward television and electronic media. According to the survey, "reading is on the decline on every region, within every ethnic group, and at every educational level."

1. _____

The day the NEA report released, the U. S. House, in a tie vote, upheld the government's right to obtain bookstore and library records under a provision of the USA Patriot Act. The House's proposal would have barred the federal government from demand library records, reading lists, book customer lists and other material in terrorism and intelligence investigations.

2. _____

3. _____

These two events are completely unrelated to, yet they echo each other in the message they send about the place of books and reading in American culture. At the heart of the NEA survey is the belief in our democratic system depends on leaders who can think critically, analyze texts and writing clearly. All of these are skills promoted by reading and discussing books and literature. At the same time, through a provision of the Patriot Act, the leaders of our country are unconsciously sending the message that readingmay be connected to desirable activities that might undermine our system of government rather than helping democracy flourish.

4. _____

5. _____

6. _____

7. _____

Our culture's decline in reading begin well before the existence of the Patriot Act. During the 1980s' culture wars, school systems across the country pulled some books from library shelves because its content was deemed by parents and teachers to be inappropriate. Now what started in schools across the country is playing itself out on a nation stage andis possibly having an impact on the reading habits of the American public.

8. _____

9. _____

10. _____

2006 年 12 月

The most important starting point for improving the understanding of science is undoubtedly an adequate scientific education at school. Public attitudes towards science owe much the   1. _____
way science is taught in these institutions. Today, school is
what most people come into contact with a formal instruction   2. _____
and explanation of science for the first time, at least in a systematic way. It is at this point which the foundations are laid   3. _____
for an interest in science. What is taught (and how) in this
first encounter will largely determine an individual's view of the
subject in adult life. Understanding the original of the negative   4. _____
attitudes towards science may help us to modify them. Most education system neglect exploration, understanding and reflec-   5. _____
tion. Teachers in schools tend to present science as a collection
of facts, often by more detail than necessary. As a result, chil-   6. _____
dren memorize processes such as mathematical formulas or the
periodic table, only to forget it shortly afterwards. The task of   7. _____
learning facts and concepts, one at a time, makes learning la-
borious, boring and efficient. Such a purely empirical ap-   8. _____
proach, which consists of observation and description, is also,
in a sense, unscientific or incomplete. There is therefore a need
for resources and methods of teaching that facilitates a deep un-   9. _____
derstanding of science in an enjoyable way. Science should not
only be 'fun' in the same way as playing a video game, but
'hard fun'—a deep feeling of connection made possibly only   10. _____
by imaginative engagement.

2006 年 6 月

Until recently, dyslexia and other reading problems were a
mystery to most teachers and parents. As a result, too many
kids passed through schools without master the printed page.   1. _____
Some were treated as mentally deficient, many were left func-
tionally *illiterate* (文盲的), unable to ever meet their potential. But in the last several years, there's been a revolution in
that we've learned about reading and dyslexia. Scientists are   2. _____
using a variety of new imaging techniques to watch the brain at

work. Their experiments have shown that reading disorders are most likely the result of what is, in an effect, faulty writing in the brain — not lazy, stupidity or a poor home environment. There's also convincing evidence which dyslexia is largely inherited. It is now considered a chronic problem for some kids, not just a "phase". Scientists have also discarded another old stereotype that almost all dyslexics are boys. Studies indicate that many girls are affecting as well —and not getting help.

3. _____

4. _____

5. _____

6. _____

At same time, educational researchers have come up with innovative teaching strategies for kids who are having trouble learning to read. New screening tests are identifying children at risk before they get discouraged by year of frustration and failure. And educators are trying to get the message to parents that they should be on the alert for the first signs of potential problems.

7. _____

8. _____

It's an urgent mission. Mass literacy is a relative new social goal. A hundred years ago people didn't need to be good readers in order to earn a living. But in the Information Age, no one can get by with knowing how to read well and understand increasingly complex material.

9. _____

10. _____

2005 年 12 月

Every week hundreds of *CVs* (简历) land on our desks.

We've seen it all: CVs printed on pink paper, CVs that are 10 pages long and CVs with silly mistakes in first paragraph. A good CV is your passport to an interview and, ultimate, to the job you want. Initial impressions are vital, and a *badly*-presented CV could mean acceptance, regardless of what's in it.

1. _____

2. _____

3. _____

Here are a few ways to avoid end up on the reject pile.

4. _____

Print your CV on good-quality white paper. CVs with flowery backgrounds or pink paper will stand out upon all the wrong reasons.

5. _____

Get someone to check for spelling and grammatical errors, because a spell-checker will pick up every mistake. CVs with errors will be rejected — it shows that you don't pay attention

6. _____

to detail.

　　Restrict yourself to one or two pages, and listing any pub-
lications or referees on a separate sheet. If you are sending your
CV electronically, check the formatting by sending it to yourself first. Keep up the format simple.

　　Do not send a photo unless specifically requested. If you
have to send one, make sure it is one taking in a professional
setting, rather than a holiday snap.

　　Getting the presentation right is just the first step. What
about the content? The rule here is to keep it factual and truth-
ful — exaggerations usually get find out. And remember to tai-
lor your CV to each different job.

7. ＿＿＿＿＿＿

8. ＿＿＿＿＿＿

9. ＿＿＿＿＿＿

10. ＿＿＿＿＿＿

2005 年 1 月

　　The World Health Organization (WHO) says its ten-year
campaign to remove *leprosy* (麻风病) as a world health problem has been successful. Doctor Brundtland, head of the
WHO, says a number of leprosy cases around the world has
been cut of ninety percent during the past ten years. She says
efforts are continuing to complete end the disease.

　　Leprosy is caused by bacteria spread through liquid from
the nose and mouth. The disease mainly effects the skin and
nerves. However, if leprosy is not treated it can cause permanent damage for the skin, nerves, eyes, arms or legs.

　　In 1999, an international campaign began to end leprosy.
The WHO, governments of countries most affected by the disease, and several other groups are part of the campaign. This
alliance guarantees that all leprosy patients, even they are
poor, have a right to the most modern treatment. Doctor
Brundtland says leprosy is no longer a disease that requires lifelong treatment by medical experts. Instead, patients can take
that is called a multi-drug therapy.

　　This modern treatment will cure leprosy in 6 to 12
months, depend on the form of the disease. The treatment
combines several drugs taken daily or once a month. The
WHO has given multi-drug therapy to patients freely for the

1. ＿＿＿＿＿＿

2. ＿＿＿＿＿＿

3. ＿＿＿＿＿＿

4. ＿＿＿＿＿＿

5. ＿＿＿＿＿＿

6. ＿＿＿＿＿＿

7. ＿＿＿＿＿＿

8. ＿＿＿＿＿＿

9. ＿＿＿＿＿＿

last fiveyears. The members of the alliance against leprosy plan to target the countries which still threatened by leprosy. Among the estimated 600,000 victims around the world, the WHO believes about 70% are in India. The disease also remains a problem in Africa and South America.

10. _____

2004 年 6 月

Culture refers to the social heritage of a people — the learned patterns for thinking, feeling and acting that characterize a population or society, include the expression of these patterns in material things. Culture is compose of non-material-culture, abstract creations like values, beliefs, customsand institutional arrangement — and material culture — physical object like cooking pots, computers and bathtubs. In sum, culture reflects both the ideas we share or everything we make. In ordinary speech, a person of culture is the individual can speak another language — the person who is unfamiliar with the arts, music, literature, philosophy, or history. But to sociologists, to be human is to be cultured, because of culture is the common world of experience we share with other members of our group.

Culture is essentially to our humanness. It provides a kind of map for relating to others. Consider how you find your way about social life. How do you know how to act in a classroom, or a department store, or toward a person whosmiles or laugh at you?

Your culture supplies you by broad, standardized, ready-made answers for dealing with each of these situations. Therefore, if we know a person's culture, we can understand and even predict a good deal of his behavior.

1. _____
2. _____
3. _____
4. _____
5. _____
6. _____
7. _____
8. _____
9. _____
10. _____

答案与解析

2006 年 12 月（新）

1. 【答案】第二个 on — in。

【解析】on the decline 为固定搭配，意为"呈下降趋势"，符合文意，也正确；

故将错误锁定在介词 **on** every region 上。on 意为 "在…之上"，而此处表示 "在任何地区/区域"，故将 on 改为 **in**（在；在…之内）。

2. 【答案】report ∧ released — ∧ was。

　　【解析】分析句子结构，the U. S. House（美国众议院）为句子主语，upheld（支持，赞成）为谓语，The day the NEA report released 是一个时间状语从句，此处关系代词 when 被省略；report 应该是被发表的，所以应在 report 和 released 之间插入 was。in a tie vote 为习惯用法，意为 "以微弱优势胜出"。

3. 【答案】demand — demanding。

　　【解析】"bar...from doing sth" 为固定用法，意为 "阻止/禁止…做某事"，故将 demand 改为 demanding。

4. 【答案】to — ~~to~~。

　　【解析】"unrelated to" 为固定搭配，意为 "与…无关"，其后须接名词；如果保留介词 to，根据语义此处需添加名词性词组 each other，这与改错题的规则不符，故将 to 去掉。unrelated 意为 "无关的，不相关的"。

5. 【答案】in — that。

　　【解析】分析句子结构，本句为介词短语提前引起的倒装句，句子的谓语 is 被提前到主语 the belief 之前。句中同时出现两个动词，系动词 is 在主句中作谓语，因此 depends 应该是从句中的谓语。our democratic system depends on leaders … clearly 是 the belief 的同位语从句；同位语从句中，当先行词为物时一般由关系代词 that 来引导，并且 that 不能省略，故将 in 改为 that。belief in 为习惯用法，意为 "相信…"，但介词 in 不能引导从句。

6. 【答案】writing — write。

　　【解析】writing 与 think 和 analyze 是由 and 连接的三个并列的动词，且三个动词都位于情态动词 can 之后，应使用动词原形，故将 writing 改为 write。

7. 【答案】desirable — undesirable。

　　【解析】be connected to 为固定用法，意为 "与…有关"，其后一般接名词。此处的定语从句 that might undermine our system of government rather than helping democracy flourish 修饰名词 activities，根据从句中的 undermine（损坏，破坏）及 rather than helping（而不是帮助）可知，这些活动（activities）应该是消极的，desirable（可取的，有利的）与语义不符，故将 desirable 改为 undesirable。

8. 【答案】begin — began。

　　【解析】"decline in" 为习惯用法，意为 "在某方面有所下降"；well 可以表示程度，意为 "相当的；充分的"，well before 表示 "早在…之前就已经"。before 表示动作已经发生，因此本句中的动词应使用过去时态，故将 begin 改为 began。

9. 【答案】its — their。

　　【解析】because 在本句中引导原因状语从句，从句中的主语 content（内容）

为不可数名词，且本句描述的是过去发生的事，故从句中的 was 单复数形式和时态都正确。此处的 its 对应的是主句中的 some books，二者在语义上矛盾，故将 its 改为 their。

10. 【答案】nation — national。

【解析】本句的主语为 what 引导的从句，故谓语为 is，主谓一致。play out 为固定搭配，意为"放出；展示"；此处表示"在全国范围的舞台上展示"，nation 意为"国家，民族"，强调国家主权和民族特征，常含政治意味；national 意为"国家级的；全国范围内的"，表示一种更高级别或更大范围，故将 nation 改为 national。

2006 年 12 月

1. 【答案】much ∧ the — ∧ to。

【解析】句子主语为 Public attitudes，故谓语 owe 保持动词原形正确；但 owe 为固定搭配，意为"因为，由于"，故在 much 和 the way 之间插入 to。句子意为"大众对科学的态度很大程度上取决于学校教授科学知识的方式"。

2. 【答案】what — where。

【解析】本行中，institutions 使用复数形式正确；most people come into 主谓一致，也正确。分析句子结构可知，is 后为一表语从句，修饰主语 school。当主语为地点时，从句应由关系代词 where 来引导。come into contact with 为固定词组，意为"开始做某事，着手"。

3. 【答案】which — that。

【解析】It is...that...为强调句型，that 不能换成 which。本句是说"人们对科学的兴趣正是基于这种想法（在学校里能够接受正规系统的科学教育）"。

4. 【答案】original — origin。

【解析】of the negative attitudes 为一介词短语，修饰对象应为名词，故将 original（原来的，起初的）改为名词形式 origin（来源；起因）。

5. 【答案】system — systems。

【解析】修饰语 most（众多的）表明此处的 education system 应使用复数形式，忽略了这一点则很容易把 neglect 改为 neglects。

6. 【答案】by — in。

【解析】a collection of 为固定词组，意为"…的集合/收藏"，后常接名词复数，故 facts 使用复数形式正确。in detail 为固定短语，意为"详细地"；often in more detail than necessary 意为"往往过于详细"，修饰 present。

7. 【答案】it — them。

【解析】此处的代词指代上文中提到的 processes，故将 it 改为 them。

8. 【答案】efficient — inefficient。

【解析】laborious（艰苦的，费劲的）和 boring（无聊的）都表示消极意义，

efficient（有效率的）与此相悖，与文意不符，故应将其改为 inefficient（没有效率的）。句子意思是"记忆事实或概念使学习变得辛苦、无聊也没有效率"。

9.【答案】facilitates — facilitate。

【解析】此处 that 引导的定语从句是在修饰 resources and methods 而不是 teaching；of teaching 为介词短语，作修饰成分，故将 facilitates 改为 facilitate。

10.【答案】possibly — possible。

【解析】此处的过去分词形式 made 表示被动，修饰 a deep feeling。make sth./sb...为固定用法，其后接形容词或名词，意为"使…变得/成为…"，此处表示"使对（事物之间的）联系的深刻感知成为可能"，故将 possibly 改为 possible。本句的意思是"科学的乐趣不像玩电子游戏那么简单，而是一种'苦中作乐'，是一种只有积极想象才有可能实现的对（事物之间的）联系的深刻感知"。

2006 年 6 月

1.【答案】master — mastering。

【解析】without 为介词，后须用名词或动名词作宾语。master 后 the printed page 为其宾语，故 master 应该改成 mastering。

2.【答案】that — what。

【解析】a revolution in 为"在…方面的一次革命"，in 为介词，in 后为其宾语，并且 we've learned 中 learned 须有宾语，that 不能满足这要求，故换成 what（= the thing which）。

3.【答案】an — 无。

【解析】通读本行可知，in an effect 中存在错误，in effect 为固定短语，意为"实际上，有效"。

4.【答案】lazy — laziness。

【解析】writing 与破折号后 lazy、stupidity 及下一行中 environment 的词性应一致，故判断 lazy 错，故改成其名词形式（laziness）。如果不通读本句，考生很可能以为 lazy, stupid 及 poor 并列而误把 stupidity 换成 stupid。

5.【答案】which — that。

【解析】evidence 为抽象名词，后通常接同位语从句，由 that 引导，故将 which 换成 that。下一句中 that 为本行 that 的原词复现，stereotype 也为抽象名词。

6.【答案】affecting — affected。

【解析】通读本行可知，本行中不存在主谓不一致或引导词使用错误等问题。affecting 为及物动词，用作主动语态时后须接宾语可断定，affecting 形式错误，故换成 affected。affected 后省略了 by dyslexia。此外，下一段中 discouraged 与 affected 语义照应。

7.【答案】at ∧ same — ∧ the。

【解析】at the same time 为固定短语，在此意为"然而，不过"，使本段与上一段构成转折关系。

8. 【答案】year — years。

【解析】year 为可数名词，在此既没有冠词，又没用复数形式，故判断 year 错。上一段中的 It（dyslexia）is now considered a chronic problem，... not just a "phase" 表明 dyslexia 现在被认为是长期的问题，而不是"某一时期暂时的"问题，故把 year 改为 years。

9. 【答案】relative — relatively。

【解析】relative 及 new 均为形容词，故其中之一肯定是错的，需把其中之一换成其副词形式才能使语义通顺。newly 修饰由过去分词转变过来的形容词，并且要置于被修饰词之前，故在此把 relative 换成 relatively。

10. 【答案】with — without。

【解析】通读本行所在句可知，no one can get 及 knowing how to read well and understand increasingly complex material 语义矛盾，故判断 with 错，应换成其反义词 without。

2005 年 12 月

1. 【答案】in ∧ first — ∧ the。

【解析】本行错误不容易发现，本行中出现序数词 first，其前要加定冠词 the。

2. 【答案】ultimate — ultimately。

【解析】ultimate 为形容词，本行中没有其修饰的成分，并且用两个逗号与前后隔开，从整句意思判断，这一词需换成其副词形式，即 ultimately。

3. 【答案】acceptance — rejection。

【解析】badly-presented CV 与 acceptance 矛盾，故断定 badly 和 acceptance 中必有一个是错的，所以使前后语义一致是解题的关键。badly-presented CV 应意味着 rejection，well-presented CV 应意味着 acceptance，但把 badly 改成 well，还是把 acceptance 改成 rejection 取决于逗号后的 regardless of what's in it。regardless of what's in it 表示"不管里面（内容）怎么样"，其中 what 指的是 content。内容当然存在 errors，mistakes 的可能性。并且，第三段中 CVs with errors will be rejected 表明，无论是 badly-presented CV 还是 well-presented CV，如果内容有错误，最后还是遭拒绝，故把 acceptance 换成其反义词 rejection。

4. 【答案】end — ending。

【解析】avoid 后只能接动名词作宾语，avoid doing sth 意为"避免做某事"。类似的用动名词作宾语的动词还有 delay，deny，enjoy，escape，fancy，mind，postpone，resist 等。

5. 【答案】upon — for。

【解析】根据上一行中的 Print your CV on good-quality white paper 可知，CVs with flowery backgrounds or pink paper（带有花边的或用粉红纸的简历）是不规范的，而且在所有的使用不当中，这种不规范最显眼。stand out 意为"清晰地显出，引人注目"，不与 upon 搭配。for ... reasons 是固定搭配，意为"由于…的原因"。

6.【答案】will ∧ pick — ∧ not。

【解析】spell-checker will pick up every mistake 表明"拼写检查装置将检出所有的错误"，这与上一行中 Get someone to check for spelling and grammatical errors（叫人检查拼写和语法错误）矛盾，即因果矛盾。由于错误在本行，故 will 和 pick 之间加入否定词 not。get someone to check for…errors 暗示拼写检查装置并不能检查出所有的错误。

7.【答案】listing — list。

【解析】Restrict 为原形动词，后用了并列连词 and，故 listing 的形式应与 Restrict 一致，即用原形动词。

8.【答案】up — up。

【解析】此句中，the format 为宾语，simple 为宾语补足语，即对宾语补充说明或表示宾语的状态。keep up 指"继续下去，保持"，后不接复合宾语。keep 作及物动词，并且后可接复合宾语，keep sth simple 表"保持…处于简单状态"，故删掉 up。

9.【答案】taking — taken。

【解析】本行中的两个 one 均指代上一句中提到的 a photo（一张相片），是 send、take 动作的承受者，故此处用 take 的过去分词形式，表示被动语态。

10.【答案】find — found。

【解析】本行前半部分中，上一行的 exaggerations 为主语，get find out 为谓语。exaggerations 指的是简历中夸张的内容，没有行为能力。并且，根据常识也可判断，简历中的瑕疵通常被面试官发现，故 find 改成过去分词形式，即 found。get 相当于动词 be，既可作系动词，又可作助动词。tailor sth to … 为固定搭配，意为"使…适应（特定需要）"。

2005 年 1 月

1.【答案】a — the。

【解析】says 与其主语 head 在数上一致。由下一行的 ninety-percent 可断定，这里谈论的不只是一个病例，可首先判断 cases 正确。a number of 表示"若干，许多"，相当于 many，修饰可数名词复数，故 a number of …cases 短语本身没有问题。around the（world）表示"遍及（世界）"，为固定短语，没有错。所以，错误范围锁定在 a number 上。says 后接的是省略了 that 的宾语从句，谓语为 has been cut，故主语也应是单数，故 of leprosy cases 是修饰 number 的后置定语，number 在此应是特指，前应加 the。a number of leprosy cases

意为"若干个麻风病病例"，重点在 cases 上，而 the number of leprosy cases 意为"麻风病病例的数目"，重点在 number 上。

2. 【答案】of — by。
【解析】由 says 的宾语从句中谓语动词用的是被动语态可知，cut of 后不能再接宾语。cut 作动词时不与 of 连用，故把 of 换成其他介词，但新的介词须与 ninety percent 搭配使用，故只有 by 符合要求。the number has been cut by ninety percent 意为"数量削减了百分之九十"。cut 作名词时可用 a cut of …percent in …结构。

3. 【答案】complete — completely。
【解析】本句中，says 后是省略了 that 的定语从句，efforts 为主语，are continuing 为谓语，to…the disease 为动词不定式短语，作宾语。故将错误锁定在 complete 和 end 上。前面的 to 为动词不定式，可知 complete 和 end 其中至少一个是动词。如果假定不改 complete，end 只能作名词，作宾语，与 the disease 衔接不上，并且 complete 不与 disease 搭配。所以只能将 complete 改为 completely，修饰动词 end。

4. 【答案】effects — affects。
【解析】effects 与 disease 在数上一致，但不与 the skin and nerves 搭配使用。此处需要一个表示"影响"的动词，而 effect 作动词时意为"实现，使生效，引起"，作名词时才意为"影响"，故将 effects 换成其形近词 affects。

5. 【答案】for — to。
【解析】damage to 为固定搭配，意为"对…的伤害"。

6. 【答案】even ∧ they — ∧ if/ though。
【解析】even they are poor 中，even 不能引导从句；由 they are poor 为完整的句子，并且与宾语从句构成转折关系断定，此处应用 even if/ though 意为"即使，虽然"，引导让步状语从句。

7. 【答案】that — what。
【解析】Instead 后的句子中，patients 为主语，can take 为谓语，后须接宾语，故断定 that is called…为宾语从句。但是，that 引导宾语从句时在从句中不承担任何成分，故将其换成 what，在从句中作主语。is called 为从句谓语，a multi-drug therapy 为主语补足语。

8. 【答案】depend — depending。
【解析】depend on the form of the disease 为动词短语，与上一行完整的句子用逗号隔开，并且中间没有并列连词，故 depend on 不是并列谓语。为动词而不作谓语的形式，即非谓语动词：动词不定式、分词、动名词。所以将把 depend 换成哪一种非谓语动词形式是本题的难点。根据 depend on the form of the disease 的意思判断，此处为一种伴随状态（即伴随状语），对句子谓语（will cure）进行补充说明。动词不定式不表示伴随状态，动名词不作状语。现在剩下分词形式，但分词分现在分词和过去分词两种，这时要看与其逻辑主语，即与句子的主语的关系。句子可改写为 The modern treatment will cure, and (the treatment) will depend on…，由此可判断，treatment 与 depend 是主动关系，故将 depend 换成 depending。

9.【答案】freely — free。
【解析】副词 freely 意为"自由地，直率地"，只修饰 given 这一动作本身，而不是 given multi-drug therapy to patients，故将 freely 换成 free（免费地，无偿地）。give sth. to sb. free 表示"免费给某人…"。

10.【答案】which ∧ still — ∧ are。
【解析】the countries 被由 which 引导的定语从句修饰。从句中，by therapy 决定谓语用被动语态形式。threatened by therapy 与第三段首句中 affected by the disease 意思相同。从句中，which 作主语，指代 countries，故被动语态助动词须用复数。still 是修饰实意动词 threatened 的副词，故将 are 加入到 which 和 still 中间。

2004 年 6 月

1.【答案】include — including。
【解析】本句的谓语动词是 refer to，故需将 include 改为非谓语动词形式，including 为现在分词作状语，表示补充说明。

2.【答案】compose — composed。
【解析】be composed of 意为"由…组成，由…构成"，是一个固定搭配。

3.【答案】object — objects。
【解析】object 为可数名词，通过句中 like 后面列举的 cooking pots, computers, bathtubs 可知有许多物件，所以应该用 object 的复数形式。

4.【答案】or — and。
【解析】不存在 both…or…的结构，所以把 both 换成 either 还是把 or 改成 and 是本题的解题关键。文章第一句讲的是文化的定义，提到文化是指一个民族的社会传统，即后天的思考、感觉和行为方式等这些方式在实体上的表现。第二句讲的是文化的构成，即文化是由非物质文化和实体组成的。这一行中，ideas 属于 non-material culture 的范畴，everything 属于 material things 的范畴。两者结合构成文化，也可以说两者通过文化表现出来，即文化同时反映两者，故把 or 换成 and。

5.【答案】individual ∧ can — ∧ who。
【解析】由 can speak 后带有宾语推断，缺的是主语，故需在 can 前加入一个能够引导从句并指代 individual 的关系代词，who 或 that 均可。

6.【答案】unfamiliar — familiar。
【解析】本行中的 unfamiliar with the arts…与上一行的 can speak another lan-

guage 在语义上矛盾。文化人是会讲其他语言的个体，也应该熟悉与其他语言相关的艺术、音乐、文学和史哲知识，故 unfamiliar 须改作 familiar。

7. 【答案】 of — of。

【解析】 because of 后面只跟名词或名词性的短语，不能跟句子；而 because 后跟原因状语从句，原文接的是一个句子所以必须改为 because，因此要去掉 of。

8. 【答案】 essentially — essential。

【解析】 原文中 be 动词后面只能跟形容词或名词，不能跟副词，所以要将副词 essentially 改为形容词形式 essential。

9. 【答案】 laugh — laughs。

【解析】 因为在原文中 smile 和 laugh 是定语从句中的并列谓语，主语是单数并且 smile 已加了 s，所以 laugh 应改为 laughs。

10. 【答案】 by — with。

【解析】 要注意句中的谓语动词 supply，与其搭配使用的介词有 to 和 with，而没有 by，根据短文意思应将 by 应改为 with。supply sb with sth 意为"给某人提供某物"。

模 拟 演 练

Test 1

Since ancient times, trees have always been very important to man who made use of them in numerous ways for their daily life. Even today trees continue to serve man in so many useful ways.

1. _____

They provide man for food, for burning and building material in the form of wood. Without trees it will be impossible to build houses, boats and even bridges. Furniture such as tables, chairs and cupboards are also made from wood.

2. _____

3. _____

4. _____

In the tropics where it is very warm throughout the year, trees protect man from the fierce heat of the sun. They are also useful in preventing good and fertile top-soil from washing away during heavy rains which are so common in the tropics.

5. _____

If there were no trees or vegetation of some sort to hold on the soil with their roots, heavy rains would wash away the rich surface soil so essential for agriculture. The result is that the land becomes useful and unproductive.

6. _____

7. _____

There are many desert areas in the world. A long, long time ago these areas must be very rich, fertile areas, but because of ignorance, people in ancient time cut down trees indiscriminately. They never bothered to plant new trees. Strong winds gradually blew away the rich surface soil and eventually the land was turned into useless deserts that nothing could grow.

8. _____

9. _____

10. _____

Test 2

A father who works, a mother who stays at home, caring for one or more children, that was the traditional American family as recent as 20 years ago. But societies have changed rapidly since the 1950's that the statements now describe less than 15% of all American homes. First, fewer women are staying at home. The number of men working at paying jobs raised by 20% between 1947 and 1975, 10 times more than the increase for men workers.

1. _____

2. _____

3. _____

4. _____

These women are also having fewer child. In 1790, there were 5.8　　5. _____
persons in the average American family. By 1965, the number had
dropped 3.7 and by 1990, the typical American family is expected to　6. _____
contain only 3 persons, about half the size it was 200 years ago. Different
kinds of families are becoming more recognized and accepted. A growing
number of people are living together without marriage. An increasing
number of children are living with only one parent. And more husbands
and wives are choosing to have no children at all.

Alone with these basic changes, there are signs that American　　7. _____
families are growing less stabler and less happy. Almost 40 % of all　　8. _____
marriages in the United States now start in divorce. About 16 % of all　9. _____
new babies are born to unmarried mothers, many of whom are less than
20 years. A growing number of Americans under 20 are drinking heavily,　10. _____
using narcotics and becoming involved in crime. And there have been
increasing reports of family violence directed against wives and children
in American homes.

Test 3

Time spent in a bookstore can be enjoyable, if you are a book-　　1. _____
lover or merely there to buy a book as a present. You may even have
enter the shop just to find shelters from a sudden shower. Whatever　　2. _____
the reasons, you can soon become totally unaware of your
surroundings. The desire to pick up a book with an attractive jacket
is resistible although this method of selection ought not to be　　3. _____
followed, as you might end up with a rather bored book. You soon　　4. _____
become engrossed in some book or other, and usually it is only much
later that you realize you have spent far too much time there and
must dash off to keep some forgotten appointment — without buy a　　5. _____
book, of come.

This opportunity to escape the realities of everyday life is, I
think, the main attraction of a bookshop. There are not many places
where it is impossible to do this. A music shop is very much like a　　6. _____
bookshop. You can wander round such places to your heart's content.
If it is a good shop, no assistant will approach to you with the　　7. _____
inevitable greeting: "Can I help you, sir?" You needn't buy
something if you don't want. In a bookshop an assistant should　　8. _____
remain in the background until you have finished browsing. Then,

only then, are his services necessary. Of course, you may want to
find out where a particular section is, since when he has led you   9. _____
there, the assistant should retire discretely and look as he is not   10. _____
interested in selling a single book.

Test 4

When people discuss education they insist that preparation for
examinations be not the main purpose. They are right in theory, but in   1. _____
practice, we all realize that important examinations are. What do you   2. _____
know about the examinations taken at English secondary schools? Here
are a few facts about some of them.

Pupils who remain at school until they are sixteen will take which   3. _____
is called the General Certificate of Education on Ordinary level. The   4. _____
examination is a subject examination. This means you can take a number
of subjects. Some pupils take as much as ten. The more subjects the better   5. _____
chance a pupil has of getting a job on leaving school. For short, this
examination is called G. C. E. "O" Level. This certificate in five or six
subjects are, if you like, the required starting point for some types of work   6. _____
and also for many types of professional training.

Pupils who remain at school when they are eighteen or nineteen   7. _____
generally take the General Certificate of Education at Advanced level —
popular known as G. C. E. "A" Level. This examination is usually   8. _____
taken in two, three or four specialized subjects. And because it is for the
specialist you have to study each subject extensively. A pupil who has   9. _____
passed two or three "A" Levels can apply to admission to a university.   10. _____

Test 5

Anna arrived far more early. Usually she left things to the   1. _____
last minute, but today was a very special occasion. It was almost
as if by getting there an hour beforehand she hoped to cause the
plane to arrive soon. Thoughts raced through her mind. "Do I   2. _____
look all right? Will he notice that I'm dress a new trouser suit?   3. _____
Will he ever recognize me?" After all, it was a year almost to the
day since she had last seen Joe. She fished a mirror out of her
handbag and inspected her face. Too much makeup? Joe have   4. _____
never made any comment but she knew that he did not approve   5. _____

heavy makeup — "*gilding the lily* (画蛇添足)", he called it. It
was funny how much importance she attached to make a good
impression on him. After all, friends don't judge each other by
appearance. All the same, it was the first meeting after a long
separation, and she wanted everything to go off right.

6. _____

Looked out of the window, Joe caught a first glimpse,
through a break in the clouds, on the town far below. This was
his third visit and looked like becoming an annual event.
Certainly it was much flattering that they had invited him to be
the guest lecturer at their Autumn Congress yet again. The
Chairman of the Organizing Committee, as a matter of courtesy,
had offered to meet him at the airport, which he had done on
previous occasions. This time, however, it was not necessary,
partly because Joe was quite familiar with the city, but mainly
because Anna had said that she could take the afternoon off in
order to come and meet him.

7. _____
8. _____

9. _____

10. _____

Test 6

Geography is the study of the relationship between people and the
land. Geographer compare and distinguish various places on earth. But
they also go beyond the individual place and consider the earth
like a whole. The word geography comes from two Greek words, *ge*, the
Greek word for "earth" and graphein, means "to write". The English word
geography means "to describe the earth". Some geography books focus on
small area like a town or a city. Other deal with a state, a region, a
nation, or an entire continent. Many geography books deal with the whole
earth. Another way to separate the study of geography is to distinguish
between physical geography and cultural geography. The former focuses
on the natural world; the latter starts with human beings and study how
human beings and their environment act upon each other. But when
geography is considered as a single subject, either branch can neglect the
other. A geographer might be described as one who observes, records, and
explains the differences between places. If all places were alike, there will
be little need for geographers. We know, however, that no two places are
exactly the same. Geography, then, is a point of view, a special way of
looking at places.

1. _____
2. _____
3. _____
4. _____

5. _____

6. _____

7. _____

8. _____

9. _____
10. _____

Test 7

Ancient Chinese reformers advocated selecting all talented people to be officials regardless of their family backgrounds. This practice is still significant, for it opposed to appoint people by favoritism.   1. _____

But it is improper for us to think that the talent can only become officials, otherwise they are stilled.   2. _____

In the course of the current reform, China needs talented persons in all trades. It is justifiable that talented personal bring their ability into full play by becoming leaders.   3. _____

But the point is who can be considered talented? Some see the holders of senior professional titles are talented; some think of who have college diplomas as talented; sane say that they are those who have made inventions or outstanding contributions to society.   4. _____

There would not be enough vacancies if all of these people are to become officials.   5. _____

It is unnecessary for all the talented to elbow their way in officialdom (官场). They can strive to become experts in philosophy, science, literature, art, history and education. There is never a limit to the number of experts in those fields.   6. _____

Albert Einstein was once invited by Israel to become its president. It was considered as a matter of course for Einstein to accept the invitation. And Einstein refused it bluntly and continued his physics study.   7. _____   8. _____

I do not mean that talented people should not become officials at all. But what I want to specify is that different people have different strength, and that not everyone is capable of becoming an official. If people without leader capacity are chosen as officials, they can only bungle thing.   9. _____   10. _____

Test 8

Here is a passage that explains that an electric refrigerator works. Before a liquid changes into a gas, it must be heated in some way. Before a gas changes into a liquid, it must be cooled. This is the principle with which a refrigerator works.   1. _____   2. _____

At the bottom of a refrigerator there is a electric pump. This pump forces the liquid through a pipe to the top of the refrigerator. Here the pipe branches out into many channels around the freezer box. The liquid spreads it out through them and becomes a gas. But before this, it must be heating, and so it takes heat from the freezer (and, of course, from any food or water around). So the freezer becomes the coldest part of the refrigerator, there water turns to ice and food frozen solid.

3. _____

4. _____

5. _____

6. _____

Any warm air in the refrigerator raises towards the freezer and helps to change the liquid refrigerant into a gas. The gas flows round to the bottom again, where the pump compresses. When this gas is compressed, it gives off, or loses heat, and it turns back into a liquid. The heat escapes from the refrigerator on the air outside. The liquid refrigerant now starts its journey again and soon reaches the freeze. There, it draws in more heat and again becomes a gas. And so the process continues, the refrigerant traveling round, taking heat from the things in the refrigerator, and lets it escape into the air.

7. _____

8. _____

9. _____

10. _____

Test 9

After the 1870's trained nurses were virtually unknown in the United States. Hospital nursing was an unskilled occupation, taken in by women of the lower classes, some of whom were sent from the prison or the alms house. The movement for reform originated not with doctors, and among upper-class women, who had taken on the role of guardians of a new hygienic order. Though some doctors approved of the women's desire to establish a nurse's training school, that would attract the daughters of the middle class, others medical men were opposed. Plainly threatened by the prospect, they objected to that educated nurses would not do as they were told — a remarkable comment on the status anxiety of nineteenth-century physicians. But the woman-reformers did not depend on the physicians' approval. When resisting, as they were at Bellevue in efforts to install trained nurses in the maternity wards, they went over the heads of the doctors to men of their own class of greater power and authority. (Florence Nightingale, who had friends high in the government, had followed exactly the same course in reforming her country's military hospitals.) Professional nursing, in short,

1. _____

2. _____

3. _____

4. _____

5. _____

6. _____

7. _____

8. _____

9. _____

emerged either from medical discoveries nor from a program of   10. _____
hospital reform initiated by physicians; outsiders saw the need first.

Test 10

The biggest safety threat facing airlines today may not be a terrorist
with a gun, than the man with the portable computer in business class.   1. _____
In the last 15 years, pilots report well over 100 incidents that could   2. _____
have been caused by electromagnetic interference. The source of this
interference remains confirmed, but increasingly, experts are pointing the   3. _____
blame to portable electronic devices such as portable computers, radio and   4. _____
cassette players and mobile telephones.

RTCA, an organization advises the *aviation* (航空) industry,   5. _____
has recommended that all airlines banned such devices from   6. _____
used during "critical" stages of light, particularly take-off and landing.   7. _____
Some experts have gone further, calling for a total ban during all flights.
Currently, rules on using these devices are left up to individual airlines.
And although some airlines prohibit passengers from using such equipment
during take-off and landing, most are willing to enforce a total ban, given   8. _____
that many passengers want to work during flights.

The difficulty is predicting how electromagnetic fields might affect an
aircraft's computers. Experts know that portable devices emit radiation
which affect those wavelengths which aircraft use for navigation and   9. _____
communication. But, because they have not been able to reproduce these
effects in a laboratory, they have no way of knowing whether the
interference might be danger or not.   10. _____

Test 11

For me, scientific knowledge is divided into mathematical sciences,
natural sciences or sciences dealing with the natural world (physical and
biological sciences), and sciences dealing with mankind (psychology,
sociology, all the sciences of cultural achievements, every kind of
historic knowledge). Apart from these sciences is philosophy. In the   1. _____
first place, all this are pure or theoretical knowledge, sought only for the 2. _____
purpose of understanding, in order to fulfill the need to understand what
is intrinsic to man. What distinguishes man and an animal is that he   3. _____
knows and needs to know.

While enjoying the results of technical progress, man must defend the primary and autonomy of pure knowledge. Knowledge sought directly for his practical applications will have immediate and foreseeable success, but not the kind of important result whose revolutionary scope is in large part unforeseen, except by the imagination of the Utopians. Let me to recall a well-known example. If the Greek mathematicians had not devoted themselves to the investigation of conic *sections* (圆锥截面) zealously and without the least suspicion that it might sometimes be useful, it would not been possible centuries later to navigate far from shore. The first men to study the nature of electricity could not imagine that their experiments, carried on because of merely intellectual curiosity, would eventually lead to modern electrical technology, without which we can scarcely conceive of contemporary life. Pure knowledge is valuable on its own sake, because of the human spirit cannot resign itself to ignorance. But in addition, it is the foundation for practical results that would not have been reached whether this knowledge had not been sought disinterestedly.

4. _____
5. _____
6. _____
7. _____
8. _____
9. _____
10. _____

Test 12

Weddings in the United States vary as much as the people do. Because many weddings, no matter where or how they are performed, include certain traditional customers.

The wedding in itself usually lasts between 20 and 40 minutes. The wedding party enters the church while the wedding march is played. The bride carry a bouquet enters last with her father who will "give her away". The groom enters the church from a side door. When the wedding party is gathering by the altar, the bride and groom exchange vows. Following the vows, the couple exchange rings. Wear the wedding ring on the fourth finger of the left hand is an old custom. After the ceremony it is often a party, called a "reception" which gives the wedding guests an opportunity to congratulate the newlyweds.

The car in which the couple leave the church is decorated in balloons, streamers and shaving cream. The words "Just Married" are painted on the trunk or back window. The bride and groom run to the car under a shower of rice thrown by the wedding guest. When the couple drive away the church, friends often chase them in cars, honking and drawing attention to them. And then the couple go on their honeymoon.

1. _____
2. _____
3. _____
4. _____
5. _____
6. _____
7. _____
8. _____
9. _____
10. _____

===== 答案与解析 =====

Text 1

1. 【答案】their — his。

【解析】本题考查代词与指代对象的一致性。此处代词的指代对象应该是 man，为第三人称单数，所以不应该用 their，应将其改为 his。for his daily life 在定语从句中作目的状语。

2. 【答案】for — with。

【解析】本题考查动词与介词的固定搭配。动词 provide 的介词搭配与其直接宾语与间接宾语的位置相关：provide sb. with sth. 或是 provide sth. for sb.。类似的搭配还有：present sth. to sb. 或 present sb. with sth.。句中 provide 接的是人，故应用介词 with 而非 for。

3. 【答案】will — would。

【解析】本题考查虚拟语气。该句为由介宾短语 without trees（假如没有树）构成的虚拟语气，对将来要发生的事进行假设，因此要将 will 改成 would。with 引导的介宾短语（假如有）也可构成虚拟，例如：What would you do with a million dollars?（有 100 万美元你会怎样用？）。

4. 【答案】are — is。

【解析】本题考查主谓一致原则。该句主语为 Furniture，是不可数名词，such as…为插入语，谓语动词还是应该和主语保持一致，故应为第三人称单数。

5. 【答案】washing — being washed。

【解析】本题考查语态。中心词 top-soil 是动词 wash away 的承受者，因此应用 wash 的被动形式。再者，wash away 又在介词 from 之后，故应为动名词的被动形式。

6. 【答案】on — back。

【解析】本题考查动词短语。hold 可以与不同的介词构成动词短语，但意义不同。hold on 意思是"坚持，不挂（电话）"，用在此处不能使语义通顺；而 hold back 则是"阻止，抑制"的意思。to hold back the soil with their root 的意思是"植物用根留住土壤"。

7. 【答案】useful — useless。

【解析】本题考查逻辑意义的一致性。useful 和 unproductive 相并列，具有逻辑上的矛盾。由前一句可知"大雨冲走肥沃的表层土"，会使 the land "无用、绝产"，所以应用 useless 保持逻辑上的合理。

8. 【答案】be — have been。

【解析】本题考查情态动词表示推测的用法。情态动词 must，may，might，can't 可用来表示推测，有三种形式：情态动词 + do/be 表示对现在情况的推测；情态动词 + have done/been 表示对过去情况的推测；情态动词 + be doing 表示对正在进行的情况的推测。由句中时间状语 A long, long time ago 可知该句是对过去的推测，因此要用情态动词 + have been 的形式。

9. 【答案】time — times。

【解析】本题考查名词的单复数。time 表"时间"时为不可数名词。但在该句中它意为"时代"，是可数名词，故应用复数形式。

10. 【答案】that — where。

【解析】本题考查用关系副词引导的定语从句。先行词 deserts 在从句中作地点状语，因此应用 in which 或 where 引导。

Text 2

1. 【答案】recent — recently。

【解析】本题考查词类。这里的 recent 是用来修饰时间状语 20 years ago 的，故应用副词形式 recently。

2. 【答案】changed ∧ rapidly — ∧ so。

【解析】本题考查固定句型。so + 形容词或副词... + that... "如此…以致…"为固定句型。

3. 【答案】men — women。

【解析】本题考查上下文逻辑关系。上一句提到"最初，只有少数妇女呆在家里"，接下来应该是工作妇女人数的增加。

4. 【答案】raised — rose。

【解析】本题考查易混词辨析。raise 意为"举起、提高、提升"，其过去式和过去分词都为 raised。rise 意为"上升、达到较高的水平"，其过去式和过去分词分别为 rose 和 risen。这里显然应该用 rise，且为过去时态，故应将 raised 改成 rose。

5. 【答案】child — children。

【解析】本题考查名词单复数。无论从句意理解上还是从前后搭配上，这里都应用 child 的复数形式 children。

6. 【答案】dropped ∧ 3.7 — ∧ to。

【解析】本题考查动词用法。drop to 后可接表示数量的名词，但 drop 不可以。

7. 【答案】Alone — Along。

【解析】本题考查形近词辨析。从文章理解来看应是"伴随这些基本变化"，所以要用 along 而不是 alone。

8. 【答案】stabler — stable。

【解析】本题考查比较级。-er 和 less 不能并用，为了保持前后一致，将 stabler 改为 stable。

9. 【答案】start — end。

【解析】本题考查逻辑关系。根据逻辑推理可知，不可能以离婚作为开始，应该为结束，故用 end。

10. 【答案】years ∧. — ∧old。

【解析】本题考查惯用法。描述人的年龄用…years old。其中的 old 不能省略。

Text 3

1. 【答案】if — whether。

【解析】本题考查固定搭配。whether 能和 or 搭配，而 if 不能。

2. 【答案】enter — entered。

【解析】本题考查时态。此处为现在完成时态，故应将 enter 改成 entered。

3. 【答案】resistible — irresistible。

【解析】本题考查逻辑关系。从上下文来看此处应将 resistible 改为 irresistible 才能使句意通顺。irresistible 和 attractive 形成语义上的照应。

4. 【答案】bored — boring。

【解析】本题考查非谓语动词。修饰一本书有什么样的特质，应该用-ing 形式，故用 boring。

5. 【答案】buy — buying。

【解析】本题考查介词用法。介词后面应用动名词形式，故将 buy 改为 buying。

6. 【答案】impossible — possible。

【解析】本题考查逻辑关系。既然书店能让人逃离现实是它主要的吸引人的地方，那么其他地方应该是做不到这点的。句子已经含有否定词 not 了，故此处应用表肯定的 possible。

7. 【答案】to — ~~to~~。

【解析】本题考查动词的用法。approach 可作及物动词，直接跟名词。

8. 【答案】something — anything。

【解析】本题考查不定代词。一般来说在否定句用应用 anything，在肯定句才用 something。

9. 【答案】since — but。

【解析】本题考查连接词。这里带有转折的意味，故不能用表原因的 since，而要用 but。

10. 【答案】as ∧ he — ∧if。

【解析】本题考查固定短语。as if 为固定搭配，意为"好像"。

Text 4

1. 【答案】be — is。

【解析】本题考查动词的用法。句中谓语动词 insist 有多个含义。当 insist 表示"坚决要求"时，引导的从句要用虚拟语气，形式为：should + 动词原形，例如：We all insist that we should not rest until we finish the work. （大家都坚决要求不完工就不休息。）。但当 insist 表示"坚持认为"的时候则不用虚拟，本句就属于后一种情况，故将 be 改成 is。

2. 【答案】that — how。

【解析】本题考查宾语从句。该从句成分不全，由 that 引导导致了意思混乱。从文中可知，该宾语从句由感叹句转换。在 what 引导的感叹句中，what 强调名词，例如：What a big house！（多么大的房子！）而在本句中，显然强调 examinations 的重要性，用 how 来强调形容词 important。

3. 【答案】which — what。

【解析】本题考查 what 引导的名词性从句。从句缺少主语，而 which 引导宾语从句时不能独立充当主语，须跟名词或代词，如 which color，which one，除非省略情况，故应改为由 what 引导的名词性从句。另外，what 表示泛指的事物，常译为"什么"或"所…的事物"。而 which 表示特定事物中的"哪一个"，因此从意思上也能将两个词区分开。例如：I believed what she told me. （我相信她和我说的话。）

4. 【答案】on — at。

【解析】本题考查固定搭配。on 和 level 搭配时只能用于 on the level 短语中，意为"诚实地，直率地"。而此处明显是要表示"处于普通程度"，因此要用介词 at。at...level 为固定搭配，表示"在某一等级"。

5. 【答案】much — many。

【解析】本题考查比较结构。as...as 结构中加形容词或副词原形。本句所加的形容词是修饰可数名词复数形式（ten subjects）的，因此应该用 many 来修饰。

6. 【答案】are — is。

【解析】本题考查主谓一致。该句主语是 This certificate （该证书），因此谓语要用第三人称单数 is。句中 in five or six subjects 这个介宾短语具有一定的干扰性。

7. 【答案】when — until。

【解析】本题考查时间状语的关联词。该句的主句谓语动词 remain 是可延续动词，意思是"逗留"，而 when 引导的状语从句意思是"当…的时候"，表示某个时刻的动作或状况，与主句相矛盾。改为 until 引导的状语从句后，意为"直到…的时候"，符合逻辑。

8. 【答案】popular — popularly。

【解析】本题考查副词的用法。中心词 known 是动词的过去分词，而形容词 popular "流行的"只能修饰名词，故应改为它的副词形式。

9. 【答案】extensively — intensively。

【解析】本题考查形近词的辨析。extensively "广泛地"与句中的 specialist "专家"相矛盾，应改为 intensively "精深地"，逻辑相符。

10. 【答案】 第一个 to → for。

【解析】 本题考查动词的习惯搭配。当 apply 表示不同的含义时，后面所跟的介词也不同。当它意为"应用"时，搭配介词 to；当表示"申请"时搭配介词 for。我们只能说申请上大学，而不能说应用大学，所以应该用介词 for。

Text 5

1. 【答案】 more → too。

【解析】 本题考查比较级。无论是句子本身还是上下文都没有暗示要用比较级，但需要一个修饰形容词 early 的副词，因为 far 作副词时一般不修饰形容词，但可以修饰形容词比较级（如 far better，far more serious）作副词，将它改成表示"过于…"的 too。

2. 【答案】 soon → sooner。

【解析】 本题考查形容词原级和比较级。根据句中的 an hour beforehand 可知安娜是早到了一个小时，她早到了，自然是希望飞机也能早一些，因此将 soon 改成 sooner，突出比较含义。句子大意为：安娜好像希望通过提前一小时到那好让飞机提前降落似的。

3. 【答案】 dress → wearing。

【解析】 本题考查近义词辨析。当表示"穿着什么衣服"时，可以用 to wear 或 to be wearing；若要用 dress 表示"穿着什么衣服"，需用下面的结构：to be dressed in。主动式 to dress 一般指经常性的动作，dress 为不及物动词，如：He always dresses in white，因此将 dress 改为 wearing。

4. 【答案】 have → had。

【解析】 本题考查时态。made 的动作在 know 之前发生，因此要用过去完成时态，即将 have 改成 had。

5. 【答案】 approve ∧ heavy → ∧ of。

【解析】 本题考查短语搭配。approve 作及物动词时意为"批准"，与句意不符；作不及物动词时后接介词 of，意为"赞成，同意"。

6. 【答案】 make → making。

【解析】 本题考查固定搭配。attach importance to sth. /doing sth. 是固定搭配，意为"重视…"，其中的 to 是介词，不是不定式的标志，因此要将 make 改为 making。

7. 【答案】 Looked → Looking。

【解析】 本题考查非谓语动词。当分词短语作状语时，其逻辑主语一般要与句子的主语一致。这里 Joe 是句子的主语，他往机窗外看，而不是被看，所以用现在分词形式。

8. 【答案】 on → of。

【解析】 本题考查固定搭配。catch/get a glimpse of 是固定短语，意为"瞥见"。

9. 【答案】much — very。

【解析】 本题考查副词用法。现在分词用 very 来加强，一些没有形容词化的过去分词用 much 或 very much 来加强，有些只作表语用的形容词不能用 very，而要用其他词来加强，例如：I'm wide awake. 我很清醒。

10. 【答案】which — as。

【解析】 本题考查关系代词。这里需要一个连词而不是关系代词。as 引导的是一个状语从句，意为："正如他以前多次做过的那样"。

Text 6

1. 【答案】distinguish — contrast。

【解析】 本题考查近义词辨析。distinguish 和 contrast 都含有"对比不同之处"之意，但是 contrast 是及物动词，而 distinguish 是不及物动词，一般用于 distinguish between A and B 这一结构中，故将 distinguish 改成 contrast。

2. 【答案】place — places。

【解析】 本题考查名词单复数。此处指的是地球上的各个地方，应用复数。

3. 【答案】like — as。

【解析】 本题考查固定搭配。当 consider 表示"认为，把…当作…"时，其后要接 as，而不是 like。

4. 【答案】graphein，∧ means — which。

【解析】 本题考查句子结构。前面已经有了谓语动词了，在没有连接词的情况下，此处不应该出现另一个主谓结构，因此要在 means 前加上 which 将这部分变为非限制性定语从句。

5. 【答案】Other — Others。

【解析】 本题考查固定搭配。前一句中有 some，能和它搭配的是 others，而不是 other。

6. 【答案】separate — divide。

【解析】 本题考查近义词辨析。separate 和 divide 都意为"分开"，但 separate 是指将连在一起的不同事物分开，divide 指将一个整体分成几个部分。文中指的显然是后者，故将 separate 改成 divide。

7. 【答案】study — studies。

【解析】 本题考查主谓一致原则。句子主语为 the latter，是单数，故将 study 改为 studies。

8. 【答案】either — neither。

【解析】 本题考查逻辑关系。根据上下文可知，地理学的两个分支谁都不能忽略谁，故将 either 改成 neither。

9. 【答案】will — would。

【解析】本题考查虚拟语气。表示对现在情况的虚拟，主句用"would + 动词原形"。

10. 【答案】however — therefore。

【解析】本题考查逻辑关系。前一句用虚拟语气说"如果所有的地方都是相似的，那么就不需要地理学家了"，此句是说"我们知道没有任何两个地方是完全一样的"，两句之间显然不是转折关系而是因果关系，故用连接词 therefore。

Text 7

1. 【答案】appoint — appointing。

【解析】本题考查惯用法。oppose 动词后必须用 to + 动名词（有时 to 可省略）即 oppose（to）doing sth. 意为"反对做某事"，因此 appoint 要改成 appointing。类似的后接 to + 动名词的动词还有 object，look forward。

2. 【答案】talent — talented。

【解析】本题考查词类。talent 为名词，指"才干、人才"，一般为不可数名词，如 talent market 人才市场。根据后文中的 they are 可知这里指的应该是一类人。英语里表示某一类人可以用 the + 形容词，因此将 talent 改为 talented。the talented 表示"有才之士"。

3. 【答案】personal — personnel。

【解析】本题考查形近词辨析。由于 personal "个人的"前有 talented 这个形容词，因此它用在此处不合适，要将其改为名词形式的 personnel，指"人员，职员"。

4. 【答案】of ∧ who — ∧ those。

【解析】本题考查定语从句的先行词。who 引导名词性从句时也可作 think of 的宾语，但它是疑问代词，只能作引导词，不能作先行词。从上下文看本段是在列举各类有才之士，所以用 those who 表示一类人。

5. 【答案】are — were。

【解析】本题考查虚拟语气。句子是对将来情况的假设，主句用的是 would，从句应为 if + were to/should，故改 are 为 were。

6. 【答案】in — into。

【解析】本题考查介词辨析。in 表静态，into 表动态。在 elbow/squeeze/force/fight…one's way into "奋力挤进"一类搭配中，动作意味很强，故用 into。

7. 【答案】as — as。

【解析】本题考查词语用法。consider 为及物动词，后面无须跟介词 as，因此将 as 去掉。

8. 【答案】And — But。

【解析】本题考查连词。前句说（大家）认为爱因斯坦接受这个邀请是理所当然的事情，本句说爱因斯坦坦率地拒绝了。由此可见，两句之间存在转折关系，故将 And 改成 But。

9. 【答案】strength — strengths。

【解析】本题考查名词单复数。strength 既可作可数名词又可作不可数名词，因此首先要判断的是 strength 在此处作何解释。在 strength 的释义中能和后文的 is capable of 形成共现的只有"长处"。当 strength 表示该意思时，是可数名词，因此此处应该用它的复数形式。

10. 【答案】leader — leadership。

【解析】本题为近义词辨析。leader 指"领导者"，不能用它来修饰 capacity。leadership 指"领导地位，领导能力"，是抽象名词，可作定语。leadership capacity 意为"领导才能"。

Text 8

1. 【答案】that — how。

【解析】本题考查逻辑一致性。谓语 explains "解释"的宾语从句应该是原因或说明，that 引导的从句 an electric refrigerator works 只是一个事实，逻辑混乱。结合全文，应该用疑问副词 how 引导由特殊疑问句转化成的宾语从句。

2. 【答案】with — on。

【解析】本题考查介词的搭配。关系代词 which 指代的是 the principle "原理"，而 principle 通常不和介词 with 搭配。能和它搭配的介词有 on 和 in。on principle 意为"根据原理；按照原则"；而 in principle 的意思是"原则上；大致上；通常"。根据句意可知，这里指的是电冰箱按照这种原理工作，因此应该用介词 on。

3. 【答案】第二个 a — an。

【解析】本题考查不定冠词。名词 pump 是可数名词单数，其前应加冠词。由于形容词 electric 是以元音音素开头的词，所以要用冠词 an。

4. 【答案】第一个 it — itself。

【解析】本题考查代词。此处的代词指代的对象是 liquid 自身，所以应该用反身代词。liquid "液体"是物质名词，故用表物的 itself。

5. 【答案】heating — heated。

【解析】本题考查被动语态。句子的主语 it（the liquid）是 heat 这一动作的承受者，所以应该使用被动语态。

6. 【答案】there — where。

【解析】本题考查定语从句。该句有两个分句，但缺少连接词，应把 there 改为 where，引导定语从句修饰先行词 the coldest part of the refrigerator。

7. 【答案】raises — rises。

【解析】本题考查近义词辨析。raise 是及物动词，例如：He raised his arms

above his head. （他把手臂举过头顶）。但句中缺少宾语，所以应该用不及物动词 rise，例如 The sun rises later in the fall. （秋季的太阳升起较晚。） any warm air 是句子的主语，为单数，所以谓语相应改为 rises。

8. 【答案】 compresses. ∧ When — ∧ it。

【解析】 本题考查及物动词。compress "压缩" 是及物动词，句中缺少宾语。句子的宾语为句首的物质名词 the gas，再次提到的名词可用代词表示，加上表物的单数人称代词 it。

9. 【答案】 on — into。

【解析】 本题考查介词。on the air 意为 "正在广播，开始播送"，用在此处语义不符。根据句意可知，热度是从电冰箱里散发到外部的空气里的，由…到…，有一个很明确的方向，所以应改为 into the air，由 from…to…这一搭配和 in the air 这一短语结合而成。

10. 【答案】 lets — letting。

【解析】 本题考查并列结构。本句主语是 the process，与动词 let 没有逻辑上的关系，所以 let 是独立主格结构。独立主格结构的逻辑主语是 the refrigerant，也是 let 这一动作的发出者，所以 let 应改成表示主动含义的 letting，与 traveling 和 taking 并列。

Text 9

1. 【答案】 After — Before。

【解析】 本题考查逻辑关系。根据常识可知，受训护士不可能在 19 世纪 70 年代以后还不为人所知，故将 After 改成 Before。

2. 【答案】 in — up。

【解析】 本题考查短语搭配。take in 意为 "吸收，接待"，显然不能说下层社会的妇女吸收或接待了看护这种职业。take up 意为 "开始从事"，符合题意。

3. 【答案】 and — but。

【解析】 本题考查固定搭配。not…but…为固定的句式搭配，故将 and 改为 but。

4. 【答案】 nurse's — nurses'。

【解析】 本题考查名词所有格。护士培训学校培养的肯定不止一个护士，因此需用复数名词所有格的形式。

5. 【答案】 that — which。

【解析】 本题考查定语从句的引导词。根据 that 前的逗号可知，本句为非限制性定语从句，故应用 which 而非 that。

6. 【答案】 others — other。

【解析】 本题考查词法。本句提及 "一些医生支持…，而其他一些男医生则反对"，但 others 和 some 对比使用时，是 "有些" 的意思而不作 "其他" 讲，故将 others 改为表"其他"的 other。

7. 【答案】 to — ~~to~~。

【解析】 本题考查动词的用法。动词 object 既可作及物动词又可作不及物动词。作及物动词时，它意为"提出…作为反对的理由"，常接 that 从句说明具体的理由；作不及物动词时，后面常跟介词 against 和 to，表示"反对；抗议"。查看句子，that 从句显然是在说明反对的理由，故将 to 去掉。

8. 【答案】 woman-reformers — women-reformers。

【解析】 本题考查复合名词的复数形式。由-man 或-woman 构成的复合名词，前后两个都要用复数形式。

9. 【答案】 approve — approval。

【解析】 本题考查词性。名词所有格 physicians' 后面应该跟名词，而 approve 是动词，故将其改成名词形式的 approval。

10. 【答案】 either — neither。

【解析】 本题考查固定搭配。neither...nor...为固定搭配。

Text 10

1. 【答案】 than — but。

【解析】 本题考查固定句式。not...but..."不是…，而是…"为固定句式，此句大意为"最大的飞行隐患不是持枪的恐怖分子，而是商务舱中携带手提电脑的人"。

2. 【答案】 report — reported。

【解析】 本题考查时态。句子中的时间状语 In the last 15 years 表明其基本时态应该是一般过去时，所以将 report 改为 reported。

3. 【答案】 confirmed — unconfirmed。

【解析】 本题考查逻辑关系。but 后面的内容意为：但是专家们却越来越多地将飞行事故归咎于便携式设备，例如：手提电脑、收音机和播放器以及手机。but 是表转折的连词，显然其前的内容应该表明电磁干扰的来源尚不明确。故将 confirmed 改成 unconfirmed。

4. 【答案】 to — at/toward。

【解析】 本题考查介词搭配。point to 和 point at/toward 均有"指向"之意，但是 point to 只能在 to 后面跟 sth. /sb.，即 point 后面不能跟宾语。而 at 和 toward 都可用于 point sth. at/toward sth. /sb. 的结构中，所以可将 to 改为 at 或 toward。

5. 【答案】 organization ∧ advises — ∧ which。

【解析】 本题考查句子结构。句子的谓语是 has recommended，an organization advises the aviation industry 是主语 RTCA 的同位语，对主语作进一步的解释说明。因此要在 organization 后面加上 which 来引导定语从句。

6.【答案】banned — ban。

【解析】　本题考查虚拟语气。recommend 后面的宾语从句要使用形式为"should + v."的虚拟语气，should 可以省略，此处直接使用动词原形 ban。

7.【答案】used 前∧ — ∧being。

【解析】　本题考查介词用法和语态。介词后面要用动词-ing 形式，但如果直接把 used 改成 using 也不对，因为 devices 并不是 use 的逻辑主语，因此这里需要采用被动语态，故在 used 前加上 being。

8.【答案】willing — reluctant 或者 are ∧ willing — not。

【解析】　本题考查逻辑关系。句中的 although 表明前后两个分句之间是转折关系。前分句意为"尽管一些航空公司禁止乘客在飞机起飞和着陆使用此类电子产品"，后分句意为"由于很多乘客想在飞行时继续办公，很多航空公司愿意彻底实施禁令"，这显然不符逻辑。句子要表达"很多航空公司不愿意彻底实施禁令"才对，故得出以上答案。

9.【答案】affect — affects。

【解析】　本题考查主谓一致。定语从句的先行词 radiation 是单数，故从句谓语动词也应该用单数。

10.【答案】danger — dangerous。

【解析】　本题考查词性。分析句子结构可知此处应使用形容词，修饰主语。故将 danger 改成 dangerous。

Text 11

1.【答案】historic — historical。

【解析】　本题考查近义词辨析。形容词 historic 的意思是"历史性的，历史上著名的"，用来修饰 knowledge，不符语义逻辑，应改为 historical。它意为"有关历史的"，historical knowledge 表示"历史知识"。

2.【答案】are — is。

【解析】　本题考查主谓一致。句子的主语为 this，尽管前面加了 all，但它仍表单数，因此谓语应改为单数形式。

3.【答案】and — from。

【解析】　本题考查介词和动词的搭配。动词 distinguish 表示"区别，辨别"时常用于以下短语中：distinguish sb./sth. from...，distinguish between...（and ...），意思都是"把…同…区别开来"。例如：People cannot distinguish between colors are said to be color-blind.（不能辨别颜色的人被称为色盲。）用作此意时 distinguish 的主语通常是人。然而表示"使…有别于，使…有特色"时，常用于短语 distinguish sb./sth. from...中，前面的主语多为物。例如：Speeches distinguishes man from the animals.（言语使人区别于动物）。本句中 distinguish 应为后一种用法，what 从句的意思是"把人和动物区别开来的是"，所

以应把句中的 and 改为 from。

4. 【答案】his — its。

【解析】 本题考查代词。此代词指代的是物质名词 knowledge，为表示物的第三人称单数，因此需把物主代词 his 改为 its。

5. 【答案】to — t~~o~~。

【解析】 本题考查不定式作宾语补足语。句中 let 后面跟的是宾语 me 和宾语补语 to recall，let 为使役动词，其后的不定式补语应省略 to。类似的动词有：let，have，make。

6. 【答案】sometimes — sometime。

【解析】 本题考查形近词辨析。sometimes "有时，间或"，常用于现在时和过去时，其含义与句子不符。而 sometime "曾经，某一天" 常用于将来时和过去时。句子中的 it might 表示的是对将来的某种推测，因此用 sometime 才符合逻辑。该句译文为："毫不怀疑它有一天会有用的。"

7. 【答案】not ∧ been — ∧ have。

【解析】 本题考查虚拟语气。If the Greek mathematicians had not devoted … zealously（如果希腊数学家没有狂热地投入对圆锥截面的研究）是对过去已发生事实的假设，因此应该使用过去完成时虚拟。主句的时间状语 centuries later 仍是一个表过去时间的状语，但相对于从句是一个将来时，故主句应该用过去将来完成时表示虚拟，即 would + have + 动词过去分词。对比原文，不难发现缺少了 have。

8. 【答案】merely — mere。

【解析】 本题考查形容词和副词。副词 merely 后是形容词 intellectual，但它实际修饰的是名词短语 intellectual curiosity 的中心词 curiosity，所以应将其改为形容词形式 mere。

9. 【答案】on — for。

【解析】 本题考查固定短语。sake 不和介词 on 搭配构成短语。for…sake of 是固定短语，意为 "为了…好处，为…着想"。

10. 【答案】whether — if。

【解析】 本题考查连词。whether 引导的从句可作主语、表语、宾语和同位语，但本句的从句是虚拟条件句，应该用 if 来引导。whether 和 if 表示 "是否" 时，可以在表语、宾语和同位语从句中互换。如 We shall soon learn whether/if it is true.（我们很快就会知道这是否是真实的。）。

Text 12

1. 【答案】Because — But。

【解析】 本题考查句际间的逻辑关系。从句法角度看，because 属于从属连词，而该句并没有主句，只有从句，这显然不对。前句提到：在美国，婚礼形式因人而异。本句讲的是：不管在哪里举行或如何举行，许多婚礼都包含一定的传统习俗。从逻辑角度看，两句间存在转折关系，故将 Because 改为 But。考生很容易犯的一个错误是：看见 many weddings 是一名词短语，就在 Because 后面加上介词 of，因为只有 because of 才接名词或名词短语。犯这种错误是完全忽视了上下文的逻辑关系和对句子整体结构的把握。

2. 【答案】customers — customs。
　　【解析】本题考查形近词的辨析。customers 意为"顾客"，显然与上下文语义矛盾。改成 customs"习俗"可使上下文语义通顺。

3. 【答案】in — in。
　　【解析】本题考查代词指代问题。反身代词 itself 指代的是前面的 wedding，其前无需使用任何介词。

4. 【答案】carry — carrying。
　　【解析】本题考查非谓语动词。仔细分析句子结构可以看出该句有两个谓语动词：carry 和 enters。主语是单数第三人称，因此首先可以判断出问题出在 carry。carry a bouquet 是新娘在执行 enters 这个动作时的伴随动作，故应用现在分词形式的 carrying。

5. 【答案】gathering — gathered。
　　【解析】本题考查语态。gather 显然不是分句主语 the wedding party 的逻辑主语，再加上 by …这个被动语态标志词，我们不难判断出这里应该用被动语态，故将 gathering 改成 gathered。

6. 【答案】Wear — Wearing。
　　【解析】本题考查句子结构。通过分析句子结构我们发现，句子的主语是一动词短语。动词是不能作句子的主语的，要使用其相应的动名词形式，故将 Wear 改成 Wearing。

7. 【答案】it — there。
　　【解析】本题考查 there be 句型。此处是指婚礼后有一个派对，因此要用 there be 句型。

8. 【答案】第二个 in — with。
　　【解析】本题考查固定搭配。be decorated with…意为"用…装饰"，是固定搭配，其中的介词 with 不能换成其他的。

9. 【答案】guest — guests。
　　【解析】本题考查名词单复数。guest 是可数名词，婚礼的客人不可能只有一个人，因此将其改为 guests。

10. 【答案】away ∧ the — ∧ from。
　　【解析】本题考查副词用法。away 含有"离开"之义，但它是副词，后面不能直接跟名词。由于是从教堂离开，因此在其后面加上介词 from。

第二篇 完形填空

题 型 透 视

一、题型特征

完形填空是大学英语六级考试 710 分改革后没有变化的一部分。《大学英语六级考试大纲》规定，完形填空共 20 题，要求考生在 15 分钟内完成。具体做法是：在一篇题材熟悉、难度适中、长度为 300 词左右的短文中，挖出 20 个空，每空为一道题；然后在文章后面给出每道题的 4 个选项，要求考生在全面理解文章内容的基础上为各题选择最佳答案，使短文的内容和结构恢复完整。该部分在六级考试中占总分值 710 分的 10% 。

为了更好地了解六级考试完形填空的特点，本书对六级所有的完形填空真题进行了统计分析，如下表所示：

时间	字数	文章题材	文章体裁
07. 12	332	爱因斯坦成名前的故事	记叙文
07. 06	328	人类与灾难	说明文
05. 06	296	一种专门为盲人设计的仪器	说明文
03. 01	203	女性管理人员在公司经营管理中的优势和特点	说明文
01. 01	296	美国托儿所早期发展史	说明文
99. 06	304	时差的起因，及如何克服时差问题	说明文

综合以上分析，我们得出完形填空题具有以下特点：

◆文章普遍较长，挖空密度小。这 6 次完形填空的选文在 200－350 个词之间，平均长度 293 个词。挖空密度平均约为 14 个词。

◆文章题材多样，但绝大多数为考生所熟悉的题材。

◆文章体裁多样，但以说明文为主。

◆考试所选用的文章难度一般低于精读课文的难度，基本上无超纲词。有个别超纲词时文中会给出中文注释。

二、测试方向

《大学英语六级考试大纲》指出：完形填空的目的是测试考生综合运用语言的能力，要求考生在掌握语篇大意的前提下运用所学的词语搭配及语法结构知识解答题目。下面按所考查能力的层次分三个方面进行讲解。

1 测试篇章理解能力

完形填空中的文章虽然被挖了 20 个空格，但是整篇文章的内容仍然是可以理解的。

首先，文章本身若要实现一定的意义表达，它的单词之间、句子与句子之间、段落与段落之间必然存在着一定的逻辑联系。这些逻辑关系，或是对比，或是并列，或是转折，或是其他。

其次，一篇文章都有一个主题。这就要求文章的主题词以及与主题词相关的一些词汇必然会以各种形式在文中多次出现。

篇章结构分析能力也属于篇章理解能力的范畴。不过由于文章比较短，篇章结构一般不会对考生理解文章构成障碍。

所有这些，都会在完形填空的考查中涉及。这一点也是完形填空题这种词汇考查题型和四六级考试改革前的词汇题的根本区别所在。

【示例】 (07-12-79)

Einstein also took time off from ___79___ revising his equations to engage in an awkward *fandango* （方丹戈双人舞） with his competitor Hilbert.	[A] casually　　[B] coarsely [C] violently　　[D] furiously

【解析】 选 [D]。考查篇章层面的理解。所填词是修饰爱因斯坦如何修正他的等式的，文章处处洋溢着对爱因斯坦赞美之意，因此所填词应表积极、肯定意义。查看选项，只有 [D] furiously "大刀阔斧地，快速地" 符合题意。[A] casually "随便地，随意地"；[B] coarsely "粗糙地，粗俗地"；[C] violently "猛烈地，激烈地" 均表否定意义，故都可排除。

2 测试词汇运用能力

《大学英语六级考试大纲》规定："填空的词项包括结构词和实义词"。结构词包括冠词、代词、介词、连词、关系词等，主要是表示语法结构关系的。因此在选用结构词时，要考虑这个词在语法结构上是否恰当。实义词有名词、动词、形容词、副词和数词，在 4 个选项中，它们或者词性相似，或者词义相似，或者以不同的搭配出现。对实义词的选择，既要看其意思用在句中是否恰当，也要看它与其它词的搭配关系是否合适。

【示例】 (07-12-70)

By the end of the summer, he realized the mathematical approach he had been ___70___ for almost three years was flawed.	[A] pursuing　　[B] protecting [C] contesting　[D] contending

【解析】选 [A]。所填词的宾语应是 the mathematical approach，能接此宾语的是 [A] pursuing，pursue for 意为"从事，追求"。 [B] protecting "保护"； [C] contesting "争论，争辩"；[D] contending "斗争，竞争"这三项均不能接此宾语。

3 测试语法运用能力

完形填空会涉及语法的很多方面，例如动词的时态、语态、语气，还有主语从句、状语从句、省略句、倒装句、强调句等等。

【真题示例】 (07-06-76)

They have got the walls to __76__ they were before Katrina, more or less.	[A] which　　　[B] where [C] what　　　　[D] when

【解析】选 [B]。空格后的 they were 是一个缺少引导词的定语从句，重建防洪墙当然是要选一个地方，故 where 正确，选 [B]。（见本书第 126 页）

三、题目类型

六级完形填空题可细分为四类题型：逻辑推理题，短语搭配题，语法结构题和词汇辨析题。我们分析了历年六级完形真题，四类题型数目的统计结果如下表：

考试时间	逻辑推理题	短语搭配题	语法结构题	词汇辨析题
07. 12	4	6	8	2
07. 06	7	6	4	3
05. 06	10	7	3	0
03. 01	9	7	3	1
01. 01	8	8	3	1
99. 06	9	7	3	1

1 逻辑推理题

根据上表可以得出，在历年完形考试中，逻辑推理题是一个十分重要的题型，所占比例相当大。这就要求考生特别注重对逻辑推理能力的培养。逻辑推理涉及的内容主要包括：（1）语境理解；（2）各种句际关系；（3）词汇的复现关系；（4）词汇的共现关系。具体内容将在下一章的第一部分"逻辑推理"中阐述。

【示例1】 (01-01-77)

By the end of the war, in August, 1945, more than 100,000 children were being cared for in day-care centers receiving Federal __77__.	[A] pensions　[B] subsidies [C] revenues　[D] budgets

【解析】选 [B]。选项中四个词都能和 federal 连用，但前面句中已经出现过 federal aid "联邦援助"，所以选同义复现的 [B] "补助金，津贴"。[A] "退休金"，[C] "税收"，[D] "预算，预算拨款"，选此三项的同学显然没有注意到 receiving 的逻辑主语是 children，既然是孩子们，那他们就不可能接受退休金、税收或是预算拨款。

【示例 2】   (07-12-78)

His first lecture was delivered on Nov. 4. 1915, and it explained his new approach, __78__ he admitted he did not yet have the precise mathematical formulation of it.	[A] so [B] since [C] though [D] because

【解析】选 [C]。空格前面的分句意为"他在第一次演讲时解释了他的新方法"，空格后的句子意为"他承认自己还不能用精确的数学公式来描述这种新方法"，由此可知两句之间存在着转折关系，故选 [C] though。[A] so 引导结果状语从句；[B] since 和 [D] because 都引导原因状语从句。

2 词汇辨析题

事实上，除了前面要讲到的语法结构题外，多数短语搭配题和逻辑推理题中也同样需要对选项的词义进行辨析。本书中的"词汇辨析题"，主要指那些词义或词形干扰程度较高的题目。

【示例 1】   (03-01-76)

These differences are __76__ to carry advantages for companies	[A] disclosed [B] watched [C] revised [D] seen

【解析】选 [D]。这种差别能给公司带来好处是人们所能看到的，所以答案为 [D]。[A] "揭露" 和 [C] "修订" 都脱离了语境；[B] watch 也能表示 "看"，但它强调专注地看，而此处表示的仅仅是随意地看，故不选。

【示例 2】   (05-06-76)

Michael Hingson, Director of the National Federation for the Blind, hopes that family will be able to buy home __76__ of Cyclops for the price of a good television set.	[A] models [B] modes [C] cases [D] collections

【解析】选 [A]。Cyclops 修饰所填词，根据原文第二段可知，这是专门为盲人设计的 computer，因此 [A] "型号，样式" 正确，model 在这里指正在研发中的新机型。[B] "方式，模式" 在词形上有一定的干扰；[C] "案例，案子"；[D] "搜藏，征收" 语义不符。

【示例3】　　　　　　　　　　　　　　　　　　　　（05-06-73）

Within a few years, Kurzweil ___73___ the price range will be low enough for every school and library to own one.	[A] estimates　[B] considers [C] counts　　　[D] determines
【解析】选 [A]。所填词为 Kurzweil 发出的动作。宾语从句的谓语 will be 以及时间状语 Within a few years 暗示了所填词应该有"预测"的含义，因此 [A]"估计，评估"正确。[B]"认为，考虑"和 [C]"计算，认为"有一定的干扰性，但它们都没有"预测"之意，因此不够准确。[D]"确定，决定"不符合逻辑。	

　　从上述例子可以看出，词汇辨析题主要有以下几种形式：
◆ 意思相近的词的辨析；
◆ 拼写相近的词的辨析；
◆ 用法相近的词的辨析。

3　短语搭配题

　　该部分题目包括固定搭配和习惯用法。其中固定搭配以动词、形容词与副词、介词构成的词组居多。这些词组出现在完形填空中，主要以副词和介词为考点。尤其是介词短语，出现的频率非常高。在下一章"考点透视"中我们会给出一些常用的短语。

【示例1】　　　　　　　　　　　　　　　　　　　　（05-06-62）

They are thereby shut off from the world of books and newspapers, having to ___62___ on friends to read aloud to them.	[A] dwell　　　[B] rely [C] press　　　[D] urge
【解析】选 [B]。四个选项都能和介词 on 构成合理搭配，那就需要对短语的意义进行辨析。既然他们不能自己阅读书籍和报刊，那么自然就会依赖于朋友，因此 [B] rely on "依赖"符合语义要求，rely on sb. to do sth. 意为"依赖某人做某事"。[A] dwell on "老是想着；详述"；[C] press on "加紧进行"；[D] urge on "竭力主张，强烈要求"都不能使上下文语义通顺。	

【示例2】　　　　　　　　　　　　　　　　　　　　（05-06-72）

Mr. Kurzweil and his associates are preparing a smaller but improved version that will sell ___72___ less than half that price.	[A] on　　　　[B] for [C] through　　[D] to
【解析】选 [B]。所填词后面直接加 price。表示某物以多少钱出售通常可以表示为 sth. sell for/at…（相当于 sth. cost…），因此选项 [B] 为答案。	

4 语法结构题

该类题型的考查主要集中在以下几个方面：（1）定语从句；（2）主谓搭配一致；（3）否定句各种否定词及双重否定；（4）句型句式。具体内容将在本书第二章第三部分"语法结构"中阐述。

【示例】 (07-06-78)

But it may be all ___78___ can be expected from one year of hustle（忙碌）.	[A] but [B] as [C] that [D] those

【解析】选 [C]。分析句子结构可知，空格处应填一定语从句引导词。当引导词前面是 all 时，该引导词必须为 that，故选 [C]。

四、专项练习

Exercise 1

A critical factor that plays a part in *susceptibility*（易感性）to cold is age. A study done by the University of Michigan School of Public Health revealed particulars that seem to hold __1__ for the general population. Infants are the most cold-ridden group, __2__ more than six colds in their first years. Boys have more colds than girls up to age three. __3__ the age of three, girls are more susceptible than boys, and teenage girls average three colds a year __4__ boys' two.

The general incidence of colds continues to __5__ into maturity. Elderly people who are in good __6__ have as few as one or two colds annually. One __7__ is found among people in their twenties, especially women, who show a rise in cold infections. __8__ people in this age group are most likely to have young children.

1. [A] real [B] true
   [C] peace [D] dear
2. [A] getting [B] averaging
   [C] receiving [D] having
3. [A] During [B] Before
   [C] After [D] At
4. [A] than [B] in
   [C] to [D] with
5. [A] increase [B] descend
   [C] degrade [D] decline
6. [A] body [B] health
   [C] taste [D] mood
7. [A] exception [B] strangeness
   [C] example [D] expectation
8. [A] if [B] although
   [C] therefore [D] because
9. [A] hesitate [B] delay
   [C] reluct [D] want
10. [A] great [B] odd
    [C] vicious [D] sudden
11. [A] economy [B] economics

Adults who __9__ having children until their thirties and forties experience the same __10__ increase in cold infections.

The study also found that __11__ plays an important role. As income increases, the __12__ at which colds are reported in the family decreases. Families with the lowest income __13__ from about a third more colds than families at the __14__ class. Lower income generally forces people to live in more *cramped* (狭窄的) __15__ than those typically occupied by wealthier people, and the __16__ increases the opportunities for the cold __17__ to travel from person to person. Low income may also __18__ influence diet. The degree to which __19__ nutrition affects susceptibility to colds is not yet clearly established, but an inadequate diet is __20__ of lowering resistance generally.

    [C] expenses   [D] payment

12. [A] frequency   [B] susceptibility
    [C] possibility   [D] opportunity

13. [A] experience   [B] tolerate
    [C] suffer   [D] burden

14. [A] best   [B] higher
    [C] superior   [D] upper

15. [A] house   [B] quarters
    [C] accommodating
    [D] accommodation

16. [A] packing   [B] swarming
    [C] massing   [D] crowding

17. [A] virus   [B] incidence
    [C] disease   [D] illness

18. [A] oppositely   [B] contrarily
    [C] similarly   [D] adversely

19. [A] good   [B] proper
    [C] poor   [D] ill

20. [A] suspected   [B] doubted
    [C] guessed   [D] supposed

Exercise 2

A punctual person is in the habit of doing a thing at the proper time and is never late in keeping an appointment.

The unpunctual man, on the other hand, __1__ does what he has to do at the proper time. He is always in a hurry and in the end loses __2__ time and his good name. There is an old saying which says, "Time flies never to be __3__". This is very true. A __4__ thing may be found again, but lost time can never be obtained again. Time is more valuable than __5__ things. In fact time is life itself, an unpunctual man is forever

1. [A] always   [B] sometimes
  [C] never   [D] often

2. [A] both   [B] either
  [C] with   [D] neither

3. [A] recalled   [B] called
  [C] returned   [D] given

4. [A] losing   [B] missed
  [C] disappeared [D] lost

5. [A] useful   [B] material
  [C] real   [D] precious

6. [A] other's   [B] other
  [C] another's   [D] others

7. [A] little   [B] not
  [C] no   [D] many

wasting and mismanaging his most valuable asset as well as __6__. The unpunctual man is always complaining that he finds __7__ time to answer letters, or return calls or keep appointments __8__. But the man who really has a great deal to do is very careful of his time and seldom __9__ of want of it. He knows that he cannot get __10__ his immense amount of work __11__ he faithfully keeps every appointment without the least delay and deals with every piece of work when it has to be attended __12__. Failure to be punctual in keeping one's appointments is a sign of disrespect towards others. If a person is __13__ to a dinner and arrives later than the appointed time, he __14__ all the other guests waiting for him. This is a great impoliteness both towards the host and the other __15__.

Friends sometimes grow __16__ towards each other, or even become enemies, because one of them has been neglectful __17__ answering letters or keeping appointment.

Unpunctuality, moreover, is very __18__ when it comes to do one's duty, whether public or private. Imagine how it would be if those who are entrusted __19__ important tasks failed to be at their proper place at the appointed time. A man who is known to be habitually unpunctual is never trusted by friends or fellow men. And the unpunctual man is a __20__ of annoyance both to others and to himself.

8. [A] earlier   [B] faster
   [C] nicely   [D] promptly
9. [A] asks   [B] complains
   [C] calls   [D] expresses
10. [A] through   [B] away
    [C] off   [D] on
11. [A] if   [B] while
    [C] although   [D] unless
12. [A] at   [B] to
    [C] in   [D] into
13. [A] wanted   [B] present
    [C] invited   [D] advised
14. [A] makes   [B] forces
    [C] keeps   [D] lets
15. [A] guests   [B] members
    [C] servants   [D] hostages
16. [A] jealous   [B] cold
    [C] angry   [D] unconformable
17. [A] at   [B] in
    [C] by   [D] of
18. [A] important   [B] harmful
    [C] serious   [D] accurate
19. [A] by   [B] at
    [C] through   [D] with
20. [A] source   [B] root
    [C] cause   [D] supply

答案与解析

Exercise 1

1. 选 [B]。短语搭配题。hold true 为固定短语，表示"适用于，对…有效"，用在此处指"适用于普通大众"，所以 [B] 正确。hold real，此搭配不存在；hold peace "缄默"和 hold dear "重视"一般以人作主语。所以其他三项不对。

2. 选 [B]。词汇辨析题。本段最后的 teenage girls average three colds a year…是一个很好的提示，根据复现原则，选 [B] averaging。本句的意思为：婴儿是最容易感冒的人群，一岁前平均感冒六次以上。其他三项均不符合题意。

3. 选 [C]。逻辑推理题。上句提到：三岁之前，男孩比女孩的感冒频率要更高。本句则提到：女孩比男孩更容易感冒。从语篇衔接上来看，本句应该是讲三岁以后的情况，因此 [C] After 符合语篇逻辑，为正确答案。[A] During、[B] Before 和 [D] At 都不符合题意。

4. 选 [C]。逻辑推理题。girls average three colds a year 和 boys' two 之间存在一种比较关系，因此要在能表比较的 [A]、[C] 两项中作出选择。[A] than 表示比较时，一般在句中要有明显的比较级，而文中没有，故不选。[C] to 也可以表示比较，例如：I prefer baseball to tennis. （我喜欢棒球胜过网球。），故为答案。[B] in 和 [D] with 不能表示比较和对比。

5. 选 [D]。词汇辨析题。上文描述了婴儿平均每年感冒六次、小男孩和小女孩的感冒情况以及青少年期的平均每年感冒两三次，由此可见，感冒的频率是随年龄的增长而逐渐降低的。因此 [D] decline "下降，减少"符合题意。[A] increase "增加，加大"不符合句子逻辑；[B] descend "（空间上）下降，（财产、权利等）遗传"和 [C] degrade "降级，退化"虽然都包含"下降"之意，但不符合本题的语境，故也不选。

6. 选 [B]。短语搭配题。能用于 be in good ~ 的结构中，且能和 colds 形成语义共现的只有 [B] health，be in good health 为固定短语，表示"身体健康"。[A] body 不能用于 be in good ~ 的结构中；[C] taste 常用于 in good taste 结构中，表示"品味高，格调高"；[D] mood 常用于 be in a good mood 结构中，表示"心情很好"。

7. 选 [A]。逻辑推理题。上文提到感冒的次数一般会随着年龄的增长而减少，但本句讲的是 20 多岁的人，尤其是妇女感冒的次数会增加。从文章逻辑上来看，这类人群是一个特例，因此 [A] exception "例外"符合题意。[B] strangeness "陌生，奇妙，不可思议"；[C] example "例子，实例"和 [D] expectation "期待，预料"语义均不符。

8. 选 [D]。逻辑推理题。本句是在解释上句提到的 20 多岁的女性感冒次数增加的原因，故 [D] because 为答案。[A] if 表条件；[B] although 表让步；[C]

therefore 是强干扰项，它也表原因，和 because 的区别在于：它适用于前因后果的语境，而 because 则适用于前果后因的语境。

9. 选 [B]。短语搭配题。选项中能接 doing sth. 的只有 [B] delay "推迟，延缓"，它常用于 delay sb. /sth. /doing sth. 的结构中。[A] hesitate "犹豫，迟疑"，常用的搭配方式为 hesitate to do sth.；[C] reluct "反对，勉强"，常用 reluct against 的搭配方式；[D] want "需要"，常用 want to do sth. 的搭配方式。

10. 选 [D]。逻辑推理题。上文提到感冒的次数一般会随着年龄的增长而逐渐减少，而本句描述的情况是不符合一般规律的，因此只有 [D] sudden "突然的，意外的"才符合上下文逻辑。[A] "伟大的，重大的"；[B] "奇怪的，单数的"；[C] "邪恶的，不道德的"均不符合语境。句子大意为：即便是那些推迟到三、四十岁生育孩子的成年妇女也还是会遭遇感冒次数突然增加的情况。

11. 选 [B]。逻辑推理题。本句话是该段的中心句。下文论述的是经济状况与感冒的关系，故选 [B] economics "经济状况"。[A] economy "节约，节省，经济制度"是强干扰项，但它通常指 "（金钱、力气、时间、资源等的）节省、节约"或用作 the economy 时表示 "（国家的）经济管理，经济制度"，而此处指的是人们的经济状况，故不选。[C] expenses "花费，开销"和 [D] payment "付款，报酬"都过于片面。

12. 选 [A]。词汇辨析题。文章通篇都在讨论每年患感冒次数的问题，能和年次数形成同义复现的只有选项 [A] frequency "频率"。本句意为：据报道，随着家庭收入的增加，患感冒的频率也逐渐下降。[B] "易感性，易受影响"；[C] "可能性"；[D] "机会，时机"都脱离了语境。

13. 选 [C]。逻辑推理题。能和前文的 cold infections 和 have more colds 等形成语义复现的是 [C] suffer, suffer from a certain disease 表示 "患某种疾病"。[A] experience "经历，体验"，[B] tolerate "容忍，忍受"和 [D] burden "使负担，使负重"都是及物动词，后面不用跟介词。

14. 选 [D]。词汇辨析题。由句子结构可知，families at the ___14___ end 应与 families with the lowest income "最穷的家庭"形成对比，故应表示 "最富裕的家庭"。英语中一般用 the upper class 表示 "上层社会"，故选项 [D] upper 为答案。与 [A] best 对应的是 worst；可以用 higher income family 表示 "高收入家庭"，但一般不用 the higher class 这一表达方式，故 [B] 项可排除；与 [C] superior "较高的"对应的是 inferior "低级的"，故也不选。

15. 选 [B]。词汇辨析题。除 [C] 之外的三个选项都能表示 "住处"之意，但根据空格前的 more 即可排除 [A]、[D]，因为它们都是可数名词，用在 more 后面要用复数形式。[B] quarters "住处"符合题意，为答案。本句的意思为：低收入往往迫使人们居住在比富人居所小得多的房子里。[C] accommodating 为形容词，意为"乐于助人的，随和的"。

16. 选 [D]。词汇辨析题。能和前文中的 live in more cramped quarters 形成语义场共现的是 [D] crowding "拥挤"。[A] packing "填塞，包扎"语义不符；[B] swarming 一般指"人群一起涌入"，此处指居住环境，因此不选它；[C] massing "集合，集中"也不符合语境。

17. 选 [A]。词汇辨析题。根据常识，在人们之间传播的应该是感冒病毒，故选 [A] virus "病毒，病菌"。[B] incidence "发生率，频率"；[C] disease "疾病，弊病"；[D] illness "疾病，生病"。本句意为：拥挤的状况为感冒病菌在人与人之间的传播提供了机会。

18. 选 [C]。逻辑推理题。前文谈论到低收入与感冒的关系，本句谈到低收入对饮食也有影响，因此 [C] similarly "同样地，类似地"能很好地衔接上下文。[A] oppositely "相对地，对立地"，[B] contrarily "反之，相反地"，[D] adversely "相反地，不利地"都与原文逻辑相悖。

19. 选 [C]。逻辑推理题。前文提到低收入能影响饮食，和低收入相伴的往往是营养不良，[C] poor nutrition 符合题意。[A] good "优良的，上等的"和 [B] proper "合适的，正确的"违背了原文的逻辑；[D] ill 虽然表示的是否定意义，但不能用它来修饰 nutrition。

20. 选 [A]。短语搭配题。be suspected of 为惯用搭配，表示"怀疑，猜想"，且和前文的 is not yet clearly established 形成语义共现。故 [A] 正确。[B] doubted 常用于 doubt about sb. /sth. 结构中，表示"怀疑某人/某事"；[C] guessed "猜，猜测"常和介词 at 连用；[D] supposed 常用于 be supposed to 结构中，表示"推测，应该"。

Exercise 2

1. 选 [C]。逻辑推理题。上文对 a punctual person 进行了解释，本句关键词 the unpunctual person 以及 on the other hand 提示本句包含着完全相反的含义，故 [C] 项正确。

2. 选 [A]。短语搭配题。both…and…为固定短语，意为"两者都…"。其他三项均不能和 and 构成合理搭配。

3. 选 [A]。短语搭配题。"光阴一去不复返"的正确表达为"Time flies never to be recalled"。故 [A] 正确，其他三项均不符合题意。

4. 选 [D]。词汇辨析题。"丢失的东西"英文表达为 a lost thing，故选 [D]。"丢失东西"应为已发生的事情，不可能用现在分词，故 [A] losing 错误；[B] missed 意为"错过的，思念的"；[C] disappeared "消失的，不见的"均不符合题目的语义要求。

5. 选 [B]。逻辑推理题。时间是一种抽象物质，与之相对的应是物质名词，故 [B] material "物质的，具体的"符合题意。[A] useful "有用的，有益的"；

[C] real "真的，真实的"；[D] precious "宝贵的，贵重的" 均脱离了语境。

6. 选 [A]。语法结构题。此处意为 "别人最有价值的财富"，和前面的 his most valuable asset 相对照，故 [A] other's 为答案，完整的句子应为 ... as well as other's most valuable asset。其他三项均不能使句子语法正确。

7. 选 [C]。逻辑推理题。根据常理推断，不守时的人总会抱怨他没时间回信，回电话等等。用在名词前表完全否定的为 [C] no。

8. 选 [D]。逻辑推理题。根据上题题解可知，该空格前已经有了否定词 no，故 keep appointments 8 应与 unpunctual 构成反义复现关系。[D] keep appointment promptly 意为 "准时守约"，符合题意，promptly 意为 "准时地，正好"。

9. 选 [B]。短语搭配题。选项中能和 of 连用的有 [B] complains 和 [C] calls。complain of... 意为 "抱怨..."，符合题意，故 [B] 为正确答案。而 call of 意为 "邀...一同去"，用在此处显然语义不符，故可排除；[A] asks 常用于 ~ sb. about sb. /sth., ~ sth. of sb. 或 ~ for 等结构中；[D] expresses 为及物动词，后面无需跟介词。

10. 选 [A]。短语搭配题。四个选项均能和 get 构成动词短语，能和 his immense amount of work 构成合理动宾搭配的只有 [A], get through "（工作）完成"。get away "逃脱"；get off "出发，动身"；get on "进展，出人头地"，所以其他三项均不符合题意。

11. 选 [D]。短语搭配题。not...unless 为习惯用法，意为 "除非...才"，故 [D] 为答案。

12. 选 [B]。短语搭配题。短语 attend to 意为 "用心（从事）..."，其中 to 不能用其他介词替代。

13. 选 [C]。词汇辨析题。根据句意可知，此处想要表达的意思为：如果某人被邀请去参加一个宴会...，故答案为 [C] invited，[A] be invited to 意为 "被邀请去..."。[A] wanted "想要"；[B] present "介绍，呈现"；[D] advised "劝告，忠告" 均不符合题意。

14. 选 [C]。短语搭配题。根据空格后的 all the other guests waiting for him 可知，所填词要能用于 ~ sb. doing sth. 的结构中，选项中符合的只有 [C] keeps，keep sb. doing sth. 意为 "使得某人做某事"。[A] makes 和 [D] lets 的用法均为 ~ sb. do sth.，意为 "使某人做某事"；[B] forces 的用法为 force sb. to do sth.，意为 "迫使某人做某事"。

15. 选 [A]。逻辑推理题。根据前文中的 ...the other guests waiting...，再根据原词复现原则可知，[A] guests 为答案。[B] members "会员，成员"；[C] servants "仆人，佣人"；[D] hostages "人质，抵押品" 均脱离了原文语境。

16. 选 [B]。逻辑推理题。根据句中的 because 可知，Friends sometimes grow 16 towards each other... 是 neglectful 17 answering letters or keeping appointment 造成的。朋友之间疏于信件或约会见面会使得关系趋于冷淡，[B]

cold "冷淡的，不热情的"。[A] jealous "嫉妒的，猜疑的" 和 [D] uncomfortable "不舒服的，不安的" 语义不符；[C] angry 不和介词 towards 连用。

17. 选 [D]。短语搭配题。be neglectful of 为固定搭配，故选 [D] of。

18. 选 [B]。逻辑推理题。不守时所带来的影响肯定是消极或负面的，因此所填词要能表消极、否定意义，据此可知 [B] harmful "有害的" 为答案。[A] important "重要的，重大的"；[C] serious "严肃的，认真的"；[D] accurate "正确的，准确的" 均表积极、肯定意义，故均可排除。

19. 选 [D]。短语搭配题。entrust sb. with sth. 意为 "委托某事给某人"，故 [D] entrust 正确。

20. 选 [A]。词汇辨析题。文章多处提到不守时的人容易制造不愉快，由此可知他们是烦恼之源，故 [A] source "来源" 正确。[B] root "根部，根源"；[C] cause "原因，理由"；[D] supply "补给，供给" 语义均不符。

考 点 透 视

一、逻辑推理

文章内部存在的各种逻辑关系，要求考生在做完形填空题时，要做到"先谋全篇，再谋一题"。考生在做题时不能只看到所填词在短语或句子里是否合适，而要时刻注意从上下文来考虑。

确定了一个空格前后存在的各种限定关系，然后再判断 4 个选项中哪一个符合这些限定关系的要求，确定答案。

在对历年真题进行分析之后，我们总结出的逻辑推理的考查重点有：

1 对语境的把握

语境就是我们通常所指的上下文。段与段之间，句子与段之间，句子之间以及词语之间都有一定的语义联系。而这一切的联系尽在语境之中，因此对语境的理解对解题至关重要。

【示例】   (07-06-69)

But a __69__ of the past year in disaster history suggests that modern Americans are particularly bad at protecting themselves from guaranteed threats.	[A] review [B] reminder [C] concept [D] prospect

【解析】选 [A]。逻辑推理题。四个选项都能和介词 of 连用，但能和空格后的 the past year in disaster history 形成语义场共现的只有 [A] "回顾"。[B] "暗示，提醒"；[C] "观念，概念"；[D] "前途，前景" 均脱离了上下文语境。

2 常见的逻辑关系

一个句子中，或者句子与句子之间，甚至段落与段落之间都可能存在一些明显的逻辑关系。这些逻辑关系常常以一些关系词为标志，下面将它们列出。

并列关系（and, while 等）；

递进关系（even, again, besides, furthermore, moreover）

转折关系（but, however, though, whereas, nevertheless 等）；

因果关系（so, therefore, thus, because, for, since, as 等）；

让步关系（though, although, despite, in spite of 等）；

条件关系（if, unless, once, provided that, in case of 等）；

解释关系（that is to say, in other words 等）；

顺序关系（before, after, and, first, then, next, finally 等）

【示例1】 (03-01-77)

| These differences are seen to carry advantages for companies, ___77___ they expand the range of techniques that can be used to help the company manage its workforce effectively. | [A] therefore [B] whereas [C] because [D] nonetheless |

【解析】 选 [C]。逻辑推理题。空格前和空格后的内容是一果一因的关系，所以选 [C]。[A] 也是表因果关系的连词，但它用于前因后果的句子中，所以不符题意；[B]"然而，反之" 和 [D]"虽然如此" 表转折，都不符合此处的逻辑关系。

【示例2】 (05-06-70)

| At present, Cyclops costs $50,000. ___70___, Mr. Kurzweil and his associates are preparing a smaller but improved version that will sell for less than half that price. | [A] Likewise [B] Moreover [C] However [D] Though |

【解析】 选 [C] 本句提到 Kurzweil 和他的同事们正在开发更加物美价廉的产品，和上句提到的 $50,000 形成转折关系，因此表转折关系的选项 [C] 为答案。

【示例3】 (01-01-72)

| ... during the First World War, when shortage of manpower caused the industrial employment of unprecedented numbers of women, ...The outbreak of the Second World War was quickly followed by an increase in the number of day nurseries in almost all countries, as women were ___72___ called upon to replace men in the factories. | [A] again [B] thus [C] repeatedly [D] yet |

【解析】 选 [A]。前文提到一战时妇女就代替男人进入了工厂，二战时的情况和一战相同，故应用 [A] again 来表示"相同情况的再一次发生"。[B] thus 与 as 语义重复。[C] 项强调的是重复多次，用于形容原文中的两次显然有点过；[D] yet 表转折，用在这里语义不通。

3 词汇的复现关系

一篇文章，由于内容的相关性，文章的主题词汇，或与主题密切相关的词汇一定会在文章中多处出现。词汇的复现，指某一个词以原词、指代词、同义词、近义词、上义词、下义词等出现在语篇中，语篇中的句子通过这种复现关系得以衔接。

　　所以，空格中要填的词汇很可能就在上下文中以其他形式出现过。考生应根据语篇中存在的内在联系来做出判断。

【示例1】　　　　　　　　　　　　　　　　　　　　　　　　　　（07-06-80）

Meanwhile, New Orleans officials have crafted a plan to use buses and trains to evacuate the sick and the disabled. The city estimates that 15,000 people will need a ___80___ out.	［A］ride　　　　　［B］trail ［C］path　　　　　［D］track
【解析】选［A］。上句提到新奥尔良官员已经制定了一项草案，计划使用公车和火车疏散病人和残疾人。本句提到，据估计，有15,000人需要…。显然所填词应该和 buses and trains 形成复现关系，［A］ride "交通工具" 符合，它和 buses and trains 构成上下义复现。［B］"踪迹，痕迹"；［C］"路线，通道"；［D］"轨迹，足迹" 都不符合题意。	

【示例2】　　　　　　　　　　　　　　　　　　　　　　　　　　（05-06-64）

Although there are …, thousands of other blind people find it difficult to learn that system. …A young scientist named Raymond Kurzweil has now designed a computer which is a major breakthrough in providing aid to the ___64___.	［A］paralyzed　［B］uneducated ［C］invisible　　［D］sightless
【解析】选［D］。根据文章首句提到 blind people 可以推测出这种计算机是为帮助盲人而设计的。根据语义复现关系可以得出［D］sightless "盲的，无视力的" 为正确答案。provide 的用法为 provide sth. to sb.，因此本题考察的相关用法是定冠词 the + 形容词表示某类人。［A］the paralyzed "残疾人" 过于笼统；［B］the uneducated "未受过教育的，无知的" 不符合语义；［C］是个强干扰项，因为它意为 "看不见的"，但 the invisible 意为 "隐形人"，故将其可排除。	

4　词汇的共现关系

　　词汇的共现关系是指词汇共同出现的倾向性。在语篇中，围绕一定的主题，一定的词就会同时出现，这种词的共现关系与语篇题材关系密切。根据这个原则，我们可以删除掉一些和语篇主题无关的选项，而将重点放在和主题相关的选项上。

【示例】　　　　　　　　　　　　　　　　　　　　　　　　　　（01-01-80）

However, the expectation that most employed mothers would leave their ___80___ at the end of the war was only partly fulfilled.	［A］nurseries　　　［B］homes ［C］jobs　　　　　［D］children

【解析】选 [C]。能和 employed mothers 形成语义场共现的是 [C] jobs。句子的大意为：联邦政府期望战争结束后妇女离开工作，回家照顾小孩，但是事实并非如此。

二、词汇辨析

在历年六级完形考题中，词汇辨析题所占比重也很大，这也是四级与六级完形题目的一个区别。词汇辨析的类型有：意思相近的词的辨析；拼写相近的词的辨析；用法相近的词的辨析。在考题中，四个需要辨析的选项的词性一般都是相同的，动词、名词、形容词、副词都会有所涉及。其中意思相近词的辨析是重点也是难点。

【示例1】 (07-12-71)

…he realized the mathematical approach he had been pusuing for almost three years was flawed. And now there was a __71__ pressure. Einstein discovered to his horror that Hilbert had taken what he had learned from Einstein's lectures and was racing to come up with the correct equation first.	[A] complex [B] compatible [C] comparative [D] competitive

【解析】选 [D]。本题考查形近词辨析。根据上下文可知，此空所在句说的是爱因斯坦目前的压力，下句对此做了解释，他的压力来自于数学家希尔伯特，故答案为 [D]，competitive 意为"竞争的"。[A] complex "复杂的，综合的"；[B] compatible "谐调的，一致的"；[C] comparative "比较的，难当的"均不符合题意。

【示例2】 (99-06-80)

…you can use a special light device to provide the necessary light __80__ for a range of activities such as reading, watching TV or working.	[A] agitation [B] spur [C] acceleration [D] stimulus

【解析】选 [D]。本题考查近义词辨析。spur 与 stimulus 都表示"刺激"：spur 原意是骑马人马靴上的马刺，后引申指激励人思想、鼓舞情绪、增加活力的刺激物，一般为概念上的，例如：The good news will be a spur to continued effort. "这个好消息一定会激励大家继续努力"。stimulus 是指生物学上能起刺激作用的东西，例如：They change automatically in response to stimuli. "在外界刺激之下，它们自动地作出反应"。本题指的是外界的光线刺激，故应选 [D] stimulus。[A] agitation "激动，焦虑"和 [C] acceleration "加速，加速度"语义不符。

下面我们分词性列出多组近义辨析的词条，考生在备考过程中可参照掌握。

1 动词（50 组）

按压 compress	condense	crush	press
保护 defend	guard	protect	secure
保留 preserve	reserve	retain	sustain
保证 ensure	guarantee	assure	swear
变弱 weaken	degrade	decay	crumble
参加 join	enter	attend	participate
颤抖 shake	tremble	quiver	shiver
抵制 resist	repel	defy	oppose
反对 object	refute	protest	retort
防止 avoid	flee	exclude	preclude
放弃 abandon	desert	discard	quit
服从 obey	conform	comply	observe
改变 alter	vary	divert	switch
忽视 neglect	ignore	omit	disregard
花费 expend	exhaust	consume	cost
获得 gain	achieve	acquire	contrive
激励 further	inspire	promote	propel
加强 intensify	consolidate	reinforce	underline
检查 inspect	investigate	scrutinize	survey
交流 contact	communicate	intercourse	correspond
禁止 prohibit	forbid	ban	bar
捐献 dedicate	donate	sacrifice	attribute
看瞧 gaze	glance	glimpse	peer
考虑 deem	consider	deliberate	ponder
扩展 extend	expand	enlarge	prolong
谴责 curse	reproach	condemn	rail
强迫 force	compel	impose	oblige
忍受 endure	sustain	tolerate	withstand
扔投 throw	cast	pitch	toss
设想 conceive	imagine	assume	speculate
使混合 blend	merge	melt	stir
使沮丧 depress	grieve	embarrass	frustrate
使困惑 confuse	perplex	bewilder	baffle
使恼怒 annoy	irritate	provoke	aggravate
使摇摆 sway	fluctuate	swing	flutter

提升 raise	heave	elevate	hoist
跳跃 bound	bounce	hop	skip
污染 pollute	spot	stain	contaminate
希望 wish	desire	urge	appetite
下降 decline	descend	diminish	shrink
限制 restrict	confine	restrain	refrain
消除 eliminate	delete	dispose	exile
消失 disappear	disperse	dissipate	vanish
修改 revise	rectify	amend	restore
压迫 oppress	repress	suppress	overwhelm
引起 arouse	generate	stir	spark
运送 carry	transport	transmit	commute
增加 increase	enhance	hike	soar
展示 show	display	illustrate	exhibit
阻碍 hinder	interrupt	interfere	intervene

2 名词（25 组）

变化 variety	variation	transformation	reform
部分 ingredient	constituent	section	proportion
产品 product	produce	commodity	cargo
刺激 spur	impulse	impetus	incentive
废弃物 rubbish	waste	refuse	garbage
混乱 mess	chaos	disorder	fuss
结果 result	consequence	impact	outcome
景色 scene	scenery	prospect	landscape
看法 bias	insight	perception	prejudice
能力 capacity	capability	faculty	ability
品质 character	temperament	integrity	virtue
契约 engagement	compact	treaty	contract
趋向 trend	tendency	inclination	current
声誉 reputation	publicity	status	glory
式样 sample	specimen	pattern	mode
视野 view	eyesight	horizon	vision
特征 characteristic	feature	trait	property
问题 question	issue	mystery	trouble
喜爱 affection	passion	appreciation	admiration
信任 confidence	belief	conviction	faith

责任 duty	burden	assignment	responsibility
障碍物 barrier	barricade	obstacle	drawback
争论 argument	controversy	debate	dispute
证据 proof	testimony	evidence	witness
种类 class	variety	category	kind

3 形容词和副词（25 组）

宝贵的 costly	precious	luxurious	invaluable
不断的 constant	chronic	consecutive	successive
出于本性的 natural	inherent	intrinsic	spontaneous
次要的 secondary	minor	inferior	trivial
粗糙的 crude	rude	coarse	rough
脆弱的 weak	feeble	crisp	delicate
独特的 unusual	exceptional	extraordinary	particular
复杂的 complicated	intricate	elaborate	tough
高贵的 decent	graceful	gracious	respectful
很可能的 liable	probable	prone	potential
基本的 radical	essential	fundamental	indispensable
静止的 calm	stationary	stable	steady
巨大的 enormous	tremendous	immense	giant
灵活的 flexible	elastic	plastic	loose
内部的 inner	inside	interior	internal
强烈的 intense	violent	robust	forceful
强制性的 arbitrary	authoritative	compulsory	imperative
清楚的 obvious	evident	distinct	explicit
始终如一的 consistent	insistent	permanent	persistent
有活力的 live	living	brisk	active
有能力的 capable	proficient	competent	able
重要的 significant	critical	urgent	crucial
著名的 prominent	outstanding	remarkable	noticeable
最重要的 cardinal	prime	primary	predominant
几乎 barely	hardly	almost	scarcely

三、短语搭配

　　短语搭配题考查的是学生基本的知识储备，这就需要学生平时多加积累。尤其是一些短语动词（look in，let out，make off 等一些固定下来作为动词使用的结构）、动词短语（动词和一些常用的名词的短语搭配）、名词短语和介词短语。

【示例1】   （05-06-61）

They are thereby shut __61__ from the world of books and newspapers, having to rely on friends to read aloud to them.	[A] up　　　　[B] down [C] in　　　　[D] off

【解析】 选 [D]。空格前有表结果的 thereby 一词，由此我们可以知道本句与上句中提到的"有数以千计的盲人难以学会布莱叶盲文点字法（Braille）"应该构成因果关系。shut off 常与 from 连用，表示"与…隔离，隔绝"，填入原文构成的句意为"与书籍和报刊隔绝"，因此，[D] 项符合题意。shut up "住口"；shut down "（使）关闭，（使）停工"；shut in "把…关在里面，禁闭"都不符合题意。

【示例2】   （03-01-81）

…a management style used by some women managers（and also by some men）that __81__ from the command-and-control style traditionally used	[A] derives　　[B] differs [C] descends　[D] detaches

【解析】 选 [B]。四个选项都能和介词 from 搭配，因此要从上下文语义衔接方面来考虑问题。文章第二段开始就指出女性管理者带来的不同，由下文中的"互动式"与"命令式"管理风格可知，此处是说这两种经营管理方式的不同，所以选 [B]，differs from…，意为"与…不同"。derives from…意为"起源于…"；descends from…意为"从…传下来"；detaches from 意为"从…分离"，它们的语义都不相符。

　　由于短语数量众多，而一般的词汇书中都会对短语动词、动词短语和名词短语作介绍，本部分主要列出一些常用的介词短语，以利大家备考复习。

1 above 构成的惯用短语

above all　尤其是，最重要的是	above suspicion　无可怀疑的
above praise　赞美不尽	above criticism　无可指责
above reproach　无可厚非	above price　价值连城
above one's head（understanding）　不可理解	above one's income　入不敷出
above the average　超过一般水平	be above oneself　兴高采烈

2 after 构成的惯用短语

after all　毕竟，到底	day after day　日复一日
one after another　接二连三	page after page　一页又一页的
year after year　年年岁岁	wave after wave　一波又一波地
bus after bus　公共汽车一辆又一辆	time after time　一次又一次

3 at 构成的惯用短语

at the sight of　看到	at the news of　听到
at one's ease/at one's leisure　在闲暇时	at the thought of　想到
at a drought　一口气	at liberty　闲暇，自在，随意
at peace　处于和平状态，心情平静	at large　自由自在
at home　安适	at one's height　酒酣
at stake　在危险中	at bay　陷入绝境
at one's convenience　在某人方便时	at the end of　在…结尾，在…末端
at rest　长眠，静止	at a loss　迷茫
at sea　茫然	at fault　迷惑
at one's will　随意	at command　掌握，可自由使用
at random　随便地	at intervals　时时
at one's mercy　任人支配，由人摆布	at expense of　以…为代价
at dusk　黄昏	at one's service　任人使用
at length　详细地	at hand　不远，在身边
at least　至少	at the risk of　冒险
at half price of　半价	at any rate　至少，无论如何
at most　至多	at cost　照原价
at a cost　亏本	at a bargain　廉价
at full speed　以全速	at a profit　获利
at the risk of　冒…的危险	at the point of　靠近，接近

4 beyond 构成的惯用短语

beyond words　难以言喻	beyond all hope　毫无希望
beyond control　难以控制	beyond belief　难以置信
beyond all comprehension　不可理解	beyond dispute　无可争议
beyond all comparison　无可比拟	beyond doubt　无可怀疑
beyond one's grasp　力所不及	beyond controversy　无可争议

5 by 构成的惯用短语

by rule　按规则	by way of　经由
years by year　年复一年	by force　用武力
by degrees　逐渐地	by heart　熟记
step by step　逐步	by persuasion　凭说服
little by little　渐渐地	by wholesale　批发
honest by nature　天性诚实	by sight　仅识其面

by trade　就职业而言

by chance　偶然

by good luck　侥幸

by mistake　弄错

by request　应邀

by accident　偶然，意外地

by turns　轮流

large by half　大一半

reduce by half　减少一半

by retail　零售

by auction　拍卖

by contract　承包

by post　邮寄

by express　以快件方式

by appointment　约定

by means of　用…方法

by all means　用一切手段，当然可以

by virtue of　凭借

by airplane　乘飞机

by boat　乘船

6 for 构成的惯用短语

cut out for　有…才能

bound for　启程前往

for all　尽管，虽然

for all I know　就我所知

for certain　的确

for life　终生

for the present　暂时

for good　永远，一劳永逸地

for the moment　暂时

answer for　负责

for the time being　暂时

7 from 构成的惯用短语

from far　从远处

from now on　从现在起

from top to bottom　彻头彻尾

from above　自上

from bad to worse　每况愈下

8 in 构成的惯用短语

in chorus　合唱

in full dress　盛装

in mourning／in white　穿丧服

in high feather　兴高采烈

in high(low, poor)spirits　情绪高昂(低沉)

in a good temper　脾气好

in a rage　盛怒

in despair　失望

in distress　悲痛

in trouble　处于困境

in any event　无论如何

in pain　在痛苦中

in whispers　低语

in disguise　假扮

in spectacles　带着眼镜

in a good mood　心情好

in violation　违反

in anger　愤怒

in hope　在希望中

in fun　开玩笑

in comfort　在安乐中

in the blues　忧郁

in conclusion　总之

in tears　流泪

in alarm　惊惶中

in astonishment　惊奇

in a fog　困惑

in debt　负债

in chaos　混乱

in haste　匆匆

in fashion　流行

in the operation　在施行

in love　恋爱

in ruins　荒废

in the right　正确

in width　在宽度方面

in shape　在外形上

in heaps　堆积

in broad daylight　在白昼

in quest of　寻求

in memory of　为纪念…而

in token of　作为的表示

in fear　在恐惧中

in dilemma　进退维谷

in good repair　情况良好

in disorder　混乱

in a fever　发烧

in force　在施行中

in labour　在分娩中

in use　在使用中

in earnest　认真地

in black and white　白纸黑字

in flower　开花

in blossom　一排排

in search of　寻求

in honour of　对…表示敬意

in revenge of　作为…的报复

in brief　简单地说

in disrepute　声名狼藉

in general　一般来说

lie in　在于

in wonder　惊奇

in horror　恐惧

in need　在危急中

in good condition　情况良好

in one's way　妨碍

in sickness　患病

in the air　传播

in progress　在进行中

in session　在开会

in secret　秘密地

in print　在印刷

in hand　在进行中，在考查中

in bloom　盛开

in the bud　含苞待放

in miniature　小型，小规模

in pursuit of　追求

in reward of　作为…的报酬

in all proportions　按各种比例

in safety　在安全中

in good order　秩序良好

in confusion　零乱

in good health　健康

in vogue　流行

in touch　联系

in public　公开地

in doubt　怀疑

in the wrong　错误

in length　在长度方面

in every respect　在每一方面

in the raw　在自然状态

in favour of　赞成

in behalf of　为…的利益

in addition　另外

in essence　在本质上

in fact　事实上

in the event of　万一

in line with　按照

in other words　换言之

in support of　支持

in stock　有库存，有现货

in part　有货

in turn　依次

in terms of　用…的术语，根据

in no time　马上

in respect to　关于

in regard to　关于

in the open　在露天

in all　总计

in time　及时

in vain　徒劳

in view of the fact that …　鉴于…这一事实

be absorbed in　专心于

indulge in　沉溺于

be engaged in　从事于

immerse in　沉湎于

9　of 构成的惯用短语

of one's own accord　自愿

of one's own choice　出于自己的选择

of oneself　靠自己

ease sb. of　减轻

relieve sb. of　接触，减轻

lighten sth. of　减轻

cure sb. of　治愈

heal sb. of　治疗

break sb. of　戒除

absolve of　赦免，免除

rid of　接触，免除

clear of　清除

break of　分离

strip of　剥夺

plunder of　抢夺

dispose of　剥夺

cheat of　骗夺

defraud of　榨取

bereave of　夺去

devoid of　没有，空的

10　on 成的惯用短语

on the ground of　基于…的理由

on account of　由于

on the wane　正在衰落，正在亏缺

on thorns　心烦

on edge　紧张

on one's mind　在沉思

on duty　值班

on guard　警戒

on leave　休假

on strike　罢工

on the market　出售

on holiday　度假

on hire　失火，愤怒

on view　展出

on display　展示

on a picnic　野餐

on the way　在途中

on the wing　飞行，传播

on the increase　增加

on fire　失火

on the alert　警惕

on the brink of　正要…的时候

on the point　濒于

on trial　受审

on the rise　上涨

on the ebb　退缩，减弱

on the watch　警戒，注意
on the verge of　处于…的边缘
act on principle　按原则办事
on this understanding　在此条件下
on such terms　根据这样的条件
on purpose　故意
on the contrary　相反的
on behalf of　代表
on the other hand　另一方面
have sth. on good authority　从可靠的方面获悉某事

on the carpet　在讨论中
on margin of　接近…的边缘
on condition that　在…条件下
on the decline　在下降
have effect on　对…有影响
on second thoughts　三思之后
on the average　平均
on the one hand　一方面

11 out of 构成的惯用短语

out of fear　出于恐惧
out of revenge　出于报复
out of sorts　不适
out of hearing　听不见
out of fashion　不流行
out of hand　失去控制
out of wedlock　未婚的
out of stock　缺货
out of necessity　出于必要
out of date　过时
out of work　失业
out of trouble　摆脱麻烦
out of place　不恰当
out of the ordinary　不平凡
out of temper　发怒

out of charity　出于仁慈
out of patience　不耐烦
out of danger　脱险
out of sight　看不见
out of politeness　不合礼节
out of step　不一致
out of print　绝版
out of practice　缺乏练习
out of pity　出于同情
out of control　失去控制
out of breath　上气不接下气
out of season　不合季节
out of proportion to　不均匀
out of one's element　不得意，不适
out of shape　健康不佳

12 to 构成的惯用短语

to a certain extent　在一定程度上
to a degree　非常
to the good　有好处
compare to　对比
to one's taste　合胃口
as to　关于，至于
to one's credit　值得赞扬
to one's advantage　有利于

according to　根据
due to　由于
to one's benefit　对…有益
to some extent　在某种程度上
to one's face　当某人的面
with reference to　关于
to and fro　来回地
be burnt to death　烧死

be moved to tears　感动得流泪

to one's regret　使人后悔

to one's shame　使人丢脸

to one's relief　使人安心

be accustomed to　习惯于

to the contrary　相反

be frozen to death　冻死

to one's joy　使人快乐

to one's disappointment　使人失望

to one's satisfaction　使人满意

in addition to　除…之外

attached to　附属

13 under 构成的惯用短语

under discussion　在讨论中

under consideration　在考虑中

under cultivation　在耕作中

under sail　在航行

under fire　被攻击

under repairs　在修理中

under way　在行动中

under construction　在建设中

under investigation　在调查中

under examination　在实验中

under trial　在实验中

under the plow　在耕作中

under the hammer　在拍卖

under the weather　患病，经济困难

under the mask of　在…假面具下

under the name of　以…的名义

under the pretence of　以…为借口

under a false name　用化名

get under　制服

keep under　抑制

serve under　在手下任职

under one's charge　由某人照顾

under order　奉命

under a cloud　受嫌疑，处于窘境

under difficulties　在困难中

under the circumstance　在…的情况下

under control　在控制之下

under the supervision　在…监督下

under direction　在…指挥中

under the control of　在…控制之下

under the command of　在…统率下

under the yoke of　受…支配

under the care of　在…照顾下

under the auspices of　在…主办下

under the influence　在…影响下

under age　未成年

under the plea of　以…为借口

under the necessity of　迫于需要

under the patronage of　在…保护之下

under one's thumb　受某人控制

under the rule of　受…统治

under the treatment of　由…治疗

under the guidance of　在…领导下

under the guise　装扮成，在…的幌子下

14 with 构成的惯用短语

tremble with fear　恐惧得发抖

in connection with　与…相连

in contact with　与…有联系

comparable with　与…相比

in accordance with　与…一致

shake with laughter　笑得全身发抖

in touch with　与…接触

in line with　与…一致

in harmony with　与…协调

be endowed with　赋有

with reserve　有保留　　　　　　　with open arms　热情地
with one accord　一致地　　　　　　with a will　坚定地
with a view to　为了　　　　　　　with the exception　除…
with a firm hand　坚决地

四、语法结构

　　尽管纯语法题在完形填空中所占比例很小，但是在四六级考试取消"词汇和语法结构"题型后，完形填空是惟一还在直接对考生的语法知识进行考查的题型。语法是语言学习的基础之一，考生尤其应该在学习中给予关注。

1 定语从句

【示例】　　　　　　　　　　　　　　　　　　　　　　　　　（07-12-75）

So in October 1915 Einstein threw himself into a month-long frantic endeavor in ___75___ he returned to an earlier mathematical strategy and wrestled	[A] how 　　 [B] that [C] what 　　 [D] which

【解析】选［D］。分析句子结构可知，in ___75___ 引导定语从句修饰 a month-long frantic endeavor，因此答案为［D］which。其他选项均不能和介词 in 共同引导定语从句。

　　定语从句主要考关系词，限定与非限定性定语从句的区别，定语从句的判别（区分定语从句与其他主从复合句）。

（1）连接词包括关系代词（who，whom，that，which，whose，as）和关系副词（where，when，why）。关系词的选择主要依据先行词在从句中充当的成分，作主、定、宾语时，选择关系代词；作状语时，应选择关系副词。例如：

　　①This is the mountain village which I visited last year.（先行词在从句中作宾语）

　　②This is the museum where the exhibition was held.（先行词在从句中作状语）

（2）定语从句有两种。一种是与主句连在一起的限制性从句，一种是用逗号隔开的非限制性从句。that 不能引导非限定性定语从句。

（3）that 定语从句特别容易和 that 同位语从句混淆，它们的区别是：定语从句中的 that 在从句中充当某个成分（主语或宾语），而同位语从句中的 that 只起连接主句与从句的作用，不充当任何成分。例如：

　　①The news that he told me is that Tom would go abroad next year. 他告诉我的消息是汤姆明年将出国。（第一个 that 引导的从句是定语从句，在定语从句中充当宾语，第二个 that 引导表语从句。）

②The news that Tom would go abroad is told by him. 汤姆将出国的消息是他讲的。（同位语从句，that 在句中不作任何成分）

2 主谓搭配一致

【示例】 （四级 01-01-84）

If they are going to read, why not give out copies of the lecture? Then we ___84___ need to go to class.	[A] couldn't [B] wouldn't [C] mustn't [D] shouldn't

【解析】选 [B]。本句表示对将来的一种假设，属于虚拟语气，因此只能用 wouldn't。

    主谓搭配一致主要考查时态、语态、语气、人称、数。虚拟语气，其一直是英语学习中的难点，更是六级考试中的重点，所以接下来我们一起来回顾一下它的相关知识点。

    If 条件状语从句中的虚拟语气，主句与从句中谓语动词的形式主要可分为以下三类：

假设类型	从句谓语动词的形式	主句谓语动词的形式
与现在事实相反	动词的过去式（be 用 were，而不用 was）	would（第一人称可用 should）+ 动词原形
与过去事实相反	had + ed 分词	would（第一人称可用 should）+ have + ed 分词
与将来事实相反	should/were to + 动词原形	would（第一人称可用 should）+ 动词原形

    虚拟语气的其他用法如下：

（1）在动词 wish 后的宾语从句中的虚拟语气，常省去宾语从句的引导词 that。

    例如：I wish I were a bird. 但愿我是只小鸟。

（2）在表示建议、命令、要求、忠告等动词的后面的宾语从句中的虚拟语气由于这些动词本身隐含说话者的主观意见，认为某事应该或不应该怎样，这些词语后面的"that"从句应用虚拟语气，且均以"should + 动词原形"表示这种语气，但事实上"should"常被省略，故此从句中谓语动词用原形。

    例如：The doctor suggested that he（should）try to lose his weight. 医生建议他要尽力减肥。

（3）在 expect, believe, think, suspect 等动词的否定或疑问形式后的宾语从句中，我们经常用"should + 动词原形（或完成形式）"，表示惊奇、怀疑、不满等。

    例如：I never thought that he should be such a brave young soldier. 我们从来没

想到他是个如此勇敢的小战士。

（4）would rather, would sooner, had rather, would（just）as soon, would prefer（希望）也用来表达主观愿望，它们之后的宾语从句中需用虚拟语气。谓语动词用过去式表示现在或将来，用过去完成式表示与过去事实相反。表示"宁愿做什么"或"对过去做的事懊悔"。

例如：I would rather he came tomorrow than today. 我宁愿他明天来（而不是今天来）。

（5）在 It is + 名词 + that 的主语从句中，常用虚拟语气，表示建议、命令、请求、道歉、怀疑、惊奇等。

例如：It is my proposal that he be sent to study further abroad. 我建议派他去国外进一步学习。

（6）当某些表示建议、请求、命令等主观意向的名词作主语时，其后的表语从句或同位语从句需用虚拟语气，其表达形式为"should + 动词原形"或直接用动词原形。

例如：My idea is that we（should）get more people to attend the conference. 我建议我们邀请更多的人来参加会议。

3 各种否定词及双重否定

该部分内容在本书"改错部分"做了详尽的阐述，考生可参照改错第二章第二节第三部分"否定"。

【示例】 (07-06-66)

And they are made much worse by our willful blindness to risk as much as our __66__ to work together before everything goes to hell.	[A] reluctance [B] rejection [C] denial [D] decline

【解析】选 [A]。由 blindness 和 risk 可知，本空应填一个含有否定意义的词，四个选项都符合。但其后能跟 to do sth. 的只有 [A] reluctance，意为"不情愿，勉强"。其他三项都意为"拒绝"。

4 句型句式

常考的句型句式包括简单句、并列句、对称结构或省略、倒装、强调等。各类句型可参见"翻译部分"第二章第二部分。

【示例】 (07-06-72)

But it turns __72__ that in times of crisis...	[A] up [B] down [C] over [D] out

【解析】选 [D]。it turns out that...为固定句型，表示"结果是…"，故选 [D]。

五、专项练习

Exercise 1

When Queen Victoria opened the Great Exhibition on 1st May 1851, her country was the world's leading industrial power, producing more than half its iron, coal and cotton cloth. The Crystal Palace itself was a triumph of pre-fabricated 1 production in iron and glass. Its contents were 2 to celebrate material progress and peaceful international competition. They ranged from massive steam hammers and *locomotives*（机车）to the 3 artistry of the handicraft trades — not to mention a host of *ingenious*（精致的）gadgets and ornaments of domestic clutter. All the world displayed its wares, but the 4 were British.

This 5 was both novel and brief. It was only half century earlier 6 Britain had *wrested*（夺取）European economic and political 7 from France, at a time when Europe itself 8 far behind Asia in manufacturing output. By 1901, 9 , the world's industrial powerhouse was the USA, and Germany was challenging Britain 10 second place.

But no country, even then, was as 11 as Britain in manufacturing: in 1901 under ten per cent of its labor 12 worked in agriculture and over 75 per cent of its wheat was imported, 13 from the USA and Russia. Food and industrial 14 materials, 15 from

1. [A] scale　　　　[B] mass
   [C] range　　　　[D] quantity
2. [A] intended　　　[B] tended
   [C] aimed　　　　[D] focused
3. [A] elegant　　　 [B] exquisite
   [C] special　　　 [D] distinctive
4. [A] minority　　　[B] popularity
   [C] prosperity　　[D] majority
5. [A] dominance　　 [B] prominence
   [C] existence　　 [D] evidence
6. [A] when　　　　 [B] which
   [C] that　　　　 [D] since
7. [A] power　　　　[B] authority
   [C] priority　　　[D] leadership
8. [A] kept　　　　 [B] lagged
   [C] remained　　 [D] upheld
9. [A] therefore　　 [B] however
   [C] then　　　　 [D] so
10. [A] for　　　　 [B] with
    [C] to　　　　　[D] on
11. [A] special　　　[B] specific
    [C] specialized　[D] professional
12. [A] vigor　　　 [B] force
    [C] strength　　 [D] might
13. [A] mostly　　　[B] roughly
    [C] rarely　　　 [D] essentially
14. [A] original　　 [B] crude
    [C] coarse　　　[D] raw
15. [A] resourced　 [B] sourced
    [C] originated　 [D] dated
16. [A] increasingly [B] decreasingly
    [C] constantly　 [D] frequently
17. [A] Or　　　　 [B] Nor
    [C] Only　　　 [D] Either

around the globe, were paid for by exports of manufactures and, __16__, services such as shipping, insurance and banking and income from overseas investment. __17__ was any other country so __18__: already in 1851 half the population inhabited a town or city; by 1901 three-quarters did so. Yet even in 1851 only a minority of workers was employed in "modern" industry (engineering, chemicals and factory-based textiles). They were __19__ concentrated into a few regions in the English north and Midlands, South Wales and the central belt of Scotland — where industrialization was __20__ by 1800.

18. [A] rural   [B] urbanized
    [C] modern   [D] suburbanized
19. [A] predominantly   [B] heavily
    [C] largely   [D] particularly
20. [A] evident   [B] distinguished
    [C] intricate   [D] projecting

Exercise 2

The first humans did not know how to talk, nor did they have fire or tools. When they dug for roots to eat, moved things or · 1 anything apart, they used their hands and teeth, Most of their time __2__ spent in a never-ending search for food, warmth, and safety. __3__ the help of tools, these early men could only rely on their __4__, still-undeveloped brains and their strong bodies to survive.

It was a million years ago. Man was new in the world. He was __5__ by powerful animals. The weather was often a __6__ enemy. Unarmed and unclothed, early man seemed to have a poor chance to survive.

__7__ he fought the greatest fight for living in the world has known. __8__ lasted hundreds of years. But man

1. [A] swept   [B] wore
   [C] tore   [D] swore
2. [A] had been   [B] was
   [C] had   [D] were
3. [A] In spite of   [B] Without
   [C] Apart from   [D] Lack of
4. [A] quick   [B] wise
   [C] fast   [D] slow
5. [A] feared   [B] fed
   [C] surrounded   [D] interfered
6. [A] a bitter   [B] a cold
   [C] an armed   [D] a terrified
7. [A] Yet   [B] Since
   [C] When   [D] As
8. [A] All   [B] He
   [C] That   [D] It
9. [A] persisted   [B] maintained
   [C] improved   [D] insisted
10. [A] nearly   [B] scarcely

_9_. He conquered his environment. Man has _10_ been defeated by mouths, the superior muscles and swiftness of his attackers, or the hardships of nature. His brain gives him _11_ strength than all of these. Within man's brain there is a remarkable power to feel, to _12_, to plan, and to invent.

He has the ability to look at a rough object and then picture in his mind _13_ he will make of it. A rock, for example, will become a hammer; a branch, a _14_; an animal bone, a knife. _15_ animal except man has this imagination and high intelligence.

Some animals can _16_ up objects found in nature and use them as tools. Yet, these animals never make new _17_ nor do they try to improve the natural _18_ that they find. Among all the animals, only man invents tools to make his work _19_. Man can also think about things that are not material at all, such as courage, truth, or humor. Man _20_ can learn from the present and the past, and then use his information to explore the future.

[C] never	[D] ever
11. [A] less	[B] fewer
[C] greater	[D] much
12. [A] cry	[B] response
[C] escape	[D] reason
13. [A] where	[B] what
[C] that	[D] which
14. [A] stone	[B] leaf
[C] handle	[D] cloth
15. [A] No any	[B] Not every
[C] None of	[D] No other
16. [A] pick	[B] make
[C] lift	[D] put
17. [A] objects	[B] courage
[C] tools	[D] picture
18. [A] uses	[B] structures
[C] manners	[D] shapes
19. [A] easily	[B] easier
[C] cease	[D] ease
20. [A] alone	[B] just
[C] merely	[D] himself

答案与解析

Exercise 1

1. 选 [B]。短语搭配题。mass production 是一个常见的修饰搭配，意为"大规模生产"。

2. 选 [A]。短语搭配题。四个选项均含有"打算，趋向"的意思，因此要从它们的用法上来作出判断。从词法的角度来看，tend 作此意解时是不及物动词，不用于被动语态，故 [B] 项可先排除。[C] aimed 的用法是 be aimed at，[D] focused 的用法是 be focused on。所以最后只能用 [A] intended，be intended to do sth. 意为

"计划，意欲做某事"，具有一定的目的性。

3. 选 [B]。词汇辨析题。这里讲的是英国水晶宫内陈设的展品，有大而重的蒸汽锤和蒸汽机，还有…的手工制品。接着在下文中提到：那些精致的小配件和小装饰品都不用提了。由此可见这些手工制品的工艺也是相当的精致，[B]"精致的"符合题意。[A] elegant 意为"优雅的，端庄的"，常用来修饰人而非物；此处突出的是这些手工制品的精致，并没有提到它们有何特别之处，所以 [C]"特殊的，特别的"和 [D]"与众不同的，有特色的"用在此处不合适。

4. 选 [D]。逻辑推理题。整篇文章讲的都是英国工业的发展，根据一切细节皆为主题服务的原则，这里应该说的是水晶宫内的大部分展品都是来自英国的，所以选 [D]"多数"。[A]"少数"；[B]"普及，流行，声望"；[C]"繁荣，旺盛"都不符合题意。

5. 选 [A]。逻辑推理题。上文说到水晶宫内的大部分展品都是英国的，选项中能和大部分形成语义共现的只有 [A]"优势，统治地位"。[B]"突出，显著"；[C]"存在，实在"；[D]"根据，迹象"都脱离了语境。

6. 选 [C]。语法结构题。句子为强调句型 It is/was…that…，因此选 [C]。

7. 选 [D]。逻辑推理题。根据上下文，此句意为"仅仅半个世纪前英国才从法国的手里夺走了全欧洲经济政治的领导地位"。同时，在第一段的开头提到过英国在维多利亚时期在全世界的工业领域处于领导地位（leading industrial power），根据同根词复现的线索，判断出 [D]"领导地位"为正确答案。[A]"权力，能力"；[B]"权威，威信"；[C]"优先，优先权"都不符合题意。

8. 选 [B]。短语搭配题。[B] lag behind 是固定搭配，意为"落后"。[A]"保持，保存"；[C]"保留，剩余"；[D]"支持，赞成"都不能和 behind 搭配。

9. 选 [B]。逻辑推理题。此空前面说英国在工业领域处于领导地位，后面说 20 世纪初，美国处于龙头地位，德国也虎视眈眈。可见前后两句是转折关系，所以选 [B] however。

10. 选 [A]。短语搭配题。challenge A for B 意为"为了 B 而挑战 A"，故选 [A]。原句意为"德国也开始挑战英国想占老二的位子了"。

11. 选 [C]。词汇辨析题。根据下文，这里要说的应当是"没有国家比英国在制造领域更专业化了"，[C] specialized 意为"专门的，专门化的"，为答案。[A]"特别的，特殊的"和 [B]"具体的，明确的"语义不符；[D]"专业的"，通常用来指人，故也可排除。

12. 选 [B]。短语搭配题。选项中的四个单词都有"力量"的意思，但是说到劳动力，一般使用的搭配是 labor force，所以选 [B]。

13. 选 [A]。逻辑推理题。根据上下文，此处句意为"英国超过 75% 的小麦都是进口的，大部分来自美国和俄国"，故选 [A]。[B]"概略地，粗糙地"；

[C] "很少地，含有地"；[D] "本质上" 都不符合题意。

14. 选 [D]。词汇辨析题。四个选项均含有 "原始的，原来的" 之意，但表示 "原材料" 要用 raw material，故选 [D] "未被加工的"。[A] "最初的，独创的"，如：original works "原作"；[B] "未经提炼的，粗鲁的"，如：crude oil "原油"，crude manner "粗俗的行为"；[C] "粗糙的，粗俗的"，如：coarse sand "粗糙的沙子"。

15. 选 [B]。词汇辨析题。由上下文可知，这里说的是原材料来自世界各地，所以选择意为 "来自…" 的 source，注意该单词在这里用作动词。[A] 意为 "向…提供资源"，不和介词 from 连用，故可排除；[C] 意为 "起源，来自"，能和介词 from 搭配使用，但它不能表示某种原材料的来源；[D] dated from 指 "起始于某个日期"，用在此处也不恰当。

16. 选 [A]。逻辑推理题。空格前面说英国大部分的原材料是进口的，后面说很多服务也进口。可见两者之间是递进关系，所以选择 [A] increasingly。[B] "渐渐减少地，渐减地"；[C] "不变地，经常地"；[D] "常常，频繁地" 都不符合文中的逻辑关系。

17. 选 [B]。逻辑推理题。根据句中的 any，可知此处应填表否定意义的词，[B] nor 符合。本句意为 "再也没有第二个国家像英国这么…"，对应该段开头部分的 But no country…was as specialized as…，这两个层次是并列关系。

18. 选 [B]。逻辑推理题。能和空格后的 half the population inhabited a town or city 形成共现的只有 [B] urbanized "城市化的，都市化的"。[A] "乡村的，田园的"；[C] "现代化的，近代的"；[D] "市郊化的" 都与文意相去甚远。

19. 选 [C]。词汇辨析题。[A] "卓越地，突出地"；[B] "很重地，沉重地"；[C] "主要地，大量地"；[D] "独特地，显著地"。从语义上看，[C] 项用于修饰 concentrated 最合适。

20. 选 [A]。词汇辨析题。原句意为 "这些地方工业化的痕迹在 1800 年已经很明显了"，因此 [A] "明显的，显然的" 符合题意。[B] "著名的，卓著的"；[C] "复杂的，错综的"；[D] "突出的，伸出的" 都不符合语义要求。

Exercise 2

1. 选 [C]。词汇辨析题。tear sth. apart 意为 "将某物撕开"，tear 的过去式为 tore，即 [C] 选项。[A] swept 是 sweep 的过去式，意为 "扫，打扫"；[B] wore 是 wear 的过去式，意为 "穿，戴"；[D] swore 是 swear 的过去式，意为 "宣誓，发誓"，这三项均不能和介词 apart 搭配，且语义均不符，故可排除。

2. 选 [B]。语法结构题。句子的主语并非 spent 的逻辑主语，且全篇的时态均为过去时，故 [B] was 为答案。

3. 选 [B]。逻辑推理题。本句是从反面来强调工具的重要性，因此选 [B] Without，说明在没有工具的情况下，人们只能…。[A] In spite of "不管" 和

[C] Apart from "除…之外" 都与原文逻辑不符；[D] Lack of "缺乏，没有" 虽然语义符合，但它是动词短语，用在此处不能使句子结构正确。

4. 选 [D]。逻辑推理题。所填词和 still-undeveloped 一起修饰 brains，因此需能和 still-undeveloped 构成语义场共现关系，查看选项，符合的只有 [D] slow "迟钝的，缓慢的"。[A] quick "迅速的，敏捷的"；[B] wise "英明的，明智的"；[C] fast "忠实的，快速的" 均与原文逻辑不符。

5. 选 [C]。词汇辨析题。在一百万年前，人们来到这个世界时是暴于野外的，因此只能说是被野兽围困，因此选 [C] surrounded，be surrounded by…意为 "被…包围"。[A] fear "惧怕，害怕"，我们不能说 "人被野兽惧怕"；更不可能是 [B] fed，be fed by "被喂养"；[D] interfered "干涉，干扰" 同样语义不符。

6. 选 [A]。逻辑推理题。本句采用了拟人手法，把天气比作敌人。暴于荒郊野外，毫无遮挡，如遇恶劣的天气人们一定会觉得十分难受，故 [A] bitter "难以忍受的，使人痛苦的" 符合题意。[B] cold "寒冷的，使人战栗的" 过于片面，因为天气还可能炎热得让人无法忍受；[C] armed "有扶手的，武装的" 其前应用 an；[D] "恐惧的，受惊吓的" 语义不符。

7. 选 [A]。逻辑推理题。上段末句提到 seemed to have a poor chance to survive，本句提及 fought the greatest fight for living in，由此可见前后内容为转折关系，故选 [A] Yet。

8. 选 [D]。语法结构题。此处是用 It 来指代上文中的 greatest fight，故选 [D]。

9. 选 [A]。词汇辨析题。此句想要表达的意思是：人类坚持一种行为即为生存而进行的博斗。[A]、[B]、[D] 三项均能表达 "坚持" 之意。[A] persisted 强调 "坚持，持续（自己所做的事）"，符合题意。[B] maintained 强调 "保持某种存在的状态" 以及 [D] insisted 侧重的是 "口头上、言语上坚持认定的一种观点"，它们均不强调行为动作。[C] improved "改进，改良" 语义不符。

10. 选 [C]。逻辑推理题。根据前文内容可以推断出，人类从没被打败过，故 [C] never 为答案。[A] nearly "几乎，密切地" 和 [D] ever "曾经，永远" 均与原文逻辑相悖；[B] scarcely 虽表示否定，但相对于 never 来说语气偏弱，意思是 "几乎不"。

11. 选 [C]。逻辑推理题。all of these 指的是上句中所列的各种困难：mouths, the superior muscles and swiftness of his attackers, or the hardships of nature。根据文章内容可知，人类战胜了自然，因此力量（strength）应该高于所有这一切，故选 [C] greater。

12. 选 [D]。逻辑推理题。观察句中一系列的动词，从 to feel 到 to plan 到 to invent，其过程是由感知到发明的一个过程，所以中间所缺环节应与思维、推理有关。[D] reason 作动词时意为 "推理、思考"，符合题意。[A] cry "叫，喊"；[B] response "回答，响应"；[C] escape "逃脱，避开" 均脱离了语境。

13. 选 [B]。语法结构题。从结构上看，所填词既能引导名词性从句，作 picture 的宾语，又在从句中充当 make 的宾语，选项中符合该用法的为 [B] what，它在此处作独立关系代词，相当于 the tool that…，在语法上起到承上启下的作用。其他选项均无此用法。

14. 选 [C]。逻辑推理题。分析句子结构可知，这里是一个省略句。由此可见，branch 与所填词的关系应等同于 rock（岩石）与 hammer（锤子）以及 animal bone（动物骨头）与 knife（刀）的关系，即所填词为 branch 能充当的某种工具。因此 [C] handle "手柄，把手" 为正确答案。

15. 选 [D]。短语搭配题。此处想表达的意为为：除了人类，没有其他的动物能有这种想象力和高智商。所以 No other…except "除了…没有其他的…，只有…" 符合题意，即 [D] 项为答案。没有 No any + n. 这种用法，故 [A] 可排除；[B] Not every "不是每一个" 语义不符；[C] None of + n. "一个也不…" 和空格后的 except man 矛盾。

16. 选 [A]。短语搭配题。四个选项均能和 up 搭配，因此要从它们的语义上来判断。[A] pick up "捡起，获得" 和句中的 found in nature 能够形成语义场共现，故为答案。[B] make up "弥补，虚构，化妆"；[C] lift up "举起，吊起"；[D] put up "举起，抬起" 语义均不符。

17. 选 [C]。逻辑推理题。前文提到，某些动物能在自然界中获得某种物体，并将它们作为工具来使用。本句句首就用了转折词 yet 将话锋一转，旨在说明这些动物不可能制造出新的工具，故 [C] tools 为答案。

18. 选 [D]。词汇辨析题。此处想要表达的意思是：动物不可能改变它们所获得的物体的自然形态。[B] structures 和 [D] shapes 都能表示 "形状，结构" 之意，但两者相比，前者侧重抽象，后者侧重具体。从上下文看，动物不可能认识抽象的结构，故选 [D] shapes。

19. 选 [B]。短语搭配题。动词 make 的用法为 make + n. + adj.，其中的形容词作宾语补足语，故选 [B] easier。其它各项均为副词或动词，故都不选。

20. 选 [A]。逻辑推理题。本句为全文总结句，意为：只有人类才有这种能力：吸取现在和过去的经验来创造未来。[A] alone "只有，唯有" 置于名词或代词后，强调独特性，符合题意。

技巧熟悉

第三章

完形填空旨在考查学生的综合语言能力，这就要求考生做题时必须通篇考虑，把握大意，然后运用自己所学的知识进行解答。根据第一章中所提到的题型特征，现总结出一些解题步骤和技巧，为考生冲刺高分助一臂之力。

一、4 大黄金法则

1 聚焦首句，了解主旨

完形填空的文章一般没有标题，因此我们只能格外注意一般不留空白的首句。全文信息始于首句，这些句子往往会揭示文章的背景知识或主题思想。因此要切记：细读首句，为后面的阅读搭桥铺路。

2 速读全文，把握大意

速读全文要一气呵成，尽管有空格、生词，仍要快速读完全文。很多考生认为阅读一篇满是空格的文章是徒劳无功的，与其这样浪费时间，倒不如看一句，填一空。其实这就陷入了一个误区。完形填空的设题有这样一条原则：去掉 20 个空格后不会影响考生对文章大意的了解。所以在答题之前通读全文时，要尽可能地把握文章的题材、大意和结构。总而言之，切忌在不了解文章大意的情况下做题。

3 定位线索，灵活解题

完形填空中的 20 个空格也是文章的一部分，也就是说每一处未知信息都处于整篇文章所包含的庞大的已知信息之中。解答每道题的关键就是要找到与这个空格所相关的信息，即定位解题线索，通过对这些关系的分析总结来推断答案。

还需注意的是，一旦开始做题，不要在某道难题上停留太长的时间。要学会根据照应关系快速做出反应。遇到难题，暂且跳过去，说不定会"柳暗花明又一村"，遇到对这道题有用的线索，豁然开朗呢。

4 通读复核，弥补疏漏

通读复核就是把空缺之处全部完成后，还要通读检查一遍，从语篇整体上去核对答案是否符合文章主题、作者态度、写作意图及文体特征；有无逻辑错误和语义含混或矛盾；有无语法错误、搭配错误等。复核过程中如果发现问题，应该重新考虑。凡不敢确定之处，必有待推敲的疑点，应依据文章的中心意思从语篇、语法、单词或短语的意思和用法等角度仔细权衡，并加以改正，以便弥补疏漏。对于个别难度较大的题目，可以坚持第一感觉作出的选择。下图中的标示是对答题步骤的简要说明。

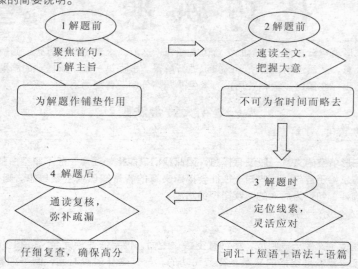

二、解题技巧

鉴于完形填空考题中的四个选项的词性一般都是一致的。本部分内容以词性为切入点，分类总结解题技巧。

1 动词

（1）看动词和主语在语法上、意义上、主谓搭配上的合适性。有时还要看主语是人还是事物，主语能不能发出这个动作。

【示例】 （四级 00-1-85）

The objectively correct answer the professor accepts and the student's personal understanding of the world can ___85___ side by side, each unaffected by the other.	[A] exist [B] occur [C] survive [D] maintain

【解析】选 [A]。exist 和主语 personal understanding of the world 搭配合理，意为"某种现象的存在"。主语不能发出 [C] survive 和 [D] maintain 这两个动作；[B] occur 指某件事情偶然发生，不符合题意。

（2）看动词和宾语的搭配是否合适。

【示例】 (01-01-75)

| Many States and local communities __75__ this Federal aid. | [A] expanded　　　[B] facilitated
[C] supplemented　[D] compensated |

【解析】选［C］。州政府和地方政府的帮助，相对于联邦政府来说也只能是［C］supplemented"增补，补充"。［A］"扩张，使膨胀"，［B］"促进，使便利"和［D］"偿还，补偿"的宾语都不能是 aid。

（3）看动词的属性——是及物动词还是不及物动词。

【示例】 (07-06-75)

| So what has happened in the year that __75__ the disaster on the Gulf Coast? | [A] ensued　　[B] traced
[C] followed　[D] occurred |

【解析】选［C］。该句后面的内容表明本段主要阐述 the disaster on the Gulf Coast 之后所发生的事情，因此本空应填入表示"后续"意义的词，从而答案锁定在［A］和［C］之间，但［A］ensued 表示"跟着发生"时为不及物动词，后面不能跟宾语，故排除。［C］项完全符合题意，故为答案。［B］"跟踪，回溯"语义不符；［D］"发生，出现"为不及物动词，也可排除。

2 名词

（1）选择名词时，要看其与前后各个成分的搭配是否合适。

【示例】 (07-06-81)

| The __81__ with neighboring com-munities are ongoing and difficult. | [A] conventions　　[B] notifications
[C] communications　[D] negotiations |

【解析】选［D］。词汇辨析题。选项中能和介词 with 搭配的有［C］、［D］两项，但 communications"通讯设施，交通工具"不能用 are ongoing and difficult 来修饰，故排除［C］选［D］，negotiation 意为"商议，谈判"。［A］"惯例，习俗"，后面通常跟介词 on，表内容。［B］"通知，布告"后常跟介词 of，表内容。

（2）选择名词还可根据语境中的同现或复现关系以及其他语义限定关系。

【示例】 (01-01-71)

| The __71__ of the Second World War was quickly followed by an increase in the number of day nurs-eries in almost all countries, | [A] outset　　[B] outbreak
[C] breakthrough
[D] breakdown |

【解析】选［B］。四个选项中能用来描述战争的自然是"爆发"，也就是［B］outbreak。选［A］"开始，开端"的同学误解了原文，是二战的爆发而不是其开端引发了各国托儿所数量的增加；［C］"突围，突破"不能和 of the Second World War 形成语义场共现；［D］breakdown 多用来指"（机器等）损坏，故障"或"（健康、精神、体力）等的衰竭、衰弱"。

3 形容词

（1）当形容词作表语时，即句子出现系表结构时，主要看主语和表语搭配的合适性。有时还要看主语是人还是物，不是所有的形容词都能修饰人或物。

【示例】　　　　　　　　　　　　　　　　　　　　　　（四级00-01-89）

...students are not ___89___ to replace them with the correct one.	［A］obliged　　　［B］likely ［C］probable　　［D］partial
【解析】选［B］。所选形容词要作表语，likely 常用于 be likely to do sth，表示"有可能做某事"。［C］probable 意思虽然与句意相符，但用法不符合句子结构，它表示"可能"时多用于 It is probable that ...句型；［A］obliged 用于被动结构 be obliged to do sth 时意思是"不得不，被迫"；［D］partial"偏爱的"语义不符。	

（2）当形容词直接修饰名词或名词性词组时，要看它们是否合适和褒贬意义的一致性。

【示例】　　　　　　　　　　　　　　　　　　　　　　（07-12-77）

...he rushes to give as lectures to Berlin's Prussian Academy of Sciences on four ___77___ Thursdays.	［A］successive　［B］progressive ［C］extensive　　［D］repetitive
【解析】选［A］。根据上下文可知，此处说的是"连续四个星期四"，故答案为［A］successive"连续的"。［B］progressive"前进的，进步的"；［C］extensive"广大的，广泛的"；［D］repetitive"重复的，反复性的"均与文意不符。	

（3）当形容词修饰的名词已经被其他成分修饰，那么要选择的形容词应根据其他的修饰成分来判断。

【示例】 (03-01-87)

All these things reflect their belief that allowing employees to contribute and to feel ＿87＿ and important is a win-win situation — good for the employees and the organization.	［A］faithful　［B］powerful ［C］skillful ［D］thoughtful

【解析】选［B］。由 and 一词可知，所填词与 important 并列，一起用来形容雇员在公司的感觉，而且是对自身的感觉，适合的为［B］"强大的"。［A］"忠实的，可靠的"；［C］"灵巧的，熟练的"；［D］"深思的，体贴的"这三个选项都不适合于用来修饰人的自我感觉。

（4）当形容词出现在总句中的时候，要通过分析总句后面的分句来判断。即要兼顾上下文的逻辑关系。

【示例】 (07-06-77)

That's not ＿77＿, we can now say with confidence.	［A］enough　　［B］certain ［C］conclusive　［D］final

【解析】选［A］。该句是对该段前面所讲的内容的一个小总结，作者很确定地认为前面列举的这些情况还不足够，因此［A］正确。［B］"确定的，必然的"；［C］"确实的，最后的"；［D］"最后的，最终的"都与上下文语义不符。

4 副词

（1）对实义副词的选择：找到副词所修饰的成分，看其是否适合于被该副词修饰，并且要看副词在意义和程度上的合适性，是否符合上下文的语义和逻辑关系。

【示例】 (01-01-67)

Although the number of nurseries in the U. S. also rose ＿67＿, this rise was accomplished without government aid of any kind.	［A］unanimously　［B］sharply ［C］predominantly　［D］militantly

【解析】选［B］。所填是用于修饰 rise 的副词，选项中能和 rise 形成共现关系的只有［B］sharply "急剧地"，说明增长的程度。［A］"全体一致地，无异议地"；［C］"占主导地位地，突出地"；［D］"好战地，激进地"都不能用来说明 rise 的程度。

（2）对疑问副词、关系副词或连接副词的选择：要看上下文之间的逻辑关系。

【示例】 (01-01-65)

In some European countries nurseries were establishes __65__ in *munitions*（军火）plants, under direct government sponsorship.	［A］hardly ［B］entirely ［C］only ［D］even
【解析】选［D］。前文提到托儿所在各地相继建立起来，本句提出在军工厂里也建起了托儿所，可见本句与前文是一种递进关系，所以选择表示递进关系的副词 even。［A］"刚刚，几乎不"；［B］"完全地，全然地"；［C］"仅仅，只不过"都不能表达语义上的递进关系。	

5 介词 ⩗

（1）看介词和其前面的动词或系动词搭配是否合适。

【示例】 (01-01-69)

Federal, State, and local governments gradually began to exercise a measure of control __69__ the day nurseries, chiefly by	［A］over ［B］in ［C］at ［D］about
【解析】选［A］。control over …为固定短语，意为"对…进行控制"，故选［A］。其他三项都不能和 control 搭配。	

（2）看介词和其前后的名词搭配是否合适。

【示例】 (05-06-77)

By pressing the appropriate buttons __77__ Cyclops's keyboard…	［A］on ［B］at ［C］in ［D］from
【解析】选［A］。所填词为介词，表示 buttons 和 keyboard 的位置关系，根据常识可知，按键在键盘上。因此［A］on 为正确答案。	

6 代词 ⩗

（1）选择哪类代词要根据句子结构或语义关系来分析。

【示例】 (07-12-67)

…his new concept of gravity, __67__ that would define how objects move into space and how space is curved by objects.	［A］ones ［B］those ［C］all ［D］none

【解析】选［A］。分析句子结构可知，所填词应能指代上文中的 the right equa-
tions，ones 有此用法，故答案为［A］。［B］those 为强干扰项，多表示特指，
而 ones 表泛指，这里没有限定范围，显然用 those 不合适。

（2）在各类名词性从句中，要对句子成分进行分析之后，选择出合适的关系代词。

【示例】 　　　　　　　　　　　　　　　　　　　　　　　（四级 03-01-75）

...but a bird has a single alarm cry, __75__ means "danger!"	［A］this ［B］that ［C］which ［D］it

【解析】选［C］。从句子结构上看，此处需要一个关系代词引导非限制性定语
从句，对前面的 a single alarm cry 进行补充说明。［A］this 和［D］it 不能引导
从句；［B］that 只能引导限制性定语从句。

（3）不定代词、人称代词以及指示代词要根据其前后的内容来进行选择。

【示例】 　　　　　　　　　　　　　　　　　　　　　　　　　（01-01-62）

Nurseries were established in various areas during the latter half of the 19th century; most of __62__ were charitable.	［A］those ［B］them ［C］whose ［D］whom

【解析】选［B］。该句和前句是以分号隔开的，所以应是个独立完整的句子，
而非上句的从句，但句子缺少主语。又根据上文可以得出，所填词是指代 nurseries 的，故［B］them 正确。其他三项都不能单独作主语。

7 连词

要根据上下文的逻辑关系来选择表示相应关系的连词。

【示例】 　　　　　　　　　　　　　　　　　　　　　　　　　（01-01-66）

__66__ the number of nurseries in the U. S. also rose sharply, this rise was accomplished without government aid of any kind.	［A］Because ［B］As ［C］Since ［D］Although

【解析】选［D］。本句的两个分句分别意为：美国托儿所的数量也在增加；但
这增加没有受到政府任何形式的帮助。由此看来，分句之间是转折关系，所以
［D］Although 正确。其他三项都是表因果关系的连词。

三、专项练习

Exercise 1

An important new industry, oil refining, grew after the Civil War. __1__ oil, or *petroleum*（石油）, a dark, thick ooze from the earth had been known for hundreds of years, __2__ little use had ever been made __3__ it. In the 1850s, Samuel M. Kier, a manufacturer in western Pennsylvania, began __4__ the oil and refining it into *kerosene*（煤油）. Refining, __5__ smelting, is a __6__ of removing impurities from a raw material.

Kerosene was used to light lamps. It was a cheap __7__ for *whale oil*（鲸油）, which was becoming __8__ to get. Soon there was a large __9__ for kerosene. People began to search for new __10__ of petroleum.

The first oil well was drilled by E. L. Drake, a retired railroad conductor. In 1859 he began drilling in Titusville, Pennsylvania. The __11__ venture of drilling seemed so __12__ and foolish that onlookers called it "Drake's Folly". But __13__ he had drilled down about 70 feet（21 meters）, Drake __14__ oil. His well began to __15__ 20 barrels of crude oil a day.

News of Drake's __16__ brought oil prospectors to the __17__. By the early 1860's these wildcatters were drilling for "black gold" all over western Pennsylvania. The boom __18__ the California gold rush of 1848 in its excitement and Wild West atmosphere. And it brought far more

1. [A] Raw   [B] Original
    [C] Crude   [D] Coarse
2. [A] but   [B] because
    [C] and   [D] if
3. [A] at   [B] in
    [C] from   [D] of
4. [A] gathering   [B] collecting
    [C] augmenting   [D] saturating
5. [A] like   [B] as
    [C] or   [D] with
6. [A] procedure   [B] process
    [C] proceeding   [D] progress
7. [A] replace   [B] supplement
    [C] surplus   [D] substitute
8. [A] higher   [B] cheaper
    [C] cleaner   [D] harder
9. [A] need   [B] demand
    [C] request   [D] necessity
10. [A] supplies   [B] offers
    [C] origins   [D] traces
11. [A] all   [B] complete
    [C] whole   [D] total
12. [A] fantastic   [B] gorgeous
    [C] empirical   [D] impractical
13. [A] when   [B] while
    [C] before   [D] as
14. [A] touched   [B] obtained
    [C] struck   [D] reached
15. [A] produce   [B] yield
    [C] assemble   [D] provide
16. [A] failure   [B] advance
    [C] venture   [D] success
17. [A] scene   [B] scenery

wealth to the prospectors than any gold rush.

    Petroleum could be refined into many products. For some years kerosene continued to be the __19__ one. It was almost sold in every grocery store and door-to-door. In the 1880's and 1890's refiners learned how to make other petroleum products such as waxes and lubricating oils. Petroleum was not __20__ used to make gasoline or heating oil.

[C] sight   [D] view

18. [A] competed
    [B] rivaled
    [C] encountered
    [D] acquainted

19. [A] principle
    [B] fundamental
    [C] natural
    [D] principal

20. [A] meanwhile   [B] now
    [C] then   [D] latter

Exercise 2

    The homeless makes up a growing percentage of American's population. __1__ homelessness has reaches such proportions that government can't possibly __2__. To help homeless people __3__ independence, the federal government must support job training programs, __4__ the minimum wage, and fund more low-cost housing. __5__, everyone agrees on the numbers of American who are homeless. Estimates cover __6__ from 600,000 to 3 million. __7__ the figure may vary, analysts do agree on another matter: that the number of the homeless is __8__, one of the federal governments' studies __9__ that the number of the homeless will reach nearly 19 million by the end of this decade.

    Finding ways to __10__ this growing homeless population has become increasingly difficult. __11__ when homeless individuals manage to find a lodging that will give them three __12__ a day and a place to sleep at night, a good number still spend the bulk

1. [A] Indeed   [B] Likewise
   [C] Therefore   [D] Furthermore

2. [A] stand   [B] cope
   [C] approve   [D] retain

3. [A] in   [B] for
   [C] with   [D] toward

4. [A] raise   [B] add
   [C] take   [D] keep

5. [A] Generally   [B] Almost
   [C] Hardly   [D] Not

6. [A] anywhere   [B] nowhere
   [C] wherever   [D] where

7. [A] Now that   [B] Although
   [C] Provided   [D] Except that

8. [A] inflating   [B] expanding
   [C] increasing   [D] extending

9. [A] predicts   [B] displays
   [C] proves   [D] discovers

10. [A] assist   [B] track
    [C] sustain   [D] dismiss

11. [A] Hence   [B] But
    [C] Even   [D] Only

12. [A] meals   [B] shelters

of each day　13　the street. Part of the problem is that many homeless adults are addicted to alcohol or drugs. And a significant number of the homeless have serious mental disorders. Many others,　14　not addicted or mentally ill, simply lack the everyday　15　skills need to turn their lives　16　. Boston Globe reporter Chris Reidy notes that the situation will improve only when there are　17　programs that address the many needs of the homeless.　18　Edward Blotkowsk, director of community service at Bentley College in Massachusetts,　19　it, "There has to be　20　of programs. What's need is a package deal."

　[C] foods　　　　　　[D] house

13. [A] searching　　　[B] walking
　　[C] crowding　　　[D] eating

14. [A] when　　　　　[B] once
　　[C] while　　　　　[D] whereas

15. [A] life　　　　　　[B] existence
　　[C] survival　　　　[D] maintenance

16. [A] around　　　　[B] over
　　[C] on　　　　　　[D] up

17. [A] complex　　　[B] comprehensive
　　[C] complementary[D] compensating

18. [A] So　　　　　　[B] Since
　　[C] As　　　　　　[D] However

19. [A] puts　　　　　[B] interprets
　　[C] assumes　　　[D] makes

20. [A] supervision　[B] manipulation
　　[C] regulation　[D] coordination

答案与解析

Exercise 1

1. 选 [C]。短语搭配题。"原油" 的英语表达为 crude oil，所以选 [C]，crude 意为 "未经提炼的"。[A] raw "未被加工的" 常和 material 连用，表示 "原材料"；[B] "最初的，独创的"，如：original works 意为 "原作"；[D] "粗糙的，粗俗的"，如：coarse sand 意为 "粗糙的沙子"。

2. 选 [A]。逻辑推理题。空格前的 had been known for hundreds of years 和空格后的 little use had ever been made 之间存在的是转折关系，所以选 [A] but。[B] 表原因；[C] 表并列；[D] 表条件。此句大意为：在美国内战之后，石油为人们所知已经很长时间了，但是却没有怎么加以利用"。

3. 选 [D]。短语搭配题。make use of 为固定搭配，意为 "利用"，所以 [D] 为答案。其他选项都不能和 make use 连用构成短语。

4. 选 [B]。词汇辨析题。[A] "聚集，搜集"；[B] "采集，集中"；[C] "增加，增大"；[D] "使饱和，浸透"。我们通常都说 "采集石油"，根据各选项的词义，不难选出正确答案 [B]。原句意为：19 世纪 50 年代，宾夕法尼亚州西部的一个制造商 Samuel 就开始采集原油，并把它加工成煤油了。

5. 选 [A]。语法结构题。原句意为：正如熔炼一样，石油精炼是一个从原材料中去粗取精的…。根据句意首先可将 [C]、[D] 两项排除。当表示 "正如…" 之意时，as 通常作关系代词或关系副词、引导定语从句，它在从句中指代全句所谈到的内容，引出非限制性定语从句，在从句中一般作主语或宾语。例如：①Metals have many good properties, as has been stated before. ②As we said before, you have done a good job. 。而此时 like 是作介词，例如：She, like thousands of others, is fascinated by this work. 。故此处应选 [A] like。

6. 选 [B]。词汇辨析题。我们都知道，石油精炼实际上是一个去粗取精的过程，因此所填词要能表达 "过程" 之意。观察选项不难发现，前三项都能符合这点，因此得仔细比较它们的用法。[A] procedure 意为 "程序"，也就是 "步骤"，例如：a long therapeutic procedure "长期的治疗过程"；[B] process 意为 "过程"，即制作或处理某一产品的一系列操作，例如：a manufacturing process "生产过程"；[C] proceeding 意为 "进程"，常用复数形式，指 "活动"，例如：watched the proceedings from a ringside seat "在看台前排座位上观看活动"。很显然，[B] 项符合题意。[D] progress 意为 "进步"，语义不符，也可排除。

7. 选 [D]。词汇辨析题。能用于 ~ for sth. 结构中的有 [B] "补充"、[D] "替代品，代用品"。此处想要表达的意思是：煤油是鲸油的廉价替代品，故选 [D]。[A] replace 也可表示 "代替"，但它只作动词，固定用法是 replace sth. with sth., 意为 "用某物代替某物"；[C] "剩余，过剩" 语义不符。

8. 选 [D]。逻辑推理题。既然都为之寻求廉价替代品，那么鲸油应该是越来越难获得了，故选 [D]。

9. 选 [B]。词汇辨析题。煤油是鲸油的廉价替代品，当鲸油难以获得时，对煤油的 "需求" 自然越来越高。[D] "必要性，必需品" 语义不符，可先排除。其他三项均能表达 "需求" 之意，但 [A]、[C] 前面均不能用 a，所以只能选 [B]。

10. 选 [A]。逻辑推理题。能和 search for new 以及 petroleum 形成语义场共现的只有 [A] supplies "供给，供应"。[B] "出价，提议，意图"；[C] "起源，出身"；[D] "痕迹，踪迹"。原句意为 "人们开始找寻新的石油供给"。

11. 选 [C]。词汇辨析题。四个单词都有 "完整的" 之意。但这里强调的是冒险的整个过程，因此 [C] whole 符合。[A] all 后面要加定冠词，所以不对；[B] complete 强调 "完成" 的意思；[D] total 强调的是 "总数"。

12. 选 [D]。逻辑推理题。根据共现原则，所填词应和空格后的 foolish 和 "Drake's Folly" 一样，也表示否定、消极含义。符合的只有 [D] "不切实际的，昧于实际的"。[A] "奇异的"；[B] "华丽的，灿烂的"；[C] "完全根据经验的，实证的" 都表积极、肯定意义，故都不选。

13. 选 [A]。逻辑推理题。解答本题要建立在第 14 题的基础之上。分析句子结构可知，he had drilled…feet（21 meters）是 Drake 发现石油之时，所以首先排除 ［C］"在…之前"。其他三项都能表示"当…之时"，但是如果选 ［B］ 的话，主句应该用进行时，故不选；［D］ 用于引导时间状语从句时，不能用于句首。［A］ 项完全符合题意，故为答案。

14. 选 ［C］。词汇辨析题。本句是 Drake 在打钻，在当他钻到 70 英尺的时候，他应该是突然发现了石油，［C］"邂逅，发现"符合题意。［A］"接触，达到"；［B］"得到，获得"；［D］"达到"都不符合语境要求。

15. 选 ［B］。词汇辨析题。原因是从钻井中自然产出的，并不涉及加工、制造，所以［A］"生产制造"和［C］"装配，组合"可先排除；［D］provide 不用于 provide sth. 的结构中。［B］"产出"符合题意，故为答案。

16. 选 ［D］。逻辑推理题。上文提到 Drake 的油井已经开始产油，这是一种"成功"，故选 ［D］ success。［A］"失败，失败者"；［B］"前进，提升"；［C］"难题，问题"都脱离了语境。

17. 选 ［A］。词汇辨析题。原句意为"Drake 成功的消息将勘探者们带到了那里"，那里指的是 Drake 成功开采到石油的地方，［A］ 指有人活动的"场景"，为答案。［B］"风景，景色"；［C］"情景，奇观"；［D］"景色，风景"都不符合题意。

18. 选 ［B］。词汇辨析题。这里是在拿 19 世纪 60 年代早期的寻油热和 1848 年加利福尼亚州的淘金热相比，［B］"相匹敌，对抗"符合题意。［A］"竞争，比赛"为不及物动词，后面要跟介词 with；［C］"遭遇，遇到"和［D］"使熟知，通知"语义不符。

19. 选 ［D］。词汇辨析题。根据后文中的 It was almost sold in every grocery store and door-to-door 可知，煤油在各种能源中依然居主要地位，［D］"主要的，首要的"正确。［A］"原则，原理"词性和语义皆不符；［B］"基础的，基本的"和［C］"自然的"都不符合语义。原句意为"石油能够被精炼成多种产品，但是数年来煤油一直是主要产品"。

20. 选 ［C］。逻辑推理题。前面说到了石油经加工后成了煤油，这里又提到了汽油等，可见是递进关系，故填 ［C］ then。［A］"同时，期间"和［B］"现在，目前"都不符合句际间的逻辑关系；［D］ 只能作形容词，不能用来修饰动词。

Exercise 2

1. 选 ［D］。逻辑推理题。前句提到"无家可归者占美国人口的比例越来越大"，本句说"无家可归者人数多得让当地政府再也无法承受"。从语意上分析，两句话之间是递进关系，［D］ furthermore "此外，而且"表递进，故为答案。［A］ indeed "确实"，用于加强语气；［B］ likewise "同样"表并列；［C］ therefore "因此，所以"表原因。

2. 选 [A]。词汇辨析题。本句的意思是：无家可归者人数多得让当地政府再也无法承受了。因此 [A] stand "经受" 符合题意。[B] cope "应付，处理"；[C] approve "赞成，满意"；[D] retain "保持，保留" 语义均不符。

3. 选 [C]。短语搭配题。help sb. with sth. 为习惯用法，意思是 "帮助某人做某事"，故 [C] 为正确答案。

4. 选 [A]。词汇辨析题。本句的意思是：为了帮助无家可归者自立，政府必须支持就业培训项目，提高最低工资以及…。由此可见，所填词应能表示 "提高" 之意，因此 [A] raise "提高" 为答案。[B] add "增加，添加"；[C] take "拿，获得"；[D] keep "保持，保存" 均不符合题意。

5. 选 [D]。逻辑推理题。下文提到，对无家可归者人数的估计从 60 万到 300 万不等，由此可知并非每个人对估计的人数都持一致的意见，故 [D] Not 为正确答案。本句的意思是：无家可归的美国人到底有多少，并不是每个人的看法都一样。

6. 选 [A]。词汇辨析题。这里想表达的意思是 "从 60 万到 300 万不等"。[A] anywhere "（表示数量不确定）大概在…之间" 符合题意。[B] nowhere "无处"；[C] wherever "无论哪里"；[D] somewhere "（在）某处，大约" 均不能使原文语义通顺。

7. 选 [B]。逻辑推理题。两分句分别意为：数字可能变化；分析家们在另一个问题上却意见一致。由此可知，空格处需填入一个表示让步的连词，故 [B] Although 正确。[A] Now that "既然"；[C] Provided "在…的条件下，如果"；[D] Except that "除了…之外" 均不符合原文逻辑。

8. 选 [C]。逻辑推理题。文章首句就提到无家可归者的人数在增加，因此所填词因能表示 "增长" 之意。查看选项可知 [C] increasing "增长，增加" 符合题意。[A] inflating "充气，膨胀"；[B] expanding "张开，发展"；[D] extending "扩充，延伸" 均不能表示数量上的增加，故都不选。

9. 选 [A]。逻辑推理题。根据句中的 will reach nearly 19 million by the end of this decade 可知这里是指对未来情况的一种预测，故 [A] predicts "预言，预报" 正确。[B] displays "陈列，显示"；[C] proves "证明，证实"；[D] discovers "发现，发觉" 均不符合题意。本句的意思是：无家可归者人数正在上升，联邦政府进行的一项研究预计，到这 10 年结束时无家可归者的人数将接近 1900 万。

10. 选 [A]。逻辑推理题。本段内容是有关帮助无家可归者的，[A] assist "援助，帮助" 符合语境要求，故为答案。[B] track "追踪，留下足迹"；[C] sustain "支撑，维持"；[D] dismiss "解散，开除" 语义均不符。

11. 选 [D]。语法结构题。only when…that… 为特殊句型，表示 "只有当…，才…"，因此 [D] Only "仅仅，只不过" 为答案。其他选项均无此用法。

12. 选 [A]。逻辑推理题。一天需要三次的只有 [A] meals "餐，膳食"，故为答案。[B] shelters "掩蔽处,庇护所";[C] foods "食物,食品";[D] house "房屋,住宅"。

13. 选 [C]。逻辑推理题。能和句中的 a good number 以及 the street 形成语义共现的是 [C] crowding "聚集,群集"。[A] searching "搜索,搜寻";[B] walking "走路,散步";[D] eating "吃饭,食用" 均脱离了语境。

14. 选 [D]。逻辑推理题。前文提到 have serious mental disorders,本句则提到 Many others… not addicted or mentally ill,很明显两句在语义上存在转折关系,故选 [D] whereas "尽管,然而"。[A] when "在…的时候";[B] once "一旦";[C] while "当…的时候,虽然" 均不符合原文逻辑。

15. 选 [C]。词汇辨析题。此处想要表达的意思为 "生存技能",故选择 [C] survival "生存",例如:the survival of the fittest "适者生存"。[A] life "生命,生活";[B] existence "存在,实在";[D] maintenance "维护,保持" 均不符合原文的语义要求。

16. 选 [B]。短语搭配题。此处讲的是这些缺乏生存技能的人需要改变他们的生活状况,故选 [B] over,短语 turn one's life over 的意思是 "将某人的生活改变过来"。[A] turn around "回转,转向";[C] turn on "开启,开始";[D] turn up "出现,突然发生" 均不符合原文语义要求。

17. 选 [B]。逻辑推理题。所填词是用于修饰 programs 的,根据 address the many needs of the homeless 可知该计划是具有积极意义的,故所填词也应能表示积极、肯定的意义,因此 [B] comprehensive "全面的,广泛的" 符合题意。[A] complex "复杂的,综合的";[C] complementary "补充的,补足的";[D] compensating "补偿的,补助的" 均不能表示积极肯定意义,故都不选。

18. 选 [C]。逻辑推理题。此处想要表达的意思为 "正如 Edward Blotkowsk 所说",故应用 [C] as。[A] so "因而,所以";[B] since "因为,既然";[D] however "然而,可是" 均无此用法。

19. 选 [A]。词汇辨析题。后文中的 "There has to be __20__ of programs. What's need is a package deal." 只是一句简单的陈述,故 [A] puts "叙述,表述" 为答案。[B] interprets "口译,解释";[C] assumes "假定,设想";[D] makes "制造,认为" 均不符合题意。

20. 选 [D]。词汇辨析题。本句的意思是:必须要有配套的规划,我们所需要的是一系列计划。四个选项中,只有 [D] coordination "配合,协同" 符合题意。[A] supervision "监督,管理";[B] manipulation "处理,操作";[C] regulation "规则,规章" 语义均不符。

真题演练

2007 年12 月

In 1915 Einstein made a trip to Gottingen to give some lectures at the invitation of the mathematical physicist David Hilbert. He was particularly eager — too eager, it would turn   1   — to explain all the intricacies of relativity to him. The visit was a triumph, and he said to a friend excitedly, "I was able to   2   Hilbert of the general theory of relativity."

  3   all of Einstein's personal *turmoil* (焦躁) at the time, a new scientific anxiety was about to   4 . He was struggling to find the right equations that would   5   his new concept of gravity,   6   that would define how objects move   7   space and how space is curved by objects. By the end of the summer, he   8   the mathematical approach he had been   9   for almost three years was flawed. And now there was a   10   pressure. Einstein discovered to his   11   that Hilbert had taken what he had learned from Einstein's lectures and was racing to come up   12   the correct equations first.

It was an enormously complex task. Although Einstein was the better physicist, Hilbert was the better mathematician. So in October 1915 Einstein   13   himself into a month-long frantic endeavor in   14   he returned to an earlier mathematical strategy

1. [A] up [B] over
   [C] out [D] off
2. [A] convince [B] counsel
   [C] persuade [D] preach
3. [A] Above [B] Around
   [C] Amid [D] Along
4. [A] emit [B] emerge
   [C] submit [D] submerge
5. [A] imitate [B] ignite
   [C] describe [D] ascribe
6. [A] ones [B] those
   [C] all [D] none
7. [A] into [B] beyond
   [C] among [D] through
8. [A] resolved [B] realized
   [C] accepted [D] assured
9. [A] pursuing [B] protecting
   [C] contesting [D] contending
10. [A] complex
    [B] compatible
    [C] comparative
    [D] competitive
11. [A] humor [B] horror
    [C] excitement [D] extinction
12. [A] to [B] for
    [C] with [D] against
13. [A] threw [B] thrust
    [C] huddled [D] hopped
14. [A] how [B] that
    [C] what [D] which

and wrestled with equations, proofs, corrections and updates that he __15__ to give as lectures to Berlin's Prussian Academy of Sciences on four __16__ Thursdays.

His first lecture was delivered on Nov. 4, 1915, and it explained his new approach, __17__ he admitted he did not yet have the precise mathematical formulation of it. Einstein also took time off from __18__ revising his equations to engage in an *awkward fandango*（方丹戈双人舞）with his competitor Hilbert. Worried __19__ being scooped（抢先）, he sent Hilbert a copy of his Nov. 4 lecture. "I am __20__ to know whether you will take kindly to this new solution." Einstein noted with a touch of defensiveness.

15. [A] dashed　　　[B] darted
　　[C] rushed　　　[D] reeled
16. [A] successive　[B] progressive
　　[C] extensive　 [D] repetitive
17. [A] so　　　　　[B] since
　　[C] though　　　[D] because
18. [A] casually　　[B] coarsely
　　[C] violently　 [D] furiously
19. [A] after　　　　[B] about
　　[C] on　　　　　[D] in
20. [A] curious　　　[B] conscious
　　[C] ambitious　 [D] ambiguous

2007 年 6 月

Historically, humans get serious about avoiding disasters only after one has just struck them. __1__ that logic, 2006 should have been a breakthrough year for rational behavior. With the memory of 9/11 still __2__ in their minds, Americans watched hurricane Katrina, the most expensive disaster in U. S. history, on __3__ TV. Anyone who didn't know it before should have learned that bad things can happen. And they are made __4__ worse by our willful blindness to risk as much as our __5__ to work together before everything goes to hell.

Granted, some amount of *delusion*（错觉）is probably part of the __6__ condition. In A. D. 63, Pompeii was seriously damaged

1. [A] To　　　　　[B] By
　[C] On　　　　　[D] For
2. [A] fresh　　　　[B] obvious
　[C] apparent　　[D] evident
3. [A] visual　　　[B] vivid
　[C] live　　　　[D] lively
4. [A] little　　　[B] less
　[C] more　　　　[D] much
5. [A] reluctance　[B] rejection
　[C] denial　　　[D] decline
6. [A] natural　　　[B] world
　[C] social　　　[D] human
7. [A] revising　　[B] refining
　[C] rebuilding　[D] retrieving
8. [A] review　　　[B] reminder
　[C] concept　　 [D] prospect
9. [A] preparing　 [B] protesting

by an earthquake, and the locals immediately went to work __7__, in the same spot — until they were buried altogether by a volcano eruption 16 years later. But a __8__ of the past year in disaster history suggests that modern Americans are particularly bad at __9__ themselves from guaranteed threats. We know more than we __10__ did about the dangers we face. But it turns __11__ that in times of crisis, our greatest enemy is __12__ the storm, the quake or the __13__ itself. More often, it is ourselves.

So what has happened in the year that __14__ the disaster on the Gulf Coast? In New Orleans, the Army Corps of Engineers has worked day and night to rebuild the flood-walls. They have got the walls to __15__ they were before Katrina, more or less. That's not __16__, we can now say with confidence. But it may be all __17__ can be expected from one year of *hustle* (忙碌).

Meanwhile, New Orleans officials have crafted a plan to use buses and trains to __18__ the sick and the disabled. The city estimates that 15,000 people will need a __19__ out. However, state officials have not yet determined where these people will be taken. The __20__ with neighboring communities are ongoing and difficult.

[C] protecting [D] prevailing
10. [A] never [B] ever
[C] then [D] before
11. [A] up [B] down
[C] over [D] out
12. [A] merely
[B] rarely
[C] incidentally
[D] accidentally
13. [A] surge [B] spur
[C] surf [D] splash
14. [A] ensued [B] traced
[C] followed [D] occurred
15. [A] which [B] where
[C] what [D] when
16. [A] enough [B] certain
[C] conclusive [D] final
17. [A] but [B] as
[C] that [D] those
18. [A] exile [B] evacuate
[C] dismiss [D] displace
19. [A] ride [B] trail
[C] path [D] track
20. [A] conventions
[B] notifications
[C] communications
[D] negotiations

2005 年 6 月

Although there are many skillful Braille readers, thousands of other blind people find it difficult to learn that system. They are thereby shut __1__ from the world

1. [A] up [B] down
[C] in [D] off
2. [A] dwell [B] rely
[C] press [D] urge

of books and newspapers, having to __2__ on friends to read aloud to them.

A young scientist named Raymond Kurzweil has now designed a computer which is a major __3__ in providing aid to the __4__. His machine, Cyclops, has a camera that __5__ any page, interprets the print into sounds, and then delivers them orally in a robot-like __6__ through a speaker. By pressing the appropriate buttons __7__ Cyclops's keyboard, a blind person can "read" any __8__ document in the English language.

This remarkable invention represents a tremendous __9__ forward in the education of the handicapped. At present, Cyclops costs $ 50,000. __10__, Mr. Kurzweil and his associates are preparing a smaller __11__ improved version that will sell __12__ less than half that price. Within a few years, Kurzweil __13__ the price range will be low enough for every school and library to __14__ one. Michael Hingson, Director of the National Federation for the Blind, hopes that __15__ will be able to buy home __16__ of Cyclops for the price of a good television set.

Mr. Hingson's organization purchased five machines and is now testing them in Maryland, Colorado, Iowa, California, and New York. Blind people have been __17__ in those tests, making lots of __18__ suggestions to the engineers who helped to produce Cyclops.

"This is the first time that blind people have ever done individual studies

3. [A] execution [B] distinction
   [C] breakthrough [D] process
4. [A] paralyzed [B] uneducated
   [C] invisible [D] sightless
5. [A] scans [B] enlarges
   [C] sketches [D] projects
6. [A] behavior [B] expression
   [C] movement [D] voice
7. [A] on [B] at
   [C] in [D] from
8. [A] visual [B] printed
   [C] virtual [D] spoken
9. [A] stride [B] trail
   [C] haul [D] footprint
10. [A] Likewise [B] Moreover
    [C] However [D] Though
11. [A] but [B] than
    [C] or [D] then
12. [A] on [B] for
    [C] through [D] to
13. [A] estimates [B] considers
    [C] counts [D] determines
14. [A] settle [B] own
    [C] invest [D] retain
15. [A] schools [B] children
    [C] families [D] companies
16. [A] models [B] modes
    [C] cases [D] collections
17. [A] producing [B] researching
    [C] ascertaining [D] assisting
18. [A] true [B] valuable
    [C] authentic [D] pleasant
19. [A] after [B] when
    [C] before [D] as
20. [A] occasion [B] moment
    [C] sense [D] event

19 a product was put on the market, " Hingson said. " Most manufacturers believed that having the blind help the blind was like telling disabled people to teach other disabled people. In that   20 , the manufacturers have been the blind ones. "

2003 年 1 月

When women do become managers, do they ring a different style and different skills to the job? Are they better, or worse, managers than men? Are women more highly motivated and   1   than male managers?

Some research   2   the idea that women bring different attitudes and skills to management jobs, such as greater   3 , an emphasis on affiliation and attachment, and a   4   to bring emotional factors to bear   5   making workplace decisions. These differences are   6   to carry advantages for companies,   7   they expand the range of techniques that can be used to   8   the company manage its workforce   9 .

A study commissioned by the International Women's Forum   10   a management style used by some women managers (and also by some men) that   11   from the command-and-control style   12   used by male managers. Using this " interactive leadership " approach, " women   13   participation, share

1. [A] confronted　　[B] commanded
　 [C] confined　　　[D] committed
2. [A] supports　　　[B] argues
　 [C] opposes　　　 [D] despises
3. [A] combination　 [B] cooperativeness
　 [C] coherence　　 [D] correlation
4. [A] willingness　　[B] loyalty
　 [C] sensitivity　　 [D] virtue
5. [A] by　　　　　 [B] in
　 [C] at　　　　　　[D] with
6. [A] disclosed　　　[B] watched
　 [C] revised　　　　[D] seen
7. [A] therefore　　　[B] whereas
　 [C] because　　　 [D] nonetheless
8. [A] help　　　　　[B] enable
　 [C] support　　　 [D] direct
9. [A] evidently　　　[B] precisely
　 [C] aggressively　 [D] effectively
10. [A] developed　　 [B] invented
　 [C] discovered　　 [D] located
11. [A] derives　　　 [B] differs
　 [C] descends　　　[D] detaches
12. [A] inherently　　 [B] traditionally
　 [C] conditionally　 [D] occasionally
13. [A] encourage　　 [B] dismiss
　 [C] disapprove　　 [D] engage
14. [A] enhance　　　[B] enlarge
　 [C] ignore　　　　[D] degrade

power and information, __14__ other people's self-worth, and get others excited about their work. All these __15__ reflect their belief that allowing __16__ to contribute and to feel __17__ and important is a win-win __18__ — good for the employees and the organization. " The study's director __19__ that "interactive leadership may emerge __20__ the management style of choice for many organizations. "

15. [A] themes   [B] subjects
     [C] researches   [D] things
16. [A] managers   [B] women
     [C] employees   [D] males
17. [A] faithful   [B] powerful
     [C] skillful   [D] thoughtful
18. [A] situation   [B] status
     [C] circumstance   [D] position
19. [A] predicted   [B] proclaimed
     [C] defied   [D] diagnosed
20. [A] into   [B] from
     [C] as   [D] for

2001 年 1 月

In the United States, the first day nursery was opened in 1854. Nurseries were established in various areas during the __1__ half of the 19th century; most of __2__ were charitable. Both in Europe and in the U. S. , the day-nursery movement received great __3__ during the First World War, when __4__ of manpower caused the industrial employment of *unprecedented* (前所未有) numbers of women. In some European countries nurseries were establishes __5__ in *munitions* (军火) plants, under direct government sponsorship. __6__ the number of nurseries in the U. S. also rose __7__, this rise was accomplished without government aid of any kind. During the years following the First World War, __8__, Federal, State, and local governments gradually began to exercise a measure of control __9__ the day nurseries, chiefly by __10__ them and by inspecting and regulating the conditions

1. [A] latter   [B] late
     [C] other   [D] first
2. [A] those   [B] them
     [C] whose   [D] whom
3. [A] impetus   [B] input
     [C] imitation   [D] initiative
4. [A] sources   [B] abundance
     [C] shortage   [D] reduction
5. [A] hardly   [B] entirely
     [C] only   [D] even
6. [A] Because   [B] As
     [C] Since   [D] Although
7. [A] unanimously
     [B] sharply
     [C] predominantly
     [D] militantly
8. [A] therefore   [B] consequently
     [C] however   [D] moreover
9. [A] over   [B] in
     [C] at   [D] about
10. [A] formulating   [B] labeling
     [C] patenting   [D] licensing

within the nurseries.

The __11__ of the Second World War was quickly followed by an increase in the number of day nurseries in almost all countries, as women were __12__ called upon to replace men in the factories. On this __13__ the U. S. government immediately came to the support of the nursery schools. __14__ $ 6,000,000 in July, 1942, for a nursery-school program for the children of working mothers. Many States and local communities __15__ this Federal aid. By the end of the war, in August, 1945, more than 100,000 children were being cared __16__ in day-care centers receiving Federal __17__. Soon afterward, the Federal government __18__ cut down its expenditures for this purpose and later __19__ them, causing a sharp drop in the number of nursery schools in operation. However, the expectation that most employed mothers would leave their __20__ at the end of the war was only partly fulfilled.

11. [A] outset   [B] outbreak
     [C] breakthrough
     [D] breakdown

12. [A] again   [B] thus
     [C] repeatedly   [D] yet

13. [A] circumstance
     [B] occasion
     [C] case   [D] situation

14. [A] regulating   [B] summoning
     [C] allocating   [D] transferring

15. [A] expanded   [B] facilitated
     [C] supplemented
     [D] compensated

16. [A] by   [B] after
     [C] of   [D] for

17. [A] pensions   [B] subsidies
     [C] revenues   [D] budgets

18. [A] prevalently   [B] furiously
     [C] statistically   [D] drastically

19. [A] abolished   [B] diminished
     [C] jeopardized   [D] precluded

20. [A] nurseries   [B] homes
     [C] jobs   [D] children

答案与解析

2007 年 12 月

1. 选〔C〕。短语搭配题。分析句子结构可知，it would turn __1__ 为插入语，句子真正的语序为 it would turn __1__ (that) he was particularly eager — too eager — to explain all the intricacies of relativity to him. 。选项中能接宾语从句的只有〔C〕，turn out "证明是，结果是"。turn up "发现，出现"；turn over "打翻，翻阅"；turn off "关掉，避开" 均不符合题意。

2. 选〔A〕。短语搭配题。convince sb. of sth. 为固定搭配，意为 "使某人确信某事"，故答案为〔A〕。〔B〕counsel "建议，劝告" 和〔C〕persuade "说服，劝说" 均用于 ~ sb. to do sth. 的结构中；〔D〕preach "鼓吹" 后面也不能接 of，preach up "赞扬；吹捧"。

3. 选［C］。逻辑推理题。根据句中的 a new scientific anxiety 可知，爱因斯坦的焦虑不止一种，而这种新的焦虑只是其中的一种，因此所填词应表示"在…之中"之意，故选［C］Amid "在…之中"。其他选项均无此意。

4. 选［B］。逻辑推理题。所填词应是不及物动词，故应首先排除［A］emit "发出，发射" 和［C］submit "提交，递交" 这两个及物动词。剩下的选项中能和空格前的 new 形成语义场共现的是［B］emerge "显现，浮现"，故为答案。［D］submerge "没入水中，消失" 与原文逻辑不符。

5. 选［C］。词汇辨析题。所填词应能和宾语 new concept of gravity 构成合理的动宾搭配，选项中只有［C］describe "描写，记述" 符合题意。［A］imitate "模仿，仿效"、［B］ignite "点火，点燃"；［D］ascribe "归因于，归咎于" 均不能接 new concept of gravity 作为宾语。

6. 选［A］。语法结构题。分析句子结构可知，所填词应能指代上文中的 the right equations，ones 有此用法，故答案为［A］。［B］those 为强干扰项，多用来指人，与文意不符。

7. 选［D］。词汇辨析题。物体当然是在宇宙中间运动的，所以选［D］through。［C］among 表示 "在众多的某物中间；在某类人/物中"，用在这里不合适。

8. 选［B］。词汇辨析题。所填词后面接的是含有定语从句的宾语从句，［D］assured 意为 "确信，担保"，其后不能接宾语从句，故可首先排除。根据上下文可知，此句大意为 "他意识到使用的数学方法有缺陷"，由此可推测所填词应有 "意识到" 之义，故答案为［B］realized。［A］resolved "决心，决定" 和［C］accepted "接受，承认" 语义不符。

9. 选［A］。词汇辨析题。所填词的宾语应是 the mathematical approach，能接此宾语的是［A］pursuing，pursue for 意为 "从事，追求"。［B］protecting "保护"；［C］contesting "争论，争辩"；［D］contending "斗争，竞争" 这三项均不能接此宾语。

10. 选［D］。词汇辨析题。根据上下文可知，此空所在句说的是爱因斯坦目前的压力，下句对此做了解释，他的压力来自于数学家希尔伯特，故答案为［D］，competitive 意为 "竞争的"。［A］complex "复杂的，综合的"；［B］compatible "谐调的，一致的"；［C］comparative "比较的，难当的" 均不符合题意。

11. 选［B］。短语搭配题。to one's horror 是习惯表达，意为 "令某人感到害怕的是"，故答案为［B］。其他选项均无此用法。

12. 选［C］。短语搭配题。四个选项均能与空格前的 come up 搭配，但根据句意 "数学家希尔伯特正奋力想最先得出正确的等式" 可知答案为［C］，come up with 意为 "得出，拿出"。come up to 意为 "达到，符合"；come up for 需和 discussion 意为 "提出讨论"；come up against 意为 "遇到，碰到" 均不符合题目的语义要求。

13. 选 [A]。短语搭配题。throw oneself into sth. 是固定搭配，意为"投身于…"，故 [A] 为答案。[B] thrust "刺，戳"；[C] huddled "拥挤，卷缩"；[D] "单脚跳，跳跃" 均无此用法。

14. 选 [D]。语法结构题。分析句子结构可知，in __14__ 引导定语从句修饰 a month-long frantic endeavor，因此答案为 [D] which。其他选项均不能和介词 in 共同引导定语从句。

15. 选 [C]。短语搭配题。rush to do sth. 是习惯表达，意为"迅速做某事"，故答案为 [C]。[A] dashed "猛击，冲撞"；[B] darted "投掷，飞奔"；[D] reeled "旋转，摇晃" 均无此用法。

16. 选 [A]。词汇辨析题。根据上下文可知，此处说的是"连续四个星期四"，故答案为 [A] successive "连续的"。[B] progressive "前进的，进步的"；[C] extensive "广大的，广泛的"；[D] repetitive "重复的，反复性的" 均与文意不符。

17. 选 [C]。逻辑推理题。空格前面的分句意为"他在第一次演讲时解释了他的新方法"，空格后的句子意为"他承认自己还不能用精确的数学公式来描述这种新方法"，由此可知两句之间存在着转折关系，故选 [C] though。[A] so 引导表法结果的并列句；[B] since 和 [D] because 都引导原因状语从句。

18. 选 [D]。逻辑推理题。所填词是修饰爱因斯坦如何修正他的等式的，对于一位伟大的科学家来说，做研究时的态度必然是严谨的，因此所填词应表积极、肯定意义。查看选项，只有 [D] furiously "大刀阔斧地，飞速地"符合题意。[A] casually "随便地，随意地"；[B] coarsely "粗糙地，粗俗地"；[C] violently "猛烈地，激烈地" 均表否定意义，故都可排除。

19. 选 [B]。短语搭配题。worried about 是固定搭配，意为"担心…"，故选 [B]。其他选项均不能与 worried 搭配使用。

20. 选 [A]。短语搭配题。be curious to do sth. 是习惯表达，意为"对…感到好奇"，故答案为 [A]。[B] conscious 通常和介词 of 搭配，意为"意识到…"；[C] ambitious "有雄心的" 也可用于 be ~ to do sth. 的结构中，但其语义不符，故排除；[D] ambiguous 意为"模糊的"，一般直接作定语。

2007 年 6 月

1. 选 [B]。短语搭配题。by that logic 是习惯表达，意为"按照那个逻辑"。其他三项无此用法。

2. 选 [A]。词汇辨析题。the memory of 9.11 still fresh 表示"对9.11事件依然记忆犹新"，故 [A] 正确。[B] "明显的，显而易见的"；[C] "显然的，外观上的"；[D] "明白的，明显的" 通常不用来修饰 memory。

3. 选 [C]。短语搭配题。live TV 为习惯表达，意为"现场直播"，故选 [C]。[A] "看得见的，视觉的"；[B] "生动的，鲜明的"；[D] "活泼的，栩栩如生的" 都不能用于修饰 TV。

4. 选 [D]。语法结构题。所填词要能修饰比较级 worse，符合的有 [A]、[D] 两项。根据后文中的 willful blindness to risk 可知，worse 的程度比较严重，所以应该用 [D] much。

5. 选 [A]。词汇辨析题。由 blindness 和 risk 可知，本空应填一个含有否定意义的词，四个选项都符合。但其后能跟 to do sth. 的只有 [A] reluctance，意为 "不情愿，勉强"。其他三项都意为 "拒绝"。

6. 选 [D]。逻辑推理题。delusion "错觉" 是一种人类行为，也就是说只有 [D] human 才能和 delusion 形成语义共现。句子大意为：不得不承认的是，一定程度的错觉也是人类状况的一部分。

7. 选 [C]。词汇辨析题。根据句中的 in the same spot 可知，当地居民是在原来的地方重建 Pompeii，[C] "重建" 符合语义，为答案。[A] "修订"，通常指对书的修订；[B] "精炼" 与上下文语义不符；前面提到 Pompeii was seriously damaged by an earthquake（庞培被地震严重破坏），因此不可能再重新获得它，故 [D] "重新获得" 也不正确。

8. 选 [A]。逻辑推理题。四个选项都能和介词 of 连用，但能和空格后的 the past year in disaster history 形成语义场共现的只有 [A] "回顾"。[B] "暗示，提醒"；[C] "观念，概念"；[D] "前途，前景" 均脱离了上下文语境。

9. 选 [C]。短语搭配题。能够用于 ~ sb. from sth. 结构中的只有 [C]，protect …from 表示 "保护…免受伤害"。[A] 常用于 be prepared for "准备着" 或者 prepare for "为…作准备" 等结构中；[B] 通常构成短语 protest against，表示 "抗议，反对，对…表示不满"；[D] 常常用于短语 prevail over/against 中，意为 "压倒，战胜"。

10. 选 [B]。词汇辨析题。空格后的 did 表明本空应填一个表过去的副词，[B]、[C] 两项符合。但是只有 [B] ever "曾经" 才能用于 more than sb. ~ ever 的结构中，符合语义。[D] before 作副词表 "从前，以前" 时，通常用于完成时或和 never 连用，且一般不单独使用，所以不选。[C] 不和 more than 连用，故可排除。句中并无否定含义，故 [A] 项也不选。

11. 选 [D]。短语搭配题。it turns out that…为固定句型，表示 "结果是…"，故选 [D]。

12. 选 [B]。逻辑推理题。由后面一句话 More often, it is ourselves. 可知，我们真正的敌人并不是这里提到的这些自然灾难，故本空应填入一个表否定意义的词，只有 [B] "很少地，罕有地" 符合题意。[A] "仅仅，只，不过"；[C] "附带地，顺便提及"；[D] "偶然地，意外地" 都不含否定意义。

13. 选 [A]。逻辑推理题。所填词是由 or 将其和 storm，quake 连接的，因此它也应该是能表示自然灾害的词，surge 表示 "因海浪引起的灾难"，故 [A] 正确。[B] "刺激，鞭策"；[C] "海浪，浪花"；[D] "飞溅，斑点"。

14. 选 [C]。词汇辨析题。该句后面的内容表明本段主要阐述 the disaster on the Gulf Coast 之后所发生的事情,因此本空应填入表示"后续"意义的词,从而答案锁定在 [A] 和 [C] 之间,但 [A] ensue 表示"跟着发生"时为不及物动词,后面不能跟宾语,故排除。[C] 项完全符合题意,故为答案。[B]"跟踪,回溯"语义不符;[D]"发生,出现"为不及物动词,也可排除。

15. 选 [B]。语法结构题。空格后的 they were 是一个缺少引导词的定语从句,根据句意推断本空应填一个表地点的引导词,故 where 正确,选 [B]。

16. 选 [A]。逻辑推理题。该句是对该段前面所讲的内容的一个小总结,作者很确定地认为前面列举的这些情况还不足够,因此 [A] 正确。[B]"确定,必然";[C]"确实的,最后的";[D]"最后的,最终的"都与上下文语义不符。

17. 选 [C]。语法结构题。分析句子结构可知,空格处应填一定语从句引导词。当引导词前面是 all 时,该引导词必须为 that,故选 [C]。这里的 that 相当于 the thing that,其中的 that things 可以省略。

18. 选 [B]。逻辑推理题。选项中能与 the sick and the disabled 以及文章主题形成共现的只有 [B]"疏散,撤出"。[A]"放逐,流放";[C]"解散,开除";[D]"取代,转移"都脱离了语境。

19. 选 [A]。逻辑推理题。前文提到新奥尔良官员已经制定了一项草案,计划使用公车和火车疏散病人和残疾人。本句提到,据估计,有 15000 人需要…。显然所填词应该和 buses and trains 形成复现关系,[A] ride"交通工具"符合,它和 buses and trains 构成上下义复现。[B]"踪迹,痕迹";[C]"路线,通道";[D]"轨迹,足迹"都不符合题意。

20. 选 [D]。词汇辨析题。选项中能和介词 with 搭配的有 [C]、[D] 两项,但 communications"通讯设施,交通工具"不能用 are ongoing and difficult 来修饰,故排除 [C] 选 [D],negotiation 意为"商议,谈判"。[A]"惯例,习俗",后面通常跟介词 on,表内容。[B]"通知,布告"后常跟介词 of,表内容。

2005 年 6 月

1. 选 [D]。短语搭配题。空格前有表结果的 thereby 一词,由此我们可以知道本句与上句中提到的"有数以千计的盲人难以学会布莱叶盲文点字法(Braille)"应该构成因果关系。shut off 常与 from 连用,表示"与…隔离,隔绝",填入原文构成的句意为"与书籍和报刊隔绝",[D] 符合题意。shut up"住口";shut down"(使)关闭,(使)停工";shut in"把…关在里面,禁闭"都不符合题意。

2. 选 [B]。短语搭配题。四个选项都能和介词 on 构成合理搭配,那就需要对短语的意义进行辨析。既然他们不能自己阅读书籍和报刊，那么自然就会依赖于朋友，rely on "依赖" 符合语义要求选 ［B］，rely on sb. to do sth. 意为 "依赖某人做某事"。dwell on "老是想着；详述"；press on "加紧进行"；urge on "竭力主张，强烈要求" 都不能使上下文语义通顺。

3. 选 ［C］。词汇辨析题。上段提到了盲人存在阅读困难，而本句提到了一个科学家已经设计出了一种可以为他们提供帮助的计算机，由此可知 ［C］ "突破，成就" 正确。［A］ execution "执行，完成"；［B］ distinction "区别，差别"；［D］ process "过程，步骤" 均不符合文意。

4. 选 ［D］。逻辑推理题。根据文章首句提到 blind people 可以推测出这种计算机是为帮助盲人而设计的。根据语义复现关系可以得出 ［D］ sightless "盲的，无视力的" 为正确答案。provide 的用法为 provide sth. to sb.，因此本题考察的相关用法是定冠词 the + 形容词表示某类人。the paralyzed "残疾人" 过于笼统；the uneducated "未受过教育的，无知的" 不符合语义；［C］ 是个强干扰项，因为它意为 "看不见的"，但 the invisible 意为 "隐形人"，故将其排除。

5. 选 ［A］。词汇辨析题。that 引导的定语从句修饰 camera。所填词为动词，和 page 构成动宾搭配，表示用照相机能够做的事情，即它的功能。四个选项中和 camera 的功能最吻合的是 ［A］ scans "扫描，全景摄影"。［B］ "扩大，放大"；［C］ "绘草图，速写"；［D］ "设计，计划"。

6. 选 ［D］。逻辑推理题。该句讲的是 Cyclops 的工作原理：先扫描书页，然后把图像转化为声音（sounds），再把声音通过扬声器（speaker）口头（orally）传出来。在这个和声音有关的语境中，可以判断所填词为 ［D］ "说话声"。［A］ "行为，举止"；［B］ "表达，表情"；［C］ "移动，运动" 均不符合语境。

7. 选 ［A］。词汇辨析题。所填词为介词，表示 buttons 和 keyboard 的位置关系，根据常识可知，按键在键盘上。因此 ［A］ on 为正确答案。

8. 选 ［B］。逻辑推理题。通过按下 Cyclops 的按键，盲人就可以 "阅读" 了，结合上句中介绍的原理可知，_____ document 指的就是上段中的 book and newspaper。这样的 document 都是印刷的，因此选 ［B］ "印刷的"。［A］ "视觉的，形象的"；［C］ "实质上的，虚的"；［D］ "口语的，口头的" 均不符合题意。

9. 选 ［A］。词汇辨析题。forward 含有 "向前" 的意思，结合上段所说的 Cyclops 解决了盲人的阅读问题，那么这个杰出的发明应该象征着巨大的进步，即向前迈出了一大步，因此 ［A］ "大步，进步"。［B］ "踪迹，痕迹"；［C］ "拖，拉"；［D］ "足迹，脚印" 都不符合题意。

10. 选 ［C］。逻辑推理题。本句提到 Kurzweil 和他的同事们正在开发更加物美价廉的产品，和上句提到的 ＄50，000 形成转折关系，因此表转折关系的选项 ［C］ 为答案。［A］ "同样地，照样地" 表类比；［B］ "而且，此外" 表递进；［D］ "虽然，尽管" 表让步，它们都不符合上下文的逻辑关系。

11. 选 ［A］。逻辑推理题。空格前后的 smaller 和 improved 形成语义上的转折，即虽然产品小了，但是性能却得到了改良，因此［A］but 符合题意。［B］表比较；［C］表选择；［D］表顺接。

12. 选［B］。短语搭配题。所填词后面直接加 price。表示某物以多少钱出售通常可以表示为 sth. sell for/at…（相当于 sth. cost…），因此选项［B］为答案。

13. 选［A］。词汇辨析题。所填词为 Kurzweil 发出的动作。宾语从句的谓语 will be 以及时间状语 Within a few years 暗示了所填词应该有"预测"的含义，因此［A］"估计，评估"正确。［B］"认为，考虑"和［C］"计算，认为"有一定的干扰性，但它们都没有"预测"之意，因此不够准确。［D］"确定，决定"不符合逻辑。

14. 选［B］。词汇辨析题。low enough 与所填词之间是隐含的因果关系，正因为这种产品的价格足够低，每所学校和图书馆才买得起，因此选［B］"拥有"。［A］"解决，安排"；［D］"保持，保留"语义都不符。［C］是个强干扰项，但它意为"投资，买进"时，为非及物动词，后面要跟介词 in。

15. 选［C］。逻辑推理题。根据后文中的 home 可知这里应该填［C］family，形成语义共现。［A］"学校"；［B］"孩子"；［D］"公司"都脱离了语境。

16. 选［A］。词汇辨析题。Cyclops 修饰所填词，根据原文第二段可知，这是专门为盲人设计的 computer，因此［A］"型号，样式"正确，model 在这里指正在研发中的新机型。［B］"方式，模式"在词形上有一定的干扰；［C］"案例，案子"；［D］"搜藏，征收"语义不符。

17. 选［D］。逻辑推理题。根据空格后的介词 in 首先将［A］"生产，制造"和［C］"确定，探知"这两个及物动词排除。再根据后文中提到的盲人给工程师提出了建议（making suggestions），推断出在对那五台机器进行测试的过程中，盲人应该是起到协助作用的，因此［D］"援助，帮助"为答案。［B］"研究，调查"不符合题意。

18. 选［B］。逻辑推理题。Cyclops 是为盲人设计的，他们亲自参与对这些机器的监测，那么他们提出的建议应该是很有价值的，因此选［B］"有价值的"。［A］"真实的"；［C］"可信的"；［D］"令人愉快的"不符合题意。

19. 选［C］。逻辑推理题。原文第三、四两段都提到，这种新机型还在研发当中，也就是说它们还没上市，即在 was put on the market 之前。因此［C］before 符合逻辑。

20. 选［C］。逻辑推理题。原文最后一句说，制造商已经是盲人了，这显然不合逻辑。前文提到，绝大多数的制造商认为让盲人帮助盲人就如同让残疾人去教其他残疾人。第四段提到，制造商请盲人参与监测。那么从这个意义上来说，制造商就是盲人。In that sense 意为"从那种意义上说"符合原文逻辑。［A］项通常和介词 on 搭配；［B］项通常和介词 at 搭配；in that event意为"如果那种情况发生"，与原文逻辑不符，故可排除［D］。

1. 选 [D]。逻辑推理题。所填词和 motivated 是由并列连词 and 连接的，因此它的感情色彩应和 motivated 保持一致，即含积极肯定之义，选项中只有 [D] "尽责的" 符合。[A] "面临的" 和 [B] "命令的" 都是中性词；[C] "限制的" 为贬义词。

2. 选 [A]。逻辑推理题。后文中由 such as 引出的 greater...的例证表明，一些研究是肯定差异的存在的，因此 [A] "支持，拥护" 符合题意。[B] "争论，辩论"；[C] "反对，对立"；[D] "轻视，蔑视" 都与文意不符。

3. 选 [B]。逻辑推理题。由 such as 可知所填词应该表示一种 attitude 或者是 skill，只有 [B] "合作，协作"；[A] "结合，联合"；[C] "一致性，连贯性"；[D] "相互关系，相关性" 这三项都脱离了语境。

4. 选 [A]。短语搭配题。空格后是不定式短语，选项中只有 willingness 才能与动词不定式搭配，意思是 "情愿做某事"，因此选 [A]。[B] "忠诚，忠心"；[C] "敏感度，灵敏性"；[D] "美德，德行"。

5. 选 [B]。短语搭配题。bear 不和介词 by 与介词 at 连用，因此首先可以排除 [A]、[C] 两项。再者 [D] bear with "忍受" 不能使上下文语义通顺。bring sth. to bear in doing sth. 用在此处表示 "在工作中做决定时融入自己的感情因素"，语义连贯，因此 [B] 为正确答案。

6. 选 [D]。词汇辨析题。这种差别给公司带来的好处是人们所能看到的，所以答案为 [D]。[A] "揭露" 和 [C] "修订" 都脱离了语境；[B] watch 也能表示 "看"，但它强调专注地看，而此处表示的仅仅是随意的看，故不选。

7. 选 [C]。逻辑推理题。空格前和空格后的内容是一果一因的关系，所以选 [C]。[A] 也是表因果关系的连词，但它用于前因后果的句子中，所以不符题意；[B] "然而，反之" 和 [D] "虽然如此" 表转折，都不符合此处的逻辑关系。

8. 选 [A]。语法结构题。根据语法关系可知，此处的动词后面的不定式省略了 to，而四个选项中只有 help 可以这样用，所以答案为 [A]。

9. 选 [D]。逻辑推理题。前文提到妇女们 carry advantages for companies（给公司带来某种优势），因此所填词应该要能表积极意义，[A] "明显地" 是中性词和 [C] "侵略地" 贬义词可先排除；[B] "正好地" 和 [D] "有效地" 在情感色彩上都符合，但从语义角度上看，effectively 用来修饰 manage 更加合适。

10. 选 [C]。词汇辨析题。所填词为句子的谓语，句子的主语是 a study，宾语是一些女经理正在使用的一种管理方法，能和主语及宾语构成合理搭配的只有 [C] "发现"。[A] "发展"；[B] "发明"；[D] "定位" 都不能使语义通顺。

11. 选 [B]。短语搭配题。四个选项都能和介词 from 搭配，因此要从上下文语义衔接方面来考虑问题。文章第二段开始就指出女性管理者带来的不同，由下文中的"互动式"与"命令式"管理风格可知，此处是说这两种经营管理方式的不同，所以选［B］，differs from…，意为"与…不同"。derives from…意为"起源于…"；descends from…意为"从…传下来"；detaches from 意为"从…分离"，它们的语义都不相符。

12. 选［B］。逻辑推理题。女性管理者带来的是新的不同的管理方式，与此相对的，男性管理者所采用的自然就是传统的方式，因此［B］项正确。［A］"固有地"；［C］"有条件地"；［D］"偶尔"都不符合题意。

13. 选［A］。词汇辨析题。所填词要能与 participation 搭配，并且要能与后面的 share power and information 以及 get others excited about their work 并列，因此应填一个表示肯定意义的及物动词，只有［A］"鼓励"符合。［B］"解散"不能和 dismiss 搭配；［C］"不同意"表否定意义，故可排除；［D］"从事，参加"也不能和 participation 搭配。

14. 选［A］。词汇辨析题。分析句子可知，所填词应该和 encourage, share 在词性和色彩上保持一致，且能与 self-worth 构成合理的动宾搭配。四个选项中只有［A］"提高，增强"符合条件。［B］"扩大，放大"的宾语不能是 self-worth 这类抽象名词；［C］"不理睬，忽视"以及［D］"（使）降级，（使）堕落，（使）退化"的感情色彩都不符合题意。

15. 选［D］。逻辑推理题。根据语境，前文讲述了女性管理者在管理方法上的种种优点，所填词要能指代这些优点，所以正确答案为［D］things。［A］"主题"；［B］"科目"和［C］"研究"三个选项均不能概括前面所述的女性管理人员的优点。

16. 选［C］。逻辑推理题。女性管理者的管理方法起作用的对象当然只能是雇员，所以正确答案为［C］employees。其他三项都脱离了语境。

17. 选［B］。词汇辨析题。由 and 一词可知，所填词与 important 并列，一起用来形容雇员在公司的感觉，而且是对自身的感觉，适合的为［B］"强大的"。［A］"忠实的，可靠的"；［C］"灵巧的，熟练的"；［D］"深思的，体贴的"这三个选项都不适合于用来修饰人的自我感觉。

18. 选［A］。词汇辨析题。破折号后的解释 "good for the employees and the organization" 说明这是一种双赢的情况，故选［A］"情况，状况"，与 win-win 形成语义共现。［B］"身份，地位"和［D］"位置，职位"语义不符；［C］项是个强干扰项，但它多用于表示"环境，形势"，且常用复数，因此也可排除。

19. 选［A］。逻辑推理题。最后一句话的意思是：该研究的负责人说这种交互式的领导模式也许会成为许多组织的管理模式的选择。句中的 may 提示这只是一种推测，所以选［A］"预知，预言"。选［B］"宣布，声明"则是忽略了线索词 may 的暗示作用；［C］"不服从，公然反抗"和［D］"诊断"则与题意相去甚远。

20. 选 [C]。词汇辨析题。此处是在讲这种管理方式可能会成为…，介词 as 能表示"作为，当作"，所以 [C] 项正确。[A]、[D] 从搭配与语义上均可排除。选 [B] 的同学可能比较熟悉 emerge from 这一短语，理所当然地认为本题的考察点是短语搭配。但从语义上判断，"交互式管理模式产生于管理方式"显然说不通，所以 [B] 不正确。

2001 年 1 月

1. 选 [A]。词汇辨析题。由第一句话可知，第一家日间托儿所于 1854 年建立，而各地的托儿所在此后相继建起，the latter part of the 19th century 即指 19 世纪的后半个世纪，符合题意，故选 [A]。选 [B] 的同学是混淆了固定用法，19 世纪下半叶用 late 的表达法是"in the late 19th century"。此外，还有 the latter part of the 19th century，它是指"19 世纪晚些时期"。[C] the other half of the 19th century 指代不明确；选 [D] 是没能正确判断句中的时间概念。

2. 选 [B]。语法结构题。该句和前句是以分号隔开的，所以应是个独立完整的句子，而非上句的从句，但句子缺少主语。又根据上文可以得出，所填词是指代 nurseries 的，故 [B] them 正确。其他三项都不能单独作主语。

3. 选 [A]。词汇辨析题。句中提到一战使得妇女们都进了工厂，孩子们自然就没人照顾了，这也就给托儿所的出现带来了推动力，故 [A] 项正确。[B]"输入"；[C]"模仿，效仿"；[D]"主动，积极性"这三个选项与正确选项只是形近，但意思相去甚远，脱离了原文语境。

4. 选 [C]。词汇辨析题。根据上下文可知，战争使得劳动力短缺，从而导致进入工厂的妇女的数量呈现前所未有的状态。因此 [C]"缺乏，不足"正确。[A]"来源，水源"和 [B]"丰富，充裕"均与原文所要表达的意思相反；[D] 项是个强干扰项，但文中并没有提到人力增加或减少的问题。

5. 选 [D]。逻辑推理题。前文提到托儿所在各地相继建立起来，本句提出在军工厂里也建起了托儿所，可见本句与前文是一种递进关系，所以选择表示递进关系的副词 even。[A]"刚刚，几乎不"；[B]"完全地，全然地"；[C]"仅仅，只不过"都不能表达语义上的递进关系。

6. 选 [D]。逻辑推理题。本句的两个分句分别意为：美国托儿所的数量也在增加；但这增加没有得到政府任何形式的帮助。由此看来，分句之间是转折关系，所以 [D] Although 正确。其他三项都是表因果关系的连词。

7. 选 [B]。词汇辨析题。所填是用于修饰 rise 的副词，选项中能和 rise 形成共现关系的只有 [B] sharply"急剧地"，说明增长的程度。[A]"全体一致地，无异议地"；[C]"占主导地位地，突出地"；[D]"好战地，激进地"都不能用来说明 rise 的程度。

8. 选 [C]。逻辑推理题。本句中的 Federal, State, and local governments gradually

began to exercise a measure of control 和上句中的 without government aid of any kind 表明两句之间是转折关系，因此 [C] however 正确。[A] "因此，所以" 和 [B] "从而，因此" 均表示因果关系；[D] "而且，此外" 则表示递进关系。

9. 选 [A]。短语搭配题。control over …为固定短语，意为 "对…进行控制"，故选 [A]。其他三项都不能和 control 搭配。

10. 选 [D]。词汇辨析题。了解了各个选项的含义，本题就迎刃而解了。[A] "用公式表述，明确地表达"；[B] "标注，分类"；[C] "取得专利权"；[D] "批准，许可，发许可证"。符合政府对托儿所采取的控制措施的只有 [D]。

11. 选 [B]。词汇辨析题。四个选项中能用来描述战争的自然是 "爆发"，也就是 [B] outbreak。选 [A] "开始，开端" 的同学误解了原文，是二战的爆发而不是其开端引发了各国托儿所数量的增加；[C] "突围，突破" 不能和 of the Second World War 形成语义场共现；[D] breakdown 多用来指 "（机器等）损坏，故障" 或 "（健康、精神、体力）等的衰竭、衰弱"。

12. 选 [A]。逻辑推理题。前段提到一战时妇女就代替男人进入了工厂，二战时的情况和一战相同，故应用 [A] again 来表示 "相同情况的再一次发生"。[B] thus 表结果，而此句是 as 引导的原因状语从句，因此如果选该项的话就会导致语义矛盾；[C] 项强调的是重复多次，用于形容原文中的两次显然有点过；[D] yet 表转折，用在 as 引导的原因状语从句中同样会造成语义上的混乱。

13. 选 [B]。短语搭配题。四个选项均有 "情形，情况" 之意，但是能与介词 on 搭配的只有 [B] occasion, on this occasion 意为 "在这种情况下"。[A] circumstance 常用的搭配为：under/in the circumstance, 意为 "在这种情况下，既然如此"，in/under no circumstance 意为 "无论如何不，决不"；[C] case 表达类似意思时和介词 in 构成短语 in the case of "在…情况下"；[D] situation 同样也是和介词 in 搭配。

14. 选 [C]。词汇辨析题。能与 government 和 $ 6, 000, 000 形成语义场共现的只有 [C] "把…拨给，分配"。[A] "调整，校正"，宾语多为声音、温度、时钟等，显然与此处的 $ 6, 000, 000 不搭配；[B] "召集，召唤"，多以人作宾语；[D] "转移，移交" 虽然能跟资金作宾语，但它后面还应该跟表示指向性的介词 to，即 transfer…to…。

15. 选 [C]。词汇辨析题。州政府和地方政府的帮助，相对于联邦政府来说也只能是 [C] supplement "增补，补充"。[A] "扩张，使膨胀"，[B] "促进，使便利" 和 [D] "偿还，补偿" 的宾语都不能是 aid。

16. 选 [D]。短语搭配题。这类日托所是用来照顾小孩的，故用 care for "关怀，照顾" 这个固定搭配。[A] by 和 [B] after 都不能和 care 搭配使用；[C] of

和 care 搭配时一般用于 take care of 的结构中。

17. 选［B］。逻辑推理题。选项中四个词都能和 federal 连用，但前面句中已经出现过 federal aid "联邦援助"，所以选同义复现的［B］ "补助金，津贴"。［A］"退休金"，［C］"税收"，［D］"预算，预算拨款"，选此三项的同学显然没有注意到 receiving 的逻辑主语是 children，既然是孩子们，那他们就不可能接受退休金、税收或是预算拨款。

18. 选［D］。逻辑推理题。所填词修饰 cut down，照应线索是后文中的 sharp drop，cut down 与 drop 是语义复现关系，因此所填词也应与 sharp 构成语义复现关系。符合的只有［D］drastically "剧烈地，猛烈地"。［A］"盛行地，普遍地"；［B］"狂怒地，暴躁地"；［C］"统计地"均不能准确地修饰 cut down 的程度。

19. 选［A］。逻辑推理题。空格前的 and later 表示一种递进关系，由 drastically cut down 到最后的 abolish "废除"是件很自然的事情，所以［A］项是正确答案。［B］"减少"与 cut down 意思相近，选此项的同学没有注意到 later 的出现，误认为 and 前后表示的还是平行关系；［C］"危害"和［D］"排除"与 cut down 偏差太大，不是 cut down 发展的趋势。

20. 选［C］。逻辑推理题。能和 employed mothers 形成语义场共现的是［C］jobs。句子的大意为：联邦政府期望战争结束后妇女离开工作，回家照顾小孩，但是事实并非如此。

模 拟 演 练

第五章

Test 1

College sports in the United States are a huge deal. Almost all major American universities have football, baseball, basketball and hockey programs, and __1__ millions of dollars each year to sports. Most of them earn millions __2__ as well, in television revenues, sponsorships. They also benefit __3__ from the added publicity they get via their teams. Big-name universities compete __4__ each other in the most popular sports. Football games at Michigan regularly __5__ crowds of over 90, 000. Basketball's national collegiate championship game is a TV __6__ on a *par with* (与…相同或相似) any other sporting event in the United States, __7__ perhaps the Super Bowl itself. At any given time during fall or winter one can __8__ one's TV set and see the top athletic programs — from schools like Michigan, UCLA, Duke and Stanford — __9__ in front of packed houses and national TV audiences.

The athletes themselves are __10__ and provided with scholarships. College coaches identify __11__ teenagers and then go into high schools to __12__ the country's best players to attend their universities. There are strict rules about __13__ coaches can recruit — no recruiting calls after 9 p. m., only one official visit to a campus —

1. [A] attribute   [B] distribute
   [C] devote   [D] attach
2. [A] out   [B] by
   [C] in   [D] back
3. [A] directly   [B] indirectly
   [C] apart   [D] indirect
4. [A] for   [B] in
   [C] against   [D] over
5. [A] draw   [B] amuse
   [C] govern   [D] handle
6. [A] spectator   [B] spectacle
   [C] spectrum   [D] spectacles
7. [A] save   [B] saves
   [C] saved   [D] to save
8. [A] flip on   [B] flap at
   [C] fling away   [D] flush out
9. [A] battle   [B] to battle
   [C] battling   [D] battled
10. [A] recruited   [B] reconciled
    [C] rectified   [D] reserved
11. [A] promising
    [B] pleasing
    [C] compulsory
    [D] professional
12. [A] contrive   [B] convince
    [C] convert   [D] convict
13. [A] which   [B] what
    [C] how   [D] whether
14. [A] ignored   [B] neglected
    [C] remembered [D] noticed

but they are often bent and sometimes __14__. Top college football programs __15__ scholarships to 20 or 30 players each year, and those student-athletes, when they arrive __16__ campus, receive free housing, tuition, meals, books, etc.

In return, the players __17__ themselves to the program in their sport. Football players at top colleges work __18__ two hours a day, four days a week from January to April. In summer, it's back to strength and agility training four days a week until mid-August, when camp __19__ and preparation for the opening of the September-to-December season begins in __20__. During the season, practices last two or three hours a day from Tuesday to Friday. Saturday is game day. Monday is an officially mandated day of rest.

15. [A] offer　　　　[B] confer
　　[C] conform　　[D] reward
16. [A] in　　　　　[B] on
　　[C] at　　　　　[D] around
17. [A] commit　　　[B] compensate
　　[C] commute　　[D] comply
18. [A] in　　　　　[B] out
　　[C] over　　　　[D] off
19. [A] recalls　　　[B] enlists
　　[C] convenes　　[D] collects
20. [A] principle　　[B] confidence
　　[C] name　　　[D] earnest

Test 2

Many people probably think of offshore drilling as a __1__ recent development __2__ since the 1969 blowout in the Santa Barbara Channel focused public attention so __3__ on the environmental aspects of these operations. __4__, producing oil from coastal water dates all the way __5__ to 1894. It began from piers built __6__ the same Santa Barbara Channel. But it wasn't until 1947 __7__ the first true offshore platform was built in fifty feet of water __8__ the Louisiana coast. Since then, some 20,000 wells have been drilled off the coast of 70 countries, and one-sixth of the world's oil is now being produced from offshore fields.

Exploring for, and producing, oil and gas offshore is expensive. It costs about four

1. [A] too　　　　　[B] quiet
　　[C] surely　　　[D] fairly
2. [A] especially　　[B] specially
　　[C] probably
　　[D] possibly
3. [A] dramatically
　　[B] interesting
　　[C] nicely
　　[D] fairly
4. [A] Apparently
　　[B] Actually
　　[C] Truly
　　[D] Absolutely
5. [A] toward　　　[B] back
　　[C] to　　　　　[D] for
6. [A] on　　　　　[B] to

times as __9__ to drill an exploratory well offshore as a similar one on land, and operations in __10__ waters will cost even more. Why then does the petroleum industry persist __11__ its underwater __12__ ?

First of all, there's the matter of __13__ and demand. Beyond that are vital considerations of continued __14__ growth and security of supply. Right now, oil and gas provide three-quarters of America's energy requirements. Meanwhile, the __15__ for energy continues to increase.

Every day, the United States consumes 650 million gallons of petroleum and over 50 billion cubic feet of natural gas.

This consumption is growing so fast that the United States is expected to use as much petroleum and natural gas in the next fifteen years as it has during the __16__ 113 years of the oil industry's existence.

In the case of natural gas, this estimate is conservative — only because supplies are severely limited. Gas is such a clean, convenient __17__ that its use would grow much faster if it were __18__ available.

Here in the U. S. , we are increasingly dependent __19__ offshore areas for natural gas, since gas is difficult and expensive to transport in anything other __20__ pipelines.

	[C] in	[D] at
7.	[A] that	[B] when
	[C] so	[D] then
8.	[A] of	[B] on
	[C] in	[D] off
9.	[A] many	[B] much
	[C] same	[D] amount
10.	[A] deeper	[B] deep
	[C] deepest	[D] depth
11.	[A] on	[B] for
	[C] in	[D] at
12.	[A] study	[B] look
	[C] find	[D] search
13.	[A] support	[B] suppose
	[C] suppress	[D] supply
14.	[A] economical	[B] economy
	[C] economic	[D] economics
15.	[A] demand	[B] cost
	[C] supply	[D] price
16.	[A] entire	[B] all
	[C] total	[D] past
17.	[A] goods	[B] material
	[C] fuel	[D] product
18.	[A] ready	[B] readily
	[C] such	[D] more
19.	[A] for	[B] on
	[C] at	[D] to
20.	[A] with	[B] for
	[C] on	[D] than

Test 3

Although Henry Ford's name is closely associated with the concept of mass production, he should receive equal credit for introducing labor practices as early as 1913 that would be considered __1__

1.	[A] advanced	[B] absurd
	[C] accessible	[D] acute
2.	[A] methods	[B] ways
	[C] means	[D] measures
3.	[A] decreased	[B] reduced

even by today's standards. Safety __2__ were improved, and the work day was __3__ to eight hours, compared with the ten-or-twelve-hour day common at the time. In order to accommodate the shorter work day, the __4__ factory was converted from two to three __5__ .

　　__6__ , sick leaves as well as improved medical care for those injured __7__ the job were instituted. The Ford Motor Company was one of the first factories to develop a __8__ school to train specialized skilled laborers and an English language school for immigrants. Some __9__ were even made to hire the handicapped and provide jobs for former convicts.

　　The most widely acclaimed __10__ was the five-dollar-a-day minimum wage that was __11__ in order to recruit and __12__ the best mechanics and to __13__ the growth of labor unions. Ford explained the new wage policy in __14__ of efficiency and profit sharing. He also mentioned the fact that his employees would be able to purchase the automobiles that they produced — in effect __15__ a market for the product. In order to qualify for the minimum wage, an employee had to establish a decent home and __16__ good personal habits, including *sobriety*（节制）, thriftiness, industriousness, and dependability. __17__ some criticism was directed at Ford for involving himself too much in the __18__ lives of his employees, there can be no doubt that, at a time when immigrants were being taken __19__ of in frightful ways, Henry Ford was helping many people to __20__ themselves in America.

[C] declined　　[D] dropped

4. [A] complete　[B] all
　 [C] entire　　[D] total

5. [A] shifts　　[B] switches
　 [C] sections　[D] classes

6. [A] However　[B] Therefore
　 [C] Furthermore[D] Whereas

7. [A] at　　　　[B] on
　 [C] in　　　　[D] for

8. [A] professional[B] practical
　 [C] technological
　 [D] technical

9. [A] effects　　[B] trials
　 [C] steps　　　[D] strength

10. [A] accession　[B] innovation
　　[C] aspiration [D] illusion

11. [A] provided　[B] assured
　　[C] offered　[D] sponsored

12. [A] maintain　[B] sustain
　　[C] retain　　[D] attain

13. [A] discourage[B] hold
　　[C] prohibit　[D] stimulate

14. [A] virtue　　[B] aspects
　　[C] relations　[D] terms

15. [A] inventing　[B] creating
　　[C] producing [D] yielding

16. [A] exemplify
　　[B] demonstrate
　　[C] improve　[D] verify

17. [A] However　[B] Since
　　[C] Then　　[D] Although

18. [A] individual　[B] routine
　　[C] usual　　[D] personal

19. [A] advantage　[B] use
　　[C] profit　　[D] interest

20. [A] distinguish[B] identify
　　[C] establish　[D] settle

Test 4

In the United States, the spirit of Christmas arrives __1__ a month before the holiday itself. Late in November, street lights and store windows are __2__ with the traditional Christmas colors __3__ red and green. Snowmen, Santa Claus, shepherds, angels, and Nativity scenes appear in countless shop windows. Fir trees, holly wreaths, and *mistletoe* (槲寄生，其小枝常用作圣诞节的装饰) are familiar sights. Families decorate their homes, inside and out, with __4__ lights and evergreens.

The manufacture and distribution of Christmas Ream is big business. Stores depend upon Christmas shoppers for about one-fourth of their __5__ sales. Smart shoppers buy their gifts in November or early December, before the "Christmas rush" makes shopping a chore. Christmas is expensive. To earn __6__ money for gifts, thousands of Americans get part-time jobs during December __7__ mail or selling gifts, trees, ornaments, or greeting cards. Many people make monthly bank __8__ in special Christmas __9__ so that they will have enough money to __10__ a nice Christmas for their families.

Although Americans enjoy the commercial gaiety of Christmas, the most beautiful and meaningful aspects of the holiday occur at home and in __11__. Many families go to church __12__ Christmas Eve and Christmas morning. After __13__, they gather around the tree and open their __14__. Then they sit down to enjoy a __15__ Christmas dinner — turkey or ham, sweet potatoes, vegetables, cranberry

1. [A] in   [B] about
   [C] before   [D] since
2. [A] adored   [B] colored
   [C] decorated   [D] painted
3. [A] with   [B] of
   [C] in   [D] from
4. [A] colorful   [B] color
   [C] colored   [D] coloring
5. [A] annual   [B] manual
   [C] year
   [D] anonymous
6. [A] change   [B] small
   [C] apparent   [D] extra
7. [A] posting   [B] throwing
   [C] carrying   [D] delivering
8. [A] savings   [B] accounts
   [C] deposits   [D] interests
9. [A] books   [B] currents
   [C] deposits   [D] accounts
10. [A] offer   [B] provide
    [C] give   [D] send
11. [A] plaza   [B] church
    [C] pub   [D] restaurant
12. [A] in   [B] at
    [C] on   [D] for
13. [A] services   [B] event
    [C] religion   [D] ceremony
14. [A] mouths   [B] gifts
    [C] boxes   [D] hands
15. [A] long   [B] plenty
    [C] traditional [D] various
16. [A] With   [B] For
    [C] In   [D] On
17. [A] during   [B] at
    [C] in   [D] when

sauce, and nuts. __16__ dessert, there is usually fruitcake, plum pudding, or *mince pie*(肉馅饼).

Perhaps children are the happiest __17__ Chrisms. They receive gifts from their parents and grandparents, they send Christmas __18__ to their companions and friends, extending good __19__ to people they love. Sometimes they even can enjoy a wonderful Christmas night with snow falling outside, dreaming __20__ Santa Claus cramming bags and bags small gifts into their shoes and socks.

18. [A] wishes   [B] cards
    [C] greetings   [D] regards
19. [A] wishes   [B] wish
    [C] wishing   [D] wishings
20. [A] with   [B] for
    [C] about   [D] of

Test 5

NBC is a/television network. In 1919 the Radio Corporation of America was founded as a manufacturer of electronic __1__ and products. Seven years __2__, in 1926, a subsidiary, the National Broadcasting Company, was organized to broadcast __3__ programs. The radio network __4__ through the years and, with David Samoff __5__ of RCA, NBC's first commercial television station, WNBT, began to broadcast out of New York City in 1941. In 1986, RCA __6__ with the General Electric Company, a major stockholder in RCA when it was formed in 1919. The purchase price was $ 6. 4 billion.

__7__, NBC has been strong in certain programming genres, although some have been marked with __8__. In its early years, the network was a

1. [A] components   [B] compacts
    [C] compartments   [D] complements
2. [A] ago   [B] after
    [C] before   [D] later
3. [A] film   [B] radio
    [C] music   [D] drama
4. [A] extended   [B] enlarged
    [C] expanded   [D] broadened
5. [A] as the chairman [B] as a chairman
    [C] as chairman   [D] be a chairman
6. [A] merged   [B] collided
    [C] changed   [D] talked
7. [A] Historically   [B] Presently
    [C] Firstly   [D] Recently
8. [A] consistency   [B] inconsistency
    [C] continuity   [D] incontinuity
9. [A] comedy   [B] tragedy
    [C] tragi-comedy   [D] drama
10. [A] dominated   [B] excluded
    [C] overlooked   [D] controlled
11. [A] Gold   [B] Golden

leader in __9__ with such successful shows as "Texaco Star Theater" and "The Colgate Comedy Hour". CBS and ABC __10__ comedy in the 1960s and 1970s, but in the mid 80s, such successful situation comedies as "The Cosby Show", "Cheers", The __11__ Girls, and "Family Ties" made NBC the number-one network.

　　__12__ the area of late-evening talk shows, the network has continuously been __13__ with its "Tonight Show", first slotted in that period in 1954. In the late 1950s and 1960s, NBC led the Western genre with __14__ fare as "Wagon Train" and "Bonanza". It also had several successful one-hour dramas, from "Dr. Killdeer", "The Man From U. N. C. L. E. ", "I Spy", and "Star Trek" in the 1960s to "Miami Vice", "Hill Street Blues", "St. Elsewhere", and "L. A. Law" in the 1980s.

　　NBC is also known for certain __15__. It has had innovative programming, such as "Rowan & Martin's Laugh", first broadcast in 1968, and "Saturday Night Live", which __16__ in 1975, in 1985 NBC began broadcasting programs to affiliates __17__ the first network to do __18__. Also that year, NBC was the first network to implement Ku-band satellite technology to __19__ programming, eliminating its dependence on interconnection facilities __20__.

	[C] Darken	[D] Ripen
12. [A] In	[B] At	
	[C] Among	[D] On
13. [A] top	[B] on top	
	[C] at top	[D] over top
14. [A] the	[B] a	
	[C] such	[D] two
15. [A] creations	[B] innovations	
	[C] inventions	[D] discoveries
16. [A] started	[B] began	
	[C] debuted	[D] performed
17. [A] in stereo	[B] in the stereo	
	[C] in a stereo	[D] at the stereo
18. [A] so	[B] such	
	[C] this	[D] it
19. [A] distribute	[B] attribute	
	[C] contribute	[D] tribute
20. [A] in land	[B] on land	
	[C] in the land	[D] on the land

Test 6

　　The human nose is an underrated tool. Humans are often thought to be insensitive smellers compared with an-

1. [A] although	[B] as	
	[C] but	[D] while	
2. [A] above	[B] unlike	

imals, __1__ this is largely because, __2__ animals, we stand upright. This means that our noses are __3__ to perceiving those smells which float through the air, __4__ the majority of smells which stick to surfaces. In fact __5__, we are extremely sensitive to smells, we do not generally realize it. Our noses are capable of __6__ human smells even when these are __7__ to far below one part in one million.

　　Strangely, some people find that they can smell one type of flower but not another, __8__ others are sensitive to the smells of both flowers. __9__ may be because some people do not have the genes necessary to generate __10__ smell receptors in the nose. These receptors are the cells which sense smells and send __11__ to the brain. However, it has been found that even people insensitive to a certain smell at __12__ can suddenly become sensitive to it when __13__ to it often enough.

　　The explanation for insensitivity to smell seems to be that brain finds it __14__ to keep all smell receptors working all the time __15__ can trigger new receptors if necessary. This may __16__ explain why we are not usually sensitive to our own smells we simply do not need to be. We are not __17__ of the usual smell of our own house but we __18__ new smells when we visit someone else's. The brain finds it best to keep smell receptors __19__ for unfamiliar and emergency signals such as the smell of smoke, __20__ might indicate the danger of fire.

	[C] excluding	[D] besides
3.	[A] limited	[B] committed
	[C] dedicated	[D] confined
4.	[A] catching	[B] ignoring
	[C] missing	[D] tracking
5.	[A] anyway	[B] though
	[C] instead	[D] therefore
6.	[A] distinguishing	[B] discovering
	[C] determining	[D] detecting
7.	[A] diluted	[B] dissolved
	[C] diagnosed	[D] diffused
8.	[A] when	[B] since
	[C] for	[D] whereas
9.	[A] That	[B] It
	[C] What	[D] Those
10.	[A] unusual	[B] particular
	[C] unique	[D] typical
11.	[A] signs	[B] stimuli
	[C] messages	[D] impulses
12.	[A] first	[B] all
	[C] large	[D] times
13.	[A] subjected	[B] left
	[C] drawn	[D] exposed
14.	[A] ineffective	[B] incompetent
	[C] inefficient	[D] insufficient
15.	[A] then	[B] however
	[C] but	[D] even
16.	[A] still	[B] also
	[C] otherwise	[D] nevertheless
17.	[A] sure	[B] sick
	[C] aware	[D] tired
18.	[A] tolerate	[B] repel
	[C] neglect	[D] notice
19.	[A] available	[B] reliable
	[C] identifiable	[D] suitable
20.	[A] that	[B] which
	[C] those	[D] it

Test 7

The increase in international business and in foreign investment has created a need for executives with knowledge of foreign languages and skills in cross-cultural communication. Americans, __1__, have not been well trained in either area and, consequently, have not enjoyed the same level of __2__ in negotiation in an international arena as have their foreign __3__.

Negotiating is the __4__ of communicating back and __5__ for the purpose of reaching an agreement. It __6__ persuasion and compromise, but in order to __7__ in either one, the negotiators must understand the ways in __8__ people are persuaded and how compromise is __9__ within the culture of the negotiation.

In many international business negotiations abroad, Americans are perceived as __10__ and impersonal. It often appears to the foreign negotiator that the American represents a large multi-million-dollar corporation that can afford to pay the price without __11__ further. The American negotiator's role becomes __12__ of an impersonal *purveyor* (传播者) of information and cash.

In __13__ of American negotiators abroad, several traits have been identified that may __14__ to confirm this *stereotypical* (老一套的) __15__, while

1. [A] however [B] hence
   [C] furthermore [D] therefore
2. [A] fulfillment [B] success
   [C] master [D] privilege
3. [A] enemies [B] counterparts
   [C] cooperators [D] entrepreneurs
4. [A] procedure [B] progress
   [C] process [D] proceeding
5. [A] forward [B] forth
   [C] before [D] towards
6. [A] includes [B] concludes
   [C] conducts [D] involves
7. [A] participate [B] indulge
   [C] attend [D] blend
8. [A] that [B] what
   [C] which [D] case
9. [A] arrived [B] gained
   [C] facilitated [D] reached
10. [A] wealthy [B] sensitive
    [C] poor [D] rude
11. [A] claiming [B] communicating
    [C] exchanging [D] bargaining
12. [A] what [B] that
    [C] it [D] those
13. [A] studies [B] discussions
    [C] investigations [D] seminars
14. [A] attach [B] compare
    [C] accord [D] serve
15. [A] concept [B] perception
    [C] realization [D] feeling
16. [A] special [B] particular
    [C] essential [D] private
17. [A] on [B] in
    [C] at [D] with

undermining the negotiator's position. Two traits in __16__ that cause cross-cultural misunderstanding are directness and impatience __17__ the part of the American negotiator. Furthermore, American negotiators often insist on realizing short-term goals. Foreign negotiators, on the other hand, may value the relationship established between negotiators and may be __18__ to invest time in it for long-term benefits. In order to __19__ the relationship, they may opt for __20__ interactions without regard for the time involved in getting to know the other negotiator.

18. [A] disgusted [B] willing
　　[C] reluctant [D] easy
19. [A] strengthen [B] proceed
　　[C] tighten [D] solidify
20. [A] direct [B] indirect
　　[C] effective [D] efficient

Test 8

IQ scores have risen sharply over the past decades. "This __1__ our belief about the __2__ of IQ," says psychologist Ulrich Neisser of Cornell University. "It's in evidence that you can indeed change it."

There's just one little problem. Leaving aside for the very real question of __3__ IQ is truly a proxy (代表) for intelligence, scientists can't explain what has made IQ scores increases. Neither nature __4__ nurture answers the question, for different reasons. Lots of data, from twin studies to adoption research, suggests that genes __5__ some 75 percent of the difference between individuals' IQ by late adolescence. Psychologists who study intelligence mostly agree that hereditary factors __6__ the lion's share

1. [A] reinforces [B] enhances
　　[C] shatters [D] explores
2. [A] seriousness [B] stability
　　[C] rigidity [D] foundation
3. [A] why [B] whether
　　[C] what [D] that
4. [A] and [B] or
　　[C] nor [D] but
5. [A] account for [B] respond to
　　[C] take up [D] match to
6. [A] resolve [B] explain
　　[C] exhibit [D] display
7. [A] dilemma [B] paradox
　　[C] contraction [D] conflict
8. [A] overwhelmingly [B] fundamentally
　　[C] admittedly [D] adequately
9. [A] retrieve [B] untangle
　　[C] repel [D] dissipate
10. [A] came [B] fit
　　[C] caught [D] teamed

of IQ difference.

"It's been a __7__ ", says William Dickens of the Brookings Institution. "The high inheritability of IQ suggests that environment is __8__ powerful. " To __9__ the mystery, Dickens __10__ up with James Flynn, who in 1987 discovered the IQ rise, now called the Flynn effect. In a study being published this week in *Psychological Review*, the duo offer an explanation that not only might __11__ the paradox but may also __12__ on the forces that __13__ intelligence. "People's IQs are affected by both environment and genes, but their environments are matched to their IQs," the researchers conclude. __14__ genes do indeed have an important effect: they cause people to seek out certain environments and life experiences. If you have a biological __15__ in intelligence, you will likely enjoy school, books, puzzles, asking questions and thinking abstractly, all of which will tend to __16__ your innate brainpower. "Higher IQ leads one into better environments, causing still higher IQ," says Dickens and Flynn. __17__ multiplier *effect* (倍数效应), you will likely study even more, haunt the library, *pester* (纠缠) adults with questions and choose bright peers as friends, boosting your intelligence yet again.

As far as scientists can tell, experiences that __18__ the intelligence of someone born with an IQ edge have

11. [A] resolve   [B] revolve
    [C] revive   [D] relieve
12. [A] start   [B] turn
    [C] shed light   [D] press
13. [A] effect   [B] shape
    [C] inspire   [D] drive
14. [A] In a word   [B] In other words
    [C] However   [D] Hence
15. [A] edge   [B] priority
    [C] effect   [D] precedence
16. [A] determine   [B] accumulate
    [C] consolidate   [D] amplify
17. [A] Despite   [B] Thanks to
    [C] Granted   [D] Provided
18. [A] boost   [B] booth
    [C] boot   [D] boom
19. [A] influential   [B] positive
    [C] potential   [D] prospective
20. [A] makes   [B] implies
    [C] suggests   [D] represents

just about the same __19__ effect on people of average intelligence. In other words, whether you seek out an IQ-boosting environment or whether it finds you __20__ no difference. In either case, experiences and the social and technological surround should work their magic. This effect may account for the IQ rise over the decades.

答 案 与 解 析

Test 1

1. 选 [C]。短语搭配题。本题要求填入一个及物动词，且能用于 ~ sth. to sth. /sb. 结构中，选项中符合的有 [B]、[C]、[D] 三项。[B] distribute…to…意为"把…分配给…"，[C] devote…to…意为"把…贡献给…，做某种专用"；[D] attach…to…意为"把…附在…上"。根据句意可知美国大学是拨专款给体育运动的，因此 [C] 项为答案。[A] attribute "品质，特征" 为名词，故可排除。

2. 选 [D]。短语搭配题。空格处要求填入一个副词，与动词 earn 搭配。前文讲到它们每年要拨款给体育运动（为支出），这里提到通过各种渠道它们能赚数百万（为收入），故 [D] back "回到原来状况" 符合题意。

3. 选 [B]。词汇辨析题。根据句中的 via their teams 可知，此种途径应该是间接获得收益，因此选 [B] indirectly "间接地"。本句的意思是：这些学校还可以通过球队所获得的知名度间接获得收益。[A] directly "直接地" 和 [C] apart "分离，分别地" 语义不符；[D] indirect "间接的" 为形容词，不能用来修饰动词 benefit。

4. 选 [C]。短语搭配题。选项 [C] compete against sb. 意思是 "与某人竞争"，符合题意，为答案。其他选项中，[A] compete for "为…竞争" 不接人作宾语，故可排除；[B] compete in 与 [D] compete over 均属搭配不当。

5. 选 [A]。逻辑推理题。能和前文中的 publicity 形成语义场共现的是 [A] draw "吸引，引起" 本句的意思是：密歇根大学的足球比赛通常都能吸引九万多观众。[B] amuse "使发笑，使愉快" 和 [C] govern "统治，支配" 脱离了语境；[D] handle "处理，操作" 不能以人作宾语。

6. 选 [B]。词汇辨析题。能和后文中的 sporting event 形成语义场共现的是 [B] spectacle "壮观场面，奇观"。本句的意思是：全美大学生篮球锦标赛是极其精彩的电视节目，与美国其他的体育赛事不相上下。[A] spectator "观众（指比赛或表演)"; [C] spectrum "光谱，型谱"; [D] spectacles "眼镜" 均脱离了语境。

7. 选 [A]。语法结构题。[B] saves、[C] saved 和 [D] to save 用在此处均不能使句子结构正确，故均可排除。[A] save 用作动词时表示 "拯救，储蓄，节约"，另外它还可以用作介词，意思是 "除了，除…之外"，在此处即用作介词。

8. 选 [A]。短语搭配题。根据后文中的 and see the top athletic programs 可知此处想要表达的意思是 "打开电视机"。选项中能表达此含义的是 [A] flip on，其中的动词 flip 意为 "轻击，轻弹"，flip on one's TV set 意为 "打开电视"，符合题意。[B] flap at "拍打" 和 [C] fling away "扔掉，错过" 脱离了语境；[D] flush out "冲洗（掉）" 不能和 TV set 搭配使用。

9. 选 [C]。语法结构题。本题考查动词 see 的用法，see sb. doing sth. 意思是 "看到某人正在做某事"，例如：I saw her crying in her room. (我看到她在房间里哭)。综合分析，选项 [C] battling 符合题意，为答案。本句的意思是：选手们在座无虚席的体育场及全国电视观众面前展开激战。

10. 选 [A]。逻辑推理题。能和句中的 provided with scholarships 形成语义场共现的是 [A] recruited "征募，吸收"，故为答案。本句的意思是：被招进大学的运动员享受奖学金。[B] reconciled "使和谐，使顺从"；[C] rectified "矫正，调整"；[D] reserved "保留，保存" 脱离了语境。

11. 选 [A]。词汇辨析题。根据逻辑可知，教练们识别出的应该是有发展前途的青少年，故 [A] promising "有希望的，有前途的" 为答案。[B] pleasing "愉快的，令人高兴的" 和 [D] professional "专业的，职业的" 脱离了语境，故不选；[C] compulsory "必须做的，必修的" 不能用来修饰人，故也可排除。

12. 选 [B]。短语搭配题。选项中 [A] contrive "发明，设计" 和 [C] convert "使转变，转换" 不能接人作宾语，故先可排除。[D] convict 意为 "证明或宣告某人有罪"，常用于 convict sb. of … "宣判某人为某罪行" 的结构中，语义和用法均不符合题目要求，故也可排除。[B] convince "使确信，使信服"，常用于 convince sb. to do sth. /of sth. /that 的结构中，符合题意，为答案。

13. 选 [C]。语法结构题。破折号后的内容：no recruiting calls after 9 p. m. ，only one official visit to a campus 谈论的是教练招收学生的途径，故选表方式的 [C] how "怎样"，它可用于引导宾语从句。[A] which 用于引导定语从句；[B] what 引导名词性从句，可作主语、宾语、表语等，但与此处的题意不符；[D] whether "是否" 也不符合题目的语义要求。

14. 选 [A]。词汇辨析题。能和 and 前的 bent (bend 的过去分词) 形成语义共现的是 [A] ignored 和 [B] neglected，两者都含有 "忽视" 之意，前者强调

"置之不理，不予考虑"，有故意的意味，后者侧重指"疏忽，不留心"。此处显然含有故意的意味，故选［A］ignored。本句的意思是：晚9：00以后不准给学生打电话，教练仅有一次参观校园的正式邀请——不过这些规定常常不能严格执行，有时还会被完全置于脑后。［C］remembered"记住，纪念"和［D］noticed"注意到，留心"语义均不符。

15. 选［A］。词汇辨析题。本句的意思是：名牌大学的足球队每年向20或30个球员提供奖学金。因此所填词需能表达"提供"之意，且能用于 ~ sth. to sb. 的结构中，四个选项中符合的是，［A］offer"提供"，offer sth. to sb. 意为"向某人提供某物"。［B］confer意为"授与，颁与（称号、学位等）"，它的用法为 confer sth. on/upon sb.；［C］conform意为"遵守，一致，符合"，为非及物动词，后面常跟介词to或with；［D］reward意为"酬劳，奖赏"，用法为 reward sb. for sth. /doing sth.。

16. 选［B］。短语搭配题。四个选项中，［A］in与［C］at均有到达某地之意，但不能与campus连用；［B］on可与campus搭配，符合句子题意，为答案。［D］around表示"到处，四周"，与题意不符。本句的意思是：这些学生球员入学后免交学费、书本费及食宿等费用。

17. 选［A］。词汇辨析题。四个选项中，能和themselves to搭配使用的只有［A］commit，commit themselves to意为"专心致志于，投身于"。本句的意思是：作为回报，学生球员要投身到他们所擅长的体育项目中去。［B］compensate"偿还，补偿"，后跟介词for；［C］commute"交换，抵偿"和［D］comply"顺从，答应"均不能和themselves to搭配。

18. 选［B］。短语搭配题。四个选项均能和work构成短语，但能和sport以及Football players构成语义场共现的是［B］work out"运动；锻炼"。本句的意思是：从一月到四月，一流大学的足球运动员每周训练四天，每天训练两小时。［A］work in"插进，引进，配合"；［C］work over"检查，研究，重做"；［D］work off"排除，清理"均脱离了语境。

19. 选［C］。词汇辨析题。所填词需为不及物动词，故先排除只能作及物动词的［A］recalls"回忆，回想"。其他三项中，语义符合的是［C］convenes"召集，集合"。［B］enlists"入伍，参军"和［D］collects"收集，聚集"均与主语camp搭配不当。

20. 选［D］。短语搭配题。为赛季开幕所做的准备工作应该是严肃而认真的，故［D］in earnest"认真地，诚挚地"为答案。［A］in principle"原则上"；［B］in confidence"秘密地"；［C］in name"名义上"均不符合题目的语义要求。

Test 2

1. 选［D］。词汇辨析题。［D］fairly"相当地"，一般表示恰到好处的程度，或赞赏的语气，符合此处的语境，故为答案。［A］too"太，过于"一般表示超出一定的程度，含有否定之意，用于修饰 recent development 不太合适，故可排除；[B] quiet "安静的，从容的" 语义不符；surely "的确地，安全地" 也明显不合题意。

2. 选 [A]。词汇辨析题。此处想要表达的意思为 "尤其是在 1969 年…以后"，[A] especially "特别，尤其"，通常用于强调许多事物中的某一类或某一件，符合题意。[B] specially "特别地，专门地"，一般表示不同于一般地，句中无此含义，故不选。[C] probably "大概，或许"；[D] possibly "可能地，或者" 语义不符。

3. 选 [A]。逻辑推理题。能和句中的 blowout 以及 focused public attention so 形成语义场共现的是 [A] dramatically "引人注目地，戏剧性地"。[B] interesting 是形容词，不能用来修饰动词 focused。[C] nicely 和 [D] fairly 均脱离了语境。

4. 选 [B]。逻辑推理题。前文说很多人认为海底钻探是近年来发展起来的，后文则说在近海中采油可以追溯到 1894 年，显然，空格处的副词含有转折意味，只有 [B] Actually 才能使文章语义通顺，其他三个选项都不符合要求。

5. 选 [B]。短语搭配题。date back to 是固定词组，意为 "追溯到，是…时代开始有的"，故选 [B] to。

6. 选 [C]。语法结构题。这里是说将码头同样建在圣巴巴拉海峡里，故用介词 in，即 [C] 答案。

7. 选 [A]。语法结构题。It wasn't until…that…为固定强调句型，正确的语序为：the first true offshore platform…was not built until 1947。因此 [A] that 为答案。

8. 选 [D]。逻辑推理题。根据句中的 true offshore platform 可以判断出答案为 [D] off "在离…不远处"，off the coast 意为 "离海岸不远处"。

9. 选 [B]。短语搭配题。指花费多少钱应用 as much as，故选 [B] much。

10. 选 [A]。逻辑推理题。根据文章意思，在海岸附近钻井的开支是在陆地上钻同样一口井的四倍，因此只有在更深的水域钻井花费才会更大，故选 [A] deeper。

11. 选 [C]。短语搭配题。persist 用作不及物动词时，多与介词 in 搭配使用，意为 "坚持干某事"，故本题答案为 [C] in。

12. 选 [D]。逻辑推理题。前文提及的 offshore drilling 意为 "海底钻探"，underwater search "水底勘探" 能与其形成语义复现关系，故 [D] search 为答案。[C] find 和 search 为同义词，也能表示 "找到，发现" 之意，但其强调的是结果，而此处强调的是过程，故不选。[A]、[B] 两项均脱离了语境。

13. 选 [D]。逻辑推理题。所填词和 demand 由 and 连接的并列结构，故它们在词性和形式上应保持一致。demand 在这里作名词，因此首先排除只能作动词使用的 [B] suppose "推想，假设" 和 [C] suppress "镇压，抑制"。与 demand（需求）对应的应该是 supply（供给），故 [D] 项为正确答案。[A]

support "支持，拥护" 语义不符。

14. 选 [C]。词汇辨析题。此处想要表达的意思是 "持续的经济增长"，故应用 [C] economic，意为 "经济（上）的，经济学的"。[A] economical 是形容词，意为 "节约的，经济的"；[B] economy 是名词，意为 "经济，节约"；[D] economics 也为是名词，意为 "经济学"。

15. 选 [A]。逻辑推理题。本段谈论的是石油的供求关系。前句谈到了供的情况，本句所谈论的应是求，因此 [A] demand 为答案。

16. 选 [A]。词汇辨析题。此处想要表达的意思是 "石油产业存在的全部 113 年"。[A] entire "整个的，全部的" 用于表示物质的、数量的、时间的完整性，符合题意。[B] all 强调所有；[C] total 强调 "总额、总数，加起来的总的数量"；如果用 [D] past "过去的，结束的"，那么文中的时态需为过去式，故不正确。

17. 选 [C]。逻辑推理题。这里将天然气和石油进行对比，说天然气是更清洁、方便的燃料，显然 [C] fuel 符合题意。[A] goods "货物，工具"；[B] material "物质，原料"；[D] product "产品，产物" 都脱离了语境。

18. 选 [B]。逻辑推理题。前文提到 is such a clean, convenient，所填这里填 readily "容易地，不困难地" 能与 convenient "方便地，便利地" 形成近义复现关系，故 [B] 为答案。

19. 选 [B]。短语搭配题。be dependent on／upon 是固定词组，意为 "依赖…，依靠…"，故选 [B] on 为答案。

20. 选 [D]。短语搭配题。管道运输是天然气运输的唯一的一种耗费不高的途径，因此 other __20__ 应表示 "除了" 之意。other than "除了" 符合题意，故 [D] other 为答案。其他三项均不能和 other 构成搭配。

Test 3

1. 选 [A]。词汇辨析题。根据后文内容，可知作者对福特在 1913 年就采取的劳工政策是持肯定态度的，故首先可排除 [B] "荒谬的，可笑的" 和 [D] "尖锐的，敏锐的"。且后文讲的是该劳工政策的先进性，故选 [A] "先进的"。[C] "易接近的，可达到的" 不符合题意。

2. 选 [D]。词汇辨析题。四个选项均有 "方式，方法" 之意，但这里要表达的意思是 "安全措施"。选项中有 "措施" 义项的只有 [D] measures。

3. 选 [B]。逻辑推理题。每天八个小时的工作时间和以前一天工作十到十二个小时相比，自然是下降了。从语义上看，四个选项似乎均符合题意，但 [A] decreased，[C] declined 和 [D] dropped 作 "下降" 之意解时，都是不及物动词，故只能选 [B]。

4. 选 [C]。词汇辨析题。四个选项是近义词，都含有 "全部" 之意，因此要注意它们之间的区别。此处强调的是 "整个工厂"，突出整体概念，[C] entire

"整个"符合题意。[A] complete 强调某件事的完整性；[B] all 强调"所有，全部"，我们可以说 all of the factories，意为"所有这些工厂"；[D] total 指总额上的"全部"。

5. 选 [A]。逻辑推理题。能和 shorter work day 形成语义场共现的只有 [A] shifts "轮班"。[B] "转化，转变"；[C] "部分，片段"；[D] "等级，种类"。句子大意为：为了适应变短的工作日，整个工厂被分成了两至三个班次进行轮班。

6. 选 [C]。逻辑推理题。前文讲了新政策的好处之一，这里开始讲其他好处，表递进，故选 [C] "此外，而且"。[A]、[D] 两项都表转折；[B] 表因果。

7. 选 [B]。短语搭配题。injured on the job 即指"因工受伤"，故选 [B] on。

8. 选 [A]。逻辑推理题。空格后出现了 specialized skilled laborers，根据同义复现原则，空格中应该填 [A] professional "专业的"。[B] "实际的"；[C] "科技的"；[D] "技术的"都脱离了上下文的语境。原句大意为：工厂创建专业学校来训练专门技术门类的工人，并且为外来的移民者创办英语学校。

9. 选 [B]。短语搭配题。能和 make 构成合理动兵搭配的有 [A] effects 和 [B] trials。前者常用于 make effects on sth. 的结构中，意为"对…有影响"，其后不接 to do sth.，且语义也不符；而后者 make trials 意为"尝试"，后常接不定式短语，意为"尝试做某事"，符合题意。[C] steps 常和动词 take 连用，意为"设法，采取措施"；[D] strength 常用于 on the strength of 短语中，意为"依凭；基于"。

10. 选 [B]。逻辑推理题。下句句首提到 the new wage policy，根据语义共现原则可知 [B] "改革，创新"为正确答案。[A] "就职，任职，添加，增加"；[C] "热望，渴望"；[D] "幻想，错觉"均不符合题目的语义要求，故不选。

11. 选 [C]。词汇辨析题。[B] assure "保证，担保"和 [D] "发起，主办"不能和 wage 搭配，故先可排除。剩下的 [A]、[C] 两项都表示"提供"之意，但是 [A] 的用法为 provide sb. with sth.，[C] offer 作"提供"之意解时，为及物动词，符合题意。

12. 选 [C]。词汇辨析题。本题考查的是近义词辨析。[A] maintain 指维持一种现状，如 law and order/good relations 等，更有保养之意；[B] sustain 指保持持续不息，如 life/economic growth 等；[C] retain 较正式，强调继续保持而不失去，如 an appearance of youth 等；[D] attain 意为"获得，达到"，如 the position of manager。此处是说为了能招募到且保留住最好的机械师，故选项 [C] 最为符合。

13. 选 [A]。逻辑推理题。采取了这么多有利于工人的措施，当然是为了阻碍工会的发展，故 [A] "阻碍，使气馁"正确。[B] hold "把握，掌握"和

[C] prohibit "禁止，阻止" 都不能和 growth 形成合理的搭配，故不选；[D] stimulate "刺激，激励" 则与原文的逻辑相悖，故也不选。

14. 选 [D]。短语搭配题。能用于 in ~ of 结构中的只有 [D] terms，in terms of 意为 "按照…"。其他三个选项的搭配分别为：by virtue of 意为 "依靠，由于"，in the aspect of 意为 "在…方面"，in relation to 意为 "和…有关"。

15. 选 [B]。词汇辨析题。福特允许工人购买本厂生产的汽车，当然是 "创造" 了市场，故选 [B] "创造"。[A] "发明"；[C] "生产，制造"；[D] "生产，生长" 均语义不符。

16. 选 [B]。词汇辨析题。原句意为：想要具有拿最低工资的资格，工人必须要建立和睦的家庭，而且要展现良好的个人素质，包括节制、勤俭、勤奋和自立"，故选 [B] "表明，展示"。[A] "例证，示例"；[C] "改善，改进"；[D] "检验，查证" 均不符合题意。

17. 选 [D]。逻辑推理题。原文两分句的意思分别为：有人批评福特过于干涉他的员工的私生活；毫无疑问，在那样一个外来劳工被压榨到极限的年代，福特帮助了很多人在美国立足。由此可见两分句之间是让步关系，故选 [D] although。[A] 表转折；[B] 表因果；[C] 表时间或先后顺序。

18. 选 [D]。逻辑推理题。前文提到 In order to qualify for the minimum wage, an employee had to establish a decent home，这说明福特有些过多地干涉到员工的私人生活了，[D] personal 为正确答案。[A] "个人的" 都一定的干扰项，但它强调个体，而原文强调的是 "私人"，故不选；[B] "日常的，常规的" 和 [C] "平常的，通常的" 语义不符。

19. 选 [A]。短语搭配题。take advantage of 为固定搭配，意为 "利用"，故选 [A]。此处若用 use，则要使用固定搭配 make use of 才行。

20. 选 [C]。词汇辨析题。选项能和句中的 immigrants，in America 形成语义场共现的有 [C] establish "使定居，建立" 和 [D] settle "安家，定居"。但 settle 为不及物动词，后面不能直接跟宾语，故选 [C]，establish oneself 意为 "使自己定居下来，立足"。[A] distinguish oneself 意为 "使扬名"，脱离了语境，不选；[B] identify "鉴别，识别" 后面不能跟 oneself，故也可排除。

Test 4

1. 选 [B]。词汇辨析题。[B] about 相当于 around，是 "大约，大概" 的意思。句子大意为：在美国，圣诞气息在节日到来前一个月左右就已经降临了。[A] [B] [C] [D]

2. 选 [C]。词汇辨析题。be decorated with 意为 "被…装点"，符合语境，故选 [C]。[A] adored "崇拜，爱慕" 语义不符；[B] colored 用在此处会造成语义重叠；[D] painted "描绘，画，涂颜料" 脱离了语境，故也可排除。

3. 选 [B]。语法结构题。the color of red 相当于 the red color，of 两侧的名词实

际上指的是同一个事物。故 [B] of 为答案。

4. 选 [C]。词汇辨析题。[C] colored 指的是在灯上的颜色，灯本身所具有的颜色，colored lights 意为 "彩灯"，符合题意，为答案。[A] colorful 是 "颜色丰富的，鲜艳的" 的意思，不强调事物本身的颜色，故不选；[B] color "颜色，色彩" 为名词，不用于修饰 lights；[D] coloring 也为名词，是 "染色，着色" 的意思，显然不符合此处语义。

5. 选 [A]。词汇辨析题。此处想要表达的意思为 "年销售量"，[A] annual "每年的，年度的，一年的" 符合题意。[B] manual "手工的，手的" 和 [D] anonymous "匿名的，无名的" 完全脱离了语境；[C] year 为名词，不用于修饰 sales。

6. 选 [D]。逻辑推理题。选项中能和 part-time jobs 构成语义共现的只有 [D] extra，extra money 意为 "外快"。

7. 选 [D]。短语搭配题。deliver mail 是一个固定搭配，意为 "送邮件"，故 [D] delivering 为答案。

8. 选 [C]。词汇辨析题。四个选项都与 "钱" 有关，但这里指的是往银行里存钱，故应选 [C] deposits "存钱"。[A] savings "存款，储蓄金"；[B] accounts 意为 "帐户，户头"；[D] interests "利息" 均不符语义。

9. 选 [D]。逻辑推理题。去银行存钱自然是存在银行账户上，故选 [D] accounts。

10. 选 [B]。词汇辨析题。选项中能用于 ~ sth. for sb. 结构中的只有 [B] provide，它通常的用法为 provide sth. for sb. 或 provide sb. with sth.，意为 "为某人提供某物"。[A] offer 是个强干扰项，它也能表示 "提供" 之意，但是它的用法为 offer (to do) sth. for sth. 或 offer sb. sth.；[C] give 的用法为 give sth. to sb. 或者 give sb. sth.；[D] send 的用法为 send sb. sth. "给某人寄送某物"，以及 send sb. for sb. "让某人去请某人"。

11. 选 [B]。逻辑推理题。根据下文中的 Many families go to church 可知此处应填 [B] church，和下文内容构成原词复现关系。[A] plaza "广场，购物中心"；[C] pub "酒吧"；[D] restaurant "餐馆，饭店" 均脱离了语境。

12. 选 [C]。语法结构题。on 常用于具体时间的前面，例如：on Sunday, on a stormy morning, on New Year's Day, on September 14th 等等，故选 [C]。

13. 选 [A]。逻辑推理题。在教堂里进行的应该是 "宗教仪式"，[A] services 和 [D] ceremony 都能表示 "仪式" 之意，但是 ceremony 一般指的是非常正式的仪式，故排除 [D] 选 [A]。这里的 services 指的是 religious services 即 "宗教仪式" 的意思。[B] event 指 "重大事件"；[C] religion "宗教，信仰" 均不符合题意。

14. 选 [B]。逻辑推理题。这句话的意思是：宗教仪式过后，他们就聚集在圣诞树的周围，打开各自的礼品盒欣赏礼品。因此 [B] gifts 为答案。

15. 选 ［C］。逻辑推理题。从后面的名词即可以看出，晚餐上的吃的都是传统的食品。因此 ［C］ traditional 符合题意，a traditional Christmas dinner 意为 "一个传统的圣诞晚餐"。

16. 选 ［B］。词汇辨析题。for 这个词表示目的，用在此处能使语义通顺，故 ［B］ 为答案。

17. 选 ［A］。词汇辨析题。此处想要表达的意思为 "在圣诞节的这段时间里"，故 ［A］ during 符合题意。

18. 选 ［B］。逻辑推理题。四个选项都符合此处语境，但 ［A］ wishes，［C］ greetings，［D］ regards 和 19 题的答案重复，故都不选。［B］ cards 在这里指 "圣诞贺卡"，符合题意，为答案。

19. 选 ［A］。词汇辨析题。wishes 经常用作复数，而不用单数。作复数用时，意思是 "祝愿，祝福"。常用短语为 to extend/give/send/offer one's good wishes to sb. 意为 "向某人传递祝福"。由此可知，［A］ wishes 为答案。

20. 选 ［D］。短语搭配题。dream of 为固定搭配，意为 "梦想，梦到"。故 ［D］ 项为答案。

Test 5

1. 选 ［A］。逻辑推理题。选项中能和 electronic 以及 product 形成语义共现的是 ［A］ components，electronic components 意为 "电子配件"。［B］ compacts "契约，合同"；［C］ complements "补充，补足"；［D］ compartments "间隔间，车厢" 均脱离了语境。

2. 选 ［D］。逻辑推理题。1919 年之后的七年正是 1926 年，表示多少日子以后，用 ［D］ later。

3. 选 ［B］。逻辑推理题。由下文可知，NBC 组建的目的是传送广播节目，故 ［B］ radio 为答案。

4. 选 ［C］。词汇辨析题。四个选项为近义词。这里指的是广播的覆盖网络有所扩张，应该用 expanded，它可以用来表示抽象意义上的扩张，故选 ［C］。［A］ extended 常指具体意义上的延伸与扩展；［B］ enlarged 与 ［D］ broadened 都有 "扩大" 之意，但往往用来表示具体意义上的扩展、壮大。

5. 选 ［C］。语法结构题。chairman 在这里是指官职，因而前面不需要加冠词，故 ［C］ as chairman 为答案。

6. 选 ［A］。逻辑推理题。由下文购买股份的陈述可知两公司是合并，故 ［A］ merged "合并，并入" 为正确答案。［B］ collided 意为 "碰撞，抵触"；［C］ changed 意为 "改变，变革"；［D］ talked "谈话，讨论" 均不符合题意。

7. 选 ［A］。逻辑推理题。完成时的运用以及下文关于 NBC 早期节目的回顾表明这一部分作者是在描述、回顾一个历史事实，由此可知 ［A］ Historically "在历史上，从历史观点上说" 为答案。［B］ Presently "目前，不久"；［C］ Firstly

"第一，首先"；[D] Recently "最近" 都不符合原文逻辑。

8. 选 [B]。逻辑推理题。连词 although 提示下面的观点与前面所述相反，由此可知所填词应表否定、消极含义。选项中符合此要求的只有 [B] inconsistency "前后不一致，矛盾"。[A] consistency "一致性，连贯性"；[C] continuity "连续性，连贯性"；[D] incontinuity "不连续，间断" 这三项均为中性词。

9. 选 [A]。逻辑推理题。下文谈论的一直都是喜剧，举的例子也全是喜剧，由此可知 NBC 的领导地位是在喜剧领域，故 [A] comedy 为答案。

10. 选 [A]。逻辑推理题。句中的 but 提示 80 年代中期 NBC 地位上升是一个转折点，因而在 60、70 年代喜剧不是由 NBC，而是由 CBS 和 ABC 控制的。由此可知 [A] dominated "支配，占优势"。[B] excluded "拒绝接纳，排斥"；[C] overlooked "俯瞰，远眺"；[D] controlled "控制，支配" 有很大的干扰性，但其侧重的是控制，而非占主导地位，故也可排除。

11. 选 [B]。语法结构题。golden girls 指很有潜力或很成功的女孩，故 [B] 为答案。[A] Gold "金色，金黄色" 一般不用来修饰人；[B] darken 与 [C] ripen 都是动词，不能用来修饰名词。

12. 选 [A]。词汇辨析题。此处想要表达的意思为 "在…领域"，故应用介词 in，即为 [A] 答案。

13. 选 [B]。短语搭配题。on top 为固定搭配，意为 "处于领先地位"。

14. 选 [C]。短语搭配题。空格后的 as 提示前面的词应为 such，两者构成固定搭配。

15. 选 [B]。逻辑推理题。下文中的 innovative programming 提示 NBC 进行的是改革而不是发明创造，故 [B] innovations "改革，创新" 为答案，与后文的 innovative 构成同根词复现关系。其他选项均脱离了语境。

16. 选 [C]。逻辑推理题。[C] debut 作不及物动词时，指 "第一次公开露面"，与前文中的 first broadcast 形成同义复现关系。[A] started 和 [B] began 语义不符；[D] performed 需以人作主语，故也不正确。

17. 选 [A]。短语搭配题。in stereo 为固定搭配，指 "用立体声传送"，stereo 前不需要加任何冠词，故选 [A]。

18. 选 [A]。语法结构题。so 在这里为代词，指上文提到的事情。

19. 选 [A]。逻辑推理题。能和主语 Ku-band satellite technology 形成语义场共现的是 [A] distribute 意为 "发送，散布"。[B] attribute 意为 "归因于，归结于"，常和介词 to 连用；[C] contribute 意为 "贡献，捐助"；[D] tribute 是名词，意为 "贡品，礼物"。

20. 选 [B]。短语搭配题。"在陆地上" 的表达为 "on land"，故 [B] 为答案。

Test 6

1. 选 [C]。逻辑推理题。空格前句子的意思为：与动物相比，人类的嗅觉器官通常被认为是不灵敏的。而空格后的句子意思为：在很大程度上这是因为，我们人类…动物，我们可以直立起来。由此可知，上下句之间为转折关系，故选项［C］but 最符合上下文逻辑。［A］although 表示让步；［B］as 表示因果；［D］while 表示并列。

2. 选［B］。逻辑推理题。根据上下文的内容和常识，人类是直立的，在这一点上和动物"不像"，因此正确答案为选项［B］"不象…，和…不同"。［A］"在…之上"；［C］"排除，排斥"；［D］besides "除…之外"都不符合逻辑。

3. 选［A］。词汇辨析题。［A］limited "限制于，局限于"，能用 be limited to (doing) sth. 的结构中，表示"将…限制在…之内"，通常是指对时间、空间、数量、能量等预先作出规定，因此符合题意，故为答案。［B］committed "忠于，承诺"和［C］dedicated "献身于"通常都以人作主语，且在语义上也不符合题意，故均可排除；［D］confined 是个强干扰项，它也能表示"局限于"，常用于 confine…to (doing) sth. 的结构中，但它强调的是禁止或不能通过的边界，含有"严格的约束、遏制"之意，故用在此处并不合适。

4. 选［C］。词汇辨析题。由于人是直立的，所以感知局限于空气中的气味，而对于绝大多数的附着在地表的气味自然就会错失，选项［C］"错过，失去"最符合句意。［A］"捕捉，发觉"；［B］"忽略，忽视"；［D］"跟踪，追踪"均不符合原文的语义要求。

5. 选［B］。逻辑推理题。此处需填入一个能正确表达句际间关系的连接词。句中两分句的意思分别为：我们对气味尤其敏感；…我们通常都意识不到这点。很显然，两分句间是转折关系，所以选［B］though "尽管如此，即便如此"。［A］"无论如何"；［C］"相反，代替的是"；［D］"因此，所以"都不能正确表示两分句之间的关系。

6. 选［D］。词汇辨析题。表达鼻子能嗅到某种气味时通常用 detect "觉察，发现"，因此选［D］。［A］"辨别，区别"；［B］"发现"；［C］"决定"都不符合题意。

7. 选［D］。逻辑推理题。能和 smells 形成语义场共现的只有［D］diffused "（光，热，气味等）扩散，散发"。［A］diluted "（液体）稀释，（力量，效果等）削弱"和［B］dissolved "（固体）溶解，（画面，景色等）消失"都不适用于气体；［C］diagnosed "诊断"更是无从谈起。句子大意为："人类的鼻子可以嗅到自身的气味，哪怕这些气味淡到只有一百万分之一以下。"

8. 选［D］。逻辑推理题。空格前句子的意思为：奇怪的是，有些人只对其中一种花的气味敏感；而空格后句子的意思为：另外一些人却对两种花的气味都敏感。从逻辑上来看，前后明显是转折关系，故选［D］whereas 表转折。［A］when 表时间；［B］since 和［C］for 都表示原因。

9. 选［A］。语法结构题。句子缺少主语，［C］What 不能单独作主语，故先可排除。此处的主语指代的是上文提到的奇怪的现象，故选［A］that。［B］It 通常指具体事物；[D] Those 为复数，而上文只提到一种现象，所以以不正确。

10. 选 [B]。词汇辨析题。本句的大意为：这可能是因为某些人的嗅觉系统中缺乏必要的基因，这些基因可以生成辨别某些花气味的特有的味觉接收器。四个选项中，[A] unusual 意为"不同寻常的，非凡的"；[B] particular "特别的，特定的，特有的"；[C] 意为 unique "独一无二的"；[D] 意为 typical "典型的，有代表性的"。综合比较，[B] particular 用于修饰 smell receptors 较为合适，故为答案。

11. 选 [C]。词汇辨析题。本句的意思为："这些接收器是一些细胞，可以觉察气味并将信息输送到大脑。"四个选项中，[A] signs "迹象，暗示"；[B] stimuli "刺激物"；[D] impulses "冲动，推动力，刺激"；[C] messages "信息"。只有 messages 符合句子意思，因此，正确答案为选项 [C] messages。

12. 选 [A]。短语搭配题。句中提及 when __13__ to it often enough，根据共现原则，可知此应填入表示时间的短语。四个选项均能和 at 搭配构成短语，但是只有 [A] at first "起初，一开始" 和 [D] at times "有时，不时" 表示时间。再根据句中的 insensitive to a certain ...suddenly become sensitive to it...可知，此处存在时间上的先后，故 [A] first 为答案。[B] at all 常用否定形式 not at all 表示 "一点儿也不"；[C] at large "详尽，普遍" 语义不符。

13. 选 [D]。词汇辨析题。所填词的宾语 it 指代的是 a certain smell，能与 smell 构成合理动宾搭配的只有 [D] exposed，exposed to 意为 "使暴露在，使接触"。[A] subjected 常用于 be subjected to 的结构中，表示"处于…情形之下，服从于…"；[B] left "留在，剩下" 和 [C] drawn "拖，牵" 均语义不符。本句的大意为：然而，人们已经发现，即便是那些起初对某种气味不敏感的人，只要经常性地接触这种气味，到一定程度也会突然变得对该种气味敏感起来。

14. 选 [C]。词汇辨析题。四个选项中，[A] ineffective 意为 "（法律，措施，药物等）无效的，没有用的"；[B] incompetent 意为 "无能的，能力低下的"，通常指人；[C] inefficient "（机器，方法等）无效率的"；[D] insufficient "不足的，不够的"。这里指的是 smell receptors，因此用 [C] inefficient 最为合适。

15. 选 [C]。词汇辨析题。空格前是说 "让所有的味觉接收器都处于工作状态，工作效率很低"，空格后是说 "如果有必要，大脑会触发这些接收器"，由此可见两分句间是转折关系，故选 [C]。[B] however 也表转折，但它不能放在句中，故可排除；[A] then 和 [D] even 也不符合句中的逻辑关系。

16. 选 [B]。逻辑推理题。前文提到 The explanation for insensitivity to smell seems ...，这里再次提到...explain why...，因此选 [B] also "也"。[A] still "仍然"；[C] otherwise "否则的话"；[D] nevertheless "然而"均不符上下文的

逻辑关系。

17. 选［C］。逻辑推理题。能和前文的 sensitive to 构成同义复现关系的只有［C］be aware of "觉察到，意识到"。［A］sure "稳当的，可靠的"；［B］sick "不舒服的，有病的"；［D］tired "疲惫的，累的" 这三项都能用于 be ~ of 结构中，但是语义不符。本句的意思为：我们不能察觉到自家的常有气味，但在别人家时，却能立即觉察到新的气味。

18. 选［D］。逻辑推理题。根据同义复现原则，所填词应能表示 "察觉到，注意到"。四个选项中符合语义要求的只有［D］notice "注意到，察觉到"。［A］tolerate "容忍"；［B］repel "击退，拒绝"；［C］neglect "疏忽，忽略" 均不符语义。

19. 选［A］。词汇辨析题。根据上下文，所填词需能表示 "处于可利用状态" 之意。四个选项中，［A］available "可获得的，可利用的" 符合题意。［B］reliable "可靠的，值得信赖的"；［C］identifiable "可识别的，可确认的"；［D］suitable "合适的，适当的" 均不符语义。句子大意为："大脑总是能使气味接收器对那些不熟悉的或紧急的信号处于戒备状态…"。

20. 选［B］。语法结构题。might indicate the danger of fire 修饰的是前文中的 the smell of smoke，加上空格前又有逗号将其与前文隔开，所以此处是非限制性定语从句，应填入［B］which。［A］that 用于限制性定语从句中；［C］those 是复数，不能用于指代 the smell of smoke，且不符合句法要求；如果选［D］it 的话，那就组成一个完整的句子了，it 前就必须添加连接词，故 it 也不适用于此处。

Test 7

1. 选［A］。逻辑推理题。前文说了国际商务交流中需要良好的外语水平和跨文化交际技巧。这里说美国人在这两方面都不在行，可见是转折关系，故填［A］however。［B］"因而，从此"，表因果；［C］"此外，而且"，表递进；［D］"因此，所以" 也表因果。

2. 选［B］。逻辑推理题。根据句中的 consequently 可知 have not enjoyed the same level of _2_ in negotiation…是 have not been well trained in either area 导致的结果，技巧不行只能导致谈判的失败，即不成功。所以［B］success "成功" 为答案，success in…通常指在某方面的成功。［A］fulfillment "实行，履行" 在词义上有一定的干扰，但它后面通常不接介词 in，而接 of；［C］master "熟练技工，能手" 和［D］privilege "特权，特别待遇" 都脱离了语境。

3. 选［B］。逻辑推理题。根据句意，所填词是指其他国家的谈判者，也就是和美国谈判者拥有相同身份的人，故［B］"对等的人" 符合题意。［A］"敌人，仇敌" 语义不符；［C］"合作者" 和［D］"企业家" 都不能指代所有的谈判者。

4. 选 [C]。词汇辨析题。谈判是一种过程，因此 [C] process 符合。[A] proce-dure 意为 "程序，手续"；[B] progress 意为 "进步，发展"；[D] process 意为 "程序，进行" 都不符合题意。

5. 选 [B]。短语搭配题。back and forth 是固定搭配，意为 "来回地"。句子大意为：谈判就是为了达成同一目的而来回交流的过程。

6. 选 [D]。词汇辨析题。persuasion（说服）and compromise（妥协，折衷）是谈判经常要涉及到的内容，[A]、[D] 两项符合。[A] include "包含，包括"，它强调 "包括作为整体的一部分"，而 [D] involve 指 "由于同主要的有联系而必须含有"，此处主要是指有联系而必须含有，故选 [D]。[B] "推断，断定" 和 [C] "引导，管理" 语义不符，故可排除。

7. 选 [A]。短语搭配题。所填词要能介词 in 连用，[A] participate、[B] in-dulge、[D] blend 三项都符合，participate in 表示 "参加"；indulge in 表示 "沉湎于"；blend in 意为 "融入，混合"。动词短语后面接的宾语 either one 指的是 either negotiating，能构成合理搭配是 [A] 项，其他两项语义不符；[C] 项为及物动词，后面不跟介词。

8. 选 [C]。语法结构题。本题考查的是定语从句的引导词。空格前有介词，从句的关系代词指的又是物，所以只能用 which 而不用 that，故选 [C]。

9. 选 [D]。短语搭配题。[D] reach a compromise 是习惯搭配，意为 "互让和解，达成妥协"。[A] 为非及物动词，不能用于被动语态；[B] "获得，得到" 不符句意；[C] "使容易，使便利" 不以人作主语，而题中的逻辑主语即为人，故不适用于此处。

10: 选 [A]。逻辑推理题。本句话是该段的中心句，后文的内容是对其的具体阐述。后文中提到 the American represents a large multi-million-dollar corporation，选项中只有 [A] wealthy "富裕的" 才能与它形成语义复现。[B] "敏感的，灵敏的"；[C] "贫穷的，可怜的"；[D] "粗鲁的，无礼的" 都脱离了语境。原句意为：在国外很多国际商务谈判中，美国人都被认为是有钱但不具人情味儿的。

11. 选 [D]。逻辑推理题。能和句中的 foreign negotiator 形成语义场共现的只有 [D] bargaining。[A] "声称，主张"；[B] "交流，沟通"；[C] "交换，交易" 都不符合题意。原句意为：国外的谈判者们通常觉得美国人代表着有着数百万美元资产的大公司，能够支付得起任何价钱，而且从来都不讨价还价。

12. 选 [B]。语法结构题。这里的引导词是引导宾语从句的，所以用 [B] that。原句意为：美国谈判者的角色演变成了一个不通人情，到处传播信息、挥洒金钱的人。

13. 选 [A]。词汇辨析题。本段话讲的都是有关于美国谈判者的研究，因此 [A] studies 为答案。[B] "讨论，辩论" 和 [D] "研究会" 完全脱离了语境；[C] investigations 有一定的干扰性，但它通常是指详尽的，正式的或官方的调查，如：the investigation of a crime 调查罪行。本段话中没有涉及到这个层面上的含义，故不选。

14. 选［D］。短语搭配题。四个选项都能和介词 to 构成动词短语，［A］attach to "使依恋，把…放在"；［B］compare to "比拟，比作"；［C］accord to "根据"；［D］serve to "用，起…作用"。根据语义逻辑可知，许多特征是用于证实这种论调的，因此［D］项为答案。

15. 选［B］。词汇辨析题。perception 和上一段开头的 perceive 构成同源词复现，故选［B］，perception 意为 "理解，感知"。［C］"实现，完成" 和［D］"感情，知觉" 语义不符；［A］"观念，概念" 干扰性比较大，但它指的是抽象、总称的概念，用在此处不合适。

16. 选［B］。短语搭配题。in particular 是固定搭配，意为 "尤其"，其他几个单词中，只有［D］private 前面可以用 in，意为 "私下的"，但语义不符，所以选［B］。［A］"特别的，特殊的" 和［C］"本质的，实质的" 用法不符。原句意为：尤其有两个特点导致了跨文化的误解，那就是美国谈判者的率直和急躁。

17. 选［A］。短语搭配题。on the part of 为固定搭配，意为 "在…方面，就…而言"，故选［A］。

18. 选［B］。短语搭配题。由句中的 on the other hand 可知本句和上句是在将外国谈判者和美国谈判者进行对比。上句提到美国谈判者是 often insist on realizing short-term goals，由此可知外国谈判者们更倾向于 invest time in it for long-term benefits，故［B］be willing to do sth. "愿意做某事" 符合题意。［A］"厌恶的，厌烦的"；［C］"勉强的，难得到的"；［D］"容易的，随便的" 都不符合语义要求。

19. 选［D］。词汇辨析题。此处想要表达的意思为 "巩固这种关系"，［A］strengthen 和［D］solidify 符合。但 strengthen 一般指加强力量，所以排除［A］，选［D］"使（巩固），使团结"。［B］proceed 意为 "进行，继续下去"，是不及物动词，后面不能直接跟宾语，故可排除；［C］tighten 意为 "拉紧"，与宾语 the relationship 搭配不当，故也不选。

20. 选［B］。逻辑推理题。前文说到美国人的特点是直率，相比之下，其他国家的谈判者会比较喜欢委婉的方式，故选［B］indirect "间接的，迂回的"，它和本段第二句话中的 directness 构成反义同现。［A］direct "直接的，径直的"；［C］"有效的"；［D］"生效的，有效率的" 均不符合上下文语义逻辑。

Test 8

1. 选［C］。词汇辨析题。根据文章内容可知，人们智商的得分在过去几十年中急剧上升，因此认为智商不变的看法是被打破而不是得到加强或巩固，所以［C］shatters "打破，动摇（主张、意见等）" 为答案。本句的意思是：我们过去认为智商是不变的，现在这种信仰被打破了。［A］reinforces "加强，加固"；［B］enhances "提高，增强"；［D］explores "探险，探测" 语义均不符。

2. 选［C］。词汇辨析题。前文提到 IQ 的得分在过去几十年中急剧上升，此处要动摇的观念应该是 IQ "无变化"，故［C］rigidity "刚性，不变，僵化，刻板" 正确。［A］seriousness "严肃，认真"；［B］stability "稳定性"；［D］foundation "基础，根本" 均不符语义。

3. 选［B］。语法结构题。根据 the very real question of 可知所填词需表疑问之意，故先可排除［D］that。再分析句子结构可知，IQ is truly a proxy for intelligence 是个完整的句子，因此所填词不在从句中充当任何成分，而要充当引导从句的连词，故［B］"是否" 符合题意。

4. 选［C］。短语搭配题。neither...nor... 为固定搭配，故［C］项为答案。

5. 选［A］。短语搭配题。本句的意思为：从双胞胎研究到收养人研究，大量数据表明青少年晚期个体智商的差异大约有 75% 是由基因导致的。据此可知，［A］account for "说明，导致或引起构成决定性的或主要的因素" 符合句子大意。［B］respond to "回答，作出反应"；［C］take up "拿起，开始从事"；［D］match to "使和…相等" 均不符合题意。

6. 选［B］。词汇辨析题。选项中能和宾语 the lion's share of IQ difference 构成合理搭配的只有［B］explain "解释，说明…的理由或原因"，它与前文中的 account for 构成同义复现关系。本句的意思是："大多数研究智力的心理学家都认为，智商差异绝大部分是由遗传因素引起的。" 四个选项中，［A］resolve "做决定，表决"；［C］exhibit "展出，陈列"；［D］display "陈列，展览" 均不符合题意。值得注意的是，句中 the lion's share 指 "最大的一部分"。

7. 选［B］。逻辑推理题。上段提到 "大多数心理学家都认为智商差异绝大部分是由遗传因素引起的"，下句又提到 "智商的高遗传性表明环境的巨大影响力"，这两句话看似是矛盾的，因此［B］paradox "似是而非的论点，自相矛盾的话" 为正确答案。［A］dilemma "进退两难的，困难的选择"；［C］contraction "收缩，紧缩"；［D］conflict "抵触，冲突" 均不符题意。

8. 选［A］。词汇辨析题。空格处要求填入一个副词，修饰后面的形容词 powerful。从语义上判断，［A］overwhelmingly "压倒性地，不可抵抗地" 符合题意。其他三个选项，［B］fundamentally 意为 "基础地，根本地"；［C］admittedly 意为 "公认地，无可否认地"；［D］adequately 意为 "充分地" 均不符合题目语义要求。

9. 选［B］。词汇辨析题。空格处要求填入一个动词，其宾语为 mystery "神秘的事物"。四个选项中，［A］retrieve 意为 "重新得到"；［B］untangle 意为 "解开，理清（某个让人迷惑或复杂难解的事物）"；［C］repel 意为 "击退，抵制"；［D］dissipate 意为 "驱散，消散，浪费（金钱或时间）"。由此可见，

untangle 最符合题意，因此选项［B］为正确答案。

10. 选［D］。短语搭配题。选项中能以人作主语，且能以人作宾语的有［C］caught up "追上，吸住" 和［D］teamed up（使）结成一队，合作，协作"，但这里要表达的意思显然不是 Dickens 追上 James Flynn，而是指他们一起合作，故［D］为答案。［A］came up "发生，出现"；［B］fit up "准备，装备（设备，房屋等）" 用法不符。

11. 选［A］。词汇辨析题。句中 the paradox 指的就是前文中的 the mystery，因此所填词要能和第9题的答案 untangle 形成同义复现关系。因此［A］resolve 意为 "决心，解决，解开（疑惑），除去或驱散（疑虑）" 符合题意。［B］revolve "旋转，考虑"；［C］revive "苏醒，回想"；［D］relieve "减轻，解除" 均不符句意。

12. 选［C］。短语搭配题。四个选项均能和 on 搭配，句中使用了 not only…but also…句型，因此 12 on 需和上题答案 resolve 构成语义复现关系，符合的只有［C］shed light on "使某事清楚明白地显示出来"。［A］start on "开始进行"；［B］turn on "开启，开始"；［D］press on "强加于" 均不符合题意。句子大意为：在本周《心理学评论》上发表的一项研究里，这对合作者提出的一种解释不仅可能消除这种似非而是的论点，而且有可能拨开迷雾，揭示决定智商的力量。

13. 选［B］。词汇辨析题。选项中能和 intelligence 构成合理动宾搭配的只有［B］shape "定形，塑造"，且和后文中的 affected 构成语义复现。［A］effect 作名词时才表示 "影响，作用"，作动词时它的意思是 "招致，实现，生效"；［C］inspire "启示，使生灵感"；［D］drive "开车，驱赶" 语义不符。

14. 选［B］。词汇辨析题。上文指出：人们的智商同时受到环境和基因的影响，但是他们的环境与智商是相匹配的。本句的意思是：基因确实起着重要的作用。由此可知，空格后的话实际上是从另一角度对前文作出阐释。因此［B］In other words "换句话说" 适用于此处。［A］In a word "总之"；［C］However "然而，可是"；［D］Hence "因此，从此" 都不能使上下文语义连贯。

15. 选［A］。词汇辨析题。本句的意思是：如果你在智力上占有先天的优势，你就极有可能喜欢上学、阅读、解题、提问以及抽象思维。四个选项中，只有［A］edge "优势，边缘" 符合题意。［B］priority "优先，优先权"；［C］effect "结果，效果，作用"；［D］precedence "优先，居先" 均不符合题意。

16. 选［D］。词汇辨析题。选项中能和 innate brainpower 构成合理动宾搭配的是［D］amplify "放大，增强"。本句的意思是：所有这些活动往往会增强你天生的智能。其他三个选项［A］determine "决定，使下定决心"；［B］accumulate "积聚，堆积"；［C］consolidate "巩固，强化" 均不能以 innate brainpower 作宾语。

17. 选［B］。逻辑推理题。multiplier effect 是 will likely study even more 的原因，

因此［B］Thanks to "由于"为答案。句子的意思是：由于倍数效应，你很有可能学到更多。［A］Despite "不管，尽管"；［C］Granted "准予，承认（某事为真）"；［D］Provided "倘若"均不符合题意。

18. 选［A］。逻辑推理题。所填词应能和上段末句中的 boosting 形成复现关系，故［A］boost 为答案。［B］booth "货摊，售货亭"；［C］boot "（长统）靴，靴子"；［D］boom "发隆隆声，兴隆"在词形上都有一些干扰，但均不符合题目的语义要求。

19. 选［B］。逻辑推理题。由上段中提到的 If you have a biological edge in intelligence, you will likely enjoy school, books, puzzles, asking questions and thinking abstractly 可知，an IQ edge 对人的智力水平是有积极影响的，故［B］positive "积极的，肯定的"为答案。本句意思见上题。四个选项中，［A］influential "有影响的，有势力的" 用来修饰 effect，语义重叠；［C］potential "潜在的，可能的"和［D］prospective "未来的，预期的"均脱离了语境。

20. 选［A］。短语搭配题。make no differenc 为固定搭配，意为 "没区别，不重要"，故选［A］makes。［B］implies "暗示，意味"；［C］suggests "建议，提出"；［D］represents "表现，象征"均不符合题意。

第三篇 翻译

第一章 题型透视

一、大纲要求

《大学英语课程教学要求》（试行）（2004）针对翻译能力提出了三个层次的要求，即一般要求，较高要求和更高要求。具体要求如下：

◆一般要求为：能借助词典对题材熟悉的文章进行汉英互译，英汉译速为每小时 300 英语单词，汉英译速为每小时 250 个汉字。译文基本流畅，能在翻译时使用适当的翻译技巧。

◆较高要求为：能借助词典翻译一般英语国家报刊上题材熟悉的文章，能摘译所学专业的英语科普文章。英汉译速为每小时 350 英语单词，汉英译速为每小时 300 个汉字。译文基本通顺、达意、无重大理解和语言错误。

◆更高要求为：能借助词典翻译应英语国家报刊上有一定难度的科普、文化、评论等文章，能翻译反映中国国情或文化的介绍性文章。英汉译速为每小时 400 英语单词，汉英译速为每小时 350 个汉字。译文内容准确，基本无误译现象，文字通顺、达意、语言错误较少。

二、题型特征

四六级考试的最后一个题型是翻译题。该部分共 5 个句子，要求考生在 5 分钟内作答完毕。答题时间有限，再加上缺乏双语翻译的训练和技巧，考生在完成这部分题目的时候会感觉压力不小。但是该题型也并非无法攻克，因为题目并非中高级口译资格证书考试的考生所形容的："翻译难，难于上青天。"，并且有一定的规律可循。

其一，考题只考查汉译英，没有英译汉。如此一来，考生训练的范围就明确很多。大学英语精读教材中，每课都有汉译英译句练习，所以考生对这一题型应该并不陌生。

其二，内容单纯，不需要专业理论知识。题目内容既没有高难度的新闻翻译、文学翻译，也不涉及科技经贸翻译中的专业知识，只是一般的短句翻译，没有大主题语境，也谈不上翻译的"信、达、雅"标准，六级程度学生完全可以处理得很到位。

其三，名为翻译，实为补全句子。考查点多为六级学习中一些重要的词汇、词组、惯用法、句型等，所填内容大多在 3～10 个单词左右。考生只需准确、规范地答题即可。

三、基本原则和评分标准

一般来说，翻译是用一种语言将另一种语言所表达的内容传达出来的活动。

翻译是实践性很强的活动，在语言操练和应用的基础阶段，学习者必须遵循一定的原则和方法。在平时的练习和六级考试中，考生们要遵循的最基本的原则是准确和通顺。所谓准确，就是把原文的意义明白无误地表达出来，没有任何偏差；通顺是指译文句子没有语法错误，符合英语表达习惯。六级考试翻译题型的评分标准如下：

◆整体内容和语言均正确，得全分。
◆结构正确，但整体意思不确切、信息不全或用词不当，得一半分。
◆整体意思正确但语言有错误，得一半分。
◆整体意思完全错误，即使结构正确也不得分。
◆大小写错误及标点符号忽略不计。

四、专项练习

1. I have had great deal of trouble _____ （跟得上班上的其他同学）.

2. The mad man was put in the soft-padded cell _____ （以免他伤害自己）.

3. A good many proposals were raised by the delegates, _____ （正如预料的那样）.

4. Most doctors recognize that medicine is as much _____ （是一门科学，也是一门艺术）.

5. Some women _____ （本来能够挣一份很好的工资） in a job instead of staying at home, but they decided not to work for the sake of the family.

6. Over a third of the population was estimated _____ （无法获得） to the health service.

7. Although punctual himself, the professor was quite used _____ （习惯了学生迟到） his lecture.

8. The price of beer _____ （从 50 美分到 4 美元不等） per liter during the summer season.

9. We'd like _____ （预订一张餐桌） five for dinner this evening.

10. There's a man at the reception desk who seems very angry and I think he means __ _____ （想找麻烦）.

答 案 与 解 析

1. 【答案】（in）keeping up with the rest of the class。
【解析】本题短语 have trouble（in）doing something "做某事有困难" 及 keep up with "赶上" the class 表示 "全体成员" 时是集合名词，另外，"the rest of + 名词" 做主语时如果这个名词是可数名词则谓语动词用复数，如果是不可数名词，谓语动词用单数。

2. 【答案】lest he（should）injure himself。

【解析】本题考查 lest "以免"，引导目的状语从句。一般要用虚拟语气，形式为 "should + 动词原形"，should 可以省略。soft-padded cell 中的 cell 是 "病室"。这是熟悉的词的不常用意思，翻译时要根据上下文判断其含义。

3. 【答案】as was to be expected。

　　【解析】考查动词不定式的被动语态结构。a good many "很多" 后面接可数名词复数。expect "预料"，这里不能换做 thought。

4. 【答案】an art as it is a science。

　　【解析】这里考查 "as much + 冠词 + 名词 + as" 结构，是 "as...as..." 结构的变形，其含义是 "同…一样多，跟…达到同一程度"。其中第二个 as 后可以接从名。Medicine "医学"。

5. 【答案】could have made a good salary。

　　【解析】本题考查 could have done 表示 "本来可以做却没有做"，for the sake of "为了"。

6. 【答案】to have no access。

　　【解析】"无法获得" 译为 have no access，这是六级词汇中的一个重要短语。在被动语态中 to 一定不能丢。

7. 【答案】to students' being late for。

　　【解析】本题考查 be used to one's doing sth. "习惯某人做某事"，although 后面省略了 he is，be late for + 名词或代词，be late to + 动词原形。

8. 【答案】ranges/varies from 50 cents to ＄4。

　　【解析】本题考查 range / vary from...to...，"在…到…范围内变化"，这里缺少谓语，因此 range 或 vary 不能少。

9. 【答案】to reserve a table for。

　　【解析】考查短语 "预定"，为多少人预定介词要用 for。

10. 【答案】to make trouble。

　　【解析】考查两个短语 make trouble "找麻烦，捣乱" 和 mean to do sth. "想要做某事"。我们还要将 "mean to do sth." 与另外一个短语 mean doing sth.（意味着做某事）区别开来。

考 点 透 视

一、词汇层次

　　仔细分析自改革以来的六级翻译真题，发现句句贴近生活，源于生活。因此我们摘录了一些贴近大学生生活的词汇。

大学学习类

application form 申请表	score/mark 分数
assessment（对学生的学习情况）评估	second Bachelor's degree 第二学位
assignment 作业	thesis oral defense 论文答辩
course arrangement 课程安排	take part in the entrance exams for post-
credit 学分	graduate schools 考研
comprehensive quality 综合素质	the craze for graduate school 考研热
dean 导师	this year's graduates 应届毕业生
diplomas and certificates 文凭	oral examination 口试
enrolment/register for 注册	participation 出勤
entry score 录取分数线	postgraduate 研究生
expand enrollment 扩招	president 校长
graduate school 研究生院	required course/compulsory course 必修课
instructor 辅导老师	school of Arts and Sciences 文理学院
letter of recommendation 推荐信	take an examination/sit an examination
optional course 选修课	参加考试
roll book 点名册	undergraduate 本科生

大学生活类

back issues 过期刊物	dormitory 宿舍
cafeteria 自助小餐厅	lecture hall 阶梯教室
call slip 索书单	library card 借书卡
campus 校园	overdue and pay a fine 过期罚款
club 学生俱乐部	renew（图书）续借
catalogue 目录	shopping mall/centre 购物中心
current account 现金账户	society 学生社团
current issues 本期刊物	student union 学生会
deposit money in a bank 存钱	student loan 助学贷款

| dining hall 食堂 | withdraw/draw cash 取钱 |

交通规则类

amber light 黄灯	red light 红灯
crash 撞车	speed limit 速度限制
cross road 十字路	traffic jam 交通拥挤
drive without license 无证驾驶	traffic light 红绿灯
excessive speed 超速	traffic police 交通警察
green light 绿灯	traffic regulation 交通规则
narrow road 窄路	zebra stripes 斑马线
parking place 停车场	

观光旅游类

check-in 登记入住	sightseeing tour 观光旅游
check-out 结账离开（退房）	star-rated hotel 星级饭店
holiday resort 度假区	tour group 旅游团队
one-way ticket 单程机票	tour guide 导游
place of sightseeing 游览胜地	travel service 旅行社
room service 客房服务	tourist attraction 旅游胜地
round-trip ticket 往返机票	vacation tour 度假旅游

社会热点类

17th CPC National Congress 中国共产党第十七次全国代表大会	net citizen 网民
assistant president 总裁助理	off line 下线
advance with times 与时俱进	New Human Being 新新人类
bid for the Olympic Games 申办奥运会	online love affair 网恋
birth control 计划生育	online shopping 网上购物
brain drain 人才外流	online trading platform 网上交易平台
bubble economy 泡沫经济	people oriented/people foremost 以人为本
care for senior citizens 关心老年人	pioneering spirit 首创精神
civil servant 公务员	preserve the ecological environment 保护生态环境
cost of living/income maintenance 生活费用	prime time 黄金时段
comprehensive national power 综合国力	puppy love 早恋
compulsory education 义务教育	rate of unemployment 失业率
computer crime 电脑犯罪	rural population 乡村人口

dropout student 失学儿童	net friend 网友
eliminate illiteracy 扫盲	self-protection awareness 自我保护意识
excusive agency 专卖店	self-service ticketing 无人售票
economic globalization/economic integration 经济全球化	shopping online 网上购物
	single parent family 单亲家庭
education for all-round development 素质教育	stock 股票
exam-oriented education 应试教育	surf the Internet 网上冲浪
fund 基金	sustainable development 可持续发展
	team spirit 团队精神
intellectual property rights 知识产权	reduce study load 学生减负
juvenile delinquency 青少年犯罪	university students' innovative undertaking 大学生创业
knowledge-based economy 知识经济	
laid-off worker 下岗职工	virtual net 虚拟网络
migrant worker 民工	win-win situation 双赢局面

二、语句层次

对单句的翻译有时还会涉及到语句层次上的知识点，以下是对翻译中常见的句型的分析：

1 否定句

（1）部分否定句

部分否定句虽然是否定句的形式，但其否定意义只局限于整体中的一部分。其形式为："概括词 all，every 等 + not + 谓语动词"，可以用于这一句型的常见词有：all，both，every，everybody，everything，everywhere，always，altogether，entirely 和 wholly 等。

【示例1】

> What we know about him is that ＿＿＿＿＿＿＿＿＿＿＿（他并非总是这么悲伤）.
>
> 【答案】he is not always so sorrow。
> 【解析】本题考查 always 在部分否定句中的应用，what 引导的是主语从句。

【示例2】

> The businessman is ＿＿＿＿＿＿＿＿＿＿＿（不可以完全信任的）.
>
> 【答案】not to be entirely trusted。
> 【解析】本题考查 entirely 在部分否定句中的应用，注意这里要用被动语态。

【示例3】

> If the conference is lacking in colloquy（自由讨论）, the people attended
> _____（不会完全同意）the program.

【答案】won't wholly /completely agree to。

【解析】本题考查 wholly/completely 在部分否定句中的应用，be lacking in "缺乏"，attended 是过去分词做后置定语。

（2）完全否定句

完全否定句是针对部分否定句而言的，这种否定是彻底的。其形式为："no，none 等否定词 + 肯定式谓语"，常见的可以用于这一句型的否定意义的词有：no，none，nobody，nothing，nowhere，anyhow，neither，never 等。

【示例1】

> After the wonderful ball, Mathilde _____（哪都找不到她丢
> 失的项链）.

【答案】can find her lost necklace nowhere。

【解析】本题考查 nowhere 在完全否定句中的应用，这是莫泊桑《项链》中的情节。

【示例2】

> Hard as it rains, but _____（我今天无论如何都得回家）.

【答案】anyhow I will go back home today。

【解析】本题主要考查 anyhow 在完全否定句中的应用，anyhow 意思是"无论如何都不"。

【示例3】

> How can we start since _____（什么都没准备好）?

【答案】nothing is ready。

【解析】本题主要考查 nothing 在完全否定句中的应用，注意疑问词直接接动词不定式的用法。

（3）双重否定句

其形式一为："主语 + cannot + help/refrain/ keep + from + 动名词"。help from，refrain from，keep from 等词具有"抑制，忍住"等否定含义，与 cannot 等连用，具有双重否定的意义。

【示例1】

> I _____（忍不住表达我的崇拜之情）his insight and resolu-
> tion.

【答案】cannot refrain from expressing my warm admiration for。

【解析】本题主要考查 cannot + help/refrain/keep 在双重否定句中的应用，from 后接动名词。

【示例2】

I _____（忍不住偷听）what he said.

【答案】couldn't help overhearing。

【解析】本题主要考查 cannot + help/refrain/keep 在双重否定句中的应用，what 引导宾语从句。

其形式二："主语 + cannot + but/choose but/help but + 动词原形"。

【示例1】

If you insist on having been here yesterday, I _____（不得不认为你在说谎）.

【答案】cannot but think you are lying。

【解析】本题主要考查 cannot + but 在双重否定句中的应用，注意 but 后面接动词原形，cannot but 在这里有"不得不"的意思。

【示例2】

Since you don't abide by the rules, I _____（我除了让你离开这所大学之外别无选择）.

【答案】cannot choose but ask you to leave this university。

【解析】本题主要考查 cannot + help/refrain/keep 在双重否定句中的应用，abide by 意思是"遵守"。

其形式三："（There be）no + 主语 + but + 谓语"。在此句型中，but 是关系代词，既代替前面的名词，又引导后面的从句，并且具有否定意义。

【示例1】

He is so devoted to his experiment that _____（没有人感觉不到他对事业的热爱）.

【答案】not a /no man but felt his love to his career。

【解析】考查双重否定句型"no + 主语 + but + 谓语"，no 相当于 not a 或 not any。

【示例2】

Don't always stick to routinism（墨守成规），and you must know _____（没有无例外的规则）.

【答案】there is no rule but has its exceptions。

【解析】本题考查双重否定句，注意这里 but 后的谓语动词要和 but 前的主语保持一致，要与 cannot help but 区别开。

2 判断句 ⌄

(1) 强调判断句

其形式一为："主语 + be + no/none + other than/but + 表语（强调内容）"。

【示例1】

The economic crisis has been created by _____（不是别人而是垄断资本家）.

【答案】none other than the monopoly capitalists。

【解析】本题主要考查 none 在强调判断句中的应用，none other than 意思是 "不是…而是"。

【示例2】

It is _____（不是别人而是你最好的朋友）who betray you.

【答案】no other people but your best friend。

【解析】本题主要考查 no other but 在强调判断句中的应用，no other but 意为 "不是…正是"。

其形式二为："主语 + be + nothing + （else）but/else than/less than + 表语"。

【示例1】

My teacher told me _____（紧张只是害怕而已）.

【答案】pressure is nothing but fear。

【解析】本题主要考查 nothing but 在强调判断句中的应用，nothing but 的意思是 "只是"。

【示例2】

Britney's behavior during the interview was nothing _____（只是彻底的妥协）.

【答案】less than compromise。

【解析】本题主要考查 nothing less than 在强调判断句中的应用，nothing less than 的意思是 "完全，不亚于"。

其形式三为："It is/was + 强调部分 + that/who + 从句"。

【示例1】

It was _____（正是由于水涨了）that they could not cross the river.

【答案】because the water had risen。

【解析】本题主要考查最基本的强调句型，因为所强调部分为原因状语，且为句子，所以应该使用 because 引导的原因状语从句，注意"水涨"要用不及物动词 rise，不用 raise。

【示例2】

All the people want to know ＿＿＿＿＿＿＿＿（可能是在什么地方发生这个事故的）.

【答案】where it might be that the accident happened。

【解析】本题既考查强调句型，又同时将其运用到充当宾语从句的疑问句中，绕了两个弯，我们可以将其还原，It might be in some place that the accident happened，转化为特殊疑句：where might it be that the accident happened，再充当 know 的宾语，即充当宾语从句，将疑问语序调整为陈述语序：where it might be that the accident happened，即最终答案。

（2）正反判断句

其形式一为："主语 + be + not + 表语 A + but + 表语 B"。

【示例】

＿＿＿＿＿＿＿＿＿＿＿＿（赚钱不应该是我们的最终目标），but a journey to realize our self-worth.

【答案】To earn money shouldn't be our destination。

【解析】本题主要考查最要的正反判断句，根据后面的 journey 一词，在这最终目标译为

其形式二："（It is）not...that（who）...，but...that（who）..."。

【示例】

The tragedy is not in that you don't know, but in that ＿＿＿＿＿＿＿＿（不知道自己无知）.

【答案】you do not know that you don't know。

【解析】本题主要考查正反判断句。这个句子 not in ...but in 后面接对等成分，翻译时不要把"无知"直接译为 ignorance，根据前半句可知这里应该和前面对称。整句话的意思是了"悲剧不在于我们无知，而在于我们不知道自己无知。

（3）比较判断句

其形式一："主语 + be + less/more + 表语 A + than + 表语 B"。

【示例1】

The suggestion you made is ＿＿＿＿＿＿＿＿（比他的建议更切实可行）.

【答案】more practicable than the one he made。

【解析】本题主要考查基本的比较判断句，注意这里比较的对象是"建议"而不是两个人，由于前面"建议"已译，后面的就要用 one 来代替，one 在比较判断句中的做代词的用法是重要考点。

【示例 2】

> The girls in your class are _____ （比我们班的女生活跃）.

【答案】more active than those in our class。
【解析】本题主要考查比较判断句，those 在这里是代词用法和上句中的 one 一样，这里代替复数名词。

其形式二："主语 + be + rather 表语 A + than + 表语 B"。

【示例】

> He who can recognize you at the second time _____ （与其说他记性好，不如说他心细）.

【答案】is rather careful than retentive。
【解析】本题考查比较判断句型"rather...than..."的用法，它的意思是"与其说…不如说…"，rather 和 than 后接对称成分。

其形式三："主语 + be + not so much + 表语 A + as + 表语 B"。

【示例】

> It's not so much that the machine is out of order _____ （而是我还没有学会操作）.

【答案】as（that）I have not learned to operate it。
【解析】本题主要考查 not so much ...as 句型，在这个句子中 A、B 是对称的从句。

3 倍数表示句型 ⟱

其形式一："主语 + be + 倍数 + that of + 被比较对象或 as + 形容词 + as + 被比较对象"。

【示例】

> Although he eat less, _____ （他的体重却是我的三倍）.

【答案】his weight is three times that of mine。
【解析】本题主要考查 that of 在倍数表达法中的应用，如果比较的对象是复数则用 those of。

其形式二："主语 + increase/rise/attain + （to）倍数 + compared with + 被比较对象"。

【示例】

> The production of integrated circuits ＿＿＿＿＿＿＿＿＿＿＿＿＿（比去年增加了两倍）.
>
> 【答案】has been increased to three times as compared with last year。
> 【解析】本题主要考查 increase 在倍数表达法中的应用，本句中要用被动语态。

其形式三："主语 + increase +（by）倍数 + compared with"。

【示例】

> People who take that medicine can increase metabolic rates（代谢率）＿＿＿＿＿＿＿＿＿（提高到原来的 2 倍或 3 倍）compared with other people.
>
> 【答案】by two or three times。
> 【解析】本题主要考查倍数表达法，注意"提高到"和"提高了"的区别。

4　比较句型

（1）等比句型

其形式一："主语 + 谓语 + as + 形容词/副词 + as + 被比较对象。

【示例】

> He studies English for only one year, so ＿＿＿＿＿＿＿＿＿＿＿＿＿＿（他英语说得不如你流利）.
>
> 【答案】he doesn't speak English as/so fluently as you。
> 【解析】本题主要考查最基本的等比句型，前一个 as 是副词，后一个 as 是连词，肯定句中前一个 as 不能换成 so。

其形式二："主语 + 谓语 + no more/less + 形容词/副词 + than + 被比较对象"。

【示例 1】

> Thinking is much ＿＿＿＿＿＿＿＿＿＿＿＿（远非做难）.
>
> 【答案】less difficult than doing。
> 【解析】本题主要考查 less…than 的用法，比较的对象 much 常修饰比较级。

【示例 2】

> Jack and John don't do well in the school work because ＿＿＿＿＿＿＿＿＿（杰克和约翰谁都不勤奋）.
>
> 【答案】Jack is no more diligent than John。
> 【解析】本题主要考查 no more than 在比较句型中的应用，意为"都不"。

（2）其他比较句型

其形式：would（had）rather…than/…rather than…和…would sooner than…。

【示例1】

> _____（与其为失败后悔），why not try again?

【答案】 Rather than regretting for the failure。

【解析】 本题主要考查 rather than 在比较句型中的应用，why not 后接动词原形。提出建议。

【示例2】

> In reality, a service requirement _____（降低义务工作的价值而非提升它的价值）.

【答案】 would sooner lessen the value of volunteering than heighten it。

【解析】 本题主要考查 sooner...than 在比较句型中的应用。

5 程度句型

（1）带 so 和 such 的程度句型

其形式一："主句 + so/such...that 从句"。

【示例】

> It was（如此精彩的展览）that I went to see it several times.

【答案】 so good an exhibition/such a good exhibition。

【解析】 本题主要考查 so/such...that，"如此…以至于"，注意不定冠词的位置。

其形式二："主语 + 谓语 + 程度状语 so/such + 形容词副词 + as + 不定式/for + 动名词"。

【示例】

> We'd _____（太自信）as to believe the business is in the bag。

【答案】 never be so cocky。

【解析】 本题主要考查 so...as to 结构，be in the bag 的意思是"胜券在握"。

（2）带 too 的程度句型

其形式一："主语 + 谓语 + too + 形容词/副词 + 不定式"。

【示例】

> Don't be conceited. _____（这个箱子太重，你搬不动）.

【答案】 This box is too heavy for you to carry。

【解析】 本题主要考查 too...to 句型，注意两点：1. 本身含有否定意义，不再用否定副词 not。2. 动词 carry 后不要有 it。

其形式二："主语 + 谓语 + only too + 形容词/副词 + 不定式"。

【示例】

_____（这对双胞胎长得像极了，不好区分）. No wonder he makes a mistake.

【答案】The twins are only too similar to tell apart。

【解析】本题主要考查 only too...to, only too "极"；tell apart "区分"。

6 倒装让步句型

其形式一："表语 + as + 主语（代词）+ 系动词，+ 主句"。

【示例】

_____（虽然他还是个孩子），he has to learn how to earn his living.

【答案】Child as he is。

【解析】本题主要考查 "表语 + as" 构成的倒装让步句型，注意表语是可数名词，前面不加不定冠词，earn one's living "谋生"。

其形式二："表语 + 系动词 + 主语（名词），+ 主句"。

【示例】

_____（出席会议的有史密斯教授和很多尊贵的客人），so make sure everything is ready ahead of schedule.

【答案】Present at the meeting are Professor Smith and many well-beloved guests。

【解析】本题主要考查表语提到系动词前的倒装句型，well-beloved "尊贵的"。

其形式三："副词或动词原形 + as + 主语…，+ 主句"。

【示例】

_____（虽然他确实很努力），he never seems able to do the work satisfactorily.

【答案】Try hard as he does。

【解析】本题主要考查 "表语 + as" 构成的倒装让步句型，does 在这是强调动词，后面接动词原形。

7 It 作形式主语时的常见句型

其形式一："It is + 形容词 + that∕wh-从句…"。

【示例 1】

It is proper that _____（你理解我所认为的我们政府的基本原则）and consequently those which ought to shape its Administration.

【答案】you should understand what I deem the essential principles of our government。

【解析】 本题主要考查 it is + 形容词 + that 句型，常用在这个句型中的形容词有 important，necessary，proper 等，that 从句要用虚拟语气。

【示例2】

It is important ＿＿＿＿＿＿＿＿＿＿＿＿＿＿＿＿＿＿＿＿＿＿（保持生态平衡）。

【答案】 that we（should）keep the balance of nature。
【解析】 本题考查 it 作形式主语的用法，英语中的主语从句有时为了避免头重脚轻，常用 it 作形式主语，而真正的主语用 that 引导放在后面。

其形式二："It + 不及物动词 + that..."。

【示例】

＿＿＿＿＿＿＿＿＿＿＿＿＿（其结果当然是那些包括经济政策在内的政治决定可以得到解释）according to the same principles and methodologies（方法论）developed within economics throughout its history.

【答案】 It follows that political decisions，including those of economic policy can be explained。
【解析】 本题主要考查 It follows that 句型，follow 意思是"其结果当然是"。

其形式三："It + be + 名词 + that..."。

【示例1】

All the activities are over. It is ＿＿＿＿＿＿＿＿＿＿（是孩子们睡觉的时间了）。

【答案】 time that the children went to bed/ high time that the children should go to bed. 。
【解析】 本题主要考查 it is time that 句型，从句中用一般过去时或 should + 动词原形。

【示例2】

He has no intention of making progress so ＿＿＿＿＿＿＿＿＿＿＿＿＿＿＿＿（你老是帮助他是没有用的）。

【答案】 it is no use that you always help him。
【解析】 本题考查 "It is no use that..." 的用法，意思是"做…是没有用的"。

其形式四："It + be + done + that..."。

【示例】

＿＿＿＿＿＿＿＿＿＿＿＿（据报道一部由不知名的导演拍的电影）won the first prize in this film festival。

【答案】It is reported that a film directed by an unknown director。

【解析】本题主要考查 it is reported/said that 句型，这类句子翻译为"据报道""据说"等。

三、专项练习

将下列句子中的空缺部分按照括号后的要求翻译出来。

1. _____（我们没有人料到主席会出现）at the party. We thought he was still in hospital. （完全否定）

2. Some young people would rather try hard themselves to go through life than _____（求助于他们的父母）with a sense of guilty. （比较句型）

3. It is a pity that _____（我们呆在家里）when we have such fine weather. （it 做形式主语）.

4. _____（周日晚餐特别受欢迎）, usually followed by musical performances. （倒装句型）

5. _____（并非所有的功能）needs to handle every possible error. （部分否定）

6. Most genius is _____（只是劳动和勤奋）. （强调判断句）

7. I am very ill, _____（不是身体上的，而是精神上的）. （正反判断句）

8. It is not that I dislike the work, _____（而是我没有时间）. （正反判断句）

9. _____（尽管他想努力自己完成）, he couldn't finish his design without others' help. （倒装句型）

10. It was amazing that _____（10 个月建成一栋 24 层的楼）. （it 做形式主语）

11. Don't you be told _____（这两件衣服并非都在打折的）. （部分否定）

12. Expensive as it is, but _____（我今天无论如何都不放弃）. （全部否定）

13. The rich have their annoyances because _____（有些人，除了钱之外一无所有）. （强调判断句）

14. The new building's area _____（将是旧楼的两倍）. （倍数表达）

15. Don't always stick to routinism, and you must know _____（没有无例外的规则）. （双重否定句）

16. The tall figure that I saw _____（不是别人，正是我们的

校长）。（正反判断句）

17. Although many people like cake, _____（但并非人人都喜欢甜食）。（部分否定）

18. He is so depressed _____（他此时此刻的心情是无法用语言来形容的）。（全部否定）

19. It is a matter of common experience _____（物体在水中比在空气中轻）。（比较句型）

20. Hardly _____（他还没做完试卷）when the bell rang（倒装句型）。

■■■■ 答 案 与 解 析 ■■■■

1. 【答案】None of us expected the chairman to turn up。

【解析】本题考查全部否定。turn up "出现"，expect somebody to do something. 意为"料到某人做某事，期待某人做某事"。注意翻译时前后句子时态要一致。

2. 【答案】turn to their parents。

【解析】考查比较句型 would rather…than…，rather 和 than 后面的成分对称，这里接的是动词不定式，turn to sb. "求助于某人"。

3. 【答案】we should stay at home。

【解析】本题考查"It is + 形容词 + that 从句"，常用在这个句型中的形容词有 important，necessary，proper 等，that 从句要用虚拟语气。

4. 【答案】Especially popular were his Sunday evening dinners。

【解析】本题考查"表语 + 系动词 + 主语（名词）+ 主句"倒装句型。followed 是过去分词做定语修饰 dinners。主语太长，为了使句子保持平衡，将表语提到句首形成倒装。

5. 【答案】Not every function。

【解析】本题考查 not every…形式的部分否定。

6. 【答案】nothing but labor and diligence。

【解析】本题考查"be nothing but + 表语"结构的比较判断句。意思是"只是…"

7. 【答案】not bodily，but mentally。

【解析】考查正反判断句型，"主语 + be + not + 表语 A + but + 表语 B"表示"不是…而是"。A、B 可以是从句。

8. 【答案】but that I have no time。

【解析】与第7题的考查点相同，只是本题这里的表语是从句。

9. 【答案】Try as he would。

【解析】考查"动词原形 + as + 主语，+ 主句"形式的倒装。As 有时可以换成

though。意思是"尽管···，但是"。

10. 【答案】a 24-story building is completed only in 10 months。

【解析】本题考查"it is + 形容词 + that 从句"句型，汉语中的无主句多翻译为被动句，翻译的时候注意。

11. 【答案】both of the clothes are not on sale。

【解析】本题主要考查部分否定句，本句的主句是一个否定的一般疑问句，后接了一个宾语从句。be on sale "在打折"。

12. 【答案】anyhow I will not give it up。

【解析】本题主要考查完全否定句，anyhow 意思是"无论如何都不"。

13. 【答案】some of them have nothing else but money。

【解析】本题考查强调判断句"主语 + be + nothing + （else）but/else than/less than + 表语"。

14. 【答案】will be attain to 2 times of the old one。

【解析】本题考查倍数表达法，of 引出比较的对象，one 指代前面出现过的 building，翻译的时候要顾及到句子的前后，不要只看所要填的部分。

15. 【答案】there is no rule but has its exceptions。

【解析】本题考查双重否定句，"（There be）no + 主语 + but + 谓语"。注意这里 but 后的谓语动词要和 but 前的主语保持一致，要与 cannot help but 区别开。

16. 【答案】was none other than our president。

【解析】本题考查强调判断句型"主语 + be + no/none + other than/but + 表语（强调内容）"，意思是"不是···正是···"。

17. 【答案】everyone doesn't like sweet food。

【解析】本题主要考查部分否定句，还要注意的一点是 although 不能和 but 连用，这里出题人设了个小陷阱，一定不要掉进去。

18. 【答案】None of the words can describe his feelings。

【解析】本题考查全部否定"None of …"。

19. 【答案】that bodies are lighter in water than they are in air。

【解析】本题考查 it 做形式主语的句型 it is + 名词 + that 从句，"物体"为 body。

20. 【答案】could he finish his test paper。

【解析】本题考查含有否定意义的副词 hardly 提到句首引起句子倒装的情况。

第三章 技巧熟悉

　　翻译的实践性决定了一个事实，即，要做好翻译，必须加强这方面的训练，因为大家都明白"熟能生巧"的道理。同时，掌握一定的翻译技巧和方法也是必需的。好的方法不但可以帮助我们解决一些翻译难题，保证我们译文的质量，而且大大地省去了动笔前考生绞尽脑汁地探求"最佳译法"的过程，为考试节约了宝贵的时间。根据六级考试新题型的特点和要求，我们有针对性地编写了一些对考生应试有所帮助的翻译技巧和方法，以供考生参考。

一、十大翻译技巧

1 词汇层次

　　对单句翻译，主要体现在词语层次方面的翻译，常见的理论有：词语选择法、词义引申法、词义褒贬法、正反译法、词类转换法、增译法、省略法等。

（1）词汇选择法

　　由于汉语和英语的表达习惯和词语搭配的不同，同一个汉语词语与不同的词语搭配时，英文译文会用到不同的词语来表达。因此，必须根据词汇的搭配关系和句子中充当的成分来确定译文所选词语。

【示例1】

> With the development of the modern weapon, ＿＿＿＿＿＿＿＿＿＿＿（没人能想象出全面核战争的后果）.
>
> 【答案】nobody can envisage the consequences of total nuclear war。
> 【解析】这里的"想象"envisage，不是视觉效果的"想象"，而是对将来的一种预测，可用 foresee 或 foretell 来解释。

【示例2】

> John is a man like imagining. ＿＿＿＿＿＿＿＿＿＿＿（他把那所房子想像成有传奇色彩的废墟）.
>
> 【答案】He visualized the house as a romantic ruin. 。
> 【解析】visualize 是指视觉的"想象"，在脑子里勾画出 picture，可用 imagine 来解释。

（2）词义引申法

　　在翻译过程中，有时会遇到一些无法找到对等英语词汇的情况，这就需要根据其基本词义进行引申。

【示例1】

> Man has always ＿＿＿＿＿＿＿＿＿＿＿＿＿（对自然界的运行规律怀有很大的兴趣）.
>
> 【答案】 had a great interest in how nature works。
> 【解析】 句中"运行"一词在英文中很难找到相对应的词语，所以译文用短语"how nature works"来表达"自然界的运行规律"，其中"work"一词就是运用其引申意义。

【示例2】

> Every life has its ＿＿＿＿＿＿＿＿＿＿＿＿＿（有甜有苦），so we must face both success and failure.
>
> 【答案】 roses and thorns。
> 【解析】 英语里通常用 rose "玫瑰" 和 thorn "荆棘" 来形容有苦也有甜

（3）词义褒贬法

　　由于在汉语的表达中褒贬意义通常很明显，而英语词汇中很多词都是中性的，其褒贬含义有时不是很明显，因此在翻译时，要尽量选择能表现褒贬色彩的词语。

【示例1】

> I didn't expect that their feudal ideas would be so ＿＿＿＿＿＿＿＿＿＿＿＿＿（顽固不化）.
>
> 【答案】 incorrigibly obstinate。
> 【解析】 obstinate "倔强的，顽固的"，多用作贬义。

【示例2】

> You will be sorry ＿＿＿＿＿＿＿＿＿＿＿＿＿（要是你在课堂上玩什么鬼花样的话）.
>
> 【答案】 if you try anything funny in class。
> 【解析】 funny 这个词有时可以是褒义词"风趣的"，也可以是中性词"蹊跷的"，还可以是贬义词"搞鬼的""放肆的"，要根据上下文语境灵活翻译。

（4）正反译法

　　由于语言习惯的不同，汉英两种语言在正说与反说方面也常常不同。英语中有些从正面说，汉语则从反面来解释；而对那些从反面说的句子，汉语则可以从正面来解释。

【示例1】

> The above facts ＿＿＿＿＿＿＿＿＿＿＿＿ （使人们不能不得出以下结论）.

【答案】insist on the following conclusions。
【解析】"不能不得出"，双重否定，而 insist on "坚持，强调"，表示肯定。

【示例2】

> She ＿＿＿＿＿＿＿＿＿＿＿＿ （要等你答应帮助以后才肯走）.

【答案】won't go away until you promise to help her。
【解析】"才走"，汉语是肯定形式，翻译成英语用 not...until 表示。

(5) 词类转换法

　　由于英汉两种语言的结构和表达方式不同，很多情况下，找不到意思对等而且词性相同的词语或短语，这时就必须根据英语的语言表达习惯，对词类进行转换。

【示例1】

> Too much exposure to TV programs will ＿＿＿＿＿＿＿＿＿＿ （大大地损坏孩子们视力）.

【答案】do great harm to the eyesight of children。
【解析】动词转名词。

【示例2】

> Thanks to the introduction of our reform and opening policy, ＿＿＿＿＿＿＿＿＿＿＿＿ （我国的综合国力有了明显的增强）.

【答案】our comprehensive national strength has greatly improved。
【解析】名词转动词。

(6) 增译法

　　在翻译时，有时为了使所翻译的译文更符合英语的表达习惯而增加一些必要的词语。指根据英汉两种语言不同的思维方式、语言习惯和表达方式，在翻译时增添一些词、短句或句子，以便更准确地表达出原文所包含的意义。这种方式多半用在汉译英里。汉语无主句较多，而英语句子一般都要有主语，所以在翻译汉语无主句的时候，除了少数可用英语无主句、被动语态或 "There be..." 结构来翻译以外，一般都要根据语境补出主语，使句子完整。英汉两种语言在名词、代词、连词、介词和冠词的使用方法上也存在很大差别。英语中代词使用频率较高，凡说到人的器官和归某人所有的或与某人有关的事物时，必须在前面加上物主代词。因此，在汉译英时需要增补物主代词，而在英译汉时又需要根据情况适当地删减。英语词与词、词组与词组以及句子与句子的逻辑关系一般用连词来表示，而汉语则往往通过上下文和语序来表示这种关系。因此，在汉译英时常常需要增补连词。英语句子离不开介词和冠词。另外，在汉译英时还要注意增补一些原文中暗含而没有明言的词语和一些概括性、注释性的词语，以确保译文意思的完整。总之，通过增译，一是保证译文语法结构的完整，二是保证译文意思的明确。

【示例1】

> The desert animals can hide ＿＿＿＿＿＿＿＿＿＿＿（白天的炎热天气）.
>
> 【答案】 themselves from the heat during the daytime。
>
> 【解析】增译了代词 themselves，hide 是及物动词后面必须有宾语，这是根据语法要求增译。

【示例2】

> Learning is endless as the saying, "＿＿＿＿＿＿＿＿＿＿＿（活到老，学到老）".
>
> 【答案】 we live and learn。
>
> 【解析】这是根据语言习惯将汉语的无主句翻译成英语时补出主语 we。

【示例3】

> Even the people in the fascist countries ＿＿＿＿＿＿＿＿＿＿＿（也被剥夺了人权）.
>
> 【答案】 were stripped of their human rights。
>
> 【解析】增译物主代词 their，整句话的意思是：即使法西斯本国的人民也被剥夺了人权。

【示例4】

> If only ＿＿＿＿＿＿＿＿＿＿＿（我能看到四个现代化实现该有多好啊）！
>
> 【答案】 I could see the realization of the four modernizations。
>
> 【解析】增译主句。

（7）省译法

汉语中为了讲究句子的平衡、气势、韵调，常常使用排比、对仗、重复等修辞手段。因此汉语句子中，一些词或词组重复使用的现象和结构类似、含义相同的几个词组连用的现象是相当普遍的。因此在翻译时，原文中含义重复的词语往往只译出其中的一个。这是与增译法相对应的一种翻译方法，即删去不符合目标语思维习惯、语言习惯和表达方式的词，以避免译文累赘。

【示例1】

> The Chinese government has always _____（重视环境保护工作）.

> 【答案】attached great importance to environmental protection。
> 【解析】省译名词"工作"。

【示例2】

> We ought to know the problem is both _____（心理和生理两个方面）.

> 【答案】psychological and physical。
> 【解析】本题考查省译技巧。译文不需添加"两个方面"这个概括性的词，因为那样使得句子听起来就不够通顺自然，所以根据句意及表达的需要，进行省译。只译"心理和生理"，因为它们在句子中作表语，所以用形容词形式。

2 语句层次

对单句的翻译有时还涉及到了语句层次上的技巧，其中包括：

（1）拆句法和合并法

这是两种相对应的翻译方法。拆句法是把一个长而复杂的句子拆译成若干个较短、较简单的句子，通常用于英译汉；合并法是把若干个短句合并成一个长句，一般用于汉译英。汉语强调意合，结构较松散，因此简单句较多；英语强调形合，结构较严密，因此长句较多。所以汉译英时要根据需要注意利用连词、分词、介词、不定式、定语从句、独立结构等把汉语短句连成长句；而英译汉时又常常要在原句的关系代词、关系副词、主谓连接处、并列或转折连接处、后续成分与主体的连接处，以及意群结束处将长句切断，译成汉语分句。这样就可以基本保留英语语序，顺译全句，顺应现代汉语长短句相替、单复句相间的句法修辞原则。

【示例1】

> The people presented point out that _____（同中国加强合作，符合美国的利益）.

> 【答案】increased cooperation with China is in the interest of the United States。
> 【解析】将前一句中的谓语动词译为非谓语，两句合并，意思明了。

【示例2】

> I wish to _____（我要感谢你们无与伦比的盛情款待。中国人民正是以这种热情好客而闻名世界的）.

【答案】thank you for the incomparable hospitality for which the Chinese people are justly famous throughout the world。

【解析】抓住第二句中的关键点"这种",将后一句译为定语从句。句中的"这个""这些"都是翻译时明显的合并信号。

（2）倒置法

　　汉语中，定语修饰语和状语修饰语往往位于被修饰语之前；在英语中，许多修饰语常常位于被修饰语之后，因此翻译时往往要把原文的语序颠倒过来。倒置法通常用于英译汉，即对英语长句按照汉语的习惯表达法进行前后调换，按意群进行全部倒置，原则是使汉语译句安排符合现代汉语论理叙事的一般逻辑顺序。有时倒置法也用于汉译英。

【示例1】

I believe strongly that ＿＿＿＿＿＿＿＿＿＿＿（英国依然应该是欧共体中的一个积极的和充满活力的成员，这是符合我国人民利益的）.

【答案】it is in the interest of my countrymen that Britain should remain an active and energetic member of the European Community。

【解析】部分倒置。

【示例2】

At this moment，through the wonder of telecommunications，＿＿＿＿＿＿＿＿＿（看到和听到我们讲话的人比整个世界历史上任何其他这样的场合都要多）。

【答案】more people are seeing and hearing what we say than on any other occasions in the whole history of the world。

【解析】部分倒置。

（3）成分转译法

　　英汉两种语言，由于表达方式不尽相同，在具体英译汉时，有时往往需要转换一下句子成分，才能使翻译达到逻辑正确、通顺流畅、重点突出等目的。句子成分转译作为翻译的一种技巧，其内容和形式都比较丰富，运用范围也相当广泛：主语可以变成状语、定语、宾语、表语；谓语可以变成主语、定语、表语；定语可以变成状语、主语；宾语可以变成主语等等。

【示例1】

China's national ball is Table tennis，＿＿＿＿＿＿＿＿＿＿＿（中国到处都打乒乓球）.

【答案】and it's played all over China。

【解析】题干包含两个分句，前分句的末尾提到了 Table tennis，因此后分句用 Table tennis 作主语能起到一个很好的衔接作用。又因为"Table tennis"是受动者，故应用被动语态。"中国到处"译为"all over China"，简洁而精确。

【示例 2】

_____（人家没告诉过她）Bette's name, or she'd forgotten it.

【答案】She hadn't been told。

【解析】没有指出具体没有告诉她的人，因此将汉语中做宾语的"她"译成主语。

二、三种基本翻译方法

翻译的技巧有若干种，且变化多端，但万变不离其宗的翻译方法有以下三种：

1 直译

直译不是死译，而是指基本保留原有句子结构，照字面意思翻译。原文结构与汉语的结构是一致的，照译即可。但如果原文结构与汉语的不一致，仍然采取直译的方法，就成"死译"了。

【示例】

The chief _____（像过街老鼠）.

【答案】like a rat crossing the street。

【解析】直译后不改变所表达的含义，可以直译，也可意译为：a bad man hated by everybody，但显然没有直译更形象。

直译最大的好处在于尽可能忠实履行翻译职责，避免越权，把解读留给读者。例如，"as timid as a hare"与"胆小如鼠"的意思是不完全吻合的，不能简单猎取现成的中文成语加以对应。"胆小如鼠"在中文里是个贬义词，带有蔑视"懦夫"的涵义，比较接近英文里的"coward"。而英文里的"timid"和"hare"都没有那么强的贬义；timid 只是一种带有羞怯或腼腆涵义的"胆小"，而 hare 并不像老鼠那么令人讨厌。所以不宜译成"胆小如鼠"。即使译成"胆小如兔"，还是容易让中国人联想到"胆小如鼠"。鉴此，还不如"羞怯如兔"更加忠实，究竟如何理解，由读者自己去领悟吧，译者就不必越权预设解读立场了。

再以"Full cup, steady hand"为例，完全可以直译成"杯满手稳"。为什么最好直译成"杯满手稳"呢？因为这句英谚在逻辑上是双向的，需要挑明的是"杯满"与"手稳"的关系。"实者沉稳，稳者充实"，如果任取半截，都可能表达不同的侧重。直译成"杯满手稳"，这种侧重的解读就完全由言者把握了。这样，翻译在避免越权方面也算尽了职，而译文也并不影响理解。

2 意译

意译不是瞎译、乱译，而是在不损害原文内容和精神的前提下，为了表达的需要，对原文作相应的调整。只有在正确理解原文的基础上，运用相应的翻译方法以调整原文结构，用规范的译语加以表达，这才真正做到"意译"。如果把"意译"理解为凭主观臆想来理解原文，可以不分析原文结构，只看词面意义，自己编造句子，势必造成"乱译"。

【示例】

There is a mixture of the tiger and the ape in the character of the imperialists.

【答案】帝国主义者的性格既残暴，又狡猾。

【解析】这里把 tiger（老虎）和 ape（猿）这两个具体形象意译为这两个形象所代表的属性："残暴"和"狡猾"。

前面讨论了直译的优势，但那是有个前提的，就是不能过分影响理解。如果直译影响了理解，就得改用意译。当然，"直译"、"意译"也只是些为了方便分类而武断的粗线条概念，理解还是因人而异的，也有一些介乎两者之间的情况稍后将顺便提及。例如，英文妙语 "When the going gets tough, the tough gets going."，两处所用"going"和"tough"不仅词性分别不同，意思也不尽相同，凑在一个句子里了。英文中象这样的东西较多，他们认为很机智（witty）。碰到这类妙语，直译如何能够达意呢？有将它译成：狭路相逢勇者胜；沧海横流方显英雄本色。在这种情况下，还是意译来得生动。再如"此地无银三百两"，如果直译，要靠长长的脚注去帮助理解，那就得把整个故事讲一遍了，不如用意译来得省事。不妨意译成：The more is concealed, the more is revealed.。

3 变通

当然，也有一种情况，就是刚才提到的介乎"直译"与"意译"之间的妙译。这里先举两个经典例子：

例：①Faults are thick where love is thin.

【译】一朝情义淡，样样不顺眼。

②You can fool all the people some of the time and some of the people all the time, but you cannot fool all the people all the time.

【译】骗人一夕一事易，欺众一生一世难。

③Out of the fullness of the heart the mouth speaks.

【译】盈于心则溢于言。

以上两个例子算"直译"还是"意译"？既相当"直接"又准确"达意"。只是对原句的情景稍作变通而已。这种介乎于"直译"与"意译"之间的"直"

与"意"的有机结合，似乎不能武断归类的。最终的翻译质量还是落实在双语基本功上；而无论直译、意译还是有机结合是见仁见智的。

三、应试方法

1 翻译考试中的常见问题

其一，考生对材料的理解不当，造成译文与原意偏差过大。由于词汇和语法等基础知识的薄弱，考生难以理清句子的结构以及句子内部的语法关系，对材料的理解存在问题和偏差，因此在这种理解基础上的表达自然谈不上正确。

其二，考生表达能力欠缺，译文不够通顺、流畅。由于平时缺乏足够的重视和训练，很多考生写出的英文句子文理不通，有点像 chinglish（中国式英语）。很多考生反映，知道汉语对应的英语单词怎么写，但就是不能把它们合理地整合起来。

2 应对方法

首先，考生在平时的学习和训练中，应当充分重视英语语言的基本功的训练，排除侥幸心理，切实打好基础。

其次，加强对英语基本句型的了解，熟悉各种方法与技巧。

3 答题步骤

◆通读题目，准确理解；
◆分析成分，划分意群；
◆选择词义，贴切表达；
◆适当调整，书写译文；
◆通读全句，检验加工。

4 检验和加工

需要提及的是，同学们在写出完成的译文之后，还应当对原文的内容进一步核实，对译文的语言进一步推敲。这是翻译实际操作中不可或缺的重要步骤，也是获取高分的重要一环。检验和加工的过程包括以下几个方面：

◆核实译文与原文内容是否一致；
◆检查译文是否符合英语表达习惯；
◆检查译文是否有错译或漏译的情况；
◆检查标点符号是否齐全、准确；
◆对译文进一步加工润色，使其精确、自然。

5 翻译练习安排

◆时间以每天 30 分钟为宜；

◆坚持每天练习；

◆5 分钟卡表做翻译。

四、专项练习

1. The bombing of Hiroshima marked _____（广岛原子弹的爆炸标志着人类历史进入到了一个新纪元）．（词语选择法）

2. Ask him what happened. _____（他看上去有些忧愁不安）．（增译法）

3. _____（中国发生了巨大的变化）since the introduction of the reform and opening policy.（倒置法）

4. I'm _____（我完全赞成你的意见）．（词类转换法）

5. I always considered him _____（工于心计又贪婪）and did my best to avoid him.（词义褒贬法）

6. She has been talking in French for two hours _____（没有出现任何错误）．（省译法）

7. 这里门庭若市。（直译）

8. 这里门庭若市。（意译）

9. He went west by stage coach and succumbed to _____（淘金热和陶银热）in Nevadas Washoe Region.（意译）

10. In his article the author _____（对人类疏忽自身环境作了批评）．（词类转换法）

11. _____（她气得浑身发抖），she promptly resigned.（合并法）

12. He came into the room _____（光着脚）．（正反译法）

13. _____（他们乐观、能干、热情），they will do everything to make your journey smooth and comfortable.（成分转译法）

14. The team lost the game, atmosphere _____（被沮丧笼罩着）．（词义引申法）

15. Everything will be better. _____（冬天来了，春天还会远吗）？（增译法）

16. _____（车子慢慢走着。在一个泥洼里陷住了）．He swore.（合句法）

17. This is _____（对牛弹琴）．（意译）

18. Huang Jinrong was _____（有名的大无赖）．（褒贬法）

19. The Premier had a lot of work to do _____（在出席会议之前）．（省译法）

20. The sun _____（有极大的影响）both the mind and body of a man.（词类转换法）

答 案 与 解 析

1. 【答案】an epoch in man's history。

    【解析】epoch "新时代，纪元"，不指历史中的朝代或统治时代，指以某重大事件或巨大变化为起点的新的历史时期；era 指历史上的"独立时代，统治时代"，因此在这选择 epoch。

2. 【答案】He looked gloomy and troubled。

    【解析】增译连词 and，使符合英语习惯。

3. 【答案】Great changes have taken place in China。

    【解析】全部倒置。因为中国是发生变化的地方在英语做状语合适，其他成分也做相应的调整。

4. 【答案】all for your opinion。

    【解析】"支持"动词，翻译时转换为介词 for。

5. 【答案】calculating and greedy。

    【解析】这两个词都带有明显的贬义色彩。

6. 【答案】without any mistakes。

    【解析】without 后面省略了动词"出现"making。

7. 【答案】The yard is like a market。

    【解析】平铺直"译"。

8. 【答案】It is a much visited place。

    【解析】意思明了，意译。

9. 【答案】the epidemic of gold and silver fever。

    【解析】将那种流行用 epidemic 一词生动地体现了出来。

10. 【答案】is critical of man's negligence toward his environment。

    【解析】名词转换为形容词。"作了批评"译成英语 is critical of。

11. 【答案】Quivering with anger。

    【解析】所要翻译部分是一个意思完整的句子，因此将其变成现在分词做伴随状语，句子简洁明了。

12. 【答案】with no shoes on。

    【解析】"光着脚"为肯定形式，转译为否定形式。

13. 【答案】Cheerful, efficient and warm-hearted。

    【解析】本题考查句子成分的转换。题干中逗号后是一个完整句子，因此可以将"乐观、能干、热情"这三个形容词性表语转换成状语。句子的意思为：他们乐观、能干、热情，总是想方设法使你一路上顺利、舒适。

14. 【答案】is clouded by depression。

    【解析】cloud 这个词可以作名词"云"使用，也可以作动词"遮蔽"使用，此处是用了它的引申义 "给…蒙上阴影"。

15. 【答案】If winter comes, can spring be far behind?

【解析】增译了表示条件的关联词 if，根据上下文语义增补词语。

16. 【答案】The lumbering cart got stuck in the mud.

【解析】将前半句中的谓语动词变为现在分词做定语。

17. 【答案】to teach a pig to play a flute。

【解析】"对牛弹琴" 是来自汉语的成语典故，在翻译成英语时要用意译法。

18. 【答案】a notorious rogue。

【解析】考查词义褒贬法。看到 "有名的"，不要立刻翻译成 famous，这里很明显带有贬义色彩，因此选择 notorious "臭名昭著的"。

19. 【答案】before the conference。

【解析】本题考查省译法。before 后面省略了动词 "出席"，attending。

20. 【答案】affects tremendously。

【解析】考查成分转译法。将汉语中的名词 "影响" 和形容词 "极大的" 分别转译成动词 affect 和副词 tremendously。

真题演练

2007 年 12 月（六级）

1. But for mobile phones, ＿＿＿＿＿＿＿＿＿＿（我们的通信就不可能如此迅速和方便）.

2. In handling an embarrassing situation ＿＿＿＿＿＿＿＿＿＿（没有什么比幽默感更有帮助的了）.

3. The Foreign Minister said he was resigning, ＿＿＿＿＿＿＿＿＿＿（但他拒绝进一步解释这样做的原因）.

4. Human behavior is mostly a product of learning, ＿＿＿＿＿＿＿＿＿＿（而动物的行为主要依靠本能）.

5. The witness was told that under no circumstances ＿＿＿＿＿＿＿＿＿＿（他都不应该对法庭说谎）.

2007 年 6 月（六级）

1. The auto manufacturers found themselves ＿＿＿＿＿＿＿＿＿＿（正在同外国公司竞争市场的份额）.

2. Only in the small town ＿＿＿＿＿＿＿＿＿＿（他才感到安全和放松）.

3. It is absolutely unfair that these children ＿＿＿＿＿＿＿＿＿＿（被剥夺了受教育的权利）.

4. Our years of hard work are all in vain, ＿＿＿＿＿＿＿＿＿＿（更别提我们花费的大量金钱了）.

5. The problems of blacks and women ＿＿＿＿＿＿＿＿＿＿（最近几十年受到公众相当大的关注）.

2006 年 12 月（六级）

1. If you had ＿＿＿＿＿＿＿＿＿＿（听从了我的忠告，你就不会陷入麻烦）.

2. With tears on her face, the lady ＿＿＿＿＿＿＿＿＿＿（看着她受伤的儿子被送进手术室）.

3. After the terrorist attack, tourists ＿＿＿＿＿＿＿＿＿＿（被劝告暂时不要去该国旅游）.

4. I prefer to communicate with my customers ＿＿＿＿＿＿＿＿＿＿（通过写电子邮件而不是打电话）.

5. _____ （直到截止日他才寄出） his application form.

2007 年 12 月 （四级）

1. _____ （多亏了一系列的新发明）, doctors can treat this disease successfully.

2. In my sixties, one change I notice is that _____ （我比以前更容易累了）.

3. I am going to pursue this course, _____ （无论我要作出什么样的牺牲）.

4. I would prefer shopping online to shopping in a department store because _____ （它更加方便和省时）.

5. Many Americans live on credit, and their quality of life _____ （是用他们能够借到多少来衡量的）, not how much they can earn.

2007 年 6 月 （四级）

1. The finding of this study failed to _____ （将人们的睡眠质量考虑在内）.

2. The prevention and treatment of AIDS is _____ （我们可以合作的领域）.

3. Because of the leg injury, the athlete _____ （决定退出比赛）.

4. To make donations or for more information, please _____ （按以下地址和我们联系）.

5. Please come here at ten tomorrow morning _____ （如果你方便的话）.

2006 年 12 月 （四级）

1. Specialists in intercultural studies says that it is not easy to _____ （适应不同文化中的生活）.

2. Since my childhood I have fond that _____ （没有什么比读书对我更有吸引力）.

3. The victim _____ （本来会有机会活下来） if he had been taken to hospital in time.

4. Some psychologists claim that people _____ （出门在外时可能会感到孤独）.

5. The nation's population continues to rise _____ （以每年 1200 万人的速度）.

答案与解析

1. 【答案】our communication would not have been so rapid and convenient。

   【解析】本题考查虚拟语气用法之———含蓄条件句，也就是不使用从句而用一些介词或短语来暗示使用虚拟语气。除了 but for "要不是" 之外还有 but that "要不是"，without "没有"，or "否则" 等。Convenient 这个词在四级的翻译中也考查到了，要引起足够的重视。

2. 【答案】nothing is more helpful than a sense of humor。

   【解析】本题考查 nothing is... + 形容词比较级 + than... 这个句型曾出现在去年 12 月的四级汉译英中 "没有什么比读书对我更有吸引力"（详见 2006 年 12 月 2 题），因此大家一定要把历年的真题吃透。

3. 【答案】but (he) refused to make further explanation (for doing so)。

   【解析】本题考查省译。在平时的语言运用中一般前面已经出现过的实义词常常省略，避免了罗嗦，使表达更简洁明了，所以我们多次强调翻译不能只看所译部分而要统筹整个句子来翻译。

4. 【答案】while animal behavior (is mostly) a product of their instinct (s)。

   【解析】本题考查在这种同样谓语结构的并列句中可以在后面省略谓语动词的用法，以及 instinct 的用法。

5. 【答案】should he lie to the court。

   【解析】本题考查否定词前置时使用部分倒装的用法。部分倒装是指只将情态动词、助动词等这些谓语动词的一部分提前。

1. 【答案】competing with foreign firms for market share。

   【解析】"为了…而和…竞争" 用的结构是 "compete with...for sth"。"市场的份额" market share 是一大难点，是个专业的经济用语。分析句子结构可知所要填写的部分在句中作补语，"竞争" 是句子主语 The auto manufacturers 所发出的动作，所以要用 compete 用现在分词形式。

2. 【答案】does he feel secure and relaxed。

   【解析】only 置于句首句子要用倒装结构。另一个考查点是 "感到…" 该如何表达。其实这个表达对大多数考生来说并不陌生，即 feel + adj。"安全和放松" 对应的形容词分别为 "secure and relaxed"。

3. 【答案】are deprived of the rights to receive education。

   【解析】本题考查一个重要的短语："be deprived of sth"。定语 "受教育的"

可以处理成动词不定式的形式，作后置定语。

4. 【答案】not to mention/let alone the large amount of money we have spent。

【解析】本题主要考查 not to mention 和 let alone 这两个短语，表示"更别提"的意思。值得注意的是它们的后面都只接动名词形式。由于 money 已经有前置词 the large amount of 修饰了，所以将另外的修饰词处理成定语从句 we have spent。

5. 【答案】have gained/caused considerable public concern in recent decades。

【解析】本题难度并不大，直译就可以。需要注意的是时态，由"最近几十年"可知应该用现在完成时。

2006 年 12 月（六级）

1. 【答案】followed my advice, you would not be in trouble now。

【解析】本题主要考查两个重要短语搭配，"听从某人的忠告"的习惯性表达为"follow one's advice"，"陷入麻烦"为"be in trouble"。此外还考查了虚拟语气，if 从句的时态为过去完成时，主句用 would + 动词原形。

2. 【答案】watched her injured son sent into the operation room。

【解析】本题考查 see/watch…sb. /sth. + done 句型，强调某动作的全过程，且宾语和动作之间是被动关系。"手术室"的表达法为"the operation room"。

3. 【答案】were advised not to travel to that country at the moment。

【解析】本题可采取直译法。"暂时"用短语 at the moment 表示。主语是复数，又可推知事情发生在过去，所以谓语动词要用 were advised。advise 常用于 advise sb to do 的结构。

4. 【答案】via E-mail instead of telephone。

【解析】本题考查介词 via "通过"和短语 instead of "而不是"。由于 via 是介词，后面需跟名词，故还采取了省译法，将"写电子邮件"和"打电话"两个动宾短语中的动作省去，只将名词译出。

5. 【答案】It was not until the deadline that he send out。

【解析】本题考查强调句型 it is not until that…，表示"直到…才"。"截止日"译为 deadline。

2007 年 12 月（四级）

1. 【答案】Owing to/Thanks to a series of new inventions。

【解析】本题考查"多亏了"的表达，翻译成 owing to 或 thanks to 要比 due to 好得多，due to 引出的原因多指导致不好的后果的原因。

2. 【答案】I am apt to/ inclined to be more easily tired than before。

【解析】本题考查比较结构。但是不能简单翻译成 I feel more easily tired。本题的考查意图还是在短语 be apt to/ inclined to 上。

3. 【答案】no matter what sacrifices I will make。

【解析】本题考查 no matter what 引导的让步状语从句。make sacrifices 是"作出牺牲"的意思。

4. 【答案】the former is more convenient and time-saving。

【解析】本题考查翻译时的变通及词类转化，注意开始的"它"如果简单成 it 会有点指代不清，用 former "前者"会好些，另外还要注意 convenient 的拼写，"省时"time-saving 这是由动词短语转化来的形容词。

5. 【答案】is weighed upon how much they can borrow。

【解析】本题翻译时要注意与后句中的 how much they can earn 句式保持一致。

2007 年 6 月（四级）

1. 【答案】include the quality of human's sleep。

【解析】fail to 后面一般接 do sth，所以解题关键在于如何把中文的"把"字句译成 do sth 的形式，其实很简单，只需将"把"后面的名词和动词调换位置就行了。动词用 include，而不用 consider，因为 consider 的主语是做"研究"的人，而不是"研究"。

2. 【答案】where we can cooperate。

【解析】所要填写的部分在句中作表语。用 where 引导一个表语从句，放在这里比较合适，"领域"一词可以省略不译。

3. 【答案】decided to quit the match。

【解析】本题答案相当明朗，用 decide to do sth 的结构，唯一的难点是要用英语中的哪个词来表示"退出"，并和"比赛"形成合理搭配。表示离开某活动、组织、工作时通常常用 quit，强调中途离开。例如，quit the army 退伍。

4. 【答案】contact us at the following address。

【解析】空格所在句是一个表请求的祈使句，因此直接用动词原形，"和某人联系，联络"通常用 contact sb。"按以下地址"是方式状语，紧跟 contact sb 就可以了。

5. 【答案】at your convenience。

【解析】本题考查习惯用语 at one's（own）convenience 在方便时。和 convenience 有关的短语是四六级考试经常考查的，类似的还有 suit sb's convenience 照顾某人的方便，at your earliest convenience 得便务请…从速，for the convenience of 为…方便起见。

2006 年 12 月·（四级）

1. 【答案】adapt oneself to living in different cultures。

【解析】常考词组 adapt oneself to 这是往年词汇部分常考的重点词组，也是大学英语教学中一直强调的知识点。其中最大的陷阱在于，其一，adapt 后面需要跟一个反身代词作泛指主语；其二，to 是介词而非动词不定式的标记，其后应该接名词或者动名词。

2.【答案】nothing is more attractive to me than reading 或 to me, nothing is more important than reading。

【解析】本题考查经典句型 nothing is more important than…这是作文老师历来推崇的精彩句子。此外，由于英汉两种语言的差异，汉语中的一些动宾结构常常在英语中以不及物动词表示，比如唱歌 singing，跳舞 dancing，开车 driving 等等。因此，"读书" 正确的译文不应是 reading books，而是 reading。本题还有一个难以确定的问题就是时态。"没有什么比读书对我更有吸引力" 是常识性内容，因此即使主句用的是过去时，从句也应是现在时。

3.【答案】would have a chance to survive 或 would have a chance of survival。

【解析】本题考点之一是与过去相反的虚拟语气的基本用法。考点之二是核心词汇 survive（幸存）和基本词汇 chance（机会）。

4.【答案】might feel lonely when they are far from home/are not in their hometown/traveling。

【解析】本题的语法考点仍是虚拟语气，考查了与 06 年 6 月份相同的考点——建议句型。本题的词汇考点是 lonely（孤独）和 alone（独自）的辨析，而"出门在外"，同学们完全可以用自己的语言表达出来。

5.【答案】at a speed/rate of 12 million per year 或 at an annual speed of 12 million。

【解析】本题基本没有语法考点，词汇考点之一是词组 at a speed of…（以…的速度）；其二是数字 1200 万人的表达，也就是 12 个百万——12 million，而 million 后面加上多余的复数 s 则是最容易出现的错误。

模 拟 演 练

Test 1

1. We were aware of _____ (那项措施中潜伏的危险).

2. By contrast, American mothers were more likely _____ (把孩子的成功归因于) natural talent.

3. On average, it is said, visitors spend only _____ (一半的钱) in a day in Leeds as in London.

4. Most of the people who die in earthquakes _____ (是正在倒塌的建筑物砸死的).

5. We must _____ (坚持把马克思主义作为我们的指导思想) because it is abreast of time.

Test 2

1. The governor _____ (宣布他将首先解决失业问题).

2. A lot of people nowadays have muscular problems in the neck, the shoulders and the back _____ (主要是由于工作中的压力和紧张造成的).

3. Poland _____ (对投资者富有吸引力) and many foreigners swarm into this country.

4. Was he sentenced to death? But he was just a _____ (他只是协助罪犯而没有在犯罪现场的一个从犯).

5. Per capita average labor wage of urban residents is 5558 yuan, _____ (比上一年同期相比增长了16.8%).

Test 3

1. With the development of computers, _____ (计算机挤掉了大批的员工).

2. Your losses in trade this year are nothing _____ (与我相比).

3. _____ (适应市场的需要), increase the rate of students' obtaining employment basing on the premise of ensuring instructional quality.

4. For miles and miles _____ (除了大火和浓烟我什么也看不见).

5. His life seems very dull and _____ (就是工作完了睡觉,

睡完觉又工作).

Test 4

1. This is _____ (正是我们要买的那本书).
2. English is _____ (没有难到不能学的程度).
3. Much British humor _____ (靠的是一语双关).
4. There is _____ (水波流动的方式与光的传播方式相似), but what we will learn is the differences.
5. _____ (他们骇人听闻的暴行) will be condemned by all the humanists (人道主义者).

Test 5

1. _____ (破产不是逃避债务的好方法) but a life-changing event that causes lifelong damage.
2. Colored people are _____ (决不次于白人).
3. Although she thinks that working in hotel is a tough job, "not for women," _____ (但是能遇上各种不同类型的人，所以她还是觉得很着迷).
4. I bet _____ (行不通) of the plan.
5. China will launch a massive survey of its underwater relics in an effort to _____ (更好地保护国家的自然遗产).

Test 6

1. Reading is to the mind _____ (和锻炼对于身体的重要性一样).
2. No matter how tough he is, _____ (他生病的时候也会很憔悴).
3. It _____ (显而易见) the enemy has no desire for peace.
4. If you join in the club, you must _____ (遵守规则) here.
5. The book will be indexed in the next edition _____ (以便让它更有价值).

Test 7

1. A gust of wind made _____ (烛光摇曳).
2. The bag was stuffed _____ (脏衣服).
3. _____ (很多朋友不在), we decided to put the meeting off.
4. Ditches were dug to _____ (排掉沼泽的水).
5. It _____ (必须指明的是) that it is one of our basic national

policies to control population growth while raising the quality of the population.

Test 8

1. _____（直到失去健康）that people know the value of health. ·

2. British scientists are on _____（即将生产出一种新药）that could revolutionize cancer treatment.

3. Plagiarists（剽窃者）are _____（老是怀疑自己的东西会被人偷走）.

4. _____（给我印象最深的）were her liveliness and sense of humor.

5. These engines are _____（不如我们制造的那些发动机功率大）.

Test 9

1. The substance does not dissolve in water _____（不管是否加热）.

2. My parents are _____（不同意）our picnic plan.

3. The swimmer caught in the whirlpool _____（挣扎着避免溺水）.

4. The emergence of e-commerce and the fast-growing Internet economy are _____（为中国的国内外贸易提供了新的增长机遇）.

5. The population of elderly people is increasing rapidly because people are living longer than before _____（发达国家尤为如此）.

Test 10

1. The club _____（采用一套新的制度）concerning its membership.

2. More than 5 million children have health insurance now, and _____（超过 250 万的家庭已经摆脱贫困）.

3. _____（除主席之外的所有成员都投票赞成我的建议）to set up a branch office in the suburbs.

4. The carpet was _____（固定在地板上）with tacks.

5. （两天了都没有走出沙漠，又没有水喝）_____ he was unquenchable.

答案与解析

Test 1

1. 【答案】the danger latent in that measure。

　　【解析】latent "潜在的，隐伏的，不易察觉的"，多用于贬义。

2. 【答案】to attribute their children's success to。

　　【解析】ascribe 和 attribute 差别不大，都可以解释为 "（中性）把…归因于，（褒义）把…归功于，（贬义）把…归咎于"，也可以解释为 "把…归属于，认为…归属于…"，基本可以互换。

3. 【答案】half as much（money）。

　　【解析】half as + 形容词原级 + as 表示 "…的一半"。因为是比较关系，把在 Leeds 和在 London 的费用做比较，所以后半句有明确的 as 一词。空缺部分是要有 as，还要有 half 和 money。关键是次序如何调理。根据比较结构中的倍数原则，倍数数字放在最开始，接下去有关于量的 as much + n. + as，因此本句要填入 half as much money。

4. 【答案】are killed by falling buildings。

　　【解析】考查分词做定语。现在分词和过去分词都可以做定语。过去分词做定语有动作已经完成的含义，现在分词做定语有动作正在进行的含义，这里 "砸到人" 肯定的正在坍塌的建筑物，因此用现在分词作定语。

5. 【答案】adhere to Marxism as Guiding Thought。

　　【解析】本题考查 "坚持" 的表达，adhere to，persist in，insist on 注意不同短语的搭配不同。be abreast of time 意思是 "符合时代要求的"。

Test 2

1. 【答案】proclaimed that he would first tackle the unemployment problem。

　　【解析】proclaim 一般指权力机关或政府领导宣布或宣称。

2. 【答案】mainly due to stress and tension in their work。

　　【解析】stress 做名词时，意思偏于精神方面的压力；pressure 做名词时，意思偏于物理方面的压力；tension 指紧张，nervousness 指神经过敏；"由于" 的表达有 owing to，due to，thanks to，on account of 等。

3. 【答案】has an abundance of attractions for investors。

　　【解析】本题考查 an abundance of "丰富的"。swarm into "涌入"，形象说明这种投资热潮。

4. 【答案】accessory who assists a criminal but is not present at the crime。

　　【解析】考查 accessory "从犯"，另外还要区分 criminal "罪犯" 指人，和

crime "犯罪，犯罪行为"。

5.【答案】with an increase rate of 16.8% compared with the same period of previous year。

【解析】本题考查倍数表达法。这是报纸新闻中常出现的句型。"as + an increase rate of + 倍数 + compare with"。这里的 increase 是名词。

Test 3

1.【答案】many employees have been displaced by computers。

【解析】displace 常指以某物挤掉另一物，含强迫之意，这里使用被动语态增强被动含义。

2.【答案】compared with mine。

【解析】compare with "与…相比"，注意这个短语多指比喻。compare A with B "把 A 和 B 做比较"。compare A to B "把 A 比作 B"。

3.【答案】Accommodate to the need of market。

【解析】本题考查 "适应" 短语的表达，accommodate 表示 "适应" 时是不及物动词，常与 to 连用，表示 "容纳" 时是及物动词。另外，obtaining employment 表示 "就业率"，premise 表示 "前提"。

4.【答案】I could see nothing but a great fire and lots of smoke。

【解析】考查双重否定句。nothing but… "除了…之外没有"。fire 当 "炉火" 讲时是不可数名词，当 "火灾" 讲时是可数名词。

5.【答案】alternates between work and sleep。

【解析】本题考查翻译时的变通，同时考查了 alternate "交替" 的用法。这里最忌讳根据汉语意思死译为 works after sleeps and sleeps after works。如果这样的话，本题完全失去了考查的意义。alternate 常与介词 between 搭配，表示相对的两种情况交替出现。如：alternated between hope and fear "处于希望和恐惧中"，alternate winter and summer "冬夏交替"。

Test 4

1.【答案】no other than the book we want to buy。

【解析】考查强调判断句。no other than "正是"。

2.【答案】not too difficult to learn。

【解析】本题考查 too…to… 的否定结构表示 "并不太…所以能"。

3.【答案】depends on ambiguity。

【解析】考查变通，同时考查短语 depend on "依靠"，及 ambiguity "含糊，不明确，模棱两可"。"一语双关" 也就是 "会让人产生歧义"，这样就找到了英语对应的单词。

4.【答案】There is an analogy between the way water moves in waves and the way light travels。

【解析】 本题考查词类转换，词义引申，本句开头已经明确给出 there be 句型，因此后面的 "相似" 就要在翻译时转换为名词。Analogy 是六级重点词汇，还要注意的地方是 "传播" travel 用的是引申义，水的 "流动" 则用 move。

5.【答案】 Their appalling violence。

【解析】 本题考查 "骇人听闻的" 表达，terrible，fearful，awful 都有 "可怕的" 意思，但 "受到所有人道主义者的谴责"，那选择程度最强的 appalling 最贴切。

Test 5

1.【答案】 Bankruptcy is not a good way to get out of debt。

【解析】 本题考查正反判断句。be not …but… "不是…而是…"，bankruptcy 名词 "破产"，另外掌握 bankrupt 形容词 "破产的"。

2.【答案】 by no means inferior to white people。

【解析】 本题考查 "决不" 和 "次于" 的表达。Inferior to 是固定搭配，"低于，劣于"，和它相对的是 superior to "高于"，两者用法相同，都含有比较的意思。不再可比较连词 than 连用。

3.【答案】 she is still fascinated by it as she can meet different kinds of people。

【解析】 本题考查 "着迷" 的表达，be fascinated by…是 "对…着迷" 的意思，翻译的时候注意两个连词 "但是" "所以"，因为前半句有了 although，所以不能再出现 but 而且 by 也暗含 "由于" 的意思，就不要再加 because 了。

4.【答案】 against the feasibility。

【解析】 本题考查成分转译，"行不通" 如果译成动词短语的话，plan 就应该放在这个短语的前面，但在这里却放在了这个短语的后面，说明这里应该填名词短语，feasibility "可行性" 是六级新增的重要词。

5.【答案】 better conserve the country's cultural heritage。

【解析】 本题考查 "保护自然遗产" 的表达，在这里 "保护" 要用 conserve，而不用 protect，conserve 有保护濒临灭绝物种的含义，而 protect 没有这层意思。

Test 6

1.【答案】 what exercise is to the body。

【解析】 考查句型 A is to B what C is to D。"A 对 B 的作用就如同 C 对 D 的作用"，这个句型多用来表示类比。

2.【答案】 he would also be feeble when he was ill。

【解析】 本题主要考查 "憔悴的" 的表达 feeble，它还有其他的含义如：a feeble attempt. 无益的尝试，a feeble brain 低能，a feeble cry 微弱的喊声。另外，

No matter how 引导的句子主句不倒装，从句将表语提前，使用部分倒装。

3. 【答案】is clear/ obvious that。

【解析】这里考查 it 做形式主语的用法。"it + be + 形容词 + that/ who…"，真正的主语是 that 后面的从句。

4. 【答案】abide by the rules。

【解析】这里考查短语 abide by "遵守，坚持"。

5. 【答案】so as to make it more useful。

【解析】考查变通的翻译方法。在这里"有价值"不能翻译为 have value，这不符合英语的表达习惯，这里要用 make sth. + 形容词。so as to "以便"在这里也可以用 in order to，但 so as to 不能放在句首。

Test 7

1. 【答案】the candles flare。

【解析】考查变通的翻译方法。短短的四个字要准确翻译出来需要下一番工夫。这里 make 指"使…处于某种状态"，flare 有"闪烁不定，摇曳"的意思，符合语境。

2. 【答案】with dirty clothes。

【解析】本题考查固定搭配 be stuffed with "被填满"的用法。

3. 【答案】With many friends absent。

【解析】这里主要是考查 absent 和 absence "缺席"的各种表达，如果按照原文"不在"翻译，显然比较生硬且与下文不符，因此要善于根据上下文推断原文意思。

4. 【答案】drain water from the swamp。

【解析】本题考查"排水"的表达，drain…from 及"沼泽"swamp。

5. 【答案】must be pointed out。

【解析】考查 it 做形式主语的句型 It be done that，"据…"，用在这个句型中的动词必须是及物动词或相当于及物动词的短语。

Test 8

1. 【答案】It is not until they lose it。

【解析】这是个 not…until 用在强调句型中的句子，另外下半句已经有 health 一词为了避免重复用来代替。

2. 【答案】the verge of producing a drug。

【解析】本题考查意译，空格前面是介词 on，可知应该是一个短语表示"即将"修饰"找到"，可以想到 on the verge of，意思是"濒临…边缘"。

3. 【答案】always suspicious of being stolen from. 。

【解析】本题考查词性转换。"怀疑"本是动词，但在空格前面有 are，所以这里用形容词形式 be suspicious of 是固定搭配，另外，这句话用的是被动语态，后面不要丢掉介词 from。

4. 【答案】What impressed me the most。

【解析】名词性从句 what impressed me the most，其中的 the 不能丢。

5. 【答案】less powerful than the ones we have made。

【解析】很多人都知道比较级，可是却往往会忽略比较级是用在形容词/副词上的，比如，这里往往有人会误用 powerful 的名词形式 power。

Test 9

1. 【答案】whether (it is) heated or not。

【解析】考查关键词和短语 "加热" heat；"不管是否"（no matter）whether… or not？，heat 与其逻辑主语 substance 之间是被动关系，即 heat 加 ed。如果 heated or not 放在句首，whether 也可以省略。

2. 【答案】averse to。

【解析】对于 "不同意" 的表述十分多，有简单的 against；复杂的 averse to；由于前面是 be 动词，这里是叙述一个事实，不应该用动词。

3. 【答案】struggled to keep from drowning。

【解析】struggle/avoid/drowning 大家都能比较好地运用起来，这里存在一个时态问题，struggle 的时态应该由 caught in the whirlpool 推导出来是过去式。

4. 【答案】providing new growth opportunities for China's foreign and domestic trade。

【解析】主要是 "国内外贸易" 的翻译是难点。China's foreign and domestic trade 这个表达较为普遍。

5. 【答案】especially in developed countries。

【解析】这题正确率也较高，主要需要注意的是千万不要漏了 in，因为去除 especially，这个句子应该是 people are living longer than before in the developed countries。

Test 10

1. 【答案】adopted a new set of rules

【解析】对 "采用" 英语表述的考查是四六级的常考点，明显这里应该使用 adopt "采用" 另外它还有 "收养" 的意思；注意：adopt 与 adapt "使适应，改编" 的区别。

2. 【答案】more than two and a half million families have been lifted out of poverty。

【解析】这题主要是对数字以及 "摆脱" 的翻译考查。250 万翻译成 2.5million 或 two and a half million 都可以，另外 "摆脱" 也有多种表达，get rid of，break away from 等，或简单地用 out 表达。

3. 【答案】 All the members except the Chairman voted for my proposal。

【解析】 这句翻译正确率较高，出现的难点主要是 vote to 还是 vote for 的问题，vote to 是指"支持某人，投票给某人"，而 vote for 不单指投票，还有"赞成某人"的意思。for 有赞成的意味，另外，"反对"可以相应表达为 against。

4. 【答案】 fastened to the floor。

【解析】 不要看到"固定"就用 fix，与 fix 搭配应该是 to（或使用 fasten to）大家可能见到后面是 floor 就一味地想到使用 on，结果答案就变成了 fixed on the floor，这样是错误的。

5. 【答案】 Having been in the desert without water for two days。

【解析】 这题是难度相对比较大的。其实是对成分转换的考查，"两天都没有走出沙漠，没有水"要注意时态、否定式、还有状语，如何安排句子？但是如果换个角度来表达为"两天都在沙漠里面没有水"，既能表现原句的意思，又符合英语的表达习惯。

第四篇 预测试题

预测试题一

Directions: *This part consists of a short passage. In this passage, there are altogether 10 mistakes, one in each numbered line. You may have to change a word, add a word or delete a word. Mark out the mistakes and put the corrections in the blanks provided. If you change a word, cross it out and write the correct word in the corresponding blank. If you add a word, put an insertion mark (∧) in the right place and write the missing word in the blank. If you delete a word, cross it out and put a slash (/) in the blank.*

Mass transportation revised the social and economic fabric of the American city in three fundamental ways. It *catalyzed* (催化) physical expansion, it sorted out people and land uses, it accelerated the inherent stability of urban life. By opening vast areas of unoccupied land for residential expansion, the *omnibuses* (公共汽车), horse railways, commuter trains, and electric trolleys pulled settled regions outward two to four times as distant from city centers than they were in the pre-modern era. In 1850, for example, the borders of Boston lie scarcely two miles from the old business district; by the turn of the century the radius extended ten miles. Now those who could afford it could live far removed from the old city center and still commute there for work, shopping, and entertain. The new accessibility of land around the *periphery* (外围) of almost every major city sparked an explosion of real estate development and fueled that we now know as urban sprawl. Between 1890 and 1920, for example, some 250, 000 new residential lots were recorded within the borders of Chicago, most of them locating in outlying areas. Over the same period, another 550, 000 were plotted outside the city limits and within the metropolitan area. Anxious to make advantage of the possibilities of commuting, real estate developers added 800, 000 potential building sites to the Chicago region in just thirty years — lots that could have been housed five to six million people.

62. _____

63. _____

64. _____

65. _____

66. _____

67. _____

68. _____

69. _____

70. _____

71. _____

Part VI
Translation
(5 minutes)

Direction：*complete the sentences by translating into English the Chinese given in brackets. Please write your translation on **Answer Sheet 2**.*

72. We can only _____（扭转这种状况）by reducing our expenses.

73. The phone is ringing, _____（她一定不在家因为没人接听）.

74. In the fast-developing world, we _____（我们除了读书来增长我们的知识之外别无选择）.

75. He admire those people who _____（在医学领域工作的人）.

76. They were stranded in the desert for one week and _____（吃光了所有能吃的东西）.

答案与解析

Part V

62. 【答案】uses，∧it — ∧and。

【解析】本题考察句子结构。三个简单句不能仅用逗号连接，故在第三个分句前加上连接词 and，使它们构成并列句。

63. 【答案】stability — instability。

【解析】本题考察逻辑一致性。前文提到 physical expansion...land uses，这些指的都是城市生活的不稳定性，因此将 stability 改成其反义词。

64. 【答案】as — more。

【解析】本题考察比较级。根据句中的 than 可知这里应该用比较级，因此要将表原级的 as 改成表比较级的 more。

65. 【答案】lie — lay。

【解析】本题考察时态。本句是在讲述 1850 年发生的事情，因此谓语动词 lie 应该用过去式。lie 这个单词有些特殊，它的过去时和过去分词会因意思的不同而有所改变。当它意为"位于，延伸，躺下"时，过去式为 lay，过去分词为 lain。当它意为"撒谎"时，过去式和过去分词均为 lied。此处的 lie 是"位于"的意思，因此过去式用 lay。

66. 【答案】entertain — entertainment。

【解析】本题考察平行结构。entertain 和前面的 work 以及 shopping 是由 and 连接的平行结构，因此它们的词性应该保持一致。work 和 shopping 在这都作名词，所以 entertain 也应用其名词形式。

67. 【答案】that — what。

【解析】本题考察名词性从句的引导词。that...sprawl 是宾语从句,该宾语从句缺少宾语,that 常用于引导宾语从句,但不能在从句中充当某种成分,故将其改成 what。

68. 【答案】locating — located。

【解析】本题考察非谓语动词。them 和 locate 是被动关系,故需用 locate 的过去分词形式。

69. 【答案】and — but。

【解析】本题考察逻辑关系。and 前是 outside the city limits(在城市分界以外),后是 within the metropolitan area(属于市区范围),前后显然是转折关系,故将 and 改成 but。

70. 【答案】make — take 或 advantage — use。

【解析】本题考察固定短语。本题将 take advantage of 和 make use of 这两个短语混用了,它们都表示"利用",因此本题有两种改法,使用其一即可。

71. 【答案】been — been。

【解析】本题考察语态。house 的逻辑主语即为本句的主语 lots,因此此处无需用被动语态,故将 been 去掉。

Part VI

72. 【答案】retrieve the situation。

【解析】本题考查"扭转状况"的表达,by 介词短语做方式状语。

73. 【答案】but there is no answer so she can't be at home。

【解析】本题考查情态动词可以表示推测的用法,can't 表示"一定不",在肯定句中表推测用 must。

74. 【答案】can't but read books to increase our knowledge。

【解析】本题考查双重否定。cannot...but do...,"除了…别无选择"。

75. 【答案】work in the domain /field of medicine。

【解析】本题考查词语的选择及词义的引申。"领域" domain,还可以用 field。

76. 【答案】ate up everything edible。

【解析】本题中宾语 everything 是不定代词,修饰它的形容词要后置。edible "可食用的"是重要六级词汇。

预 测 试 题 二

Directions: *This part consists of a short passage. In this passage, there are altogether 10 mistakes, one in each numbered line. You may have to change a word, add a word or delete a word. Mark out the mistakes and put the corrections in the blanks provided. If you change a word, cross it out and write the correct word in the corresponding blank. If you add a word, put an insertion mark (∧) in the right place and write the missing word in the blank. If you delete a word, cross it out and put a slash (/) in the blank.*

Until very recently, the songs of colonial American were known only in small, isolated areas of the United States. They were handed over within a family circle, and them was no way for   62. _____

them to become known over the whole country or be a real part of   63. _____

the nation's culture. Since each generation tended to remember its own songs and to forget the older songs it once knows, much of   64. _____

the nation's song *heritage* (遗产) may have disappeared.

The first step toward preserve America's song heritage was   65. _____

taken by scholars, collectors and researchers who gathered and studied songs; next, singers became interested, and soon folk songs could be heard nationally by the radio. Finally, America's   66. _____

rediscovered musical heritage was spread to the schools, becom-   67. _____

ing part of every child's experience.

Many colonial songs were rediscovered in the Southern Appalachian Mountains. Universities, the Library of Congress, and many individual collections added up to the *treasury* (作品集) of   68. _____

song. In some parts of the nation old Scottish, Irish, Welsh, or English song had not been pushed out of existence by newer mu-   69. _____

sic. There collectors found ten, twenty, even thirty versions of the same ballad — sometimes with a different ture or story, but always recognizable and always originating in the same old song. In few isolated places, the ballads still existed in what was proba-   70. _____

bly the form that sung in colonial days, but since the songs were   71. _____

transmitted orally, individual variations have probably crept in.

Part VI　　　　　　　　Translation　　　　　　（5 minutes）

Direction：*complete the sentences by translating into English the Chinese given in brackets. Please write your translation on **Answer Sheet 2.***

72. If you are a man, you can point out that most poets and men of science are male；if you are a woman, ＿＿＿＿＿＿＿＿＿＿＿＿＿＿＿（你可以反驳说多数罪犯也是男人）.

73. It's a pity. ＿＿＿＿＿＿＿＿＿＿＿＿＿（你本应该邀请她来参加你的毕业典礼的）.

74. The blackboard and chalk ＿＿＿＿＿＿＿＿＿＿＿＿＿（正在被电脑和投影机所取代）.

75. His books are so popular and be said that ＿＿＿＿＿＿＿＿＿＿＿＿＿（他具有杰出的写作天赋）.

76. If too old to work much, the retired worker is ＿＿＿＿＿＿＿＿＿＿＿＿＿（对社区工作非常热心）.

━━━━━━━ 答 案 与 解 析 ━━━━━━━

Part V ....

62. 【答案】over — down。
    【解析】本题考查固定短语。hand over 意为"让渡：放弃或让出（财产）给别人"，用在此处显然不符合上下文的语义要求。"hand down"意为"传下去"，尤指"家传，祖传"，和 within a family circle 形成语义共现。

63. 【答案】or ∧ be — ∧ to。
    【解析】本题考查平行结构。整句结构为 there was no way for them to become …and to be a real part…。and 引导两个并列的不定式，它们是平行结构，在形式上要保持一致，因此 be 前面的 to 不能省略。

64. 【答案】knows — knew。
    【解析】本题考查时态。句中 once "从前"是明确的过去时间状语，因此需将 knows 改成 knew。

65. 【答案】preserve — preserving。
    【解析】本题考查介词的用法。toward 是介词，后面应加名词或动名词形式，因而将 preserve 改成 preserving。

66. 【答案】by — on。
    【解析】本题考查固定搭配。by…表示"通过某种方式"，其后直接跟媒介，而不跟冠词，如 by air，by bus 等。但在本题中，如果将 the 去掉，那就是留下 by radio，它的意思是"通过广播"，而这里表达的显然不是通过广播之意。改成 on the radio "在广播里播放"才符合题意。

67. 【答案】was — was。

【解析】本题考查动词用法。spread 在大多数情况下用作不及物动词，当它用作及物动词时多以人作主语，指传播消息、疾病等等。它在此处是不及物动词的用法，因此不能用被动语态。

68. 【答案】up — up。

【解析】本题考查短语搭配。add up to 意为"加起来总共"，例如：The cost added up to 80 yuan. 。这里显然不是表示总数，而是加入。故应改为 add to "加入，汇入"。句中的 treasury of song 是习惯性表达，意为"歌曲总集"。

69. 【答案】song — songs。

【解析】本题考查名词单复数。此处不是单独提到某一首歌，而是泛泛而指，所以应用复数名词 songs。

70. 【答案】In ∧ few — ∧ a

【解析】本题考查逻辑关系。从句子主干部分可知本句是肯定语气，"still"更重了肯定语气。"在一些与世隔绝的地方，民谣仍然以殖民地时期被歌唱的形式存在着"。few 表示否定，与句子主干部分的逻辑不符，应把它改成表肯定的 a few，即在其前加上 a。

71. 【答案】that — that。

【解析】本题考查引导词。"sung in colonial days"为过去分词作后置定语，相当于"the form that was sung colonial days"，因此其前无需用引导词引导。

Part VI

72. 【答案】you can retort that so are most criminals。

【解析】本题考查"so + be/do/must… + 其他"句型以及翻译时词语的选择，"so + be/do/must… + 其他"表示"…也是如此"，在这里 so 后面的助动词要根据前面的动词而定，前半句用的是 are，因此这里用 are。"反驳"用 retort。

73. 【答案】You should have invited her to your graduation ceremony。

【解析】本题考查"情态动词 should/ought to + have done"的用法，这个句型多用于评论过去应该做而实际并未做的动作，含有批评的意思。

74. 【答案】is being replaced by the computer and the projector。

【解析】本题考查词语选择的同时也考查了被动语态的现在进行时，"取代"replace，substitute，但是 replace 常含有被动的意味，用在这里较合适。

75. 【答案】She is endowed with great writing ability。

【解析】考查短语 be endowed with "具有…方面的天赋"。

76. 【答案】very enthusiastic about neighborhood affairs。

【解析】本题考查 be enthusiastic about "热衷于某事"。整句话的意思是"虽因年老不能多操劳，但这个退休工人对里弄工作非常热心。"

预 测 试 题 三

Part V   **Cloze**   **(15 minutes)**

Directions: *There are 20 blanks in the following passage. For each blank there are four choices marked [A], [B], [C] and[D] on the right side of the paper. You should choose the ONE that best fits into the passage. Then mark the corresponding letter on Answer Sheet 2 with a single line through the centre.*

Generally speaking, a British is widely regarded as a quiet, shy and conservative person who is __62__ only among those with whom he is acquainted. When a stranger is at present, he often seems nervous, __63__ embarrassed. You have to take a commuter train (市郊火车) any morning or evening to __64__ the truth of this. Serious-looking businessmen and women sit reading their newspapers or dozing in a corner; hardly anybody talks, since to do so would be considered quite offensive. __65__, there is an unwritten but clearly understood code of behavior which, __66__ broken, makes the offender immediately the object of __67__.

It has been known as a fact that the British has a __68__ for the discussion of their weather and that, if given a chance, he will talk about it at __69__. Some people argue that it is because the British weather seldom __70__

62.	[A] relaxed	[B] frustrated
	[C] amused	[D] exhausted
63.	[A] yet	[B] otherwise
	[C] even	[D] so
64.	[A] experience	[B] witness
	[C] watch	[D] undergo
65.	[A] Deliberately	[B] Consequently
	[C] Frequently	[D] Apparently
66.	[A] unless	[B] once
	[C] while	[D] as
67.	[A] suspicion	[B] opposition
	[C] criticism	[D] praise
68.	[A] emotion	[B] fancy
	[C] likeliness	[D] judgment
69.	[A] length	[B] peace
	[C] random	[D] large
70.	[A] follows	[B] predicts
	[C] defies	[D] supports
71.	[A] dedication	[B] compassion
	[C] contemplation	[D] speculation
72.	[A] Still	[B] Also
	[C] Certainly	[D] Fundamentally
73.	[A] faith	[B] reliance
	[C] honor	[D] credit

forecast and hence becomes a source of interest and __71__ to everyone. This may be so. __72__ a British cannot have much __73__ in the weathermen, who, after promising fine, sunny weather for the following day, are often proved wrong __74__ a cloud over the Atlantic brings rainy weather to all districts! The man in the street seems to be as accurate — or as inaccurate — as the weathermen in his __75__.

Foreigners may be surprised at the number of references __76__ weather that the British make to each other in the course of a single day. Very often conversational greetings are __77__ by comments on the weather. "Nice day, isn't it? Beautiful!" may well be heard instead of "Good morning, how are you?" __78__ the foreigner may consider this exaggerated and comic, it is worthwhile pointing out that it could be used to his advantage.

__79__ he wants to start a conversation with a British but is at a __80__ to know where to begin, he could do well to mention the state of the weather. It is a safe subject which will __81__ an answer from even the most reserved British.

74. [A] if   [B] once
    [C] when   [D] whereas

75. [A] propositions   [B] predictions
    [C] approval   [D] defiance

76. [A] about   [B] on
    [C] in   [D] to

77. [A] started   [B] conducted
    [C] replaced   [D] proposed

78. [A] Since   [B] Although
    [C] However   [D] When

79. [A] Even   [B] Because
    [C] If   [D] For

80. [A] loss   [B] bargain
    [C] profit   [D] cost

81. [A] stimulate   [B] constitute
    [C] furnish   [D] provoke

Part VI   Translation   (5 minutes)

Direction: *complete the sentences by translating into English the Chinese given in brackets. Please write your translation on* **Answer Sheet 2.**

82. The criminal wanted to _____ (对逮捕者复仇).

83. _____ (必须立即采取有效措施) to eliminate sandy storms.

84. We can't (choose) but _____ (承认他们在科技的某些方面领先于我们).

85. The present armed clash on the border was _____ (是让

他们国家的人忘记国内经济困境的一次转移).

86. Enemy agents _____ (蓄意破坏了军工厂).

████████ **答 案 与 解 析** ████████

Part V

62. 选［A］。逻辑推理题。根据句中的 only 可知所填词应与前文提到的"安静，害羞，保守"形成对比。查看选项可知，［A］relaxed"放松的，宽舒的"符合题意。［B］frustrated"失败的，落空的"；［C］amused"愉快的，开心的"；［D］exhausted"耗尽的，疲惫的"均脱离了语境。

63. 选［C］。逻辑推理题。embarrassed（尴尬）较之于 nervous（紧张）来说，在困窘的程度上更进一层，故两者之间应用［C］even"甚至"来连接。本句的意思是：当有陌生人在场时，英国人常常显得紧张，甚至会感到尴尬。［A］yet"然而，但是"，表示转折；［B］otherwise"否则"，表示转折；［D］so"因而，所以，那么"，表示因果。

64. 选［B］。词汇辨析题。后文中的 Serious-looking businessmen and women sit … quite offensive 即为 the truth of this，而这一切都是需要亲眼目睹才能知晓的，因此所填词需能表达"目睹"之意。选项中符合的只有［B］witness"目睹，目击"，故为答案。［A］experience"经验，体验"和［D］undergo"经历，遭受"脱离了语境；［C］watch"看，注视"虽然语义恰当，但其不能与 the truth 搭配，故也不选。

65. 选［D］。逻辑推理题。空格处要求填入一个副词作状语。前文叙述了一系列亲眼目睹的事情，能和 witness（目睹）形成语义场共现的只有［D］Apparently"显然地"。［A］Deliberately"故意地"；［B］Consequently"从而，因此"；［C］Frequently"常常，频繁地"均不符合语境要求。

66. 选［B］。逻辑推理题。根据句意可知，当这种行为准则（code of behavior）被打破时，冒犯者就会变成…，［B］once"一旦"和［C］while"当…的时候"在语义上都符合，while 用于引导时间状语从句时，主句的时态应为现在进行时，因此它不能用于此处。［B］once 在语义上和用法上均符合题意，故为答案。［A］unless"除非"；［D］as"像，因为"语义不符。

67. 选［C］。逻辑推理题。根据常识，打破了行为准则招来的应该是批评，故［C］criticism"批评，批判"为答案。［A］suspicion"猜疑，怀疑"；［B］opposition"反对，相反"；［D］praise"赞扬，称赞"均不符合语义要求。

68. 选［B］。短语搭配题。have a fancy for sth. 为固定搭配，意为"偏好于某事物"，故选［B］。［A］emotion"情绪，情感"；［C］likeliness"可能"和［D］judgment"看法，评价"均不符合题意。

69. 选［A］。短语搭配题。四个选项均能和 at 构成短语搭配。［A］at length 意为

"详细地"；［B］at peace 意为 "和平，心情平静"；［C］at random 意为 "随便地，胡乱地"；［D］at large 意为 "自由自在"。其中能和 has a fancy for 在语义上形成照应关系的是 ［A］at length 意为 "详细地"，故为答案。

70. 选 ［A］。词汇辨析题。［B］predicts "预言，预报"；［C］defies "公然反抗，藐视"；［D］supports "扶持，支持" 这三项均需以人作为主语，故都可排除。［A］follows "遵循" 符合题意。句子大意为：有人争辩说，英国人喜欢谈论天气是由于天气预报不准，因而天气成为人人都感兴趣…的话题。

71. 选 ［D］。词汇辨析题。人们谈论天气，也只能对其作出 "猜测"，不可能是 "贡献、怜悯或者沉思"。因此只能选 ［D］speculation "推测"。［A］dedication "贡献，奉献"；［B］compassion "同情，怜悯"；［C］contemplation "沉思，企图" 语义均不符。

72. 选 ［C］。逻辑推理题。解答本题需建立在 12 题的基础上。空格后的内容为 a British cannot have much faith in the weathermen（英国人不能太相信天气预报员）和前文中的 the British weather seldom follows forecast 意思相符，且在语气上更加肯定。据此我们可以得出，［C］Certainly "的确，（口语）当然，行" 用在此处最为恰当。［A］Still "尽管如此，依然"；［B］Also "也，同样"；［D］Fundamentally "基础地，根本地" 均不符合题意。

73. 选 ［A］。短语搭配题。have faith in sth. 为固定短语，意为 "对某事有信心，相信某事"，故 ［A］为答案。［B］reliance "信心，依靠" 常用于 place/have put reliance on/in sb. 结构中，意为 "信任，依赖某人"；［C］honor "尊敬，荣誉" 和 ［D］credit "声望，荣誉" 均不能用于 have ~ in sth. 的结构中。

74. 选 ［C］。逻辑推理题。本题要求填入一个关系副词，引导时间状语从句。［C］when "当…的时候"，常用于引导时间状语从句，同时也符合句子意思，故为答案。［A］if 引导条件状语从句；［B］once "一旦"，可用于引导时间状语从句，但语义不符；［D］whereas "然而"，表示转折，也不合题意。本句的意思是：情况也许是这样。的确，英国人无法过于相信天气预报者，他们常常保证第二天会是个好天气，结果第二天，当大西洋面飘来云层，所有地区雨水涟涟时便证实天气预报者说错了。

75. 选 ［B］。逻辑推理题。能和 the weathermen 形成语义场共现关系的是 ［B］predictions "预报，预言"，故为答案。［A］propositions "主张，建议"；［C］approval "赞成，承认"；［D］defiance "蔑视，挑衅" 均不符合逻辑要求。

76. 选 ［D］。短语搭配题。名词 reference 与其动词形式 refer 一样，都与 to 搭配使用，故选 ［D］to，reference to 表示 "提及，参考"。本句的意思是：外国人也许会对英国人一天之中如此频繁地提及天气而感到惊奇。

77. 选 ［C］。逻辑推理题。文章多出提到英国人的谈话内容通常为天气，由此可以推断出谈话中的问候常常被天气评论给替代了。所以本题答案应为 ［C］replaced "取代，替换"。［A］started "开始，着手"；［B］conducted "引导，管理"；[D] proposed "建议，向…提议" 语义均不符。

78. 选 [B]。逻辑推理题。本句大意为：外国人会认为这很夸张很滑稽，有一点
    还是值得一提，即外国人可以利用这一点。由此可知从句与主句间属于让步
    关系，故选 [B] Although "虽然，尽管"。[A] Since "自…以来，因为"，
    表原因；[C] However "然而，可是"，表转折；[D] When "当…时"，表时
    间，这三项均不符和原文逻辑，故都可排除。

79. 选 [C]。逻辑推理题。本句想要表达的意思是：如果他想开始与一个英国人
    谈话而又不知从何说起，那他完全可以谈论天气情况。由此可知，[C] If
    "如果" 符合题意。[A] Even "甚至"，表递进；[B] Because "因为"，表原
    因；[D] For "因为"，也表原因。

80. 选 [A]。短语搭配题。根据上题提到的句意可知，[A] at a loss "迷茫，不
    知所措" 符合本题的语义要求。[B] at a bargain "廉价"；[C] at a profit "获
    利"；[D] at a cost "亏本" 都脱离了语境。

81. 选 [D]。词汇辨析题。本句的意思是："这是一个很保险的话题，甚至可以
    让最保守的英国人开口回答。" 四个选项中，[D] provoke "引起，使…出现"
    符合句意要求。[A] stimulate "激励，鼓励；使兴奋"；[B] constitute "制定
    （法律），建立（政府）"；[C] furnish "提供，装备" 均不符合语义要求。

Part VI

82. 【答案】take revenge on his captors。
    【解析】本题考查词语的固定搭配。"复仇"，take revenge on sb.，revenge 做
    动词时是及物动词，后面直接跟宾语。revenge for …意为 "为…报复"。

83. 【答案】Effective measures must be taken immediately。
    【解析】汉语的无主句通常翻译成英语的被动语态，eliminate "排除，消除"。

84. 【答案】admit that in certain aspects of science and technology they are ahead
    of us。
    【解析】本题考查双重否定句型 cannot choose but do "不得不" but 后面接动
    词原形，翻译时注意。ahead of "领先于"。

85. 【答案】a diversion to make their people forget the internal difficult economic situ-
    ation。
    【解析】本题考查介词短语作后置定语的用法。本句是一个表语带长定语的
    主系表结构的简单句，翻译时要将其译为不定式做定语。diversion "转移"，
    armed clash "武装冲突"。

86. 【答案】sabotaged the arms factory。
    【解析】考查词义褒贬法。"蓄意破坏，阴谋破坏" sabotage 含有明显的贬义
    色彩，而 destroy, demolish 都是中性词，没有 sabotage 用在这里合适。"军工
    厂" arms factory。

预测试题四

Directions: *This part consists of a short passage. In this passage, there are altogether 10 mistakes, one in each numbered line. You may have to change a word, add a word or delete a word. Mark out the mistakes and put the corrections in the blanks provided. If you change a word, cross it out and write the correct word in the corresponding blank. If you add a word, put an insertion mark (∧) in the right place and write the missing word in the blank. If you delete a word, cross it out and put a slash (/) in the blank.*

Every human being has an unique arrangement of the skin on 62. _____
his fingers and this arrangement is unchangeable. Scientists and
experts have proved the uniqueness of finger-prints and discovered
that no exactly similar pattern is passed on from parents to children, therefore nobody knows why. 63. _____

The ridge structure on a person's fingers does not change with
growth and is not effected by superficial injuries. Burns, cuts and 64. _____
other damages to the outer part of the skin will be replaced in time 65. _____
by new one which bears a reproduction of the original pattern. It is
only when the inner skin is injured then the arrangement will be de- 66. _____
stroyed. Some criminals make use this fact to remove their own 67. _____
finger-prints but this is a dangerous and rare step to take.

Finger-prints can be made very easily with printer's ink. It 68. _____
can be recorded easily. With special methods, identification can
be achieved successfully within a short time. Because of the sim-
plicity and economy of this system, finger-prints have often been
used for a method of solving criminal case. A suspected man may 69. _____
deny a change but this may be on vain. His finger-prints can 70. _____
prove who he is even if his appearance has been changed by age
or accident.

When a suspect leaves finger-prints behind at the scene of a
crime, they are difficult to detect with the naked eyes. Special 71. _____
techniques are used to "develop" them.

Part VI　　　　　　　　Translation　　　　　(5 minutes)

Direction：*complete the sentences by translating into English the Chinese given in brackets. Please write your translation on **Answer Sheet 2**.*

72. We must _____ （保卫国家的利益）.

73. It was so dark outside that _____ （他勉强能在黑暗中分辨出道路）.

74. _____ （打捞工作彻底失败了） because of lacking in enough machines.

75. No one helps us now and we _____ （靠不了别人只能靠我们自己）.

76. Please also take caution in _____ （处理你的现金卡）.

■■■■■■■■■■■■■■■■■■■ 答案与解析 ■■■■■■■■■■■■■■■

Part V

62. 【答案】an — a。
　【解析】本题考查不定冠词。冠词 an 应加在以元音为首音节的单词前。unique 的首个音节并非元音，所以应用冠词 a。

63. 【答案】therefore — though。
　【解析】本题考查句子的逻辑关系。therefore 表示的是因果关系，但本句的前后两个分句应该是让步关系，该句译文为：科学家和专家们已证明指纹的唯一性，并发现父母遗传给孩子的纹路也没有完全一样的，尽管没人知道原因。

64. 【答案】effected — affected。
　【解析】本题考查形近词的辨析。当 effect 表示"影响"时，是名词，不能应用于本句的被动语态中。当 effect 作动词时，意思是"生效，实现"，此含义不符句意。显然是把 effect 和形近的动词 affect "影响"混淆了。

65. 【答案】damages — damage。
　【解析】本题考查名词的单复数。damage 表示"损害、伤害"时是不可数名词，不应该用复数形式。

66. 【答案】then — that。
　【解析】本题考查强调句型。强调句型的结构为 it is…that…。纵使本句强调的是时间状语 when the inner skin is injured（当内皮层受伤时），也应该用 that 来引导。

67. 【答案】use ∧ this — ∧ of。
　【解析】本题考查动词短语。make use of sth. "利用某物"是固定搭配，文中遗漏了介词 of。

68.【答案】It — They。

【解析】本题考查代词指代的一致性。句中的代词代替的应是上一句的 finger-prints "指纹"，是复合名词的复数形式，所以代词也要相应地用第三人称的复数。

69.【答案】for — as。

【解析】本题考查介词。本句想要表达的是指纹通常被当作是破案的一种方法，是表媒介、手段，因此不能用表目的的介词 for，而应该用 as。短语 be used as，意思是"被作为"，类似的还有 be served as，be treated as，be seen as 等。

70.【答案】on — in。

【解析】本题考查短语搭配。下文提到：即使他的外表随岁月发生了变迁，或因意外而发生了改变，他的指纹仍能证明他的身份。由此看来，嫌疑犯否认改变是徒劳的。vain 表示"徒劳的，无益的"的时候，和介词 in 搭配构成固定短语，表"徒然"，故应将 on 改成 in。

71.【答案】eyes — eye。

【解析】本题考查固定短语。eyes 常以复数出现，因为人有两只眼睛。但在固定短语 the naked eye "肉眼"中，用单数形式。

Part VI

72.【答案】safeguard our national interests。

【解析】本题结构简单，明显只是单纯考查"保卫国家利益"的表达，safeguard national interests 可以当作固定搭配来记忆。

73.【答案】he was just able to discern the road in the dark。

【解析】本题是 so...that...句型，just 在这里有"勉强"的意思。discern "分辨"。需要有一定的判断力。

74.【答案】The salvage operation had been a complete failure。

【解析】本题考查词语的选择。"打捞"salvage 多指从灾难中救出。既可以做名词也可以做动词。

75.【答案】depend on none but ourselves。

【解析】本题考查强调判断句。强调"不是别人而是我们自己"。

76.【答案】handling your cash card。

【解析】本题考查 take caution in doing sth. "谨慎做某事"。

预 测 试 题 五

Part V   Error Correction   (15 minutes)

Directions: *This part consists of a short passage. In this passage, there are altogether 10 mistakes, one in each numbered line. You may have to change a word, add a word or delete a word. Mark out the mistakes and put the corrections in the blanks provided. If you change a word, cross it out and write the correct word in the corresponding blank. If you add a word, put an insertion mark (∧) in the right place and write the missing word in the blank. If you delete a word, cross it out and put a slash (/) in the blank.*

Nearly everyone has heard of the popular alcohol drink, 'sherry'. Not everyone knows, however, that the home of sherry is a tiny corner of southwest Spain — an area where the climate and local conditions are exceptionally good for growing the grapes from that sherry is made.

Probably long ago as 700 BC the vine was being cultivated in the fields around the town where Jerez now stands. Certainly when the Moors invaded southern Spain in 711 AD they found a flourish sherry-making industry. The 13th century Spanish king, Alfonso the Wise, won the little town of Jerez back with the Moors, and did much to boost the wine trade in the area. It was the English merchants who settled in Jerez in the 15th century, however, who first introduced sherry into England, and who gave to the British people taste which they have never lost.

During the reign of Queen Elizabeth I sherry was enjoyed by people in the highest of circles and in the lowest of taverns. Indeed, Sir Francis Drake stole 3, 000 casks of sherry when he entered Cadiz harbour at his famous raiding expedition of 1587. In the 19th century the Duke of Wellington is said to have enjoyed sip sherry whilst on his great military campaigns, and Lord Nelson was supplied with a cask of sherry before the battle of Trafalgar. Back at home no drawing-room was complete with its decanter of sherry on the sideboard. Nowadays Great Britain is the largest importer of sherry in the world, and about 600, 000 gallons of sherry are shipped to the British Isle every year.

62. _____

63. _____

64. _____

65. _____

66. _____

67. _____

68. _____

69. _____

70. _____

71. _____

Part VI   Translation   (5 minutes)

Direction: *complete the sentences by translating into English the Chinese given in* *brackets. Please write your translation on **Answer Sheet 2.***

72. Such words simply _____ (在铁的事实面前碰得粉碎).

73. You should _____ (和律师协商一下这个案子).

74. He had to _____ (以事情本来可能会更糟糕这样的想法来安慰自己).

75. I walked around the house _____ (不住地吮着阵阵作痛的手指), and eventually arrived at the telephone.

76. His failure was _____ (完全是由于他自己的粗心).

答案与解析

Part V

62. 【答案】alcohol — alcoholic。

【解析】本题考查词类。这里需要用 alcohol 的形容词形式 alcoholic 来修饰名词 drink。

63. 【答案】that — which。

【解析】本题考查定语从句引导词。当引导定语从句时，如果引导词前有介词，那就应该用 which 而非 that。

64. 【答案】Probably ∧ long — ∧ as。

【解析】本题考查固定搭配。as…as…为固定搭配，任何一个 as 都不能省略。

65. 【答案】flourish — flourishing。

【解析】本题考查此类。flourish 为动词，这里需要将其改成现在分词形式的形容词来修饰 industry。

66. 【答案】with — from。

【解析】本题考查固定搭配。前面提到 the Moors invaded southern Spain，所以应该是从 the Moors 手里把 Jerez 给赢回来了，故需将介词 with 改成 from，win…back from…意为"从…赢回…"。

67. 【答案】people ∧ taste — ∧ a。

【解析】本题考查名词单复数。taste 指某一一种东西的味道时为可数名词。

68. 【答案】at — on。

【解析】本题考查固定搭配。expedition 不和介词 at 而和介词 on 搭配。

69. 【答案】sip — sipping。

【解析】本题考查惯用法。enjoy 后面跟 doing sth.，因此要将 sip 改成 sipping。

70. 【答案】with — without。

【解析】本题考查逻辑关系。根据上下文内容，客厅里应是没有葡萄酒就不能算完整。

71. 【答案】Isle — Isles。

【解析】本题考查名词单复数。英国由多个岛屿组成，故应为复数。

Part VI

72. 【答案】shatter themselves on the hard fact。

【解析】本题考查词语的选择"撞得粉碎"。shatter themselves，shatter 指彻底碾碎，无法恢复原状。crush 也有"粉碎"的意思但它强调挤压或踩的动作，毁坏程度不如 shatter 深，这里显然用 shatter 好些。"铁的事实" hard fact。在这里 words 指"言论"。

73. 【答案】confer with the lawyer about this case。

【解析】本题考查固定搭配 confer with sb. about/ on sth. 和某人协商某事。

74. 【答案】console himself with the thought that it might have been worse。

【解析】本题考查虚拟语气及固定搭配。短语 console oneself with sth. "用某事来安慰自己"。从句用 might haven done 表示"本来会发生但却没有发生的事"，是一种虚拟。

75. 【答案】sucking my very painful finger。

【解析】本题考查现在分词做伴随状语。由于"吮手指"和前面的 walk around the house 是同时发生的所以在这不要翻译成并列的谓语，而翻译成伴随状语较好。suck "吮，吸"。

76. 【答案】due to nothing else than his own carelessness。

【解析】本题考查强调判断句。be nothing else than… "不是别的…正是…"。"由于"前面有了 was，很明显这里用 be due to。

预 测 试 题 六

Part V   Cloze   (15 minutes)

Directions: *There are 20 blanks in the following passage. For each blank there are four choices marked [A]、[B]、[C] and[D] on the right side of the paper. You should choose the ONE that best fits into the passage. Then mark the corresponding letter on **Answer Sheet 2** with a single line through the centre.*

With the start of BBC World Service Television, millions of viewers in Asia and America can now watch the Corporation's news coverage, __62__ listen to it.

And of course in Britain listeners and viewers can turn into two BBC television __63__ , five BBC national radio services and __64__ of local radio stations. They have brought sport, comedy, drama, music, news and __65__ affairs, education, religion, parliamentary coverage, children's programmes and films for an annual license fee of £ 83 per __66__ .

It is a remarkable record, __67__ back over 70 years — yet the BBC's future is now __68__ doubt. The corporation will survive as a publicly broadcasting organization, at least __69__ the time being, but its role, its size and its programmes are now the __70__ of a nationwide debate in Britain.

The debate was launched by the

62. [A] as well   [B] as well as
    [C] may as well [D] may well
63. [A] channels   [B] chances
    [C] changes   [D] charges
64. [A] dozes   [B] doles
    [C] dozen   [D] dozens
65. [A] currency   [B] current
    [C] currently   [D] currant
66. [A] housewife   [B] housework
    [C] household   [D] housing
67. [A] striking   [B] strengthening
    [C] striding   [D] stretching
68. [A] in   [B] without
    [C] beyond   [D] no
69. [A] at   [B] in
    [C] for   [D] from
70. [A] subject   [B] style
    [C] sub   [D] subsidy
71. [A] for   [B] on
    [C] with   [D] at
72. [A] which   [B] what
    [C] that   [D] it
73. [A] worthful   [B] worth
    [C] worthy   [D] worthwhile

Government, which invited anyone __71__ an opinion of the BBC — including ordinary listeners and viewers to say __72__ was good or bad about the corporation, and even whether they thought it was __73__ keeping. The reason for its inquiry is that BBC's royal charter runs __74__ in 1996 and it must decide whether to keep the organization as it is, or to __75__ changes.

Defenders of the corporation — of whom there are many — are fond of __76__ the American slogan "If it ain't broke, don't fix it." The BBC "ain't broke", they say, __77__ which they mean it is not broken (as distinct from the word "broke", meaning having no money), __78__ why bother to change it?

Yet the BBC will have to change, because the broadcasting world around it is changing. The commercial TV channels — ITV and Channel 4 — were required by the Thatcher Government's Broadcasting Act to become more commercial, __79__ with each other for advertisers, and cutting costs and jobs. __80__ it is the arrival of new satellite channels — funded partly by advertising and partly by viewers' subscriptions — which will bring __81__ the biggest changes in the long term.

74. [A] across   [B] down
    [C] out   [D] off
75. [A] bring   [B] keep
    [C] do   [D] make
76. [A] quoting
    [B] quitting
    [C] quizzing
    [D] questioning
77. [A] by   [B] for
    [C] at   [D] toward
78. [A] and
    [B] because
    [C] so
    [D] as
79. [A] quarrelling
    [B] comparing
    [C] compiling
    [D] competing
80. [A] And   [B] So
    [C] For   [D] But
81. [A] forth   [B] about
    [C] off   [D] out

Part VI   Translation   (5 minutes)

Directions: *complete the sentences by translating into English the Chinese given in brackets. Please write your translation on **Answer Sheet 2**.*

82. _____ (他们不仅带了小吃和饮料), but they also brought cards for entertainment when they had a picnic in the forest.

83. The man who betrayed me was _____ (不是别人，正是我最好的朋友).

84. We have no need to run after luxury, because _____ (高价格并不一

定意味着高品质）.

85. _____（你过去是，现在是，将来仍是）my beloved friend.

86. _____（国家间的国际性合作）is an urgent necessity, because new infectious diseases threaten world economy.

答案与解析

62. 选［B］。短语搭配题。本句的意思是：随着BBC（英国广播公司）电视服务的诞生，现在成百上千万亚洲及美洲观众不仅可以听到，而且可以看到BBC的新闻节目。因此［B］as well as"也，又"符合题意。［A］as well"也"，一般放在句尾；［C］may as well意为"最好"；［D］may well意为"有充分的理由可以"。

63. 选［A］。词汇辨析题。能和句中的BBC television形成语义场共现的是［A］channels"频道，渠道"。［B］chances"机会，可能性"；［C］changes"变化，改革"；［D］charges"费用，主管"均脱离了语境。

64. 选［D］。短语搭配题。根据前文的two，five可知，所填词也应能表示数量，故将答案锁定于［C］dozen和［D］dozens这两项。但［C］dozen不和介词of连用，故可排除；［D］dozens常与of搭配，意思是"许多的"，符合题意，为答案。［A］dozes"瞌睡，假寐"；［B］doles"施舍品，救济金"均不符语义。

65. 选［B］。词汇辨析题。能和news形成语义共现关系的是current affairs"时事"，故选［B］。［A］currency"流通，流行"；［C］currently"普遍地，当前"；［D］currant"（无核）葡萄干，［植］黑醋栗"均不符合题意。

66. 选［C］。词汇辨析题。本句的意思是：…每年的收视费为每户83英镑。四个选项中，只有［C］household"一家人，家庭"才能表示"户，家"。［A］housewife"主妇，家庭主妇"；［B］housework"劳动，家务事"；［D］housing"供给住宅，住宅群"语义均不符合。

67. 选［D］。逻辑推理题。选项中能和back over 70 years形成语义场共现的是［D］stretching，它可以表示"穿越一段给定的时间"，故为答案。本句的意思是：这是一个非凡的记录，可以追溯到七十多年以前。［A］striking"显著的，惊人的"；［B］strengthening"加强，巩固"；［C］striding"大步行走，跨过"均脱离了语境。

68. 选［A］。短语搭配题。根据前文可知，BBC曾经有过辉煌的历史，但从yet一词可知，现在BBC前途未卜。因此［A］in doubt"不能肯定的，可怀疑的"为答案。［B］without doubt"无疑的"；［C］beyond doubt"无疑的，确切的"；［D］no doubt"无疑"均与原文逻辑相悖。

69. 选 [C]。短语搭配题。for the time being 为固定搭配，意为"暂时，目前，眼下"，故 [C] 为正确答案。本句的意思是：公司将以公共广播的组织形式而存在，至少目前是这样…。

70. 选 [A]。逻辑推理题。能和 a nationwide debate 形成语义场共现的只有 [A] subject "题目，主题"。本句的意思是：…但是它的作用、规模及节目现在却是全英国人民争论的话题。[B] style "风格，时尚，文体"；[C] sub "潜水艇，低能者"；[D] subsidy "补助金，津贴" 均脱离了语境。

71. 选 [C]。词汇辨析题。政府邀请的应该是对 BBC 有想法的人，因此所填词应能表示"具有，拥有"之意。查看选项，符合的是 [C] with "有，以，用"。[A] for "为了，因为"；[B] on "在…之上，依附于"；[D] at "在…方面"均不符合题意。

72. 选 [B]。语法结构题。所填词既要能引导名词性从句充当主句的宾语，又要能在从句中作主语，选项中有此用法的是 [B] what "什么"，它可用来引导名词性从句，作主语、宾语或表语。[A] which "哪个，哪几个" 和 [C] that "那，那个" 能够用于引导从句，但它们都不能在从句中充当某种成分，故均可排除；[D] it "它"，不用于引导从句，故也可排除。

73. 选 [B]。短语搭配题。四个选项都表示"值得"，因此要从它们的具体用法上来作出判断。[B] worth 后面常跟 doing sth.，意为"值得做某事；有做某事的价值"，符合题意。[A] worthful "有价值的，宝贵的" 无此用法，它一般用作定语；[C] worthy 为形容词，既可作表语，也可作定语，作表语时常用于 be worthy of sth. /to do sth. 的结构中；[D] worthwhile 为形容词，常用于有形式主语的句子中，即 It is worthwhile to do sth.。

74. 选 [C]。短语搭配题。根据句中的 it must decide whether to keep the organization as it is（公司必须决定是要维持公司现状，还是作出改变）可知，BBC 的皇家特许证于 1996 年就到期了。所以 [C] runs out "完成，被用完" 符合题意。[A] runs across "偶遇，跑着穿过"；[B] runs down "停止，撞倒"；[D] runs off "逃跑，流掉" 均不符合题目的语义要求。

75. 选 [D]。短语搭配题。本题考查名词 change 的固定搭配。change 意为"改革，变化，转变"，可与 make 搭配，表示"作出改变或更改"，因此 [D] 为正确答案。

76. 选 [A]。词汇辨析题。本句的意思是：公司众多的维护者喜欢引用一句美国式口号"没坏就别补"。四个选项中，[A] quoting 意为"引用，引证"；[B] quitting 意为"离开，辞职"；[C] quizzing 意为"测验，提问"；[D] questioning 意为"询问，审问"。综合分析，quoting 符合句子意思，因此 [A] 为正确答案。

77. 选 [A]。短语搭配题。本题考查的是介词 by 的用法，短语 sb. means…by…意思是"某人说…意思是…"，故 [A] 为答案。

78. 选［C］。逻辑推理题。本句的意思是：BBC 还未到山穷水尽的地步，因此为什么要费事去改变它呢？从语意上分析，空格前后是因果关系，空格前是原因，空格后是结果，故选［C］so，表结果。［A］and 表示并列关系，故不选；［B］because 和［D］as 都用于前果后因的场合，故也可排除。

79. 选［D］。短语搭配题。四个选项除［C］项之外都能和介词 with 搭配，但能和前文 commercial 形成语义照应的是［D］competing "竞争"，与 with each other 搭配时表示 "相互竞争"，符合题意。［A］quarrelling with each other 意为 "相互争吵"；［B］comparing with each other 意为 "相互比较"。［C］compiling "编译，编辑，汇编" 为及物动词，后面无须跟介词再接宾语。

80. 选［D］。逻辑推理题。上句讲的是变革带来的消极影响，而本句讲的是变革带来的积极影响，因此，本句与前一句是转折关系，故选［D］But 表转折。［A］And 表并列；［B］So 表结果；［C］For 表原因，均违背原文逻辑。

81. 选［B］。短语搭配题。本题考查动词 bring 的固定搭配。四个选项中，［A］bring forth 意为 "提出，出示"；［B］bring about 意为 "使发生，带来"；［C］bring off 意为 "救出，完成"；［D］bring out 意为 "出版，生产"。根据空格后的 the biggest changes 可知，bring about 最符合句子意思，故［B］正确。

Part VI

82. 【答案】Not only did they bring snacks and drinks。
    【解析】本题考查倒装。当具有否定意义的词 no，not until，not only，no sooner，by no means，in no case / way，at no time 等位于句首时，要用部分倒装。

83. 【答案】no other than my best friend。
    【解析】本题考查的句型是：主语 + be + no/none + other than/but + 表语（强调内容）。betray "背叛"。

84. 【答案】a high price does not necessarily mean good quality。
    【解析】本题考查部分否定的表达法：概括词 + not + 谓语动词。用 a high price 表示泛指。

85. 【答案】You were，you are and you remain to be。
    【解析】本题考查考生的变通能力。题干中的 "过去是"、"现在是"、" 将来仍是" 完全可以通过英语中的时态准确去表达出来。"were，are，to be" 分别表示 "过去，现在与将来"。

86. 【答案】International collaboration between countries。
    【解析】本题考查 "国际性合作" 的表达 international collaboration。另外，in collaboration with 也是常用的固定搭配，表示 "与…合作"。

预 测 试 题 七

Directions: *This part consists of a short passage. In this passage, there are altogether 10 mistakes, one in each numbered line. You may have to change a word, add a word or delete a word. Mark out the mistakes and put the corrections in the blanks provided. If you change a word, cross it out and write the correct word in the corresponding blank. If you add a word, put an insertion mark (∧) in the right place and write the missing word in the blank. If you delete a word, cross it out and put a slash (/) in the blank.*

One of the greatest mysteries of the world, for that scientists have so far been unable to find some satisfactory explanation, is the Bermuda Triangle, sometimes called "The Graveyard of the Atlantic". This is an area of the western Atlantic between Bermuda and Florida, roughly triangular in shape, there since 1945 at least a hundred ships and planes and over a thousand people have disappeared. No wreckage has been found, no bodies, lifebelts or any other evidence of disaster. It is as if these planes, ships and people never existed. In some cases a radio message has been received from aircraft reporting everything in the order a few minutes before all contact was lost, in other a weak S. O. S. message has been picking up and, in perfect weather, inexplicable references to fog and loss of bearings. In the extraordinary case of five U. S. navy planes disappearing on a routine mission from Florida, the rescue plane sent to locate them vanishing also. There have been references to the curious white light or haze which is a feature of the sea in part of this area, and it is interesting to note that not only were this light, or streaks of light, observed by the astronauts on their way to space, but was also noted by Columbus, five centuries before. Whether this light has any	62. _____ 63. _____ 64. _____ 65. _____ 66. _____ 67. _____ 68. _____ 69. _____ 70. _____ 71. _____

connection with the mysterious disappearances is unknown — it is just another curious circumstance as yet unexplained.

Part VI　　　　　　　Translation　　　　　　　(5 minutes)

Directions: *complete the sentences by translating into English the Chinese given in brackets. Please write your translation on **Answer Sheet 2**.*

72. The method of scientific investigation is _____ (只不过是人类思维活动的必要表达方式).

73. Our restaurant tries to _____ (满足顾客的各种需要).

74. _____ (我去过的地方很多) I have never seen anyone who's as capable as John.

75. On summer vacations, I _____ (宁可在家看电视而不愿去度假).

76. The earth _____ (是月球大小的49倍).

答 案 与 解 析

Part V

62. 【答案】 that — which。
　　【解析】 本题考查定语从句的关系词。当定语从句的关系代词前有介词时，不能用 that，要用 which。要注意，当介词放到后面时，就没有此限制了，例如：This is a date that we are all proud of. （这是一个我们都感到骄傲的日子）。

63. 【答案】 some — any。
　　【解析】 本题考查不定代词。some 通常用于肯定句和表示建议的句子，而 any 常用于否定句和疑问句。句中的 unable 含有否定含义，使句子成为一个否定句，故应将 some 改成 any。

64. 【答案】 there — where。
　　【解析】 本题考查地点副词所引导的定语从句。本句是复合句，但前后两句缺少连接词。应把副词 there 改成 where，引导非限制性定语从句修饰先行词 an area of the western Atlantic。

65. 【答案】 never ∧ existed — had。
　　【解析】 本题考查虚拟语气。由 as if 引导的从句要根据实际情况来决定是否进行虚拟。从上文可知 these planes, ships and people 曾经存在，所以该从句是假设的条件，对过去发生的事情进行假设要用过去完成时，即 had + 过去完成分词。

66. 【答案】the — the。

【解析】本题考查固定短语。在固定短语 in order "状况良好"中，名词表示泛指，其前不加定冠词。

67. 【答案】other — others。

【解析】本题考查不定代词的用法。句中的 in other 同 in some cases 相对应，other 指代的是前面的 cases，为保持一致性，应改为复数形式 others，相当于 other cases。如 I haven't brought many cakes. Could you get some others? （我没有多买糕点，你有多余的吗?）

68. 【答案】picking — picked。

【解析】本题考查动词的被动语态。动词短语 pick up 同本句的主语 a weak S. O. S. message 应是动宾关系，即主语是该动作的承受者，故应改成被动语态形式。

69. 【答案】vanishing — vanished。

【解析】本题考查句子结构。分析结构可知句子缺少谓语。句子的主语是 the rescue plane，动词 sent...them 为过去分词短语作后置定语，而谓语缺失。应把 vanishing 改为 vanished 作谓语。句子大意为："一个显著案例是，五架美国海军飞机从佛罗里达起飞执行常规任务时失踪，而派出寻找他们的救援机也消失了。"

70. 【答案】were — was。

【解析】本题考查主谓一致原则。本句是 not only 引导的倒装句，主语为 this light，其后的 or streaks of light 为插入语，并不影响主语。因此谓语应为第三人称单数，和主语保持一致。

71. 【答案】before — ago。

【解析】本题考查副词 ago 与 before 的区别。ago 意为"从现在起何年（月、日等）以前"，而 before 却用来指"过去某一特定时间的以前"，即"从当时起何年（月、日等）以前"，因此 ago 常与过去时连用，而 before 却多与间接引语中的过去完成时搭配使用。例如：His father died three years ago. He said his father died three years before.。本句中的"五个世纪以前"是指从现在起五个世纪以前，所以应将 before 改为用于一般过去时的 ago。

Part VI

72. 【答案】nothing but the expression of the necessary mode of working of the human being。

【解析】本题考查强调判断句及翻译时的变通。be nothing but... "只不过是…"前面已经讲了很多，这里不再细说。本题"表达方式"前面带了很长的定语，翻译时将其断为几个 of 结构。

73.【答案】cater for the need of the customers。
　　【解析】本题考查短语 cater for "满足需要，配备食物，投合"。

74.【答案】Much as I have traveled。
　　【解析】本题考查倒装。"副词＋as＋主语＋助动词＋主句"，翻译时一定要看完整个句子后再决定所填部分所需的结构，例如 这句话，但看要翻译的汉语部分根本无法确定用倒装。后面定语从句中包含 as…as 结构的比较句型。

75.【答案】would rather watch TV at home than spend a vacation。
　　【解析】本题考查 "would rather … than …" 句型，意思是 "宁愿…而不愿…"。spend a vacation "度假"，要区分开另一个相近词 vocation "职业"。

76.【答案】is 49 times the size of the moon。
　　【解析】考查倍数表达法，倍数表达法除了前面我们在理论部分讲的几种结构之外，在简单句中表达 "A 是 B 的几倍" 时用 "A is ＋倍数＋ the size of ＋ B"。

预测试题八

Part V   **Error Correction**   (15 minutes)

Directions: *This part consists of a short passage. In this passage, there are altogether 10 mistakes, one in each numbered line. You may have to change a word, add a word or delete a word. Mark out the mistakes and put the corrections in the blanks provided. If you change a word, cross it out and write the correct word in the corresponding blank. If you add a word, put an insertion mark (∧) in the right place and write the missing word in the blank. If you delete a word, cross it out and put a slash (/) in the blank.*

Housing has remained a headache for many a country for decades. Families of multi-generations over-crowding one room and the homeless wandering among the sky-scrapers and rambling in the parks is the common outlook of big   62. _____ cities. These phenomena often cause social destruction and even crimes.

However, most victimized countries are in the develo-   63. _____ ping world. The major problem is population. The pace of house-construction can not keep down with the rapid growth   64. _____ of population. Another reason lays in the most developing   65. _____ countries are poor and fail to invest enough money into house-building. The unjust social distribution of wealth also play a part.   66. _____

With a handful of rich people live in luxurious and   67. _____ spacious houses on one hand, many poor people are driven out of his houses because of lack of money on the other   68. _____ hand.

In order to solve these problems, necessary measures must be done to develop the economy, control the growth   69. _____ of population and improving the existing system of wealth   70. _____ distribution. Only in this way can we fight a way ahead.   71. _____

Part VI　　　　　Translation　　　　　(5 minutes)

Directions: *complete the sentences by translating into English the Chinese given in brackets. Please write your translation on **Answer Sheet 2**.*

72. This substance _____（反应速度是另外那种物质的三倍）.

73. Some math problems in that book are _____（我实在解不出来）.

74. No one knows who wrote that play, but it is _____（归功于莎士比亚）.

75. It is strange that _____（女孩子的皮肤总是比男孩们更容易被碰青肿）.

76. You should try to get a good night's sleep, however _____（你还必须做多少工作）.

答 案 与 解 析

Part V

62.【答案】is — are。
　【解析】本题考查主谓一致原则。主语为"Families of multi-generations over-crowding one room and the homeless wandering among the sky-scrapers and rambling in the parks"，故谓语应用复数形式，即将 is 改为 are。

63.【答案】However，∧ most — ∧ the。
　【解析】本题考查形容词最高级。victimised 的最高级为 the most victimised。

64.【答案】down — up。
　【解析】本题考查固定搭配。keep up with 意为"跟上（某人或某物），与（某人或某物）同步前进"。

65.【答案】lays — lies。
　【解析】本题考查易混词辨析。lay：放下；铺，砌，下（蛋），产（卵）；设置，布置；使处于（某种状态）；提出，主张。lie：躺，平放；位于；处于（某种状态）；展现，伸展；（in, with）（问题、事情等）在于，说谎。句子意思为：另一个原因在于，大部分发展中国家都很贫穷，不能投足够的钱在房屋建设上。很显然，应将 lays 改成 lies。

66.【答案】play — plays。
　【解析】本题考查主谓一致原则。主语为 the unjust social distribution of wealth "社会财富的分配不均"，故谓语用单数第三人称形式 plays。

67.【答案】live — living。

【解析】本题考查非谓语动词的用法。分析句子结构可知，with...hand 在句中作伴随状语，因此 live 要用现在分词形式，充当 rich people 的宾语补足语。

68. 【答案】his — their。

【解析】本题考查代词指代的一致性。此处代词的指代对象为 many poor people，故应用 their。

69. 【答案】done — taken。

【解析】本题考查固定搭配。"采取措施"应用 take measures，而没有 do measures 这种用法。

70. 【答案】improving — improve。

【解析】本题考查平行结构。由 and 连接的并列成分在形态上需保持一致，以保证句子结构的平衡，故这里 improving 也应和前面的 develop 和 control 保持形式上的一致，改为 improve。

71. 【答案】ahead — out。

【解析】本题考查固定搭配。fight sth. out 意为"通过斗争使（争论等）得到解决"，其中的 out 不能用 head 来代替。

Part VI

72. 【答案】reacts three times as fast as the other one。

【解析】本题考查倍数表达法。"倍数 + as + 形容词/副词 + as"。

73. 【答案】more than I can work out。

【解析】考查比较句型及直译。我们常见的比较句型 than 后面多为单个的词，这其实是省略了从句中与主句相同的成分。More than I can...可以当作固定句型，意为"超出了我所能…的范围"。

74. 【答案】often ascribed to me。

【解析】本题考查词语的选择。"把…归功于"可以 ascribe to...，attribute to...两个短语都可以表示"归功于"，但？ascribe to...还多用来指"认为是…的作品"，翻译本句时还要注意应用被动语态。

75. 【答案】girls are much easier to bruise their skin than boys。

【解析】本题考查 it 做形式主语的句型"it is + 形容词 + that 从句"、比较句型及翻译时的变通。汉语比较一般是具体的方面，例如"女孩的皮肤"，但英语习惯是先说大的比较范围再说具体的方面。girls...their skin。翻译时注意英汉的不同语言习惯，bruise"碰青，擦伤"本身已经含有被动的意思，翻译时不再用被动语态。另外它还可以做名词"瘀伤"。

76. 【答案】much work you have to do。

【解析】本题考查倒装。however 在这里不是连词而是副词"无论如何"的意思，"however + 形容词/副词"放在句首时句子要倒装。

预测试题九

Part V **Cloze** (15 minutes)

Directions: *There are 20 blanks in the following passage. For each blank there are four choices marked [A], [B], [C] and[D] on the right side of the paper. You should choose the ONE that best fits into the passage. Then mark the corresponding letter on* **Answer Sheet 2** *with a single line through the centre.*

More and more, the operations of our businesses, governments, and financial institutions are controlled by information that exists only inside computer memories. __62__ clever enough to modify this information for his own purposes can __63__ big reward. Even worse, a number of people who have done this and been caught __64__ it have managed to get away without punishment.

It's easy for computer crimes to go __65__ if no one checks up on what the computer is doing. But even if the crime is detected, the criminal may walk __66__ without punishment but with a __67__ recommendation from his __68__ employers.

Of course, we have no statistics on crimes that go undetected. But it's __69__ to note how many of the crimes we do know about were detected by __70__, not by systematic inspections or other security __71__. The computer criminals who have been caught may have been the victims of __72__ bad luck.

62. [A] Everyone [B] Someone
    [C] Anyone [D] Nobody

63. [A] acclaim [B] reap
    [C] reach [D] reclaim

64. [A] at [B] with
    [C] of [D] by

65. [A] unfound
    [B] undetected
    [C] discharged
    [D] underestimated

66. [A] aside [B] out
    [C] on [D] away

67. [A] redundant
    [B] glowing
    [C] terrible
    [D] formidable

68. [A] preceding
    [B] prior
    [C] former
    [D] proceeding

69. [A] annoyed [B] deliberate
    [C] persistent [D] disturbing

70. [A] accident [B] incident
    [C] coincidence [D] case

__73__ other lawbreakers, who must leave the country, __74__ suicide, or go to jail, computer criminals sometimes __75__ punishment, demanding not only that they not be charged but that they be given good recommendations and perhaps other benefits. All too __76__, their demands have been met.

Why? Because company executives are afraid of the bad publicity that would result if the public found out that their computer had been misused. They __77__ at the thought of a criminal __78__ in open court of how he *juggled* (诈骗) the most confidential __79__ right under the noses of the company's executives, accountants, and security __80__. And so another computer criminal __81__ with just the recommendations he needs to continue his crimes elsewhere.

71. [A] procedures　　[B] process
　　[C] progress　　　[D] precedence
72. [A] unluckily　　　[B] uncommonly
　　[C] recklessly　　　[D] subjectively
73. [A] Like　　　　　[B] Despite
　　[C] Unlike　　　　[D] Though
74. [A] commit　　　　[B] do
　　[C] make　　　　　[D] carry
75. [A] avoid　　　　　[B] violate
　　[C] escort　　　　　[D] escape
76. [A] usual　　　　　[B] often
　　[C] much　　　　　[D] rarely
77. [A] contemplate　　[B] manifest
　　[C] hesitate　　　　[D] contrive
78. [A] elaborating　　　[B] simulating
　　[C] proposing　　　[D] boasting
79. [A] records　　　　[B] figures
　　[C] deficits　　　　[D] matters
80. [A] stuff　　　　　[B] facility
　　[C] staff　　　　　[D] faculty
81. [A] separates　　　[B] divides
　　[C] cuts　　　　　[D] departs

Part VI　　　　　　　Translation　　　　　(5 minutes)

Directions: *complete the sentences by translating into English the Chinese given in brackets. Please write your translation on **Answer Sheet 2**.*

82. The room was _____ (弥漫着咖啡的芳香).

83. It is not heroes that make history, _____ (而是历史创造了英雄).

84. Don't trust them. They acted _____ (他们和贪官污吏狼狈为奸).

85. People as a rule tend to notice things or people that _____ (偏离常规).

86. His physical injuries had quickly healed, but _____ (精神上的创伤却在心灵上留下了一个永久的疤痕).

答案与解析

62. 选［C］。词汇辨析题。原句意为：任何一个足够聪明，为了自己的目的而修改这些信息的人的都能…，因此选［C］Anyone。

63. 选［B］。词汇辨析题。选项中能和 big reward 构成合理的动宾搭配的是，［B］reap "收获，收割"。［A］acclaim 意为 "称赞，欢呼"；［C］reach 意为 "到达，达到"；［D］reclaim 意为 "要求归还，收回" 在语义上都不符合题意。

64. 选［A］。短语搭配题。be caught at sth. /doing sth. 为惯用法，意思是 "在做某事时被当场抓住"，因此选 at。原句意为：更糟糕的是，很多这样做了而且当场被抓住的人最后都可以设法逃脱惩罚。

65. 选［B］。逻辑推理题。后文提到 But even if the crime is detected，再根据反义复现原则可知，［B］undetected "未被发现的，未被查出的" 为答案。［A］unfound 意为 "未被找到的"；［C］discharged 意为 "放电的，泻出的"；［D］underestimated 意为 "低估的" 均不符题意。

66. 选［D］。短语搭配题。［D］walk away 意为 "走开"，符合题意。没有 walk aside 这种说法，故［A］先可排除；［B］walk out 意为 "罢工" 和［C］walk on 意为 "继续行走" 均不能使原文语义连贯。

67. 选［B］。逻辑推理题。所填词是修饰 recommendation 的形容词，根据空格前的 without punishment but with a 可知，犯罪者得到的推荐信一定不是不好的，也就是说所填词一定是表积极、肯定意义的形容词，查看选项，只有［B］glowing "生动的，有力的" 符合题意。［A］redundant "多余的，冗长的"；［C］terrible "很糟的，极坏的"；［D］formidable "可怕的，艰难的" 均为贬义词，故都可排除。

68. 选［C］。词汇辨析题。根据常识可知，推荐信一般是前任雇主或老板给发出的，所以此处需要填入一个能表 "以前" 之意的词，这点前三项都符合，因此需要区分它们具体的用法。［A］preceding 意为 "在前的，前述的"，如：preceding chapter "前述章节"；［B］prior 意为 "优先的"，如：prior to "在前，居先"；［C］former 意为 "时间上靠前的" 或者 "前任的"，如：former classmate "以前的同学"，former president "前任总统"。由此可见，显然［C］former 最符合题意，为答案。［D］proceeding 意为 "进程，行动"，语义不符。

69. 选［D］。词汇辨析题。［A］annoyed 和［C］persistent 一般用于指人，故先可排除。［B］deliberate 意为 "故意的，深思熟虑的" 显然不符合原文语义。［D］disturbing 意为 "引起烦恼的，令人不安的" 符合题意。原句意为：令人感到烦恼的是，很多电脑犯罪是意外被发现的，而不是通过系统的检查或其他安全程序发现的。

70. 选［A］。短语搭配题。by accident 为固定短语，意为"意外地，偶然地"。

71. 选［A］。词汇辨析题。根据句意，这里指的是"安全程序"，故选［A］procedures "程序，手续"。［B］process 意为"过程，作用"；［C］progress 意为"前进，进步"；［D］precedence 意为"优先，居先"均语义不符。

72. 选［B］。词汇辨析题。所填词是用来修饰 bad 的，从语义上看，［B］uncommonly "非常，极其"正确。［A］unluckily 和 luck 语义重复，故不选；［C］recklessly "鲁莽地，不顾一切地"和［D］subjectively "主观地"语义均不符。

73. 选［C］。逻辑推理题。整篇文章的中心都是在讲电脑犯罪者不同于其他罪犯，即使犯罪，也没有什么严重的后果，因此［C］Unlike 正确。

74. 选［A］。短语搭配题。commit suicide 为固定的动宾搭配，意为"自杀"。

75. 选［D］。逻辑推理题。文章第二段提到过，the criminal may walk away without punishment，根据同义复现原则可知，［D］escape "躲避"为正确答案。［A］avoid 意为"避免"；［B］violate 意为"违犯"；［C］escort 意为"护送"均不符合题意。句子大意为：其他罪犯一旦罪行败露，就必须离开国家、自杀或者进监狱。不同于他们的是，电脑犯罪者有时可以逃避惩罚，并且要求雇主不但不控告他们，还要给他们写着好言好语的推荐信或者其他的好处。

76. 选［B］。短语搭配题。all too often 为固定短语，意为"时常"，故选［B］。

77. 选［C］。短语搭配题。根据题意可知，所填词需为不及物动词，并且能和介词 at 搭配使用。据此，可以得出选项［C］hesitate "犹豫，踌躇"为答案，hesitate at sth. "为某事而犹豫，踌躇"。［A］contemplate "凝视，沉思"；［B］"表明，证明"；［D］"发明，设计"均为及物动词，故均可排除。

78. 选［D］。词汇辨析题。根据空格后的 in open court of how he juggled…以及语义共现原则可知，［A］elaborating "详细描述"和［D］boasting "自夸"符合题意。但 elaborate 为不及物动词，要使用固定搭配 elaborate on，故可排除。［B］simulating "模仿，模拟"和［C］proposing "计划，建议"语义不符。

79. 选［A］。逻辑推理题。confidential records 意为"机密档案"，故［A］records 为答案。［B］figures "数字"；［C］deficits "赤字"；［D］matters "事件，物质"都不符合题意。

80. 选［C］。逻辑推理题。能和 executives, accountants 成语义场共现的只有 security staff，故选［C］。［A］stuff "原料，材料"，［B］facility "设备，工具"；［D］faculty "系，科，全体教员"脱离了语境。

81. 选［D］。逻辑推理题。根据句末的 continue his crimes elsewhere 可知，犯罪分子离开了原来的地方，故［D］departs "离开"正确。［A］separates 意为"分开，隔离"；［B］divides 意为"划分，分开"；［C］cut 意为"切（割、

削）" 都不符合题意。

Part VI

82. 【答案】saturated with the aroma of coffee。

【解析】本题考查词语的固定搭配及词语的选择。"弥漫" be saturated with，aroma "芳香" 指植物、香料或食物发出的香味，fragrant 一般多指植物散发出的香味，所以这里用 aroma。

83. 【答案】but history that makes heroes。

【解析】本题考查正反判断句。It is not…that，but that…两部分结构相同。

84. 【答案】in collusion with corrupt officials。

【解析】本题考查翻译时的词义褒贬法及意译。"狼狈为奸" 在英语中没有对应的词，in collusion with "与…勾结" 意思和感情色彩都相符。corrupt "腐败的，贪污的" 它还可以用作动词，意思是 "贿赂"。

85. 【答案】deviate from the routine。

【解析】考查固定搭配 deviate from… "偏离…"，本句是一个定语从句先行词既有人又有物时关系代词要用 that。

86. 【答案】the spiritual damage left a permanent scar on his mind。

【解析】这里考查词语的选择。首先，精神上的 "创伤" 要用 damage，injury 多指外伤。其次，"伤疤" scar 既可以指身体上的，也可以指精神上的。

预 测 试 题 十

Directions: *This part consists of a short passage. In this passage, there are altogether 10 mistakes, one in each numbered line. You may have to change a word, add a word or delete a word. Mark out the mistakes and put the corrections in the blanks provided. If you change a word, cross it out and write the correct word in the corresponding blank. If you add a word, put an insertion mark (∧) in the right place and write the missing word in the blank. If you delete a word, cross it out and put a slash (/) in the blank.*

Today's trumpet is one of the world's oldest instruments. It is the result of many centuries of development. Although it looks something like its ancestors, but there are many similarities. All trumpets are hollow tubes. They are all brown. And they all use the player's lip to produce the basic sound.

62. _____
63. _____

64. _____

The trumpet developed as players and makers worked to improve its design, size, shape, material, and method of construction. They wanted to create a instrument that would produce beautiful and attractive tone, enable the performer to play all the notes of scale, extend the range higher and lower, make it possible to play more difficult music, and in general, is easier to play good. The remarkable way in which the modern trumpet achieves these goals is a measure of the success of all those which struggled to perfect this glorious instrument.

65. _____

66. _____
67. _____

68. _____

The trumpet is actually the leading member of an entire family of relative instruments. There are trumpets of several different sizes, and in several different keys. There are cornets, bugles, flugelhorns, and a number of other that are all similar to the trumpet in the way they are made and played. From the use of trumpets in ancient religious ceremonies to the part they play in modern bands, the trumpet

69. _____

70. _____

family of instruments have much to tell about
civilization and its development.

71. _____

Part VI　　　　Translation　　　　(5 minutes)

Directions: *complete the sentences by translating into English the Chinese given in brackets. Please write your translation on* **Answer Sheet 2.**

72. _____ (控制"非典"的主要任务是隔离"非典"病人) from non-SARS patients in respects of the use of the equipments, examination rooms

73. What the man said was _____ (简直是一派胡言).

74. I could _____ (我体会到他越来越恼火), so I got up and left.

75. There were _____ (多达1000人) people at the meeting.

76. It's improbable that _____ (商人图谋占领市场) via the inappropriate methods.

答案与解析

Part V

62. 【答案】something — nothing。
【解析】本题考查句子的逻辑一致性。句首的 Although 表示两个分句存在转折关系，something like "有点像"和后分句中的 there are many similarities "有很多相似点"矛盾。将 something 改为 nothing 后，逻辑变得合理。nothing like 的意思是"丝毫不像"。

63. 【答案】but — but。
【解析】本题考查连词的用法。该句开头已有转折连词 although，再用 but，出现重复，故将 but 删除。在英语中，表达同种逻辑关系的连词不能用在同一个句子中，如 because 和 so。

64. 【答案】lip — lips。
【解析】本题考查名词的单复数。根据常识可知吹奏喇叭必须用双唇，且 lip 又是可数名词，所以应把 lip 改为 lips。

65. 【答案】a — an。
【解析】本题考查冠词的用法。instrument 是以元音音素开头的可数名词的单数，所以应该加上不定冠词 an。

66. 【答案】is — be。
【解析】本题考查主谓一致性。is 与 produce，enable，extend 和 make 由并列

255

连词 and 连接，一起充当 that 定语从句里的谓语。从句中有情态动词 would，因此谓语应该用动词原形。

67. 【答案】good — well。

【解析】 本题考查形容词和副词的用法。good 是形容词，不能修饰动词 play，要改成意思相同的副词 well。

68. 【答案】which — who。

【解析】 本题考查定语从句的关系代词。those 为先行词时通常指人，而 which 指的是物，应该将其改为指人的 who。

69. 【答案】relative — related。

【解析】 本题考查形容词的辨析。表达"有关的"意思时，relative 要与 to 连用，而且不能作前置定语，例如 All the details relative to the matter at issue under discussion. （所有的细节都与正在讨论的事情有关。）所以要将它改为符合这一用法的 related"有关的；相关的"。

70. 【答案】other — others。

【解析】 本题考查代词的使用。短语 a number of"许多的"后接可数名词的复数形式，所以相应的代词也应该是复数形式，故应把 other 改为 others。

71. 【答案】have — has。

【解析】 本题考查主谓一致性。该句的主语是 the trumpet family"喇叭家族"，可为单数或复数，视具体情况而定。由句末的 its development 可以推断出，这里 the trumpet family 是被视为一个整体，因此谓语应为第三人称单数形式。

Part VI

72. 【答案】The major role in SARS control is the segregation of SARS。

【解析】 本题考查词性转换及成分转化。本题要翻译的句子出现了三个动词"控制""是""隔离"，因此"控制""隔离"都要用名词短语。

73. 【答案】nothing else than nonsense。

【解析】 本题考查翻译时的灵活变通及强调判断句型。be nothing else than..."完全是，实在是"。

74. 【答案】sense his growing irritation。

【解析】 本题考查词类转化及变通技巧。"越来越…"可以用一个词 growing 表达。所以就将从句译成了由现在分词的复合结构作宾语的简单句。

75. 【答案】no less than one thousand。

【解析】 本题考查词语的选择。no less than"多达，不亚于"强调数量多。not less than 连写时，意为"不少于"，无数量多或少的含义。

76. 【答案】businessmen contrive to dominate market。

【解析】 本题考查 it 做形式主语及翻译时的词义褒贬法。"it is + 形容词 + that 从句""图谋"带有明显的贬义色彩，因此应用 contrive to 而不用 try to。

预测试题十一

Part V Error Correction (15 minutes)

Directions: *This part consists of a short passage. In this passage, there are altogether 10 mistakes, one in each numbered line. You may have to change a word, add a word or delete a word. Mark out the mistakes and put the corrections in the blanks provided. If you change a word, cross it out and write the correct word in the corresponding blank. If you add a word, put an insertion mark (∧) in the right place and write the missing word in the blank. If you delete a word, cross it out and put a slash (/) in the blank.*

An undergraduate course consists of a series of lectures, seminars and tutorials, and, in science and engineering, laboratory classes, which in total account about 15   **62.** _____
hours per week. Students studying for a particular degree will take a series of subject which run in parallel at a fixed   **63.** _____
time in each week and may last one academic term or the whole year. Associated with each lecture course is seminars, tutorials and laboratory classes which draw upon, an-   **64.** _____
alyze, illustrate or amplify the topics presented in the lectures. Lecture classes can vary in size through 20 to 200,   **65.** _____
although larger sized lectures tend to decrease as students progress into the second and third year and more options become available. Seminars and tutorials are on the whole much bigger than lecture classes and in some departments   **66.** _____
can be on a one-to-one basis. Students are normally expected to prepare work in the advance for seminars and tutorials   **67.** _____
and this can take the form of researching a topic by discussing, for writing essays or by solving problems. Lectures,   **68.** _____
seminars and tutorials are all one hour in length, whilst laboratory classes usually last either 2 or 3 hours. Much emphases is put on how to spend as much time if not more   **69.** _____
studying by themselves as taught. Each student has a tutor   **70.** _____
whom they can consult on any matter whether academic

or personal. Therefore the tutor will help, moti-
vation for study is expected to come from the
student.

71. _____

Part VI　　　　　　Translation　　　　　(5 minutes)

Directions: *complete the sentences by translating into English the Chinese given in brackets. Please write your translation on Answer Sheet 2.*

72. _____ (从山谷中传来一阵令人恐怖的声音) which scared me.

73. _____ (正是 Jefferson 写了) *the Declaration of Independence.*

74. Don't care too much about it and there is _____ (人皆有过).

75. He is so devoted to his experiment that _____ (没有人感觉不到他对事业的热爱).

76. The food was cold, the guests quarreled — _____ (整个晚宴是一次彻底的失败).

答案与解析

Part V

62.【答案】account ∧ about — ∧ for。
　【解析】本题考查动词的用法。account 作及物动词时，意为"认为"，用在此处语义不符。account for 意为"占"，符合句意。

63.【答案】subject — subjects。
　【解析】本题考查名词单复数。subject 为可数名词，用于表"一连串的"的 a series of 后面应该用复数形式。

64.【答案】is — are。
　【解析】本题考查主谓一致。句子为倒装句，真正的顺序应为 Seminars, tutorials and laboratory classes are associated with each lecture course...，所以应该将 are 改成 is。

65.【答案】through — from。
　【解析】本题考查固定搭配。要表示"大小在…到…之间变化"，应该用 vary in size from...to...，而不能用 through。

66.【答案】bigger — smaller。
　【解析】本题考查语义逻辑。前文提到 Lecture classes can vary in size from 20 to 200，而本句则说 Seminars and tutorials...in some departments can be on a one-to-one basis。由此可见，Seminars and tutorials 要比 lecture classes 小，故将

bigger 改成 smaller。

67.【答案】the — ~~the~~。
【解析】本题考查固定短语。in advance 意为"预先"，advance 前不加定冠词 the。

68.【答案】for — by。
【解析】本题考查并列结构。or 表选择，故其前后内容应保持一致，所以将 for 改成 by。

69.【答案】emphases — emphasis。
【解析】本题考查主谓一致原则。根据谓语动词 is 和句首的 much，可知应该用 emphases 的单数形式 emphasis。

70.【答案】as ∧ taught — ∧ being。
【解析】本题考查语态。teach 这个动作的逻辑主语不是 themselves，即 student，故应用被动语态。

71.【答案】Therefore — Although。
【解析】本题考查逻辑关系。前分句意为：导师会提供帮助；后分句意为：他们希望学生在学习上有自主性。两分句间不能构成因果关系。将 therefore 改为表让步关系的 although 即能使语义通顺。

Part VI

72.【答案】From the valley came a frightening sound。
【解析】本题考查倒装句。表示方位意义的介词短语或副词短语位于句首作状语，谓语动词为 be、表示"位于，存在"的动词或"位置移动"的单个不及物动词时，句子要用全部倒装。

73.【答案】It was Jefferson who wrote。
【解析】考查强调判断句，"it is + 被强调的部分 + who/ that"。

74.【答案】no man but has his faults。
【解析】考查双重否定句及正反翻译的方法。双重否定更能增强肯定的语气，更有说服力。

75.【答案】not a /no man but felt his love to his career。
【解析】考查双重否定句型"no + 主语 + but + 谓语"，no 相当于 not a 或 not any。

76.【答案】the whole dinner turned out to be a catastrophe。
【解析】本题考查固定搭配。turn out to be a catastrophe "结局糟透了"，是固定搭配。catastrophe "悲惨的结局，彻底的失败"还可以指"（突如其来的）灾难"。

预测试题十二

Part V

Cloze (15 minutes)

Directions: *There are 20 blanks in the following passage. For each blank there are four choices marked [A], [B], [C] and[D] on the right side of the paper. You should choose the ONE that best fits into the passage. Then mark the corresponding letter on* **Answer Sheet 2** *with a single line through the centre.*

Teachers need to be aware of the emotional, intellectual, and physical changes that young adults experience. And they also need to give serious __62__ to how they can be best __63__ such changes. Growing bodies need movement and __64__, but not just in ways that emphasize competition. __65__ they are adjusting to their new bodies and a whole host of new intellectual and emotional challenges, teenagers are especially self-conscious and need the __66__ that comes from achieving success and knowing that their accomplishments are __67__ by others. However, the typical teenage lifestyle is already filled with so much competition that it would be __68__ to plan activities in which there are more winners than losers, __69__, publishing newsletters with many student-written book reviews, __70__ student artwork, and sponsoring book discussion clubs. A variety of small clubs can provide __71__ opportunities for leadership, as well as for practice in successful __72__ dynamics. Making

62. [A] thought   [B] idea
     [C] opinion   [D] advice
63. [A] strengthened
     [B] accommodated to
     [C] stimulated
     [D] enhanced
64. [A] care   [B] nutrition
     [C] exercise   [D] leisure
65. [A] If   [B] Although
     [C] Whereas   [D] Because
66. [A] assistance   [B] guidance
     [C] confidence   [D] tolerance
67. [A] claimed   [B] admired
     [C] ignored   [D] surpassed
68. [A] improper   [B] risky
     [C] fair   [D] wise
69. [A] in effect   [B] as a result
     [C] for example   [D] in a sense
70. [A] displaying
     [B] describing
     [C] creating
     [D] exchanging
71. [A] durable   [B] excessive
     [C] surplus   [D] multiple

friends is extremely important to teenagers, and many shy students need the __73__ of some kind of organization with a supportive adult __74__ visible in the background.

In these activities, it is important to remember that the young teens have __75__ attention spans. A variety of activities should be organized __76__ participants can remain active as long as they want and then go on to __77__ else without feeling guilty and without letting the other participants __78__. This does not mean that adults must accept irresponsibility. On the __79__ they can help students acquire a sense of commitment by __80__ for roles that are within their __81__ and their attention spans and by having clearly stated rules.

72. [A] group   [B] individual
     [C] personnel   [D] corporation

73. [A] consent   [B] insurance
     [C] admission   [D] security

74. [A] particularly [B] barely
     [C] definitely   [D] rarely

75. [A] similar   [B] long
     [C] different   [D] short

76. [A] if only   [B] now that
     [C] so that   [D] even if

77. [A] everything [B] anything
     [C] nothing   [D] something

78. [A] off   [B] down
     [C] out   [D] alone

79. [A] contrary   [B] average
     [C] whole   [D] advance

80. [A] making   [B] standing
     [C] planning   [D] taking

81. [A] capabilities [B] responsibilities
     [C] proficiency   [D] efficiency

Part VI   Translation   (5 minutes)

Directions: *complete the sentences by translating into English the Chinese given in brackets. Please write your translation on Answer Sheet 2.*

82. Scarcely had she fallen asleep _____ (一阵敲门声就把她吵醒).

83. She stumbled and _____ (把脚踝扭得很疼).

84. The child is adept at _____ (用笑话或赞美的话来平息他父母的怒气).

85. _____ (人们不能不被他的事迹所感动) after knowing the bachelor has adopted five orphans.

86. If *The New York Times* _____ (在图像旁边配上文字说明), why shouldn't everyone be able to have them?

答案与解析

62. 选［A］。词汇辨析题。从语义上看，四个选项似乎都符合题意：［A］thought "关怀，关心"；［B］idea "主意，思想，观念"；　［C］opinion "意见，看法"；［D］advice "忠告，建议"。但 idea 和 opinion 均为可数名词，前面要加不定冠词 an，且 give an idea to 和 give an opinion to 的对象都应是人，故可将它们排除；而 advice 要想与后面的从句衔接，必须使用介词 on，故也不选。综合分析，thought 用在此处最为合适，故［A］为正确答案。

63. 选［B］。词汇辨析题。能和 such changes 构成合理搭配，且能和前文的 experience 形成照应的是［B］accommodated to "适应"。［A］strengthened "加强，巩固"；［C］stimulated "刺激，激励"；［D］enhanced "提高，增强" 语义均不符。

64. 选［C］。逻辑推理题。能和空格前的 movement 形成语义场共现的是［C］exercise "训练，锻炼"。［A］care "注意，照料"；［B］nutrition "营养，营养学"；［D］leisure "空闲，悠闲" 这三个选项都脱离了语境。本句的意思是：成长中的身体需要运动和锻炼。

65. 选［D］。逻辑推理题。本题考查的是前后两个句子间的逻辑关系。"他们正在调整以迎接许多新的生理、思维和情感方面的挑战" 是 "十几岁的青少年特别害羞…" 的原因，因此［D］Because "因为"。［A］If 表条件；［B］Although "虽然，尽管"，表让步；［C］Whereas "然而，尽管"，表转折。

66. 选［C］。逻辑推理题。能和前文的 especially self-conscious 以及后文中的 comes from achieving success 形成语义场共现的只能是 need the confidence，故［C］confidence "信心" 为答案。［A］assistance "援助，补助"；［B］guidance "指导，领导"；［D］tolerance "宽容，忍受" 均脱离了上下文的语境。

67. 选［B］。逻辑推理题。能够符合得到信心应该是因为自己的成就被别人欣赏，而不是被声称、忽视或超过，所以选［B］admired "赞美，钦佩，羡慕"。［A］claimed "声称，主张"；［C］ignored "不理睬，忽视"；［D］surpassed "超越，胜过" 都不符合原文逻辑。

68. 选［D］。逻辑推理题。青少年的生活方式里充满了竞争，所以计划一些赢者多于输家的活动是明智的，故［D］wise "英明的，明智的" 正确。［A］improper "不合适的，不正确的"；［B］risky "危险的"；［C］fair "干净的，公平的" 脱离了语境。

69. 选［C］。逻辑推理题。本题考查上下句之间的逻辑关系。联系上下文可知，选项前后是例证关系，故选［C］for example。［A］in effect "有效"；［B］as a result "结果"；［D］in a sense "在某种意义上" 均不符合题意。

70. 选［A］。逻辑推理题。文中提到这些活动是为了使青少年获得信心的，那应该是要将他们的作品进行展示才对，故选［A］displaying "展示，展览"。［B］describing "描写，记述"；［C］creating "创造，创作"；［D］exchanging "交换，调换"，都不符合原文逻辑。

71. 选［D］。词汇辨析题。本句依旧是在讲为青少年提供信心的措施，所填词是修饰 opportunities 的，因此需表积极、肯定意义。符合的有［A］durable "持久的，耐用的" 和［D］multiple "多样的，多重的"，但 durable 不能用来修饰 opportunities，故排除［A］选［D］。［B］excessive "过多的，过分的" 和［C］surplus "过剩的，剩余的" 均为贬义词。

72. 选［A］。逻辑推理题。根据前文内容，既然能锻炼领导才能，那肯定是与他人在一起，因此［A］group 符合题意。［B］individual "个人" 和［C］personnel "人员，职员" 语义不符；［D］corporation "公司，企业" 虽然也是一个团体，但是它不能涵盖所有的团体，故不选。

73. 选［D］。逻辑推理题。本句讲的依旧是为青少年提供信心的途径，四个选项中，符合语境的只有［D］security "安全感，安心"。［A］consent "同意，赞成"；［B］insurance "保险，保险单"；［C］admission "允许进入，供认" 都不脱离了语境。

74. 选［B］。逻辑推理题。既然组织能带给青少年们自信，那大人们只能在背后支持他们，不能让他们知道，故选［B］barely "仅仅，几乎不"。［A］particularly "特别，尤其"；［C］definitely "明确地，干脆地"；［D］rarely "很少地，罕有地" 都与原文逻辑不符。

75. 选［D］。逻辑推理题。本段讲的是如何组织活动，使学生保持持久的兴趣和注意力，之所以如此，是因为青少年的关注周期不够长，这一点根据常识也可判断出来，所以［D］short "短的" 为正确答案。［A］similar "相似的，类似的"；［B］long "长的，长期的"；［C］different "不同的，差异的"。

76. 选［C］。逻辑推理题。空格后的内容是空格前的内容的目的，所以要选择能引导目的状语从句的［C］so that。［A］if only "只要"；［B］now that "既然"；［D］even if "即使" 都不能使上下文语义连贯。

77. 选［D］。逻辑推理题。空格处及后面的内容泛指别的活动，所以只有［D］something 符合句子意思。［A］everything "每件事物，万事"；［B］anything "任何事"；［C］nothing "无，无关紧要之事"。

78. 选［B］。短语搭配题。四个选项均能和 let 构成短语，但能和 feeling guilty 形成语义场共现的只有［B］let down "使失望，辜负"。［A］let off "放出，饶恕"；［C］let out "放掉，泄露"；［D］let alone "不管，不打扰" 在语义上均不符合题意。

79. 选［A］。短语搭配题。上文提及，这并不意味着大人就没有责任。本句讲的是大人们能够帮助学生获得一种责任感…。由此可知，空格前后的句子在逻辑上存在强烈的对比关系，因此［A］On the contrary "正相反" 为答案。［B］On the average "平均，按平均数计算；一般地说"；［C］On the whole "大体上，基本上"；［D］On the advance "（物价）在上涨" 均不符合题意。

80. 选［C］。短语搭配题。四个选项都能与 for 构成固定搭配，因此只能从它们的词义上来辨析。［A］making for "走向，有利于"；［B］standing for "代表，象征"；［C］planning for "为…作计划，打算"；［D］taking for "认为，以为"。本句谈的是大人如何帮助学生，因此［C］planning 符合句意。

81. 选［A］。词汇辨析题。能和介词 within 搭配的有［A］capabilities "能力，接受力" 和［B］responsibilities "责任，职责"。值得注意的是，空格前的 their 指的是 students，因此只能选［A］capabilities，within capabilities 表示 "在能力范围之内"。本句的意思是：这些角色应该在学生的能力范围和关注周期内，并且要有陈述清晰的规则。［C］proficiency "熟练，精通" 和［D］efficiency "效率，功效" 均不符题意。

Part VI

82. 【答案】when a knock at the door awakened her。
　　【解析】本题考查 scarcely…when…结构。"刚…就…"。Scarcely 后面部分要用部分倒装结构，过去完成时。when 后面部分不用倒装，一般过去时。"唤醒" awaken，awake to，注意区分两个词。

83. 【答案】gave her ankle a painful wrench。
　　【解析】本题考查 "扭伤" wrench，一般这样用 "gave + 身体部位 + a wrench" "扭伤某个部位"。

84. 【答案】appeasing her parents' anger with a joke or compliment。
　　【解析】本题考查两个固定短语 be adept at doing sth. "熟练于做某事" 及 appease one's anger with sth. "用某事平息某人的怒火"。

85. 【答案】One cannot but be moved by his deeds。
　　【解析】本题考查双重否定 cannot but 句型，cannot but 的意思是 "不能不"，另外 "人们" 不要生硬地翻译成 people。

86. 【答案】has captions on their images。
　　【解析】本题考查词类转化。caption 可以做名词 "字幕，说明" 也可以做及物动词 "加上说明"，在这句话中如果用 caption 的动词形式，将 image 做其宾语的话不能完全体现出原文所要表达的 "在…旁边" 的意思，因此这里将汉语中的动词 "配说明" 转译为名词那就比较合适了。

预测试题十三

Directions: *This part consists of a short passage. In this passage, there are altogether 10 mistakes, one in each numbered line. You may have to change a word, add a word or delete a word. Mark out the mistakes and put the corrections in the blanks provided. If you change a word, cross it out and write the correct word in the corresponding blank. If you add a word, put an insertion mark (∧) in the right place and write the missing word in the blank. If you delete a word, cross it out and put a slash (／) in the blank.*

As the cost of gas and oil for home heat has gone up, many Americans have switched from these fuels to wood for heating their homes. In 1973, approximate 200, 000 wood-burning stoves, intended for home use, sold in the United States. By 1979, this figure had reached one million; and by the end of 1981, there were as many asseven million home-owned wood-burning units in operation in the U. S. A.	62. _____ 63. _____
In addition low fuel bills, many people choose these stoves because their initiative cost is very low (the prices range from $ 50 kit to $ 5, 000 top-of-the line models), and because new technology has made wood fires more efficient, cleaner, and, therefore, safe than ever before. One new technological feature of this type is the catalytic combustor which adds about $ 100 to $ 200 to the cost of the stove, but which causes to much more complete combustion of the wood and therefore burns up more of the pollutants left by incomplete combustion and produces more heat.	64. _____ 65. _____ 66. _____ 67. _____
A second cost-saving innovation is a device which agitates the wood, increasing the number of oxygen that the center of the wood pile, and leads to more efficient combustion. The real advantage of the device is that it allows the owner to make use of cheap sources of wood such	68. _____ 69. _____

as dirty wood chips (an industrial by-product)
that has almost no commercial value, cost as
little as $ 20 a ton, but burn very inefficiently
in furnaces without an agitator.

70. _____

71. _____

Part VI　　　　　　　　Translation　　　　　(5 minutes)

Directions: *complete the sentences by translating into English the Chinese given in brackets. Please write your translation on* **Answer Sheet 2.**

72. _____（人们听见正是 Jim 这个无情的家伙）shouting at his mother in the dead of night.

73. His proposal was that _____（他们成立一个专门委员会来检查这个问题）.

74. This would _____（缓解学生的压力）and would allow students to develop both socially and intellectually in a healthier school environment.

75. He jumped into the pool to save the child _____（结果却摔断了自己的腿）.

76. Rescue vehicles _____（包围了泰国一架坠毁的飞机的残骸）in Phuket September 16, 2007.

答 案 与 解 析

Part V

62. 【答案】heat —— heating。
　　【解析】本题考查近义词辨析。heat 和 heating 都能作名词，但意义不一样。heat 指"热，热度"，heating 指"供暖系统，供暖装置"。能和 home 形成语义共现的是 heating。

63. 【答案】use，∧ sold —— ∧ were。
　　【解析】本题考查语态。sold 的逻辑主语不是句子的主语 wood-burning stoves，所以此处应该用被动语态，并且要注意句首的时间状语 In 1973，说明应该用过去时态。

64. 【答案】addition ∧ low —— ∧ to。
　　【解析】本题考查固定短语。in addition to 为固定短语，to 不能省略。

65. 【答案】initiative —— initial。
　　【解析】本题考查形近词辨析。initiative 为名词，意为"自主，主动性"。initial 为形容词，意为"最初的，初始的"。根据句意，这里想要表达"初始成本"之义，故应用 initial。

66.【答案】 safe — safer。

【解析】 本题考查比较级。根据句中的 than ever before 可知，此处应该用 safe 的比较级。

67.【答案】 to — ~~to~~ 。

【解析】 本题考查动词用法。cause 为及物动词，后面可直接跟名词，无需再用介词。

68.【答案】 number — amount。

【解析】 本题考查近义词辨析。the number of sth. 意为"某事物的编号/号码"，而 the amount of sth. 指的是"某物的总数"。综观全句，此处应该指后者。

69.【答案】 leads — leading。

【解析】 本题考查平行结构。leads to more efficient combustion 和 increasing the … wood pile 是用 and 连接的平行结构，故它们在形式上应保持一致。所以要将 leads 改成 leading。

70.【答案】 has — have。

【解析】 本题考查数的一致性。that 定语从句修饰的是 dirty wood chips，因此要将 has 改成 have。

71.【答案】 but — and。

【解析】 本题考查逻辑关系。burn very inefficiently in furnaces without an agitator 和前文的 no commercial value 并不存在对比或转折的关系，而是并列的关系，故将 but 改成 and。

Part VI

72.【答案】 It was Jim, the heartless fellow, who was heard。

【解析】 本题考查强调句，强调主语。

73.【答案】 they (should) set up a special board/committee to examine this problem。

【解析】 表示"建议、命令、要求、想法"的名词所接的表语从句通常用"(that) sb. (should) do"的虚拟形式。

74.【答案】 alleviate students' stress。

【解析】 本题考查固定搭配 alleviate one's stress，"缓解某人的压力"。Alleviate "减轻，缓和" 在这里也可以用 lighten 或 ease 来代替。

75.【答案】 only to break his own leg。

【解析】 本题考查表达"意料之外的结果"的方法，only to "但是却…"。

76.【答案】 surround the wreckage of a crashed Thai airliner。

【解析】 本题考查过去分词做定语。过去分词做定语表示的动作已经完成。crashed "坠毁的"。wreckage "残骸"。

预测试题十四

Part V   Error Correction   (15 minutes)

Directions: *This part consists of a short passage. In this passage, there are altogether 10 mistakes, one in each numbered line. You may have to change a word, add a word or delete a word. Mark out the mistakes and put the corrections in the blanks provided. If you change a word, cross it out and write the correct word in the corresponding blank. If you add a word, put an insertion mark (∧) in the right place and write the missing word in the blank. If you delete a word, cross it out and put a slash (/) in the blank.*

    Son of Zeus and Hera, Ares was appointed god of war. He was terrible and majestic, and his march shook the world. Of all the major divinity at Olympus, he was the   62. _____
most hateful, loving strife and war and ever thirsty of   63. _____
blood. On the other hand he signified courage and victory in battle, and was devoutly worshipped by warriors going to war. Prayers were addressed for him before the war and   64. _____
spoils presented at his altar after it.

    He was the one god who ever had to submit the supremacy of his inferiors. At one time lack of tact and discretion led to his disgrace. He was fighting with two giants, Otus and Ephialtes, and find himself no match for the   66. _____
two monstrous creatures, surrendered and was imprisoned in chains. He was set free in the end by the wileful Hermes, but not before he had suffered all the humiliations the giants chose to inflict on him.

    He was as discreet as he was savage. A son of   67. _____
Poseidon's, attempting to kidnap his daughter, incurred the war-god displeasure, so that he slew the youth without demur. In retaliation, Poseidondragged him before a group of Athenian magistrates for trial. The court was held on a hill outside Athens. Ares presented his case and was acquitted.

   65. _____

The hill was ever after called Areopagus, "the hill of Ares", and the magistrates received the name of Areopagitae.

　　But Ares was altogether without gentle feelings. From his union with Aphrodite (Venus), ridiculed as it was, sprang three beautiful children, Harmonia, Eros (Cupid) and Anteros. He fell in love with the charming Vestal virgin, Ilia, who born him the twins, Romulus and Remus. The former was destined to become the founder of Rome. As he loved the riot way of Roman life, Ares took the city under his protection and received a great worship there than elsewhere in the ancient world.

68. ＿＿＿＿＿＿＿＿＿

69. ＿＿＿＿＿＿＿＿＿

70. ＿＿＿＿＿＿＿＿＿
71. ＿＿＿＿＿＿＿＿＿

Part VI　　　　　　　　　Translation　　　　　　(5 minutes)

Directions: *complete the sentences by translating into English the Chinese given in brackets. Please write your translation on* **Answer Sheet 2.**

72. He denied ＿＿＿＿＿＿＿＿＿＿＿＿＿ (偷看了同桌的试卷).

73. It was advised that ＿＿＿＿＿＿＿＿＿＿＿ (在居民区设更多的流动商店).

74. They cannot ＿＿＿＿＿＿＿＿＿＿ (无法抑制他们的兴趣和敬佩之情) to the new book.

75. You must ＿＿＿＿＿＿＿＿＿＿＿ (向他们赔礼道歉) for the insult.

76. Since some countries ＿＿＿＿＿＿＿＿＿＿ (根据早先的教育计划将学生分配到各个学校), some differences in average school performance are there by design.

＝＝＝＝＝＝＝＝＝　答 案 与 解 析　＝＝＝＝＝＝＝＝＝

Part V

62. 【答案】divinity — divinities。
　　【解析】本题考查名词单复数。前面有 all the major 来修饰 divinity，故应用 divinity 的复数形式，divinity 作"神"讲时为可数名词。

63. 【答案】of — for。
　　【解析】本题考查固定搭配。thirst 和其形容词形式 thirsty 后面都跟介词 for，而非介词 of。be thirsty for sth. 意为"对某事很渴望"。

64. 【答案】for — to。
　　【解析】本题考查固定搭配。address to sb. 为固定搭配，意为"向某人说"。

65. 【答案】submit ∧ the — ∧ to。

【解析】本题考查固定搭配。submit to sb. /sth. "向某人或某事屈从，顺从"。

66. 【答案】find — finding。

【解析】本题考查平行结构。find 和前面的 fighting 是由 and 连接的并列结构，因此它们在形式上应该保持一致，如果将 fighting 改成 fight，那前面的结构就成了 was fight，是不正确的。因此将 find 改成 finding。

67. 【答案】discreet — indiscreet。

【解析】本题考查逻辑关系。本段旨在描述 Ares 轻率的性格，故应将 discreet 改为 indiscreet。

68. 【答案】was ∧ altogether — ∧ not。

【解析】本题考查逻辑关系。本段讲述的是 Ares 的婚姻爱情，指出他还有温柔的一面。

69. 【答案】born — bore。

【解析】本题考查近义词辨析。这里是指 Ilia 为他生了（bear）双胞胎，且这里应该用过去式，即为 bore。born 是指某人出生，而非生育。

70. 【答案】riot — riotous。

【解析】本题考查词类。这里应用形容词修饰 way。riot 的形容词为 riotous。

71. 【答案】great — greater。

【解析】本题考查比较级。后面有 than，所以前面的形容词 great 应用其比较级 greater。

Part VI

72. 【答案】having peeked at his neighbor's test paper。

【解析】考查 deny having done sth. "否认做过某事"，动名词的完成式作 deny 的宾语。

73. 【答案】more mobile shops (should) be set up in the residential area。

【解析】表示"建议、命令、要求、想法"的动词所接的主语从句通常用"（that）sb.（should）do"的虚拟形式。注意用被动语态。

74. 【答案】withhold their interest and admiration。

【解析】本题考查"抑制"的表达，在这里 cannot withhold 有"忍不住流露出"的意思。

75. 【答案】make amends to them。

【解析】本题考查六级重要词组 make amends to sb. "向某人赔礼道歉"。amend "修订，改进"。

76. 【答案】allocate students to schools according to their prior educational performance。

【解析】本题考查 allocate …to… "把…分配到"。prior "最初的，先前的"。

预测试题十五

Directions: *There are 20 blanks in the following passage. For each blank there are four choices marked [A], [B], [C] and[D] on the right side of the paper. You should choose the ONE that best fits into the passage. Then mark the corresponding letter on **Answer Sheet 2** with a single line through the centre.*

Taste is such a subjective matter that we don't usually __62__ preference tests for food. The most you can say about anyone's preference, is that it's one person's opinion. __63__ because the two big cola companies — Coca-Cola and Pepsi Cola are marketed so aggressively, we've wondered how big a __64__ taste preference actually plays in brand loyalty. We set __65__ a taste test that challenged people who identified themselves as __66__ Coca-Cola or Pepsi fans: Find your brand in a blind testing.

We invited staff volunteers who had a strong liking __67__ either Coca-Cola Classic or Pepsi, Diet Coke, or Diet Pepsi. These were people who thought they'd have no trouble __68__ their brand from the other brand.

We eventually __69__ 19 regular cola drinkers and 27 diet cola drinkers. Then we fed them four __70__ samples of cola one at a time, regular colas for the one group, diet versions for __71__. We asked them to tell

62. [A] conclude [B] condense
    [C] conduct [D] confess
63. [A] But [B] And
    [C] If [D] So
64. [A] roll [B] role
    [C] rock [D] rod
65. [A] off [B] up
    [C] in [D] aside
66. [A] none [B] both
    [C] neither [D] either
67. [A] with [B] to
    [C] at [D] for
68. [A] telling [B] differing
    [C] distinct [D] separate
69. [A] loaded [B] located
    [C] locked [D] lodged
70. [A] unidentified [B] identified
    [C] identifying [D] identify
71. [A] the others [B] the other
    [C] another [D] other
72. [A] if [B] whether
    [C] either [D] if not
73. [A] strenuously [B] steadily
    [C] still [D] statistically

us __72__ each sample was Coke or Pepsi; then we analysed the records __73__ to compare the participants' choices __74__ what mere guess-work could have accomplished.

Getting all four samples right was a __75__ test, but not too tough, we thought, for people who believed they could __76__ their brand. In the end, only 7 out of 19 regular cola drinkers __77__ identified their brand of choice in all four __78__. The diet-cola drinkers did a little __79__ — only 7 of 27, identified all four samples correctly.

__80__ both groups did better than chance would predict, nearly half the participants in each group made the wrong choice two or more times. Two people got all four samples wrong. Overall, half the participants did about as well on the last round of tasting __81__ on the first, so fatigue, or taste burnout, was not a factor. Our preference test results suggest that only a few Pepsi participants and Coke fans may really be able to tell their favorite brand by taste and price.

74. [A] for [B] to [C] with [D] from
75. [A] easy [B] rough [C] tough [D] enough
76. [A] recognize [B] realize [C] admit [D] specify
77. [A] wrongly [B] correctly [C] correspondingly [D] costly
78. [A] triangles [B] trains [C] trails [D] trials
79. [A] best [B] better [C] worst [D] worse
80. [A] While [B] When [C] If [D] However
81. [A] than [B] so [C] as [D] and

Part VI　　　Translation　　　(5 minutes)

Directions: *complete the sentences by translating into English the Chinese given in brackets. Please write your translation on* **Answer Sheet 2.**

82. No matter how difficult life is going to be, please _____ (为了你的父母、朋友和在乎你的人，珍视你的生命)!

83. The cat tried to _____ (用爪子抓住边缘).

84. A survey shows that _____ (加重税收会牵制私营经济的发展).

85. It seemed that the pay of the workers had risen, however, _____ (增长被通货膨胀抵消了).

86. Children are often the quickest and _____ (做出响应最多的成员) of the audience

答案与解析

Part V

62. 选 [C]。词汇辨析题。句子的宾语为 tests（调查），四个选项中，能和其构成合理动宾搭配的是 [C] conduct "进行，实施"，conduct a test 意为 "展开调查"，故 [C] 为答案。本句的意思是：个人的味觉极具主观性，所以我们通常不会去调查人们喜欢哪些食品。[A] conclude "推断，断定"；[B] condense "（使）浓缩，精简"；[D] confess "承认，坦白，忏悔" 在语义上均不符合题意。

63. 选 [A]。逻辑推理题。文章首句提到我们通常不会去调查人们喜欢哪些食品，但本句又提及 we've wondered…taste preference actually…。显然，本句和前文在语义上为转折关系，故 [A] But 为答案。[B] And 表并列或递进；[C] If 表条件；[D] So 表结果，这三项均不符合原文逻辑。

64. 选 [B]。短语搭配题。play an important role in 为习惯表达，意思是 "在…中起重要作用"，故选项 [B] role "角色，任务" 为正确答案。[A] roll "(一) 卷，卷形物"；[C] rock "岩石，暗礁"；[D] rod "杆，棒" 均不符合题意。

65. 选 [B]。短语搭配题。根据语义复现原则，set __65__ 应和首句中的 conduct 构成同义复现关系。查看选项，符合的是 [B] up，set up 意为 "建立（事业）；成立（组织）"。[A] set off "出发，动身"；[C] set in "开始，到来"；[D] set aside "留出，不顾" 均不符合题意。

66. 选 [D]。短语搭配题。either…or…为 [D] 为答案。[A] none "一个也没有"，不能与 or 搭配；[B] both "双方，两者"，与 and 搭配；[C] neither 与 nor 连用，表示 "既不…又不"。

67. 选 [D]。短语搭配题。liking 为名词，意思是 "爱好，嗜好"，与介词 for 连用，故选 [D]。

68. 选 [A]。短语搭配题。have no trouble (in) doing sth. 为习惯用法，意为 "做某事不费事"，故先可排除 [C] distinct "独特的，截然不同的" 和 [D] separate "分离，隔离"。[A] telling "讲，说，叙述"，可与 from 搭配使用，tell … from …意思是 "将…和…区分开来"，符合题意。[B] differing 意为 "不一致，不同"，differ from …意为 "不同于；和…不同；和…意见不一致"，语义不符，故排除。

69. 选 [B]。词汇辨析题。查看选项，[A] loaded 意为 "装填，使担负"；[B] located 意为 "通过寻找、检查或试验而找出"；[C] locked 意为 "锁，锁上"；[D] lodged 意为 "临时住宿，寄宿"，其中能以 19 regular cola drinkers 以及 27 diet cola drinkers 作宾语的就只有 [B] located，故为答案。

70. 选 [A]。逻辑推理题。既然是做实验，那叫参与实验的人品尝的应该是没有明确标明品牌的可乐，故 [A] unidentified "未经确认的"为答案。本句的意思是：然后我们让他们先后品尝了四种没有标明品牌的可乐。

71. 选 [B]。词汇辨析题。句中提到一组人品尝传统型可乐，而低糖型可乐自然是由另一组品尝，与 the one group 相对的是 the other group，故选 [B] the other "另一个"，特指两个中的另一个。[A] the others "其余的"，表示在一定范围内的其他全部；[C] another "另一个，另一个人"，为泛指；[D] other "其他的，另外的"指代不明。

72. 选 [B]。语法结构题。所填词需能引导宾语从句，且能和 or 搭配使用，选项中只有 [B] whether "是否"符合，故为答案。[A] if 也具有"是否"的意思，但不与 or 搭配使用，因而不可选；[C] either 能和 or 搭配使用，但它不用于引导从句；[D] if not "不然的话，否则"不能使上下文语义连贯。

73. 选 [D]。逻辑推理题。空格处要求填入一个副词，修饰动词 analysed。选项中能和 analysed the records 形成语义场共现的是 [D] statistically "统计上地，统计地"，故为答案。本句大意为：然后我们对他们的答案进行了统计分析，以便将他们的答案与随意猜测的结果进行比较。[A] strenuously "奋发地，费力地"；[B] steadily "稳定地，有规则地"；[C] still "还，仍"均不符合题意。

74. 选 [C]。短语搭配题。本题考察动词 compare 的惯用搭配。compare 只能和 [B] to 以及 [C] with 搭配。compare...to...意为"比作，比喻为"，而 compare...with...意为"把…与…作比较"。此处显然是指将两者进行比较，故选 [C] with。compare 不能与 [A] for 和 [D] from 连用。

75. 选 [C]。逻辑推理题。根据下文中的 but not too tough 可知，所填词应与 tough 形成语义复现关系，因此 [C] tough "困难的，费力的"为答案。本句的意思是：要准确无误地确认四种样品的品牌不是一件容易的事。[A] easy "容易的，安逸的"；[B] rough "粗略的，大致的"；[D] enough "足够的，充足的"均脱离了语境。

76. 选 [A]。逻辑推理题。文章通篇都在讲辨认不同品牌的可乐，故所填词应能表示"辨认"之意。选项中符合的只有 [A] recognize "认出，辨认"，故为答案。句子大意为：但对这些相信自己能够辨认出自己所喜欢的品牌的人来说似乎也不是太难。[B] realize "认识到，了解"；[C] admit "容许，承认"；[D] specify "指定，详细说明"语义均不符。

77. 选 [B]。逻辑推理题。根据句中的 identified their brand of choice in all four 可知他们是正确地品尝出了自己喜欢的品牌，故 [B] correctly "恰当地，正确地"为答案。本句的意思是：最终，19 名只喝传统可乐的人中有 7 人在四次试验中正确辨认出了自己喜欢的品牌。[A] wrongly "不正当地，错误地"；[C] correspondingly "相对地，比照地"；[D] costly "昂贵的，贵重的"均不符合原文语义。

78. 选［D］。逻辑推理题。本段依旧在讲试验的情况，故［D］trials "试验，考验" 为答案。［A］triangles "（数）三角形"；［B］trains "火车，列车"；［C］trails "踪迹，痕迹" 均不符合语境要求。

79. 选［D］。逻辑推理题。根据上下文，19 名只喝传统可乐的人中有 7 人能在四次品尝中正确辨认出自己喜欢的品牌，而 27 名低糖可乐的饮者中只有 7 名能识别出自己的品牌，说明后者的成绩要差一些，因此只有［D］worse 符合句子意思，为答案。

80. 选［A］。逻辑推理题。句子两分句的意思分别为：两组人的成绩要优于随意猜测可能得到的结果；每组中都有将近一半的人有两次或两次以上的识别错误。由此可见，两分句间为转折关系。［A］While "虽然，但是，然而" 和［D］However "然而，可是" 都能表转折关系，但是 However 用于句首时，要用逗号将其与后面的内容隔开，故排除不选。所以答案为［A］While。［B］When "在…的时候"；［C］If "（表条件）如果，（表假设）要是"。

81. 选［C］。短语搭配题。本题考查固定搭配 as…as… "和…一样"，故［C］as 为答案。［A］than，［B］so 及［D］and 都不符合题意及语法要求。本句的意思是：综观几轮试验，有一半参加品尝的人，第四轮和第一轮的品尝结果是一样的。

Part VI

82. 【答案】cherish your life, for your parents, for your friends, and for those who care you。

【解析】本题考查 "珍视" 的表达及 those 做代词的用法，本题是 no matter how 引导让步状语从句，后半句中的连用了三个 for 介词短语做状语。

83. 【答案】cling to the edge by its claws。

【解析】本题考查 "抓住" 的表达，tackle、seize 、catch hold of 、get hold of、clutch at 都有抓住的含义，注意搭配的介词。

84. 【答案】heavy taxes hamper private business。

【解析】本题考查 "牵制" 的英语表达及词性转译。hamper "牵制，妨碍" 是六级重要单词，"加重税收" 做 that 引导的宾语从句中的主语，因此在翻译时将 "加重" 由动词改为 "重的" heavy 作定语修饰 taxes。

85. 【答案】the raise was offset by inflation。

【解析】本题考查基本的、常用的经济术语，"抵消" offset，及 "通货膨胀" inflation。在这里还要注意后半句的 "增长" 是名词用 raise，不要受前面 rise 的影响。

86. 【答案】most responsive members。

【解析】本题考查 "做出响应的" responsive 的表达，注意要和 responsible "有责任的，可靠的" 区分开。

图书在版编目(CIP)数据

大学英语六级考试直击考点——综合测试/ 王长喜主编.
– 北京:中国社会出版社,2003.7
　ISBN 978-7-80146-709-6

　Ⅰ. 大... Ⅱ. 王... Ⅲ. 英语 – 综合 – 高等学校 – 水平考试 – 自学参考资料
Ⅳ. H310.42

中国版本图书馆 CIP 数据核字(2003)第 060754 号

丛 书 名:大学英语六级考试直击考点
书　　名:大学英语六级考试直击考点——综合测试
主　　编:王长喜
责任编辑:杨晖　张国洪

出版发行:中国社会出版社　　　邮政编码:100032
通联发行:北京市西城区二龙路甲 33 号新龙大厦
　　　　　电话:66016392　　　传真:66016392
欢迎读者拨打免费热线 8008108114 或登录 www.bj114.com.cn 查询相关信息
经　　销:各地新华书店

印刷装订:保定华泰印刷有限公司印刷
开　　本:850×1168 毫米　　1/32
印　　张:44
字　　数:916 千字
版　　次:2008 年 1 月第 3 版
印　　次:2008 年 1 月第 1 次印刷

书　　号:ISBN 978-7-80146-709-6
定　　价:39.20 元